MANGROVE
MAMA

Also by Janwillem Van de Wetering

The "Dutch Cop" Series
Outsider In Amsterdam (1975)
Tumbleweed (1975)
Corpse On The Dike (1976)
Death Of A Hawker (1977)
The Japanese Corpse (1978)
The Blond Baboon (1979)
The Maine Massacre (1980)
The Mind Murders (1981)
Streetbird (1982)
Rattlerat (1983)
The Sergeant's Cat (1985) (short stories)
Hard Rain (1987)
Just A Corpse At Twilight (1994)
The Hollow-Eyed Angel (forthcoming, 1996)

Other Fiction
Bliss And Bluster (1982) (novel)
The Butterfly Hunter (1984) (novel)
Murder By Remote Control (1986) (graphic novel)
Inspector Saito's Small Satori (1986) (short stories)
Seesaw Millions (1986) (novel)

Autobiographical
*The Empty Mirror (1971) (experiences in a Japanese Zen
  monastery*
*A Glimpse Of Nothingness (1973) (experiences in an American
  Zen center)*

Biography
Robert van Gulik: His Life, His Work (1983)

Children's Books
Little Owl (1979)
Hugh Pine (1980)
Hugh Pine And The Good Place (1981)
Hugh Pine And Something Else (1983)

In Preparation
Afterzen (Buddhist Essays)
The Cannibal And The Living (Amsterdam Cop series)

MANGROVE MAMA

& OTHER TROPICAL TALES OF TERROR

~

JANWILLEM VAN DE WETERING

1995

Many of these stories have appeared in *Ellery Queen's
Mystery Magazine* and in other magazines on both sides of
the Atlantic. "Madremonte," "Using People,"
"Thunderhole Exit," "Prawns With Evil Faces,"
"Quicksand," and "Crime & Punishment in Timeless
Japan" appear here for the first time in English.

FIRST EDITION
Published November 1995

Dustjacket by the author with the help
of the trusted Barones.

ISBN 0-939767-23-6

DENNIS MCMILLAN PUBLICATIONS

2421 E. SPEEDWAY BLVD.

TUCSON, ARIZONA 85719

CONTENTS

To Rudy DeHarak

LADY HILLARY

Good day, Ma'm Tourist Group Leader from America. Welcome to the Tariand Isles of Niugini. Your tourist group likes my little Pacific isle? I'm glad. I'm the chief here, just a little chief, my great-grandfather Waku was a great chief, who became ruler, after much carefully planned and brilliantly executed inter-island warfare, of all the Tariand Islands here in Pangea Bay on the East Coast of Niugini. Niugini is our name for Papua New Guinea. PNG (we call it that, too), is, next to the immensity of Greenland, this planet's biggest island. Even so, few people know our country, except experienced travelers, like yourself, Ma'm, and your group.

I don't know America, but I did travel to Europe. After Independence, in 1978, we thought we should introduce to our former masters, the British, the Germans, the Dutch, the Portuguese. I was part of the retinue of our Prime Minister. We wore three-piece suits and headgear made out of casuari feathers. Everywhere we went we were mistaken for representatives of some newborn African nation. We kept saying "Papua New Guinea, north of Australia" and a departmental secretary would say ". . . Ah . . ." and buy us lunch maybe. Hamburgers. French fries. In Bonn we were fed sushis, that was nice, actually. We do care for fresh fish.

During the Second World War we were important though and even American warriors admitted that my grandfather,

1

Witu of the Tariand Crocodile Clan of Niugini, was a great Papuan island chief. Lieutenant James Cosby of the US Marines came back to issue my grandfather with a Legion of Merit medal. We keep it in our Long House, it has its own shelf.

The medal came with this beautiful ribbon that I wear on my belt, between these parrot feathers. Just one moment, I have to undo its clasp. Here you are, M'am, you can pass the ribbon along to your fellow tourists. Chief Witu earned the great honor because he kept you Allieds informed about Japanese naval movements. My grandfather once tricked a Japanese destroyer (by observing and copying Japanese light signals) into breaking up on a reef. Chief Witu was also known for his cunning counsel.

My grandfather's wisdom once saved your Marine Corps' face. Shall I tell you what happened or would you rather take your group skindiving?

Your group's itinerary allows for an extra hour to spend on trivial matters? Good. We can sit in the shade of the banyan tree there. See where the tree's air roots have formed a little cabin? That's where my throne is, I can look down on the people and direct their formal dancing. But there's no need for formality now. Some other time, perhaps, maybe some of you would like to learn about our sacred dances, but for now . . . let me tell you . . .

The Marine Corps face-saving matter was tricky, both personal and political. Lieutenant James Crosby, "Jim Bwana," as he liked us to call him, was accused of raping Leia, my beautiful sister, and cutting her throat afterward. Our murder suspect Jim Bwana was a splendid man, of course, not just a Marine warrior but a graduate of the, ahhh, I can never say it right, *Havvard* School as well. Do I pronounce that right? *Havvard*, yes? The American school of wizards? Good. Even so, in spite of his qualifications, Jim Bwana, liked

2

and admired by all of us, nearly lost name and fame here, but was saved by my father's father, chief Witu.

Isn't war fun?

I was only a boy then but never will I forget the glorious days when your war birds dueled with their Japanese counterparts in our sky, when our giant crocodiles slid into the lagoons looking for parachuted corpses, when dried chicken eggs and other exotic foods were served out of little green cans, when we tore gold braid off Japanese officer tunics and used it in our hairdos together with polished pieces we cut from spent canon shells. Later the fun improved, there were Japanese landings, causing brief fights between the sharp eight feet high alun alun grasses—we used our weapons.

I'm sorry, I'll try to be brief. I forgot the other items in your program, skindiving, was it? I hope you won't be naked. We hear nakedness is rude in America and we can't abide rudeness. You won't be rude? That's nice. I am glad.

As I said, my mind wanders back sometimes, to throwing spears, or swinging them, like clubs.

We play golf now. Have you seen our course? Japanese tycoons fly their business jets out to Port Moresby on the mainland, then ferry across Pangea Bay in their hydrofoil. When they come ashore here I charge big money for entry and dues. Would you like to be a member? The memory of Jim Bwana will warrant a discount. Here is my card, for you, Sir. We don't allow ladies on our course. You and your colleagues, when you plan to come out again, can fax me at my office so that I can confirm reservations. Winter months are quite busy.

We, male members of the Crocodile Clan, follow the warrior path. I'm glad to see white hair on your party's gentlemen's heads, it means the gents will remember the great War of the Forties. Once in a while the sight-seeing schooner out of Port Moresby brings us your anthropology students who need to fill up their laptop computers. I get paid by the Tourist Agency to answer their questions. I tell them our war stories. It's all news to them. Sometimes those bright young folks stare at me as if they don't know nothing.

Oh dear, . . .

Wearing a pig's tusk through my nose doesn't excuse use of the double negative. If Sister Cissy could hear me she'd rap my knuckles with that *bad* wooden ruler. Sister Cissy was an Australian nun who taught school here, before Independence of course. The young Papuan sister who met you at the dock is now in charge of the Mission.

Pardon?

Yes, Ma'm, when our nation was considered old enough to make its own decisions, we, on this island, retained the Roman Catholic faith. We didn't make religious changes, but appearances changed somewhat. We're in the tropics here. You will have noticed the heat. So our sisters go topless, as far as we are concerned we consider that quite polite.

I'm sure Sister Cissy forgives that change but I'm equally sure my use of the double negative will infuriate her spirit. I apologize to her spirit. You see, Sister, now that we're seeing modern movies we tend to pick up bad language, but as for me, I do make an effort to practice your Queen's English.

Does America have a queen? I get confused sometimes. I only traveled to Europe you see. You do have one now, right? The Lady Hillary? No? I thought I read that somewhere. *Time* magazine? No? She was on the cover. A lovely lady.

America, to me, is kind of a dream. Like movies.

What was that, Ma'm? You were saying that violence on TV has an unfortunate influence on us native people?

That may be so, but here in Niugini we don't have TV yet. So far the Prime Minister says we don't need more advertising. He sees TV in Australia in hotel rooms and he says it's repulsive. All dead babies and fast food. We do see movies, though. In the Long House, the very tall building with the sloping roofs over there, I keep a VCR and a large size monitor that a Japanese group gave us. The old Caterpillar generator Sister Cissy left makes it go. My cousin the schooner captain brings out video tapes that he copies at Port Moresby. Kick-ass movies are great fun, Ma'm. The language may be bad but the action is simply splendid. We particularly like Chief Schwarzenegger, he who married Lady Hillary of the Kennedy tribe.

Oh, I see. Pardon our ignorance, Ma'm. We don't get too many newspapers here. Clint? Clint Eastwood? Wrong again? Clint Ton? I see, *Clinton*. Just a president, you say? I'm glad you explained. I'll try to remember.

Shall I tell your group about the time your Marine Corps nearly lost face, about splendid Jim Bwana and my poor sister Leia?

Jim Bwana and his men were dropped off a US Navy motorpatrolboat when the Battle of the Coral Sea was going on. As you remember, a flotilla of Japanese invasion vessels, aimed at Australia, was defeated between Guadalcanal and these islands. It is impossible to forget the views we enjoyed then. The first great happening was Japanese warships sailing by in formation. I had never seen anything like it–those big light-gray colored vessels with their smoothly swiveling guns, the bright flags used for communication, their sea planes being catapulted off their rear decks, scouting everywhere. Whenever the warships came by, theirs or yours, it didn't matter, I ran along our beaches, with the other boys behind me, screaming and waving, we had no idea what we were looking at but we were so happy it drove us crazy. Like the Speechless One here, but she is always that way, . . .

Then you folks, in Mustangs, suddenly dove out of the sky and bombed us. You thought the Japanese had taken over our village and lands but what you saw were women tilling our fields (they still did that then, now they insist we take turns) and little girls manning bamboo lookout towers, keeping seed-eating birds away. The Mustang pilots must have been nervous, they kept strafing and bombing. Us males happened to have an important ceremony going on, me and some other boys were being prepared for coming of age. Dressed in my parrot-feather creamy white skirt and bright-red clay ghost mask I was stomping about the village square, and suddenly air devils dove down and the village was burning. Wasn't that an intimidating initiation? I thought I had done something wrong at first. Fortunately you missed our two community temples. Both the Long and Boys Houses are considered as kind of holy. There are treasures inside. Used to elevate our spirits. You didn't miss my father and brother. They both got hit. My brother Masset died instantly, my father took his time, having many helpful hallucinations before he floated off on the spirit turtle shell.

Yes, Ma'm, quite a few women and girls were hit, too.

Then the Japanese sent a boat ashore, to see why you bombed us.

No, Ma'm, Sister Cissy had left us already. She died before the war and the other Australian nuns had fled to their convent in Brisbane. They had been teaching us knitting and Jesus and how to wash hands and relieve ourselves before dinner and be respectful to our masters. I forgot how to knit but we still love Jesus. The Japanese had Buddha, he lives in a little mahogany box, with hinged doors that open, you get to burn incense and clap your hands and sing. I like Buddha, too. We keep him in the Long House, in the box that we captured from the Japanese captain. Our holy sisters keep a little Jesus in their church but we have our own big Jesus in the Long House. My brother Masset carved him long ago, from specially selected pieces of driftwood that he dovetailed together. The big statue is still in service, in spite of the squirrel living in Jesus' stomach. The squirrel has long whiskers, he takes part in some of the ceremonies, running about and squeaking. We also have Elvis Presley, he is a painting done by the Speechless One here. We started with a poster that a sea captain gave us, but the paper wore out. The Speechless One loves him.

Yes, Ma'm? How did Sister Cissy die? Unnecessarily, I'm afraid. There is a hill behind the village that we can climb after we have purified ourselves. It's just for sitting, gazing, quietness, that sort of thing. Sister Cissy wanted to grow tomatoes on that hill's slope. We warned her but she was somewhat strong-minded and started pulling up weeds, tearing the soil, and one of the hill's devil-lizards bit her bottom. Those devil-lizards are quick. They're big, too, ten feet long, including the tail of course. They like to eat our goats but they eat us too if we make ourselves defenseless by not paying attention. Sister Cissy got bitten badly. Afterward she hit the lizard with her rake and he backed off and hid in the bushes. This happened over fifty years ago, before penicillin.

Let me sing you the story while the Speechless One plays her bones. All set?

Go!

Devil-lizard doesn't mind being chased off, he can think. He waits behind bushes, for Sister Cissy to weaken. My grandfather, chief Witu, can think, too. Devil-lizard concentrates on Sister Cissy and grandfather concentrates on devil-lizard, and gets him. We roast devil-lizard, have a death-feast for the Sister. Devil-lizard enters by the mouth, Sister Lizzy enters by the ear. Bone music. Bone music.

Don't let the sacred Speechless One frighten you. She carries the craziness of this island, but we keep her in check. We always have one, you see. Craziness is so useful.

No, the Speechless One is not always female. In fact, I think there is a mistake here, but somehow this generation's Speechless One entered a woman. Could it be the greenhouse effect? Or nuclear carelessness somewhere? Worrying, somehow, very.

Okay, Speechless One, that's enough now. Sit down. Yes, you have lovely legs. Fold them. That's better. Thank you. Please relax, dear.

Where was I? Sister Cissy's bottom? We used herbs on Sister Cissy's wound but couldn't stop the lizard bite's infection. A high fever set in, that resulted in death. We buried the body for a while, within view of the Long House, within earshot, too. We did a lot of drumming and chanting and so forth, to prepare Sister Cissy's bones.

Yes, Sir. It does get a tad chilly here in the evenings, could be the sea breeze. Makes you shiver doesn't it? I have the same trouble.

Any other questions?

What the Japanese were like?

A little fishy, Ma'm, reminded me of that seagull I ate when my canoe broke on a reef during a storm, and I had to wait for my father to find me. We are what we eat. That makes seagulls flying fish. Japanese are walking fish. Australian soldiers, we met quite a few of those, too, with those hats that curl up on one side, Australians are sort of muttony and Americans kind of beefy.

Haha.

Sorry, Ma'm. Just kidding–I beg your pardon. We're not cannibals on the Tariand Isles. We do have some customs, of course–what tribe hasn't?–but for really consuming human flesh I'd have to refer you to the mainland. Foreign rule stopped flesh eating for some time, as you know, we were colonized for, oh, over a hundred years I should think. There were the Dutch out West side, the Germans up North side, the British/Australians down here, South and East, and roving Portuguese in the Past. Your white tribes' customs differ a little but all you folks agreed that we shouldn't catch and eat each other. "Headhunting," as you called our pastime, took up too much time. You'd rather had us pick coconuts to make margarine or kill off birds of paradise to stick feathers in your girlfriends' hats. All work, no fun for us, all fun, no work for you. Tribal warfare is our fun though, and now that we're on our own again it's drifting back on the mainland.

Ancient customs, something to keep us busy.

How about us island people? Well, everything changes so fast—I'm not too sure. I have no way of knowing for certain but maybe some of our young men still practice a few customs. The young men are very much on their own, you see. We allow our boys some privacy, to grow up in. Adults live rather dull lives, they'll have enough of that later. Eventually they'll be like I am now, I just like to play a little golf. Some fishing in the afternoon. A nap. Watch Chief Arnold in the Long House. Chief Schwarzenegger, on the big monitor, with the VCR the Japanese gave us—that's right, Ma'm.

What kind of customs do our young ones practice?

Our young fellows, from fourteen through seventeen, not an easy age as you may recall, live in the Boys House over there. With the skulls on the veranda. They're plastic, you know. I bought them in London, they came in flat cartons, all broken up in parts, we had to glue the parts together. I had sticky fingers for a week. The skulls do look real, don't they now?

Well, yes, we do train our boys a little, but apart from weekly Instruction we pay no attention to what our successors are doing. For Instruction the boys join us in our Long House. There's ritual, there's story-telling by the chief—our sorcerer, Mr. Waya, is in charge of ritual. We beat wooden drums and shake lizard skin tambourines (baby rat skulls are the djingles) and the Speechless One rattles Sister Cissy's thigh bones. The Long House is dark but the shadows are dancing. Hollow-eyed images of the ancestors look down from the rafters.

9

There is always a draft in the Long House, even if there is no wind outside; it rustles the ancestors' grass skirts and Leia's coral necklace. Mr. Waya's herbal student burns twigs, roots and leaves. The wooden Jesus statue, pale white, lifts its arms while Buddha smiles quietly in his box. The foreign chiefs smile, too, especially chief Elvis when we do his "You're Nothing but a Hound Dog." You know the hymn? Big Bart's Marine fighting knife squeaks in its sheath. We don't have Sergeant Big Bart's bones here but the Speechless One made a mask that catches his likeness. Now that you mention it, I haven't seen that mask lately. I hope she didn't take it out of its niche.

Well, never mind.

So our big boys are humming; the younger ones, with the clear high voices, chant. "Heart Break Hotel." We also have our own hymns. After an hour of good chanting and burning there's that strong acrid smell that shows things are beginning to jump a little.

HA!

Excuse me. I get too enthusiastic.

No, Ma'm, girls are not allowed either in the Long House or in the Boy's House.

After Instruction in the Long House our young men go back to their Boy's House.

What they do there? Play cards I think. Smoke Benson & Hedges, I imagine, that's a brand of cigarettes that is advertised on billboards here: the pictures show handsome warriors in ceremonial dress impressing attentive beautiful girls that look like my dead sister Leia. Everybody smokes. Or the boys drink Budweiser maybe. The schooner brings beer once a week, taking wood sculptures in return. We like to chisel palmwood on this island. Our specialty. Here's an example of our art. See? Big penis on one side, gun butt on the other. The butt side of the art-object curves. The Portuguese raiders, a hundred years ago, were armed with that kind of handgun. Portuguese "blackbirders" didn't do too well here, though. We caught some but most of them died by natural causes. Or so I heard.

Yes. That's true, Ma'm. I did live in the Boys House myself and do recall that in my time. . . of course. . . for instance. . . but I don't know if such a pastime would still be popular now. Each of our Tariand islands had a custom then, when I was a boy–but, as I said, that's a long time ago now–of "hunting *Her*."

"Hunting *Her*" involved sending scouts to the neighboring islands to look for *Her,* for that island's female principle. My sister Leia, on this island, was a candidate to be the female principle, we knew that, but the custom said that we could only use a *Her* from another island. It meant that we had to protect Leia, for boys from another island would be likely to be attracted.

So, when I was a boy living in our Boys House . . .

What the new building is on the other side of the village? Ah, you noticed, did you? It's the Girls House. Oh, some newfangled idea we haven't quite dealt with. We may have to pull that building down soon, but please don't interrupt, Ma'm. I'm trying to tell this story.

So once our scouts determine what girl *Her* inhabits in one of the other islands we would carefully note that girls' habits, her timetable and so forth, when and where she might be alone. Then . . . you really want to hear the story, Ma'm? You're sure? Not too rough for your group? I notice it's mostly female. Okay, I continue.

There might be some sick boys who would stay behind on our home island's Boys House to light and tend fires, burn twigs, make the acrid smoke I mentioned. Us others would sneak out in a war canoe shaped like a two-headed crocodile. You saw the canoe boats in our harbor? Tourist display now,

11

but they were all in use once. We keep our paddles razor sharp so that they can also serve as weapons. Us boys, naked, rubbed with oils, honed by all sorts of war games that we used to play all the time, were weapons ourselves. We would have waited for a moonless, windless night. Once on the chosen island (we have six islands here) we would hide in the jungle that surrounds the village, wait for daybreak, for *Her* to show herself, catch the girl, sling her body from a pole, race back to the canoe, wait for nightfall, paddle home.

And then?

Hmmm. I don't know whether your anthropologists ever got that part of our customs right. Eating human flesh is not for sustenance, you know. We keep pigs for that. The "locating *Her*" custom intends to join spirits, there is no room for the stomach. If boys partake of *Her* it's to harmonize their manhood.

Oh yes, I'm afraid, in those long begone days, we did eat *Her.* There were other sacred customs, too, that came first.

Pardon? You say "rape?"

How could we? Poor girl. Perhaps. But think of the honor though, how the chosen one knew that she did represent the highest, the most elevated part of half of what goes on. How she was the essence of what all men are looking for? Forever?

Think of the custom's aftermath, too. To us, participating boys, the adventure was fraught with danger. If we were caught we died. There was always revenge when the boys from the other island would notice that their divine one was missing and send their scouts to even things out. If they found us they'd have to kill us. Of course they'd also come to find *Her* on this island. Keep us on our toes, so to speak.

Disgusting, you say?

Remember First Lieutenant James Colby, "Jim Bwana?"

What was he suspected of doing? How come Leia got raped, then murdered?

Guilty?

Perhaps you'd like to drink some coconut juice first? We serve Heineken, too. A Perrier for the ladies?

You are refreshed?

Good.

Leia and I had different mothers. Leia's mother was a *Her* who never got caught. We knew Leia was *Her* too and made an effort to guard her.

You saw our girls when you walked up the ramp from the schooner this morning? Arranged into two rows, facing each other, leaving just enough space so that our visitors can shuffle through? Wearing grass-minis? Perfumed with squirrel secretion? Chanting "we love Jesus, we love Jesus?" Bopping while the Speechless One taps her bones to carry the chant? The girls brushing the gentlemen in your party with their breasts? Our new local nuns clapping and smiling?

Leia was many times as attractive.

The American Marines liked to look at Leia but she had eyes for Jim Bwana only. The lieutenant and his men came to set up radio equipment and to train us as spotters but when the Japanese landed patrols too, the Marines stayed on. In order not to attract attention the Marines killed with their knives.

Later when the Japanese had left the area and the Marines had little to do, Jim Bwana had a long jetty built into the ocean. The Marines constructed a little thatch covered hut at the end of the jetty. Jim Bwana liked to sit there quietly for hours on end. I think he was thinking of Leia. He probably knew she was *Her*. Leia kept showing herself to the lieutenant, finding things to do in the yard when he came back from his jetty, smiling, reaching up to pick flowers or fruits.

Even good men are bad sometimes. You have noticed? There was a good bad man in Lieutenant Jim's war group. His name was Big Bart. The sergeant was driven crazy by

Leia's smiles and movements, directed at Jim Bwana, who seemed not to notice. Not expecting a raid from a neighboring island—the Great War was still on—us boys weren't paying attention. Big Bart broke into my sister's cabin one night and raped her. That same night Jim Bwana, made bold by my sister's seductive invitations, finally gathered the courage and knocked on Leia's door. Inside Leia was about to scream for help. Big Bart, hearing the lieutenant's voice, cut Leia's throat. Big Bart escaped through the window. The lieutenant, perturbed by Leia's throaty death-gurgle, entered the cabin. He tried to help Leia, had her leaning against his chest. There was blood all over his tunic. Big Bart had left his knife. The lieutenant wasn't armed. Seeing Leia was dead, the lieutenant panicked. He left, leaving footprints.

We found Leia's corpse in the morning, the blood, the knife, the footprints that enabled us to track the lieutenant, who was waiting for us in his thatched hut at the end of the jetty.

We liked Jim Bwana fine, and we understood what he had been doing, but custom demanded the intruder's death.

We were all very sorry but our brothers, the huge lagoon-crocodiles, were hungry now. We would have to feed them.

The lieutenant told my grandfather, Chief Witu, that he was innocent, but the evidence (although we didn't understand he hadn't tried to eat her) was overwhelming. Even the Marines didn't believe their own chief. Chief Witu kept quiet. He just nodded, had the lieutenant locked up in the bamboo cage behind the Long House and appointed me as a guard. That night I heard my grandfather ask Jim Bwana if his Havvard (I wish I could say it right) training suggested a solution. Jim Bwana said it did not. He had no idea who was the real killer. When he entered Leia's house there was just blood, and the dying woman.

Sergeant Big Bart had gone off to check radio equipment on a hill on the other side of our island.

While all this happened word came from the mainland that the Great War was coming to an end, and we knew our friends, the Marines, were waiting to be picked up by a warship.

There were some twenty victorious white Marines and some five thousand of us black friendly armed and war-trained *Fuzzyheads,* that's what we were called then. It was a term of endearment. We had been of use. There were a few million of us in the islands and on the mainland. It was rude to repay us for our help during the war years by what a Marine lieutenant had done to Leia, daughter of a chief.

As I said before, the matter was tricky.

The Speechless One of that time played Sister Cissy's thighbones and Mr. Waya, after consulting a cracked tortoise shell in the Long House while my father made the acrid smell, set a date and time for pronouncing a verdict. My grandfather's decision could be predicted. Weren't the facts clear? My sister's dead body on the straw mat? The Marine fighting knife on the floor? A man's seed in her shell? Lieutenant Jim's bloody trail leading out of the house toward the jetty, ending in the thatched hut at the end where we found him crying?

So what to do?

My father said that, as the tortoise shell indicated that his final decision had to be reached late that night, it might be nice to have a knife throwing match first. All available Marines and quite a few of our warriors entered the contest. The target was a female figure cut from a lizard's skin that was strapped between bamboo poles. Just as the first contestant was about to throw his knife a heavy rain poured down, as it always did at that time during that part of the rainy season. My father ordered that all knives had to be put on a table while we waited for the downpour to stop. While Mr. Waya beat a drum and the Speechless One danced I replaced one of the Marine's knives with the one that had killed Leia.

15

The rain stopped, everybody went to the table to pick up his knife. One Marine said his weapon was missing. I pointed at the sharp flat dagger that was left on the table.

"Not mine."

"Whose?" my grandfather asked.

All the Americans studied the knife. Although Marine knives are standard issue and apparently look alike they don't stay that way. After a while each Marine knows his own weapon, and those of his friends, by individual dents, stubborn rust spots, blemishes on the handle, or just the feel of the weapon.

Several Marines declared the murderous knife to belong to Sergeant Big Bart. As they were prepared to swear to the truth of their statements, Jim Bwana was released at once.

Beg pardon, Ma'm?

Ah, you want to know what happened to Big Bart, the sergeant? He wasn't there. Feeling guilty, Big Bart was wandering all over our island, on all sorts of errands–catching Japanese stragglers, looking for downed pilots, that sort of thing.

Well, we first had a feast. We were ready, of course. Prize pigs were slaughtered, big fresh grouper fish were lanced with skewers to be rotated above coals, a multi-vegetable stew simmered, crackly tree bugs were being roasted, the girls were lining up for their dance. Us boys were shaking the rain sticks. Leia's image moved in the breeze. We drank captured sake. Big Bart came back in the middle of the party, felt something was wrong and took off again.

No, Ma'm, a lizard got the sergeant. Us boys found Big Bart on the same hill slope as Sister Cissy. Wound fever had almost killed him by then. Sergeant Big Bart died as we carried him in. The Marines had left, we sent the metal tag we took off Big Bart's neck to the mainland, by schooner.

The body?

Crocodiles ate the body, Ma'm. We are of the Crocodile Clan, as I said.

You have to go now?

Thank you, Ma'm. We appreciate presents but on this island we sometimes do things the other way around. Today we don't accept presents. Here is a cassette for each of you. Mr. Waya composed the music. Here, I'll play one for you on this boom-box.

You liked the music?

You heard the thighbones?

Excuse me, Ma'm?

The crying in between the Speechless One's percussion? No, that isn't Big Bart, that's just the sound of large bats with flat faces that fly between the palm tops, looking for coconuts. I tried to chase them away when we were making the recording but my efforts made the Speechless One unhappy. Yes, the big bats do sound rather guilty. Like little male ghost voices, you say? Sorry for catching all those girls? Well, we only caught one girl once every three years or so. It's a custom, you see, with a very deep meaning. Religious, you might say.

So . . . have a safe journey home and please give my regards to Lady Hillary, do tell her to be careful.

Yes, aren't our girls noisy? The Girls House is having a ceremony again. Preparing for something or other? Yes, it does rather seem so. Why they keep chanting "Abau, Abau?" I don't really know. "Abau" is our word for "male principle." What those war canoes are doing in the cove near their building? Our nuns have been encouraging the girls to learn how to paddle.

Times are changing?

Who that handsome boy is? He is my son Kokoda, isn't he an exceptional fellow? A perfect smile. A little fearful maybe.

What is troubling you, Kokoda? The idea that the girls on the other islands, in their newfangled Girls Houses, are chanting "Abau," too?

1985   PAPUA NEW GUINEA   (author's note)

"The grass is always greener on the other side of the fence." Away is always further away when you get there. Australia seemed the ultimate goal but once I settled in Brisbane there was New Guinea, at a distance bridged by a mere hour's flight. Papua New Guinea, land of magic cannibals, tropical beaches, rain forests where the giant casuwari bird stalks, snow mountains, penis sculptures and redhaired dancing women.

While in Brisbane I couldn't go anywhere. I had to work. The desire remained, however, and twenty years later fate grinned. Traveling along the PNG's empty eastern shores, and sailing among the thousand islands that include the sizeable landscapes of New Ireland and Bougainville, time returned to a Now that I could only have partly imagined.

Even cannibalism sounded exciting. The boat's captain told me about a famous German missionary who, when he got old and feeble, asked the local tribal chiefs to please kill and eat him so that his spirit would blend with theirs, the souls of his good friends. The chiefs respectfully declined. New Guinea was still under white rule and the chiefs, although they loved their white brother and would like nothing better than to ceremoniously consume his temporary shape, didn't want to dangle from gallows.

The missionary started the old Diesel engine in his launch and crossed over to the next archipelago. After patiently trying he eventually had himself captured by a distant tribe and became part of a sacred dinner. "Poor bastards got themselves shot and hung by the white Police," my boat captain said. "The old man only wanted to become part of the present."

The foregoing story is not as far-fetched as it seems . . .

LET'S GO
BANANAS

Not my fault, I assure you. What happened to my former employer and tormentor, Herr Huber, was done to him by Madame Pele. Pele is a Hawaiian goddess, and extremely cruel. I couldn't have possibly thought of the punishment Pele inflicted on Herr Huber. I tell you, I had little to do with it. although maybe I was, somehow, the instrument that helped inflict all that pain. Could also be that it had to do with the "Zeitgeist"–you must have noticed that there is a shifting of balance between the sexes now. Perhaps I was the weak human mini-male manipulated by the all-powerful divine giant female.

Yes, I know what you are saying, "Befehl is Befehl," is out of date, that I can't shift blame to higher authority. That's okay if you look at relationships between human beings. I'll have you know that we aren't talking Nazis here, or Hutus vs. Tsutsis, or Serbs against Croats, we are talking about a human being helpless in divine hands.

Remember what the Baghwan said? That Indian guru who drove a stable of Rolls Royces in Oregon and claimed all sorts of insights? The Baghwan said he had met God and that "God is not a nice man, He is not your uncle."

Well, I tell you, I met with Madame Pele twice and Madame Pele is not a nice woman, She is not your aunt.

I'm sorry, you don't know what I am talking about. Okay, I will explain this further. I'm talking about the goddess who rules Hawaii, more specifically rules what Hawaiians call "the Big Island," which consists of two huge volcanos with several live craters, and a lot of gelled lava all around those craters, that has turned into land, for the time being.

Volcanos are miraculous phenomena, they connect the planet's thin surface of illusion with its real core. Truth bubbles up like red-hot liquid fire. You think I exaggerate? Well, look down into the Kilauea volcano, Pele's mouth. The fire is always there and gushes out of the mountain at regular intervals. You try and build a house within the triangle formed by the villages of Naalehu, Kelakekua and Kurtistown. You can if you pay cash. The banks won't grant a mortgage and nobody will insure your home.

You know what Pele can do when she gets angry? Sit back in your hotel room and watch the video of the latest Kilauea eruption, see little people run for their lives as their houses explode into flames behind them and sparks chase them like little birds of death.

My name is Martin Schuppke. I was a journalist then, well, that is exaggerated a bit. I was a "travel writer." Herr Huber had sent me to Hawaii to write nice stuff about a new Japanese-owned hotel there.

Herr Huber owned Huber Verlag then. Yes, it still exists, you must have seen our travelogues, guidebooks and so forth. You can find them in most book stores. In the old days the Verlag liked to do advertising booklets, too. I would get sent all over the world, on cheap tickets, preferably on charters that were being sold out at the last minute, in the back row where the smokers sit (I don't smoke myself) to visit hotels that wanted more business.

That's how I got to the Hualalai Hotel on the Big Island. I was happy there until Herr Huber caught up with me, he and Jutta. Herr Huber was a handsome man who dressed in tailormade clothes. Jutta worked for a Hamburg escort club. He had hired her for the trip. She was, still is, a most beautiful woman, with, normally, a nice disposition. Herr Huber arrived at the Hualalai in a tropical costume and a wide-brimmed linen hat. His full blond beard was trimmed neatly, his sea-blue eyes sparkled. Jutta has long shapely legs, so Herr Huber dressed her in the shortest of miniskirts. She has nice breasts, too, so he made her wear a low-cut blouse and had her push up her bosom so that she looked like a blown-up Barbi doll.

Jutta's appearance had to help convince people that Herr Huber was special. Herr Huber doesn't really care for adult women, he likes young girls, but not too many people know that. I do, of course, for I like young girls too, but for different reasons. I admire their innocence. I think I might like to have daughters, be a father to them, take them ice skating, or to the zoo, help them with their homework. Jutta can't have children, an abortion went wrong and she lost her uterus.

Herr Huber likes to abuse young girls. He used to buy videos where that sort of thing goes on.

Yes, I am Martin Schuppke. When Herr Huber used to address me he would accent the first syllable and pronounce the second in a derogatory way, like some people say "ski." Schupp-ke. As if I came from Outer Siberia or somewhere, and as if that were bad.

"Ah, Schupp-ke," Herr Huber said when he saw me on the terrace of the Hualalai Hotel. He pointed me out to Jutta, as if I were an insect, a "Schupp-ke," a local species of cockroach. He didn't introduce us. She got pointed out, too. She was no

21

insect, but a whore, that he had rented. "Jutta does as she is told, Schupp-ke. If she doesn't she gets into trouble with the Agency, because I will complain, and they'll send her back to the street, eh? Darling?"

She didn't answer. He stared at her. "Answer me, darling."

"Yes, Herr Huber."

I never asked Jutta what she thought of me that time. I didn't ask because I knew. Look, I'm an undersized chinless big-nosed type with large feet. My head is big, too, and I have small eyes. They're colorless and stare stupidly through thick glasses. They're too close together. My eyes aren't my best feature.

These days I dress better, but at that period I still wore my father's clothes: double-breasted jackets and too-wide trousers and frayed silk neckties with gaudy coloration. I couldn't afford to buy clothes on what Herr Huber paid me.

Herr Huber's arrival spoiled the evening for me. The Hualalai is a too-expensive hotel (rooms start at $600 a day) and everything is kind of ridiculous there but the music is fantastic. The Kahuku Song Boys were on that evening. I had heard the group before and was looking forward to the concert.

Native Hawaiian music is special. We hear stuff in Europe that is cracked up to be Hawaiian and is played by imitators. We believe that those silly long twangs on metallic strings and childish voices going on about sunsets and pineapple juice are the real thing, especially when some Asiatic women wobble their hips and make grass skirts flop.

Not so at all. The Kahuku Song Boys are immensely fat men and don't wobble or flop anything, except perhaps the immense folds of their bellies. I couldn't believe what I saw the first time. The singers showed themselves as human puddings sitting on steel stools (the "boys" are too heavy to stand up for more than a few seconds), with small heads on top, like decorative cherries. Their tiny instruments are ukuleles, that disappear into the jelly of their huge bellies. When the musicians pluck the strings it looks like they are masturbating. I wanted to laugh or blush but forgot my amazement when the music started up. The flow of these Hawaii-originated songs seemed to fill the universe. For once my silly mind stopped babbling and pretty soon it had gone altogether. There was only the music, the long notes those pure voices poured out in all directions. The magnificent sunset around us–the hotel is built on a hilltop–became part of the song. My spirit, or whatever I had changed into, joined the vast living stillness of the Pacific Ocean. I suddenly began to see that perhaps everything was all right after all, that there was no reason to be either happy or sad, that all and I were identically godlike.

The evening Herr Huber and Jutta showed up I wanted to hear that amazing music again but Herr Huber insisted on talking and laughing and ordering drinks loudly and eating noisily.

The music became mere background and the sunset looked like colored wallpaper as Herr Huber belittled Jutta and me. He described me as a defective genie he had found in a beer bottle, as his low-cost projection that he sent cheaply from place to place to collect impressions. He told Jutta that he had to edit all my work, that my writing, even after years of practice, was still either flat or expressed on a *"schwaermend"* pubertal level. "Schupp-ke still suffers from *Weltschmertz,* darling. *You* don't do that, do you?" Herr Huber painfully tweaked Jutta's cheek. "Whores are tough. They know true values, and truth is pretty cheap, nothing our guides advertise is worth all that much. We paint the product up with clichés, call it what we know the traveling sheep will go for. All we do is help herd them to their hotels so that they

23

can be properly shorn for the season. Then they can fly home to grow more money again."

In a way he was right. Huber Verlag's advertising aims at the common denominator, at what the average middle class tourist expects to collect in return for what he can borrow on his credit card. My mistake, often, is that I delve too deeply. When Herr Huber asked me what I had been doing the last few days I stupidly told him that I had been researching the folklore of the Big Island. I even told him about my interest in the awesome Madame Pele. As soon as he understood what I was trying to tell him Herr Huber shut me up rudely. "Scuba diving, you asshole, that's what you're paid for to find out about. The foreign food, for God's sake, cheap fish or whatever. How safe everything is out here. That nothing can possibly happen to the suckers our travelogue targets. The free guided tours the hotels throw in, did you get details on those? You have notes on the excellent medical provisions here, included in regular health insurance? That kind of crap, Schupp-ke, garnished with a few mynah birds that talk back when tourists say Hello, and a palm tree or two, not the kind that drops coconuts on silly people's heads. Who the fuck cares about a forbidding goddess or the local bullshit fairies? You want to scare our precious clients?"

Jutta was supposed to laugh at my ignorance but she didn't. She wanted to excuse herself but Herr Huber wouldn't even let his expensive escort go to the bathroom. Jutta could do that on her own time, he needed her now to show off her "T and A."

Jutta didn't know that expression.

"Tits and ass, darling."

"When is my own time?" Jutta asked.

"When I am in bed, darling, you know I have no need of you there." Herr Huber's perfect teeth showed in a lopsided grin. "Don't want to catch some vile disease, do I now?"

24

Fortunately, Herr Huber over-indulged other appetites. He bought Jutta a tuna sandwich—he wouldn't even let her look at the menu—because, he said, she had to watch her diet. "Living off your beautiful body, darling, like you do . . . eh?"

I had to pay for my own tonic water, no lime. Fortunately the potato chips were complimentary and I managed to get a double helping.

Herr Huber himself feasted on baked lobster and all the trimmings. He polished off a $100 bottle of wine that looked like it had just been dusted. For desert it was "Let's go Bananas," the most expensive item the menu listed. The dish was assorted ice creams over fruit in a little silver bucket that the waiter filled up with a Hawaiian liqueur.

A double cognac finally did the trick for Herr Huber. Jutta and I watched with fascination when our respective client and employer suddenly froze. He stared straight ahead. He became pale. Then his sinuses emptied out via his nostrils.

It was disgusting to see those two parallel stalactites of slow flowing phlegm reaching down to his plate overloaded with after-dinner mint bon-bons.

The waiter, after making sure Herr Huber signed his voucher, including a tip filled in by the waiter himself, looked at Jutta and me. When we both shook our heads he called over an athletic busboy to guide, and support, the hotel's star guest back to his suite.

Once Herr Huber was gone I invited Jutta for a snack in downtown Kona. She drove Herr Huber's rented Cadillac down to the city where we found a reasonably priced restaurant. Jutta insisted on paying for our broiled sole and fresh salads. Her income was better than mine, she said. She hoped I didn't object to the way she made her money.

I stuttered—I must admit that I was taken by Jutta right from the start—that I didn't mind at all what she chose to do with her life.

Jutta is trained to please her company and she remembered my attempt to tell Herr Huber about my study of Hawaiian folklore. I now told Jutta about the legend of Madame Pele. There were two things that enraged her divine presence. The Hawaiian goddess was said to become upset when women were abused, and when tourists took things away from the island.

"Things?" Jutta asked.

"Shells," I said, "rocks, flowers, any kind of memento."

According to my research this last item on Pele's "No No" list was well documented. Many tourists who had taken parts of the Big Island home later mailed them back to Hawaii. The Kona and Hilo Post Offices are used to a steady stream of parcels containing the sort of things tourists tend to pick up or pull off or dig up, neatly packed in tissue paper, accompanied by bank notes and polite letters, asking the Post Master to please take the trouble to return the enclosed items to beaches, fields or forests.

"Pele puts a curse on the tourists?" Jutta asked. "Those people had a traumatic experience, you think?"

The articles I had read in the Kona Public Library hadn't mentioned any details in that respect. I suggested that the offenders might have nightmares, that Pele told them in their dreams that they should return their booty, or maybe they suffered physical discomfort associated with the shells or stones.

"An allergy?" Jutta suggested.

Could be. Hives. Shingles. Boils. Who knows. Could be that the bodily symptoms were linked with feelings that called up the articles the tourists had taken home.

"You could try it out," I joked. We were sitting outside on the restaurant's porch. I pointed at a small piece of driftwood lying nearby. "Put it in your handbag, see what happens."

"Not me," Jutta laughed.

26

Jutta wanted to know what Madame Pele looks like.

My information said that the goddess, being divine, could show herself in any form or shape, but seemed to prefer to appear either as a Polynesian old woman, almost bent double with age and disease, or as a young beautiful local girl. I also remembered that Madame Pele, although her punishments were supposed to be harsh and painful, always did give due warning.

Herr Huber needed a few days to recover from the emptying out of his skull's cavities. Jutta had to take care of his needs and I worked on my travelogue in the servant's room the hotel made me sleep in.

"Schupp-ke," Herr Huber said, when he found me again. "Why don't you take me and Jutta for a drive. By now you must know the island. I still feel weak. I'll sit in the back of the car and doze a little, with my head on Jutta's lap, and you wake me up when there is something to see."

There you go again. Are you telling me that I shouldn't have taken Herr Huber to the bubbling burning crater? It is true that there are plenty of other attractions on the Big Island. There's the huge and spectacular Parker's Cattle Ranch with Hawaiian cowboys, with a nice steak restaurant. There's the spectacular rain forest on the East Coast. I could have driven Herr Huber across mountain roads, shown him USA Special Forces, maneuvering their Humvee war-vehicles, the kind Arnold Schwarzenegger drives, on the Alpine Meadows. But no, I had to choose the volcano. Well, damn it, maybe I did have to take Herr Huber there, perhaps I was under some compulsion. I don't recall planning that hellish trip as a means to revenge myself on Herr Huber.

We arrived at Kilauea and I woke Herr Huber and suggested he'd walk the rest of the way and look down into the living volcano. I thought he might refuse, being still tired and ill, but he got out of the car with some gusto. It turned out that he wanted to pick up strangely formed white lava rocks that can be found all over the mountain's slopes. I should have told him to leave the rocks alone but I didn't feel like being yelled at again. Jutta didn't say anything either. While Herr Huber was picking up some fair-sized rocks and putting them into the rented Cadillac's trunk, a young girl approached him. She looked just like the picture on a box of candy Herr Huber had bought earlier on and that he had been eating from during the journey. He didn't offer Jutta and me any of course, claiming that the chocolate-covered macadamia nuts were "too damned expensive to waste on servants and pleasure girls." The likeness between the picture on the candy box and the live girl was amazing. She looked pure Hawaiian, with a golden skin, long brown hair and delicate features. The mouth seemed rather sexy and inviting for a twelve-year-old girl but Hawaii is tropical and Polynesian girls grow quickly. She wore a crown of leaves decorated with little red wild berries. The girl's flaming red cotton blouse was off the shoulders and showed the outline of budding breasts and her skirt was made out of rough plaited linen. She wore a double necklace of red coral.

Although the girl's eyes were large and innocent, I did get an impression of savage wisdom.

Amazingly enough the girl spoke German without any accent. She smiled briefly at us and then skipped over to Herr Huber asking him what he wanted to do with the rock he had just picked up. Herr Huber, leering at the girl, said he wanted to use it to mark a path in his garden in Stuttgart. "Why don't you help me?" he suggested. "If you point out some nice rocks, behind those bushes over there, I will pay you big dollars." He took out his billfold to show her how fat it was.

"Don't you have any rocks in your own country?" she asked.

28

Herr Huber kept smiling and showing her his money and pointing at the bushes.

The two of them went off. Jutta and I both thought–we discussed what happened afterward–that the girl seemed capable enough to either push the sickly Herr Huber over, should he bother her, or to run away, and that there was no need to protect her at this stage of the proceedings.

You may say that by then I knew something dangerous was going on and should have mentioned the matter to Herr Huber. Well, okay, you may say whatever you like but the truth of the matter was that Jutta and I had sudden headaches. We later agreed that we felt as if our brains were zapped with long insidious flames.

Herr Huber came back alone, muttering that the girl had suddenly disappeared. "I didn't even get a chance to touch her. Bitch didn't want to take any money either." He shook his head. "That girl can move. Her feet hardly touched that hot rock."

In my defense I should mention here that I did ask Herr Huber whether he noticed that the girl had spoken to him in German. He just growled at me. He growled again when I asked whether he had asked the girl for her name.

Later that day, after we had looked down into the bubbling and boiling crater, we stopped off at a village restaurant for lunch. As is customary in Hawaii we ate on a wide porch with a thick straw roof. From where we sat we had a good view of the village main street. Herr Huber went out of his way to put Jutta down. He said that as she probably never had much formal training, and therefore didn't know much about any of the arts, he felt that, as a publisher, he should fill her in on modern literature. Had Jutta ever heard of the French prize-winning *Story of O?* Well, O was a fairly common woman Jutta's age, also with long legs and big breasts, who fell in love with a man of the Parisian upper classes. As her lover thought she needed training he passed her along to his older friends. O obediently succumbed to these men's perverted wishes and humiliated herself in every way her masters demanded. Herr Huber then described, in detail, all sorts of male-arousing tortures O underwent. While Jutta and I ate our cheeseburgers, and Herr Huber picked at an appetizer of roasted quails before getting into his fillet mignon, in between gulping two double martinis, his voice got louder. He spoke English so that other guests could enjoy Jutta's discomfort. As the alcohol took over Herr Huber thought it would be fun to pretend slashing Jutta's nipples with his steak knife. Just as I thought I could stand it no longer and contemplated slapping Herr Huber's beautifully bearded face, a police car entered the village street.

Two burly white cops, corseted into tight black uniforms, ran to one of the pretty wooden cottages shaded by blossoming frangipani trees. They came out a minute later pushing an old man ahead of them. The old man, a native Hawaiian, dressed in a kimono, looked like a sage with a personality problem. He was wobbling his tufted eyebrows as he looked over his shoulder. He berated the two constables in a squeaky, angry voice. Behind him a little old woman, bowed down by osteoporosis, stood in the open doorway of the cottage, arms folded, smiling up at the scene. I kept looking at her. It was the same thing as with the young girl on the volcano. I sensed an aura of extraordinary power.

"Schupp-ke," Herr Huber ordered. "Go over there and find out what the hell is going on."

I went out, napkin in hand, and asked the constables why they had handcuffed the old gentleman. The biggest of the cops thumbed back at the old lady in the cottage. "The missus got tired of this fool of a husband abusing her." The constable showed me a long knife. "We have had complaints before. Suspect keeps threatening to cut her with this saber if she doesn't hurry up dinner. We have warned subject before, this time we take him in on a charge of attempted manslaughter, maybe that'll teach the old moron a lesson."

"And he'll be convicted, you think?" I looked at the old man, who was rattling his handcuffs while mumbling to himself.

"For sure," the other cop said. "Old man Makika will be spending time in jail." He pushed his prisoner. "Jails ain't much fun here."

Although the conversation took place within Herr Huber's hearing distance my boss wasn't impressed. He sliced his steak and guffawed. "That'll teach that cute old nigger."

The next day Herr Huber had me pack his bizarrely-shaped white lava rocks into a carton with some batiked sarongs and other Asian clothes he had bought. Jutta drove the parcel to Kona Post Office and had it airfreighted to Herr Huber's address in Stuttgart. Herr Huber himself spent the day on the beach where he found a rusted cylinder of propane gas, the kind that's used on ships for cooking. He told me later that the cylinder hissed when he hit its top with a rock and that he had thought that it would be fun if he could light the escaping gas. He had enjoyed martinis for lunch again. Suffering from impaired judgement he was chuckling to himself when he lit a match.

Surfers who happened to be coming in on a large wave told me that they saw Herr Huber running about the beach. His hair and skin were ablaze. Being blinded he ran away from the water. The surfers turned him round and doused the fire in the sea but by then there had been considerable damage. He was wrapped in a blanket, which aggravated his wounds, and driven to a hospital and later helicoptered to Honolulu. Jutta and I flew along. There was a problem with Herr Huber's insurance and the hospital in Honolulu, after exhausting Herr Huber's credit cards and the cash he carried, suggested that the patient be flown home on Lufthansa.

I never quite found out what was the trouble with Herr Huber's policy, but in Germany there didn't seem to be proper coverage either. Of course, as a high income earner, he was responsible for his own insurance. The skin grafts and other operations Herr Huber underwent were immensely expensive. Huber Verlag, without a leader, lost money. Herr Huber had to sell his house and most of the shares of his now failing company. As I knew the routine of the company quite well a bank was willing to finance Jutta's take-over.

Herr Huber became a minor shareholder and stayed on as an employee.

Jutta's savings were considerable; that helped a lot.

Jutta and I had married by then.

The rocks that Herr Huber took? We sent those back of course, with a check to the Hilo Post Master and a request to return the rocks to the slopes leading up to the Kilauea crater. We also wrote a note of apology to Madame Pele, that we asked the Postmaster to drop into the "mouth of Pele." Herr Huber signed the note. His wounds healed a bit better after that.

Herr Huber has recovered but the ordeal has changed his looks. In order to make the new skin grow the doctors told him to eat a lot so now Herr Huber is obese. He is also quite bald, for none of the burned hair grew back. He no longer shaves and he looks like a misshapen gigantic baby. He can't walk well so he mostly uses a wheelchair.

I don't know why Jutta keeps him. Huber works hard, of course, writing the travelogues from notes that Jutta and I bring back from our trips. He keeps the place organized, even clean, as he likes to tie the vaccuum cleaner to his wheelchair. But he is such a sight that I worry that he will make a bad impression on our clients. I keep telling my wife that the business is so profitable that we can easily afford better looking staff.

My assistant calls me "Herr Schuppke" now, without the hyphenating that made me feel ethnic. It seems that he can never do enough to please "Frau Direktor."

Jutta usually ignores him but when she hands down orders she calls him "Hub-ke."

FRIENDS

W e mostly look back when we get old. That's one of those home truths we won't believe in until later, when proof stares us in the face. I don't like looking back–I prefer going ahead, toward ever-receding landscapes– but I don't make the laws of life: another home truth old age offers to displease us.

As there was little more to be done, fate had me surrendered to an existence within repetitive flashbacks, viewed from the terrace glued to my retreat in the Florida Keys. My sole companion was a parrot who didn't like me. He should have liked me in return for liberal daily helpings of Miami-supplied bird deli and overpriced spring water originating hundreds of miles away, but he called me "con man." He pronounced the term delicately, with his head held to the side, whispering, pushing the insult from the tip of his tongue, as if he entrusted me with delicious confidential information. He knew I was a con man because when things got bad, he heard me as I walked into the barren fields stretching toward my cove and shouted, "Jannie Jansen, you're a con man!"

Actually, I'm more than that. I'm also the tormentor of my dear deceased wife, who I humiliated for many long years, never giving in, always interrupting her conversation, always telling her what to do and what not to. I also dodged paying taxes and cared for no one but myself.

A baddie, right?

Sure. However, I do keep trying to provide excuses. It sometimes pays off. I didn't really spoil my wife's life on purpose. She invited trouble, too–the blunt, double-edged knife of daily disharmony was expertly handled by the both of us. Crooking the I.R.S.? Listen, old buddy, you don't really expect me to fund our debt-producing bureaucracy, do you? And if I don't pamper myself, who will? I'm a lonely old geezer, lost, wandering about sadly in my eleven-room "cottage" (that's what we call our dwellings here to impress tourists with our modesty), prey to my own wealth. Who has choices, anyway? Aren't we humans programmed for badness?

I do plead guilty to choosing to be a con man, however. My conscience won't budge there. It's right, I assume guilt.

I used to do real estate in Boston, in partnership with young Frank, who then owned a quarter of our successful enterprise. I was good at what I did and I made our business profitable, but the older I got the less I did. I would mostly disperse approving nods. After a few thousand of those, Frank had done well enough. My patience was rewarded. I wanted out.

"Listen here, Frankie," I said, "either you buy my three quarters or I'll offload my share of the shares to our dishonorable competition." I stared his protests down. "Don't forget," I told him, "with seventy-five percent, I'm king of the castle. I can sell to anyone who offers a reasonable price."

Frankie put on his hangdog mask.

"I don't think," I said, "you'd care to work for the competition, right?"

Frank had to agree. There's no way in the world of real estate that Frankie could work with that bunch of cutthroats.

He didn't mind paying my price if I was willing to finance. I backed off in disgust. "None of that, Frankie. Your senior partner is looking for cash." My figure was steep, for there's such a thing as taking care of the future. Business was booming then, buyers were begging, you couldn't shove pricey property down their throats fast enough, but real estate is a business, and like all business it moves in waves. What soars up crashes down. Fat years turn into lean years. Capitalism roars, capitalism weeps. 'Twas ever thus, and well I knew, having seen prosperity wane into misery and vice versa again and again.

Frank didn't share my foresight. He believed my optimistic sales talk and was still too inexperienced to see through my self-serving bluffing. He gave me what cash he had and borrowed the balance from the greediest of banks. I grabbed the loot, rushed south, and hardly got myself settled into the luxury of Florida reef life when the market turned and Frank's house of cards began to slide.

A bad business indeed, but good young Frank refused to blame me. He worked even harder and managed to stay more or less upright. He denied himself and his family to keep making payments on his bank loan. I shouldn't have pushed him into that predicament.

Was I punished? Well, yes, I think I was. I'm short of breath these days, my heartbeat sometimes slips into uncontrolled solos, and my stomach tends to cramp. Bad conscience, what else? My wife sighed and left for housewife heaven and the loneliness that replaced her hurt me about as bad as my body.

I do the Key things—some fair-weather planing in my 400 HP Suzuki bayboat, a bit of downbeat whoopee that Miami callgirls drive down to hand out now and then—I even motor to Key West once a week to share my sunset with the weirdos. But where others see a dapper senior citizen in a Tom Wolfe suit filling in the long vacation, I define myself as an agonized asshole.

Can guilty pains be soothed? My wife's ashes were sprinkled into the cove and I regularly float roses on the spot. It's a bother to get fresh roses sometimes, what with pushy tourist traffic during season and my dimmed eyesight that makes me slow down and infuriates the rig drivers up back. Even so, I keep going. My Jaguar shivers while the hurricane roars up to mile-long bridges, tropical rain-storms flood my windscreen. I make a dramatic effort, not without danger. Once the Jaguar got pushed across two lanes, steel railing sparked, I lost consciousness, and the car got hit by a truck—nearly flipped into the Gulf of Mexico—but I kind of liked that.

What else do I do to reduce the weight of sin? I pay into a fund for the homeless and am easy on others, even when she is a new-to-the job waitress spilling blood-red chowder over my British striped suit and Thai silk tie. "Never mind, dear." I smile, tip double, call up my probation angel, point out the good deed, and hope the blessed one takes note.

I also think of young Frank. I know exactly how much I took him for and would like to pay that back, but I know him too well. He'd tear up the check.

Sometimes things get too much for me in this impossible paradise of clear water and sky, with exotic imported fauna to liven up mangrove jungle and sparse bushes of the native pine, and especially the wondrous, everlasting show provided by abundant and splendid birds: fisheagles nesting on billboards, white herons daintily treading their way through the weeds, pelicans patiently dive-bombing the cove. Then, overcome, I catch the Boston plane.

Back home, I stay at the best hotel. Whoever cares to notice me (nobody does, but I may fantasize my suppositions) sees me in winter plumage above the burnt-in tan: three-piece tweed, Bogart-style fur-lined raincoat–affluent and empty-handed.

First lunch, traditionally, is with young Frank, who politely wants to know how things are.

"Good," I assure him. "Everything is smooching along as planned. How about you, meboy?"

Frank doesn't want to load me down with his worries. Isn't he keeping up the firm's good name? He wants me to believe things couldn't be better. Most of our staff is gone, the old half-page advertising splendor is reduced to a square inch in a cheap place, and the Beacon Hill office is moved to a Cambridge alley, but we won't mention any of these trifles.

Frank holds onto a big smile.

"Anything wrong, meboy?"

So Frankie tells me, after all–in bits and pieces connected by the slight stutter that's part of his tarnished image these days. The Dutch dark beer I like to lunch on and which I urge on submissive Frank helps to open him up. Business is disastrous, but (his smile recalls days long past) there's still one good chance to get back, contained within a four-story waterfront warehouse near Fosters Wharf that he bought outright at an auction, cheap.

"Big building, meboy? Refurbishable? Future lofts for the wealthy?"

"Yessir. Badly abused, of course, but the possibilities are in place." Frank warms up. "Splendid location–adjacent properties have been remodeled as elegant condominiums.

It's a solid project that can easily house five huge apartments. The view reaches all the way across the harbor. There shouldn't be a finance problem, either. The bank had a look and the loan officer loves the project."

Great. Just what young Frank needed. So why didn't his smile hold?

"I can't get into the building," Frank said.

Squatters? Squatters are rough these days. Big-time drug-dealers back them up, they like having slums for trading in, but the police, when properly approached, take an interest in clearing infested real estate. And there are other ways, too. Could I help?

"Even squatters can't get entry, Mr. Jansen."

"Wild rats? Big bugs?"

Frank belched softly behind a politely raised hand. "A ghost."

I didn't laugh that one off. I have some experience with ghosts. I won't admit to the gift in public, but I'm a bit of a medium myself—a "channeler," as they call it these days. I meet with dead people at times. They don't bother always to step aside nicely.

First one was Uncle Jerry, most unexpectedly met with in the upstairs corridor of our old house in Charles Street. I must have been five years old when the incident occurred, and urgently motivated by a pressing piddle. There Uncle strutted along, under his wide-rimmed felt hat, behind his silvertopped cane. Uncle always behaved like a good guy, so I wasn't supposed to be frightened—although I had no idea what he could be doing in our corridor in the early hours, and how come I could suddenly look through his neat old shape? It was the night Uncle died. He was known for his politeness and I think now he wanted to say goodbye.

Later on I saw other ghosts. A gentleman who had been run over by a truck and walked calmly, and in good order, toward the sky, leaving his mashed body on the tarmac. Then–a more recent experience–there was Sam, our cat, being ripped apart by the ferocious Doberman from up the road and simultaneously wafting away through the abundant foliage of our poinciana tree.

Much farther down the Florida Keys, close to the mainland, next to an extensive cemetery, I ran out of gas once and had to listen to the residents' thin crying while observing their vague movements.

"A ghost holds up your money project?" I asked Frank.

Frank nodded. "I didn't want to believe it, either, Mr. Jansen, but I did try to spend a night in the building's loft. The last inhabitant left some furniture and I relaxed on his couch for a minute, must have dozed off." Frank dabbed at sweat drops on his forehead. "I had a bad time, Mr. Jansen. I couldn't stand it–rushed out after a while, fell down, hurt my ankle. Cut my shin, too. I haven't dared to go back." Businessmen try to be pragmatic. Frank is a good Catholic.

"Get a priest," I said. "Your religion accepts ghosts. The priest shows up with his incense burner and all spooky spoilsports take themselves somewhere else."

Frank smiled shakily. "Yes, Mr. Jansen. I did get an exorcist, but it didn't work at all. The priest is seeing a therapist now– a Zen Trappist monk." He tried to laugh cynically.

I might have entered into a discussion, but I suddenly saw what I was about to do. I presented my suggestion.

"You?" Frank asked. "But, sir, you've got heart trouble–you should take things easy."

"I'd like to see the project, Frank," I said.

We made an appointment and met that evening in front of Frank's building. I couldn't help rubbing my hands gleefully when I saw the property's strong lines, solid foundation, and framing. If Frank could get this project to move, he'd make up his losses and have plenty to spare. I could see it all: gut the inside, construct plastered and white-washed interior walls, put up mahogany wainscoting in the living rooms and studies, use marble floors for the halls, install huge picture windows to maximize on-the-waterfront views, throw in jacuzzis, go all out on the industrial-sized elevator (I envisioned a little Victorian anteroom, complete with Empire easy chairs on a Persian rug), rig laundry chutes to the basement, and a centralized vacuum cleaner with outlets everywhere. Oh dear-dear-dear, prices could be jacked skyhigh and an easy half million made forthwith.

I congratulated Frank on his lucky find.

"Thank you," Frank said. "But what good is it if nobody can spend any time in the building? I won't allow you to go in, either, sir. I plan to auction the property, and hopefully I'll get my investment back."

To improve Frank's mood, I took him to one of the cozy new eating places near Battery Street and loosened his resistance with whiskey up front and cognac for dessert. During the evening he gave me the building's key.

Guilt causes courage, but not enough in my case. I was sorry before I closed the door behind me. The light switch didn't function. The flashlight Frank had given me illuminated a dust cloud that preceded me into the creaky elevator. A momentarily visible rat and his rustling companions made me groan with fear and I dropped the flashlight and broke it.

The elevator's cast-iron harmonica door squeaked sarcastically when I reached the top floor. I groped about shakily, managed to find the loft's entry, and more rusty hinges complained as I pushed open a door and contemplated the huge hole behind it. Finally mustering enough courage to enter, I was caught by a curtain that wrapped itself around

42

my neck. I tore free and the curtain retreated to a window, sucked back by a draft.

Streetlights helped me see the curtain's folded face, and I heard its voice, built up out of the hinges' creaking, a car that snarled by on the quay, the ploppering of a helicopter high above the harbor.

"Heeheehee," an old man laughed. "Coming to vihihisit?"

I could hear my heart's rattle bouncing off my ribs.

The curtain embraced me again and I struggled with it weakly.

The little light that sneaked in from the street seemed cold and uncaring. I sat on the windowsill. The old man had somehow managed to grow a shape that could float free—I saw him as a wasted derelict, a streetperson strayed indoors. Hollow sounds ejected from between his bony jaws, scarcely covered by dried-out skin. I noticed his long and slender canines, green-edged with age, but still strong and sharp. There was a sparkle of deeply socketed eyes under brows that looked bent from rusty wire.

So Frank's apparition did exist: a sketchy but fearsome reflection of a past human form. The ghost dressed himself in paint-splashed pants dangling from frayed pink suspenders. He came closer again, clawing his long bone-fingers, stabbing with blackened doglike nails, then backed off and searched in the rear of the vast room, rummaged in a cupboard where glasses tinkled. Then, evidently not finding what he was looking for, he moved away, shuffling on old-fashioned checkered slippers.

Okay, so this demon stood between Frank's and my financial recovery. What could he do to me? I tried to remember good old Uncle Jerry—*he* didn't harm me, and neither did the spooks partying above the cemetery near Miami. I managed to still my shaky nerves and moved away from the windowsill, aiming for a filthy couch. I found an empty wine bottle on the way and picked it up, considering it to be somewhat of a weapon.

The loft smelled of mold. Something moved from a large crack in the wall facing me and became an oversized moth, shaking itself free of crumbly cement. It flapped close and I swung the bottle, missing the foe but managing to knock off my glasses with my other hand. I was on the floor groping for them, finally locating them and putting them on again, when I saw a rat's beady eyes looking at me. The foot-sized beast stepped briskly forward, ears pointed, bare tail curled up. The moth's wings touched my neck. The ghost shuffled by, stopped, turned toward me, and scratched its thin nose as if suddenly surprised. "Hey." I cleared my throat. "Sir?" "You're not to use that couch," he shrieked. "Ef off. I sleep there."

"You're dead, Mr. Ghost," I said slowly, as if peeling the words off my tongue.

"What if I am?" he asked. "You're still on my couch." I noticed that some of his words got away from him and trilled along as if blown out of a pathetic pennywhistle.

Rat and moth rushed and flew about, straight through my ghostly host—the rat traversed his skinny ankles, the moth pierced his head.

He pointed at me. "A drop?"

"What was that?" I asked.

"A drop. Gimme that bottle."

I made my reluctant body get up from the couch. Maybe the ghost would respond to a bit of good manners. I bowed, said my name.

His claw rushed at me, grabbed the bottle, slapped its bottom, approached the neck with his beaklike nose, and inhaled noisily.

I asked what his name was.

He put the bottle on the floor-carefully, as if he was saving its precious contents. "Nothing to do with you, effah," he croaked. "Here, here, you eff off, right? Or–" He pranced closer, clapping his hands.

"I can't leave," I said.

His hands dropped. "Why not?"

"Because of my former partner," I said. "The man you chased away. He paid good money for this building and now you won't let anyone near the place. I'm here to make you see it's you who has to leave."

The rusty eyebrows moved up. "Your man bought my building? So where's the cash?"

"You're dead, sir," I said. "Money is no good to you."

His claws closed slowly around the frayed pink suspenders. "Cash buys booze. *Give,* you effah." The recessed eyes twinkled. He evidently liked the expression. He said it again. "Effah!" He laughed.

"Maybe the cash passed to your heirs," I said.

The suddenly released suspenders hit his ribcase. "Don't have none."

"So what's left for you here?" I asked. "Why don't you go to heaven where you're awaited? Heaven is supposed to be quite a pleasant place."

"Listen," he squeaked, "maybe I can't call the cops any more but there's lots of devils here. You want me to set a few on you?" He looked over his shoulder. "The man here wants your home. Come on, boys, get him." His transparent finger poked through my chest.

The rat showed up and sat half within the old man's feet, the animal's face more clearly drawn than the ghost's outline. The rat was real."And so am I real," the ghost said. "More so even."

Telepathy. Why not? Released from the body, ghosts should be better equipped with subtle senses than us.

The spook's finger wobbled. "You've no idea what we can be up to here."

"You're insubstantial," I said. "You can't hurt me."

"You're an effah. As soon as you're asleep, your mind is mine and once I chew it a bit it should have trouble getting back." He giggled. "How's that for substance? Remember how the other guy gave in? The priest? So are you leaving now maybe? Or do you want me to tear at your substantial soul while Ratty here nibbles on your toes? Pain is pain and you're about to feel it." He waved both arms. "Here's your last chance. We get you at the count of three. Uh-one, uh-two-"

The moth frightened me more than the ghost or the rat. The huge insect came fluttering toward me from the old man's navel. I tried to catch the wicked insect, but it evaded me smartly. The old man laughed at my hectic dance of fear.

I was getting tired, but there was no way I could allow myself to nod off. Unfortunately, I do tend to fall asleep suddenly of late and I can't do without naps. I sleep helplessly in cabs, planes, waiting rooms.

The ghost read my mind and sneered. He pointed at the couch.

"Go ahead, lie down, relax-heh heh."

I did have to lie down. He tiptoed around the couch—I could hear the joints in his foot bones crackle. I tried to sit up so I could ward off his blows, but I felt too weak. The alcoholic dinner was a bad mistake. Sleepy, drunk, and fighting a demon—all this would hardly improve my fate. The old man soon had his fangs in my throat. "Nice booze," he murmured.

"Vampire," I groaned.

"Nah." He withdrew and briefly touched his mouth with the back of his hand. "I only need the vapors. Real blood would be gross." He gestured toward the door. "Okay, I'll let you go." His eyes glinted briefly. "Get lost."

I staggered to the door. Frank would just have to excuse me—each man has his limit. I'd come dangerously close to mine.

A cruising cab stopped and took me to the hotel. The phone in my room was ringing. "Thank heaven," Frank said. "How did it go?"

"Yes, yes," I said vaguely. "Frank—what's the old geezer called?"

"Max Polski."

"What else do you know?"

"He was an eccentric miser," Frank said. "He used to let the building out to sweatshops, but he kept raising the rent and finally everybody left. Then he moved in himself and spent most of his time drinking. Didn't pick up his mail one week, and when the postman got the police to break down the door old Max had been dead on his couch for quite a while. The city auctioned the place to collect unpaid taxes. We're up against the devil here, sir."

"Frank," I said, "unfortunately, I'm not a quitter. Phone some cleaning outfit as soon as you hit your office. I want them to go there right away with a sizable crew—safety in numbers—and scrub out that place good. All the furniture and curtains—whatever clutters the place up gets into a dumpster and away. Have them clean out cobwebs, soak the floors with whatever dissolves vermin, sprinkle rat poison around, blow killing gas into the cracks."

"Any idea of the cost, sir?" Frank asked sadly.

"No problem—I pay," I said brightly.

Frank stood his ground. "Please, Mr. Jansen, you're wasting your money. Nothing works against that kind of evil. Even the priest—"

"The priest prepared our way," I said. "Max must be weaker since the good man whacked him with incantations and incense. I probably got through to him a little, too. His morale should be low now. Get that cleaning crew, Frank. Today. On the double."

I felt Frank weakening. The building mattered to him as much as it did to me. He must have understood by then that I wanted to even things out with him. My brain may be obsolete but I can still do simple sums. The profit Frank could make on Polski's place would equal what I suckered him for on that goodbye deal I set up for him when we split. If I could get Max out, it should lessen my load of guilt.

The next night I showed up at the building again. The smell of cleaning products nearly knocked me over. Polski's wafty appearance waited for me on the top floor. His ratty friend was around but seemed rather listless and the moth was nursing a torn-up wing.

"You did all this to me?" Polski asked softly.

"Max," I said, "do me a favor and think of others for a change. You're dead. Go where the dead have a good time and leave the living so that we can get some peace down here."

Polski hooked his thin arms and dropped his chin. "Nobody pushes me into hell, mister. I'm okay right here, this is my turf."

I sighed. "Okay. What do we do—have another fight? You're very welcome, Max." I showed him a trembling fist. "Here we go again."

There he came, behind his bony sharp fists, but all his uppercuts passed right through me. "You wait," he screamed. "You'll be asleep in a minute and I'll tear you up properly again. My mind against yours. You got heart trouble, right?

48

Won't have it in the morning, you effah! Know why?" He laughed thinly. "Because your heart will have stopped."

I grinned as I walked through him, but I knew he wasn't bragging. I had to lie down sometime soon, allowing Max free play.

This time he treated me with visions. Dissolving corpses dripped from the ceiling and walls, the floor rotted away, and I fell into moving caverns where I nearly suffocated in my own filth. All my past mistakes were acted out on stages cut out into the living rock, with superb actors in correct settings, showing me the sordid pettiness of my miserable existence. Unable to tear myself away, I also watched what my foul behavior was doing to other people's lives. It seemed as if nothing I ever did had produced anything but trouble.

Fortunately, I did manage to wake up every now and then so that I could recuperate somewhat, wandering about in the thoroughly scrubbed building, but then I'd nod off again and slide into where Polski was waiting, aiming his lobster-sized moth at me.

"Please," I said, groveling at his feet, "give in, Max. You can't win. I'll get through this night and I'll still be around in the morning. I'll bulldoze the building—you'll have nowhere to stay."

He called me lyrical but foul names.

"Yell away," I said. "Waste your time and effort—once you're done you'll go where you belong."

"Never." His voice wavered even higher.

The sun finally floated subtly designed abstract art on the loft's back wall. Polski faded and I went back to the hotel. I had Frank send some men down with sledgehammers and a pneumatic drill under orders to make a racket but do little real damage. No business like show business to impress the foolish.

That night Max agreed to talk.

"No deals," I kept assuring him. "You just have to leave."

"Where to?"

"To the destiny that your activity here created for you." (Dear me, hear me–Mum was right, I could have been a preacher.)

Polski had little faith in rewards in the hereafter. He described his earthly activities for me. I had to agree that they added up to a wasted life, with a bad start and a bad end, and much misery in between.

"Alone, always alone," squeaked Max. "Never a friend."

I sighed. "Same here."

"And I won't go." Polski's canines ground horribly. "Go ahead, work on the building, remodel–the minute you put the apartments on the market you'll find me back again."

I was nodding off and could see him clearly: a human scarecrow lost between heaven and earth. I left but he stayed within my thoughts.

He gave in the following night. We sat next to each other on the floor. Max socialized a bit, wanted to know where I lived, what I did, whether I had a good time with it. I politely answered all his queries: "On a lesser known bridge-connected mangrove and coral-based is land off the Florida coast." "I'm retired, just tootle around. Sure, I drink–every night under the banyan tree when it isn't too hot and the mosquitos lighten up." "Yes, Max, it's very nice down there."

"That's in the tropics?"

"Absolutely," I said.

Max huddled up, arms wound tightly around his knees, and shivered. Then he smiled. "Jansen, sir?"

"Mr. Polski?"

He shrugged. "Okay. You win. Tell young Frank the building is his, I'm moving out." There were tears in his eyes, no doubt caused by the vapors of the cleaning products. Or maybe they were tears of rage due to the loss of his spacious living quarters and tastefully arranged furniture. Perhaps the gassed roaches that crunched under my feet infuriated him. Or might we suppose that some heavenly light had finally penetrated his shadows, that Max suddenly realized that others have needs, too? "You're serious, Max?"

"I am," Polski said quietly.

We left the place together, waved goodbye by the coughing rat and the wounded moth. Polski's shape was erased by glaring headlights as a car passed us as we stepped into the street. I waited around for a few minutes for him to reappear but he didn't show up.

Until the next evening, when the lights in the Miami-bound airplane flicked out for a moment and he sat next to me, his raggedy appearance penetrated by soft moonlight, on the seat where I was storing my new hat. I whipped it through his ghostly appearance. He grinned and faded, but returned again in my car on the highway connecting the Keys, attentively studying the Gulf of Mexico on one side, the Atlantic Ocean on the other.

Azure versus cobalt waters, we don't lack for striking colors here.

"This isn't heaven, Max," I said.

His canines showed in the widest of smiles. "Good enough for me, Mr. Jansen."

"Please get lost," I pleaded.

Max shook his grisly head. "If I do, I'll head back for the Boston building."

Impossible. I had promised young Frank that I'd done away with all obstructions. I drove on in glum silence. Max admired a group of turkey vultures circling some carrion on an islet that seemed to have floated out of the mangrove tangle on our right. The birds were landing, one by one, dark wings extended, claws and beaks ready to bite and tear. Max sighed happily. "I wouldn't mind a drop of something or other. Happen to have anything on board?"

I found a miniature bourbon bottle, souvenir from the plane, sipped its contents, then let him sniff. "Aaaah," he said.

Once home, I rigged up a hotplate on the terrace, where I steamed up more whiskey in a small kettle. Bourbon vapor turns out to be Max's favorite ticket to Higher Insight. Every night I see him kneeling on the terrace, inhaling deeply. After that, he sometimes engages in dance and song or recites poetry with an Irish accent.

He isn't as much bother as I feared. When bored, he occasionally wanders about my quarters, but he usually manages to stay fairly busy and out of my way.

Some squatters drowned when they wrecked their boat on the coral across our cove last year and Max likes to invite their ghostly remains to share his vapors. When the moon is full, he flaps rhythmically around the banana trees and I can vaguely hear the eerie beat of voodoo drums, maybe associated with memories of runaway Haitian slaves, shipwrecked here a century ago. As time goes on, he avoids me more and more, except when I'm late heating his whiskey, then he thickens his shape and hangs about, whispering exotic curses he's picked up from his contacts.

The parrot has stopped insulting me, for he's a channeler/visionary too, and very likely aware of recent changes. He also can perceive our new non-paying tenant, and shakes his wings and screeches enthusiastically whenever Max's semi-transparent form glides past his cage.

Frank phoned the other day to inform me of recent progress. The condo is by no means completed, but he sold one of the five apartments, collecting a down payment that even at this early stage does away with all his financial worries.

While I type these notes, an oversized night moth tries to break down my screen door, a rat rustles along a wall in a nearby room, and my live-in spook floats above the terrace, humming a Seminole Indian hunting hymn. The parrot screeches sleepily. It's late. Soon I'll get up from the desk, straighten my aching back, yawn luxuriously, and wish all my friends a most sincere goodnight.

MANGROVE MAMA

Jamy is kind of foolish but I didn't think that he would kill his girlfriend Mangrove Mama. Still, Jamy said he did, staring at me with his twelve-year-old eyes. Jamy is close to forty, but spiritually retarded. He killed, he said, Mangrove Mama by kicking her in her pregnant belly. Unintentionally of course. He just happened to be emotionally upset at the time, and stoned on cocaine somewhat.

Circumstances have inadvertently come about making me Guardian of this Key. This Key is Egret Key, Florida, temporary heaven for the wealthy. Why me? I think a Guardian was needed and I looked like I could fill the vacancy. Nobody, of course, except soliciting TV preachers and fighting mullahs, ever dares look angels in the face, but if Nobody runs into me, Nobody might confuse this kindly and harmless old codger with that of an incarnate venerable power.

Hi! Jannie is the name. I was born in the Netherlands town of Rotterdam, emigrated along with my parents, made out OK as a small-time real estate tycoon in Boston.

Long years ago I retired here, on my acre estate facing Egret Cove and, on the horizon, Eagle Island. I came with my dear wife, who never liked me but got used to me, but she died, and my dear parrot, who never got used to me but learned to like me.

Lately Parrot no longer screeches when we meet but snuggles up on my shoulder, probes and nibbles my ear and gently, ever so gently, does his piped-down imitation of the neighbor's dog yapping.

"Arf arf arf," Parrot goes softly, then pants: "huh huh huh," then breathes in sharply. I stiffen in fear, for a parrot's close-by screech easily punctures human ears, but no, Parrot's final chorus is a melodious "arf arf arf" again.

Parrot was into his doggie act while drunken Jamy again admitted to doing away with long-legged high-breasted beautiful Mangrove Mama, mother of his unborn child.

"That's not good, Jamy," I agreed, pouring bourbon. We had dined on chewy stone crabs, served with butter and French bread, followed by fluffy Key lime pie and Cuban coffee. We puffed Dominican cigars. "Then what happened?" I asked.

Then, Jamy explained, Bad George, his skipper, and Sopwith, his servant, shouted "Oooh" and "Aaaah."

The scene? Eagle Island, where Jamy resides in a look-alike T'ang Dynasty Buddhist temple, partly raised above a lagoon. Dolphins dally while Jamy dines. All of Eagle Island—after Jamy, three years back, had it razed of any wildlife—was arranged by Zen architect "Goldy" Yamamoto for a cool million or two. The resulting luxury is grossly overdone, even along fabulous Key standards.

I avoid Eagle Island now. Its human refabrication looks distasteful to me. Inside the building an endless expanse of pastel-colored walls surround furniture carved out of elephant tusks upholstered with snow-tiger skins. Jamy runs a wooden-spoked 1920 Lincoln convertible on his few miles of hot-topped highway. The temple's drive is lined with helicopter-transported, elegantly peeling mahogany trees, ever-blossoming frangipani, and a carefully guided banyan hedge, doubling yearly in size. Jamy's marina is decorated by a row of symmetrically placed traveller palms; fan-shaped trees waving welcomes. Lifesize plastic pelicans, herons, ospreys, even—damn the dear boy's soul—bald eagles perch on curved gates and flared roofs. An Olympic swimming pool is walled in by giant mirrors, the nine-hole golf link is freshened by piped-in dollar-a-gallon water. Servant Sopwith climbs the coconut palm grove to pick giant nuts that might smash Jamy's dear head, when he hammocks down underneath, composing poetry:

. . . one evening, dancing in Mallory Square meeting my luv, luv, LUVVV . . .

Leatherbound copies of the completed poem, handprinted on parchment, will be distributed to select recipients some day soon. That includes me. Oh, Jamy is indeed a dear boy, though irritating at the best of times. If I could show you his Yamamoto kitchen, with walls lined by stainless steel counters and floors of genuine marble, complete with a display of culinary machinery (kept spotless by Sopwith), including a cakery and a puddingery . . . and what does Jamy normally have for dinner? A TV tray, zipped in by Bad George on the speedboat. No wonder Jamy likes to drop in at my place, and if I happen to be broiling fresh snapper, or another fine marine-deli Egret Cove provides during my daily outing in the rowboat, well now, seeing that Jamy considers himself to be a friend, he may sit down and dig in vigorously.

I'm stuck here in my old house, bought long before the Keys became fashionable. I dread the growl of Jamy's powerboat covering the distance between Eagle Island and my shore in mere minutes. I never have time to get away. I fear Jamy's repetitive monologues, leaving headaches for Parrot to smoothe away with more "arf arf huh huh arf," but I almost forgave Jamy when he presented me with his murder.

How exciting. Kicked Mangrove Mama in the belly, did he now? And in the presence of mutinous slave Sopwith and jealous former pal Bad George?

Aha!

If my fellow Keysians project divine qualities onto my humble presence I may as well use that free glory. Besides, I enjoy manipulating the multitude, and I suddenly saw, while Jamy sobbed and slobbered, a chance to work some things out.

So what have we here? I tell you what we have here: a delightful set of circumstances, pointing toward planetary improvement.

Let me provide some background here.

Before our Florida Keys became a maddening, over-populated, tourist-trappy bozo-bonanza, Eagle Island was one of many raised mangrove swamps that attracts birds. Weren't the silver-gray pelicans, that its wilderness supported, a great sight as they delicately glided about, before noisily nose-diving for their daily fish? White herons displayed themselves too, and slate-colored egrets, some iridescent ibises, a charming bunch of little sandpipers and, of course, the lone turkey vulture on everlasting patrol, but I was mainly fascinated by a pair of bald eagles. Bald eagles are spectacular beings, rare, an endangered species.

Jamy shot those two eagles.

How do I know? Because he told me, at another after-dinner session, also bourbon-related.

I believe the eagle murderer as Suspect was properly motivated that time. Killing harmless wildlife is what self-centered dear boys do, especially when they are rich and extra-damned by prolonged parental absence during early formative years.

What proper motivation?

Vanity. Jamy originally bought Eagle Island to show off. He wasn't contented with sharing a regular Key with other happy folks, no, he needed an entire island all to himself. Then "Goldy" Yamamoto meets Jamy in a Key West strip joint and Yamamoto turns out to be a specialist in architecting antique Chinese surroundings. A contract is signed forthwith, but before bulldozers dash out of landing craft to shred the island's flora, our conspirators check out the area and observe nesting eagles.

Nesting eagles interfere with the granting of building permits.

Jamy, sniffed full of cocaine, boards his super speedboat, shoulders his twelve gauge automatic, zooms out on Egret Cove and blasts two rare eagles—six foot wingspan, immaculate white heads and tails, beautiful specimens indeed. Didn't I watch and admire them many a morning, roosting so quietly on their nest tucked high in the mangroves?

BLAM! BLAM!

Jamy shoots the ibises and the pelicans too, for good measure.

Zen architect Yamamoto submits his plans to Egret Key's planning board. I was away at the time. My fellow members saw no reason to refuse the request. They checked the island but there were no endangered life forms around—nobody but ducks and cormorants, both still plentiful species.

You wonder how I could feed Jamy my fine dinners after he told me what he did to beautiful birds?

Sages stay cool.

Permit me more outline of background.

Jamy's father made millions in oil, skin, highrise and other Texanias of the highflying days. Jamy's mother, meanwhile, was made by macho men.

Jamy himself decorated his handsome head with a garland of bluebonnets, dropped out of everything and surfaced in our capital, Key West. Like that most independent little city itself, "the unwanted child seemed to welcome parental neglect."

I surmise he was happy here during these footloose years. In spite of all bad habits Jamy is still attractive today; in his youth he was surely stunning. He met Mangrove Mama, a perfect mate, an unmatched package of Lorelei-like sex. There were other members of the tribe: gangling Bad George, peddling dope, and nerdy Sopwith, attracted to serving German gents. We are talking flower children here, latter-day hippies, making a dollar if they had to, mostly hanging out in far-out space, drunk, doped, no need for sense.

. . . *One evening, dancing in Mallory Square* . . .

Jamy, part time kitchenscrape, pimped a bit on waitress Mangrove Mama hooking lone tourists on the side. A good time, no doubt, was had by all.

Another sunset comes along and sees our gang dancing again to guitars strummed by Cuban and Haitian refugees, with New York poets going crazy on bongos.

The same sunset, a short while earlier, saw Jamy's dad having a terminal heart attack in his 1958 white Cadillac (only eight thousand instant collectors' items sold). The car careens wildly between San Antonio and Austin, slips off the highway, projectiles through a row of model homes. Salesmen and their customers jump off balconies and hurt themselves. Jamy Sr. is dead throughout the rampage.

The same sunset, a less short while earlier, filtering through plastic blinds in a Montana motel, saw Jamy's mom, a wispy woman, squeezed away by an over-enthusiastic trucker.

Orphan Jamy is rich.

Now what does he do?

For a while Jamy gets going on the togetherness idea. He shares his fortune. Mama immediately crashes the Jaguar Jamy buys her as a token of communal bondage. Sopwith pulls a four-cylinder Honda motorcycle over on himself while trying to be early Marlon Brando. Bad George, in his role as Popeye, loses a pricey yacht off Bimini due to gusting wind and open portholes. All together they wreck a mansion by knocking down supporting walls to create undivided space.

Eager to economize, Bad George and Sopwith use communal funds to buy a used school bus. While restoring the rustbucket, fifty gallons of old gas are drained into a city sewer. Better burn that dirty gas. A dropped match causes bad explosions. The city presents a bill for new concrete. In none of the above calamities was any insurance taken out. Jamy, while settling claims, protests, not so much about accumulated losses but because nobody pays respect. He dismantles the commune.

Not having learned to sit still yet he rushes into more trouble.

Jamy is buying properties to impress others, who are impressed until the closings. Jamy is also stood up by dates. His dates think he is crazy. They're mostly women he meets in bars. Jamy tells them what properties he owns, scribbling additions of bonds, shares, warrants, bullion, cash reserves in foreign currencies on napkins. He invites his new found partners for rides on the *Queen Elizabeth* and the Concorde. They don't show up at appointed places. He can't figure why.

Mangrove Mama is having a hard time too. She is in her addictive stage. Trading sex for drugs doesn't work for her. She is raped in a van and dumped on a beach. A disturbed lover tosses her clothes out of a window of a not good hotel. There are other bizarre events that she doesn't remember too well but policemen keep showing to ask odd questions. To escape incomprehensible hassle Mama finds a canoe and paddles between the outer Keys where an abandoned cocaine cruiser offers refuge. She starts living on seaweed and raw fish.

Bad George crews on a flying transport of Mexican marijuana. The old crate crashes in the Everglades. He is ambulanced to jail.

Sopwith is riding blue rented bicycles with lone male Germans again but no tourist wants to keep him. Sopwith branches into gardening, feeding heavy palm fronds into noisy chippers. He cheats on his hours and keeps getting fired.

Now, really, don't we agree that these children need a Guardian's help?

Except for Mangrove Mama, blonde Lorelei siren gone wild and canoeing about Egret Cove, I haven't met any of these kids yet. Mama and I get on good. I take out gourmet lunches to her cruiser at times.

Now we get the goings-on on Eagle Island. I discover, to my grief and fury, that the eagles have disappeared. The island is stripped of its mangroves, Yamamoto builds his infernal temple mansion, Jamy moves in.

Jamy and I meet on the cove, where I yell at him when his powerboat's wake nearly overturns my dinghy. The dear boy's profuse apologies instigate my wining and dining the scoundrel.

Mostly unemployed Sopwith and paroled Bad George are gardening for me at the time and Jamy meets them on the premises. He hires them away respectively as the butler and captain, assuring his former friends that there will be no more Mr. Nice Guy.

Sopwith drops in occasionally to complain about his master keeping him and Bad George at long arms' lengths. I hear about Mangrove Mama also trying to re-establish her relationship with Jamy but only succeeding in staying occasional nights.

So much for history. I hope I succeeded in sketching out relevant lines of cause and effect. Now let's see where they cross each other. Maybe their meeting points will indicate a more pleasant picture than that of Mangrove Mama's bleeding corpse.

I tipped the bottle again and handed out more cigars. Key lime pie rested easily on glowingly digesting stone crabs. I could feel Parrot's little dry feet moving about on my shoulder.

"Arf arf," the bird muttered sleepily. Another lovely evening under the palm trees enjoyed by friends.

"Kicked Mangrove Mama to death, eh?" I asked. "Now run that by me again, Jamy. Keep nothing back."

Jamy got up, postured and gestured. There he stood again at the scene of the crime, at the side of his lagoon, and there Mama's begging sharp fingers plucked annoyingly at his sleeve. She wanted to stay the night. He didn't want her to stay the night. He wanted to listen to New Age compact discs on the sound system that Bad George installed and that Sopwith explained.

"Arf arf huh-huh-huh . . ."

Dear Parrot.

"And then you kicked Mama?" I asked.

Jamy said he remembered pushing Mama, watching her fall, seeing lots of blood on the floor.

"But did you *kick* her?"

Jamy couldn't recall. Bad George claimed Jamy kicked her, and Sopwith likewise, so surely Jamy kicked Mama. Here we had two sober witnesses and Jamy, the perpetrator, brimful of coke.

"You were woozy, dear boy?"

Jamy admitting to having sniffed away for a while, preparing proper reception of New Age jazz on his new CDs.

"You remember pushing Mama?"

He did.

"You don't remember kicking her?"

He did not. Sure? Sure. He did remember the blood, though, lots of blood, coming from underneath Mama, who was losing her baby because Jamy had kicked her. Jamy's baby. So said Sopwith and Bad George, later.

"Mama told you she was pregnant?"

She had not.

"So how could she lose the baby? Your baby? Why *your* baby?"

Jamy said he had been sleeping with Mama at times.

I said that Mama is over forty now. Forty-year-old women are known to get pregnant sometimes, but what with Mama's frugal lifestyle, canoeing about all day, living on seaweed and raw fish . .

"Have you ever made any woman pregnant?" I asked.

He said that, ah, now that I mentioned it, ah, no, . . .

"Now Mama dies," I said. "We have her on your marble tiles next to the lagoon in the Zen lounge, and she dies."

No, no, Jamy said I got that wrong. Mama was alive then, but very sick, bleeding, and he was stoned, quite incapable of dealing with the situation. However, Bad George and Sopwith were sober and able, so he ordered them to take Mama to Key West hospital to get her fixed up. Bad George said hospitals don't take in single women that bleed, not without money. Jamy shelled out money.

"How much?"

A thousand dollars, Jamy said. While he got the cash Bad George and Sopwith wrapped Mama up in a blanket, lowered her into the powerboat—off shoots the rescue party into the dark night. The speedboat planes on the small waves of Egret Cove, the roar of its twin outboards recedes in the black expanse.

"You stayed home, Jamy?"

Yep, he said. Jamy hates blood and he hates suffering women. There were still the new CDs to listen to. While Mangrove Mama got fixed up by modern medicine Jamy planned to relax on the intake of smooth wide-spaced New Age sounds, cresting his spiritual energy, to be telepathized to Mama so that she would get better pronto. She didn't get better pronto. She died before she reached the hospital's shore. Bad George and Sopwith brought the body back, still wrapped securely in the bloody blanket. Mama's long blonde hair hung out at one end and her dead feet at the other. An unbearable sight, which made Jamy switch off his sound equipment.

"Where's the body, Jamy?" I asked, but I had to go on hold. Jamy was off in alcoholickies. He shuffled around my chair, flailing his arms, wailing his lament. How he loved Mangrove Mama, Jamy lamented, how he wished to make repairs, to her, to all, to everything. The world was going to wreck and ruin, and he had been playing with his millions, adding to destructive waste and pollution, adding to the ozone hole— while he could have been another Saint Jacques-Yves Cousteau, captaining a Greenpeace cruiser with Mama as his mate, torpedoing Japanese whaling vessels, or flying a glider plane on solar energy, patrolling Russian nuclear waste sites that interfere with the supply of chanterelle mushrooms that could feed New York bag-ladies.

"Yes," I said, "yes."

While helping Parrot, who had had enough, too, into his cage—the tired little thing almost dropped off my hand—I switched to analysis.

Was it the French novelist Stendhal who said that successful businessmen make good philosophers for they dare to see things clearly? Money makers see what goes on, rather than what they would like to see go on, and profit by accepting bad truths.

What would I like to see go on? Justice, of course. Let's have Jamy in irons, pulling weeds at the side of the road, while a sadistic wad-chewing southern guard gestures with a shotgun.

Jamy, no-good slob, miserable halfwit, look at him blabbermouthing away . . .

Egret Key's Guardian forces himself to stay calm, benevolent, benignly detached, while he works harder on

65

himself. Yes, even angels are tempted, but I wasn't about to join Lucifer. Not until the move suited me, that is.

"Did you throw the corpse into the sea?" I asked. My breathing became a tad irregular. This was the question on which my solution hinged.

"Had Mama buried," Jamy sobbed.

"Where, dear boy?"

"On Bad George's Pissing Rock," Jamy sobbed.

Better, much better. The little clump of riprap, overgrown by poisonous Florida holly and acid-dripping cottonwood trees, is about halfway between Eagle Island and my house. We named it after Bad George began using it for sanitary stops, interrupting his ferrying across the Cove.

"Let's go have a look," I said.

Jamy, worn out by his groveling, fell asleep on my floor. I poured out my watering can's contents on his face. He whimpered but got up.

Parrot woke. "Arf?"

"No, you stay home, little friend." I found a spade, dragged Jamy to my dock and dumped him into the rowboat. Jamy clawed my knees. "Please, Jannie, let Mangrove Mama's body be."

He stayed in the boat, slumped over, head in hands, while I rowed over, got out, started digging. Bad George and Sopwith had done a good job, the body was six feet under rocks and rubble, but it was not Mangrove Mama's. I thought I recognized the old girl who *had* used this body. On the far side of Egret Cove an ever-changing colony of squatters exists on a flotilla of dying vessels. This woman once lifted a bottle at me, as I rowed by, while she suggested a carnal meeting. I constructed a theory that fitted all the facts. Drunk again, she fell in and drowned. Her body bobbed about that fateful night and drifted afoul of Bad George and Sopwith taking Mangrove Mama to Key West hospital.

My flashlight revealed Mangrove Mama's blonde locks, cleverly braided into the dead woman's matted hair. Who had gone to such grisly trouble? Mama was supposedly ill. Squeamish Sopwith? While Bad George stood over him, raising a threatening fist? I had to smile as I imagined the scene: the lapping of the waves, owls hooting, the flutter of bats' wings, eerie sounds that accompany Sopwith's feeble protest. His squeak sounds like Stan Laurel's thin crying, and Bad George, who sports a bowler hat and who has put on weight, is the pathetic introvert's unrelenting Oliver Hardy. Mangrove Mama stars as the beautiful woman that paired comics need to use for contrast.

I bowed to the dead body, shoveled the rubble back, stamped the grave tight again, got back into my dinghy.

"How is Mama?" Jamy asked.

"Just fine," I said. We rowed to my house in silence. I put Jamy up in the guest room. The next morning, while watching me eat breakfast, Jamy stirred in his cloud of cigarette smoke and suggested that I should hold his hand while he gave himself up to the sheriff.

"No need," I said. "I can save you, dear boy, on certain conditions."

Jamy, properly awed, whispered, "You can bring Mangrove Mama back to life?"

"Why not?" Egret Key's sage asked his unenlightened disciple.

A glimmer of hope made the blood in Jamy's eyes glow.

As I said, my neighbors credit me with certain powers. It's this infernal New Age. We have all sorts of rich self-appointed spiritualists here and the general trend is to force growth of the soul. Most seekers on this shore aim for Buddhahood so in order to flavor the general quest I profess to be into Tao.

Taoists, apart from walking the nameless road named Tao, perform tricks. Local legend points at my pool that "magically mirrors the spirit," my age-old hibiscus tree, "a set-off point for jumping astrally into space," my barbecue rack, "alchemic instrument for preparing invisibility potions." My age is guessed at one hundred plus. Being born in Europe I am credited with remembering World War One and the Belgian freedom struggle. I will, if pressed, confirm that I studied Tantric Lamaism with the Tsarist spy Gurdjieff in Kum Bum Monastery, Tibet. On a recent Smithsonian-sponsored visit to New Guinea I acquired a skull drum that accompanies my full-moon Penobscot Indian dances. I often chant Dutch children's rhymes and I can juggle telephone books in the W. C. Fields manner. No wonder Jamy wanted to believe me.

"Jamy," I said, "you did foully, egotistically and ignorantly, which are three sides of the same coin, murder a pair of magnificent eagles, at least four endangered pelicans and a rare group of ibises in order to take over their island. You are a true tyrant ape. I can give you Mangrove Mama again but must insist on your speedy evolution."

Jamy drooled and mumbled.

"OK?"

"OK," Jamy whispered.

"Well now," the Guardian said, while stroking white whiskers, while flashing steel-blue eyes, "you will have Mama back, to love and cherish. You and our karmic brethren, Sopwith and Bad George, plus the muse to be revived by me, will together realize your true purpose and assist Saint Jacques-Yves Cousteau. After–"

"Arf?" asked Parrot from his cage.

"Yes?" asked Jamy from his hell.

"–you see the authorities," I said from my cloud, "and tell them you want to restore a bird sanctuary for endangered species and that you require permission to wreck your eyesore house. Persoanlly oversee burning your building, blasting your driveway, exploding your marina. Transfer Eagle Island to Egret Key Wetlands Conserving Society and authorize me, its chairman, to have it legalized as a nature reserve forever." I pointed at the door. "Dear boy, do that now!"

Jamy folded his hands. "And you will bring Mama back to me?"

I said I would do that small thing.

I released Parrot. Together we watched Jamy being reborn, at the beginning of a busy day. Jamy, once he knows what it is he knows, knows how to get it going.

I rowed out to locate Mama, who, of course, was living quietly in the abandoned cocaine cruiser, her home of some years. She hid at first but I had brought lunch and its good smells made her canoe float out from between mangrove roots.

"So our little plan won't work," she said after she had worked herself to the bottom of my hamper.

"It's working very well," I said. "How's the bleeding, Mama?"

She blushed under her woman-of-the-islands tan. "A female complaint, Jannie. I'm of a certain age now, this granola life doesn't balance things out. It's either all or nothing."

I blushed too. "No pregnancy gone wrong?"

"No," she said.

"It all just happened?" I asked. "You didn't find the old lady's dead body first, anchored it somewhere, then produced it at the right moment to set up your lover within a blackmail scheme?"

It all just happened again, Mangrove Mama cried, like everything always just happened. First she happened to collapse, bleeding, then the drunken woman's body banged the boat Bad George and Sopwith were using to take her to the hospital, then the blackmail plan blundered along; they would cut off Mama's hair, braid it into that of the corpse, pretend that the corpse was Mama's . . . Mama cried.

"All is well," I said, "Jamy loves you."

I sang: *"One night, dancing in Mallory Square . . ."*

I pointed at her short hair. "Looks attractive."

Mama kept on crying.

"No need," I said. "Wait here some more. The prognosis is good."

That evening me and Bad George and Sopwith watched the fireworks of Eagle Island's plastic temple compound's destruction.

"I'd like to help out there," Bad George said, "but Jamy will be mad at me, I think."

"Bad George," I murmured. "Fussing with the dead old lady and telling lies for money is not quite what your Scout Master had in mind."

Bad George bowed his fat head and Sopwith did the Stan Laurel squeak again. They wanted to know when the sheriff was coming to pick them up.

"Angels don't squeal on pals," I said, "but there will have to be some changes."

Half a year passed.

Jamy returned from detox. The white coats did a good job. The patient even quit smoking. Mangrove Mama helps him in restoring an old schooner. Bad George and Sopwith are on the job too, and the gang attends a Coast Guard navigation course. Whoever passes the exam first will be the *Saint Cousteau's* captain and take the vessel out on patrol, pursuing polluters, liberating whales from loose floating nets.

Jamy says I can come along and watch.

Patiently waiting I admire an eagle soaring above the Cove, gliding down every now and then to check out the Eagle Island. The mangroves have grown back there. I installed, near the location where "Goldy" Yamamoto's Ch'an temple once raised its roof, a wooden wheel on a post. It hasn't yet met with the bird's approval.

MOSTLY ME

Listen," Deputy Sheriff Wacko said, "this was for real. I was all pumped up, adrenaline everywhere. I knew I was in danger, I was *afeared.*" Wacko touched his toothbrush moustache. "The mother was *after* me, Jannie."

"So you didn't have a steady hand," I said.

Wacko laughed. "I missed him twenty-eight times, Jannie. And then I got him in the T-zone.

"You know what the T-zone is?" Wacko asked.

"Two inches wide, spans above eyebrows, intersects in the middle with a line that extends down to the navel," Wacko said.

"Get them there and they're dead," Wacko said.

"I'll tell you," Wacko said, "I don't really know for sure where I got him. But must have been in the T-zone, right?

"Because he is dead," Wacko said. "I got him with my twenty-ninth slug. Jeez, Jannie, you should have been there. It was a battle. I kept sneaking around the cruiser and the palm trees and the bushes, and those damned little carbine bullets kept whining, and all the glass in the cruiser got smashed and I kept shouting at Barnie to stop, and firing over his head, and

71

then by and by I started trying to get him–and then I got him." Wacko was sweating. "Got him in the T-zone, Jannie."

And Barnie missed Wacko fifty-nine times in any zone, I thought. With a carbine. A carbine is a rifle with a short barrel. But a short barrel on a carbine is a lot longer than the barrel on Wacko's service gun.

"Was Barnie drunk?" I asked.

"You're kidding?" Wacko asked, trying to squeeze his pot belly back into his pants. "His car was waving all over Egret Key Avenue. When I put on my blues, he wouldn't stop. When I switched on the siren, he swung off so wide he crumpled up on a royal palm. That should have stopped him, but he came out, anyway, shooting that goddamn carbine." Wacko's white handkerchief polished his bald skull.

I knew Barnie wasn't a problem drinker. I knew Barnie's carbine, I had fired it myself. It's a short plastic rifle, twenty-two caliber, made by a Brazilian outfit under a Remington license. To load the weapon, you unscrew a plastic loading pin in the butt and take it out, then you drop in fourteen cartridges one by one–little things, they are–then you screw the loading pin back again. It's a fiddly job–easy to drop cartridges next to the butt even when there's good light. It's also easy to lose count and drop in too much ammo, in which case you have no weapon for the carbine won't work.

So, here we have Barnie, a seventy-year-old man, reloading that little well-made precision rifle accurately in the dark several times, and he's *drunk?*

"Wacko," I asked, opening another alcohol-free beer and pushing it across the table on my porch, "did you count the shots?"

"Yes," Wacko said, "like when I shoot basketball, I always count. You know? When we practice."

Wacko and I live across from each other on Egret Key Avenue. Wacko lives with a bunch of raccoons that line up between the Florida bushes every evening for dogfood and I live with Parrot, who imitates the dead neighbor's dead dog: "Arf arf, huh-huh-huh, arf arf." Wacko and I are good neighbors. He comes over in the mornings sometimes and we shoot balls through the basket I have rigged next to my driveway. We keep throwing as long as we score. We play for an hour. The guy with the longest score wins. Loser makes breakfast. Wacko is good at stews on toast. My thing is ginger pancakes.

"I counted the shots," Wacko said. "Both Barnie's and mine. And the detectives out of Key West counted the empty cartridges that were lying about the scene. I got to fifty-nine, counting the number of times the carbine cracked at me, and the detectives counted the empty cartridges lying around on the tarmac. They got to fifty-nine too."

"They didn't find any good cartridges?" I asked.

Wacko clacked his dentures. "Why?"

"I'm wondering whether Barnie dropped any cartridges while reloading, I said.

"Barnie *fired* his cartridges," Wacko said. "At *me.*"

And Barnie was drunk, I thought, and he didn't drop any of those small cartridges while reloading the carbine.

"Nah," I said.

"Something wrong?" Wacko asked.

We were sharing breakfast and I pushed a plate of pancakes across the table. It was two mornings after the shootout resulting in Barnie's loss of life. Barnie demised at nine P.M. at the end of Egret Key Avenue, near the wastelands–the mangrove swamps where bad bugs breed. Wacko was on patrol in the area, cruising around, looking for couples throwing empties out of their cars, and saw Barnie's white Caddy careering around.

Barnie was a retired fishing-fleet owner from Maine, spending lonely winters here in a palatial home sprawling nearby on the shore of Egret Cove—a little porcupine of a man, but pleasant enough when spoken to politely. I sometimes stop off at his dock when I'm out rowing. We boasted about the few investments we made that went right and drank iced coffee. Last time he showed me the carbine, too.

"Eskimo rifle, Jannie," he said. "Alaska Eskimo takes it out in his kayak, gets it wet, just shakes out the wet, gets it dirty, shoots out the dirt, hits the odd seal he needs to get through the winter. Never misses. Beats bow and arrows."

He set up some cans at thirty feet and I shot each and every one, hitting their dead centers. I'm not really a very good shot, but with the carbine that didn't matter.

Barnie was the last smoker. He dangled an empty pack of Marlboros from a few feet of fishing line attached to a palm frond, took careful aim from quite a distance, hit the packet in its red spot. Good shot.

Barnie missed Wacko fifty-nine times?

"Jeez," Wacko said. "I *knew* the guy. Bad-tempered old codger *lives* here. Why do I have to get an old codger personally known to me in the T-zone, hey?"

Because you wanted to, Wacko, I thought, but I wasn't sure. The doubt was creeping up. The doubt was saying that it wasn't only Wacko's mind directing his service Magnum .375 that killed Barnie. It wasn't even Giuliano's mind so much. What took out Barnie was probably mostly me.

Why use Wacko as my extension?

Wacko is ahead in ideas. He claims he got himself incarnated on a mad planet by mistake. He says he hates it here. I've told him he hates the planet because his wife moved in with her fat boss in return for an imported sportscar with transmission trouble and a stack of Trump paper, and Wacko says that is so but it's also because of garbage taking over the seas, and the dead eyes of the Mexicans that served him during his last holiday, and TV fundamentalist-preaching, and all the other bad guys that fix the price of oil. Wacko, to symbolize his protest, wants to hit a bad guy. "Just one."

Wacko told me that after he lost on early-morning basketball again.

"In the T-zone?" I asked.

"Right." Wacko walked back to his house across the road to get the book on street survival he sent for out of a law-enforcement catalogue. It showed a picture of a naked man with a beard aiming a gun, and you saw the bad guy's guts and liver and lungs. But that wasn't where to hit him so as to stop the mother—you had to get him in the T-zone, from the forehead straight down the middle: nose, mouth, chest, upper intestine. Wacko said he'd been practicing up on paper targets. He said he got the paper targets good.

I remembered telling Barnie, in between sipping iced coffee and shooting beer cans, that Deputy Sheriff Wacko wanted to take out "just one bad guy" and that Barnie thought that was cute. I told you Barnie was a porcupine of a man. He had hair sticking out of everywhere around his blueberry eyes. He was normally kind of crusty, but Wacko's desire seemed to cheer him.

"Wacko is the guy with the raccoons and run-off wife?" Barnie asked. "Crazy cop that lives in the junk-tower he built himself out of beach stuff floating up?"

I said that was so.

"And taking out just one bad guy would make him feel better?"

I said that was so, too.

"Cute," Barnie said.

"I've seen you on the bridge," he said, "fishing with Giuliano."

I said that was so.

"I hung Giuliano's dog," Barnie said. "In nineteen forty-five; a woolly pooch called Button. Cute little dog. Nice ears. I hung him."

A long pause drifted by, filling up the wide sky above Egret Cove.

"Did Giuliano tell you?" Barnie asked me.

Pelicans were plunging into the cove for fish. A frigate bird planed effortless above us.

"Gives me bad dreams," Barnie said.

Two vultures flapped by.

"So Wacko wants to kill just one bad guy?" Barnie asked. That was a bad moment. If it had been a movie, there would have been some glossy music oozing out of your set's speaker. You know that something nasty is about to happen, events that you're imagining vaguely and that you know the director won't really allow to flash from screen to your poor innocent eyes—but then he does. Trouble with directors is that they don't ask their audience for permission. And trouble with Barnie was that he was asking me for permission. And trouble with me was that I grunted. "Erch erch." Like if I agreed.

Giuliano says I look like his idea of a god. I say I look like a heron. I am tall and thin on spindly legs, with long monkey arms swaying about, and my brow is high and I have lots of long white curls that grow into my guru beard. My voice is bass, which is sort of silly for such an elevated skinny guy. Here on the lower Keys, some sillier folks have made me part of their legend. They project all sorts of insights and magic into my robed form flapping about on retread sandals. Being vain, I've never stopped the imagery that turns sillier folks on. In fact, I add to all that foolishness by rowing about in moonlight, chanting and playing bongos, meditating in a gazebo Wacko built in the shape of a teepee, listening endlessly to people's monologues. Sometimes I grunt.

The grunts are taken for approval. I grunted when Wacko said he wanted to get his bad guy–just one–and I grunted when Barnie volunteered that Wacko's murderous desire was cute. I didn't grunt when Giuliano said he had a bad heart and could croak any minute now and that maybe he should be excused if he let Barnie go. Giuliano was born in a stable on Sicily and a pig sat on his leg and crushed it a bit. He grew up in New York. When World War II started, the partly lame leg kept Giuliano out of the service. All his brothers invaded Italy and fought the fascists while Giuliano kept the family business going by supplying the U.S. Navy off Manhattan with ladies and liquor. In order to do that, he cut in Barnie, who was with the Coast Guard patrolling the Hudson River.

"So I missed a payment once," Giuliano said, when we were fishing for snapper off Flagler Bridge, "so Barnie warned me. But everything was going wrong and I couldn't find cash. So Barnie warned me again. So next was Button dangling from a rafter on the Tribeca loft I used for working out of."

Dogs are good guys. I agree with Wacko that Homo sapiens is evolution's most serious mistake and that dogs are different. Dogs greet you when you come home and snuggle up in your back when your spine hurts and grin sillily after bad barks because the wind is away from them and you're not moving and they think maybe you're the burglar at last and now what?

Dogs shouldn't hang from rafters.

Giuliano retired to Egret Key, too. He got an architect to build him an Ibiza stucco villa. He drives a Rolls. He has a wife who looks like his granddaughter and was a model. She does a good job. Everything is good with Giuliano except his heart that has been bypassed by the best but keeps going wrong regardless. What with all the luxury and the fishing and the sex and the physical problem, Giuliano didn't jump when fate turned up Barnie forty-five years too late.

"I should have taken him out then," Giuliano said, "but the war was over and my brothers needed me in free Sicily to sell surplus to the poor. Barnie got demobbed somewhere and I postponed and *you* know how it goes."

I didn't grunt. Suppose something would happen to Parrot. Suppose I would come home one day and Parrot wouldn't arf and huh-huh-huh but hang from a rafter.

"Barnie used a noose?" I asked.

"One of my own silk ties," Giuliano said. "Barnie thought I was Mafia and that's what Mafia does–horrors, you know? Treat them to what they know. But I never did horrors." Giuliano touched his heart. He sighed.

I've been doing Taoist exercises lately, with burning herbs, and reciting mantras in Chinese, and standing on one leg. The activity is supposed to make you see the dreams of others. I was seeing Giuliano dreaming his way into Mafia heaven and the padrone wouldn't give him a cloud to sit on.

"You wouldn't want to spend eternity standing around with no cloud to sit on," I said.

Giuliano gave me his funny look. Sometimes he would like to replace me, but, as in the case of his lovely wife, too, replacing your environment gets harder with old age. As his only friend, I'm prepared to come over and enjoy his squid sauce on spaghetti, and I drive him to his hospital checkups when Katarina has her massage or *Beauty and the Beast* is on rerun or she is sunning naked on the back porch and the Red Baron tourist plane out of Key West is flying out to see sights.

We left it at that. I wouldn't grunt. I went home quietly. And now Barnie got taken out by Wacko.

There was a missing link somewhere.

The morning after Barnie's suicide, Giuliano was feeling better. He was in his hammock and Katarina walked around on high heels serving fruit juice.

"What happened?" I asked.

"Giuliano tried," Katarina said. "Really, Jannie, he tried, but there was something wrong with the gun."

Katarina never did any of the burning herbs or the mantras or the standing on one leg and she can *still* read my dreams. Maybe it's different for women.

Giuliano uses a Walther PPK, same as James Bond. A Walther is made by Germans the way Germans used to make Walthers. A Walther lies in your hand and you just touch the trigger and *whap!*–into the T-zone. It's the kind of gun that directs itself. You can't miss. Not even bypass-Giuliano could miss.

"Listen," Giuliano said, "it was more than the gun being broke. Listen, Jannie. First of all, there's Barnie turning up here. Why retire on Egret Key? There are lots of keys."

We had been through that before. Giuliano is religious. He believes in the guiding hand, in growth through suffering, the flaming sword, the blind lady with the scales, karmic conclusions. You name it and Giuliano folds his hands and mumbles. Katarina says it's because he's old and his heart is bad.

"So what do I do?" Giuliano says. "I do the right thing. I could have put out a contract but I tried it myself."

"To show he was sorry," Katarina said, serving more fruit juice. "But there was the problem with the gun."

"Please," Giuliano said, "put something on and don't interrupt me. There was nothing wrong with the gun when I left here to do my duty. I had everything right. Five-thirty in the A.M. Sun wasn't up yet. Nobody around. I took my bicycle, not the car. No sound."

"You got a bicycle?" I asked.

"For training," Katarina said. "He never trains."

"Please," Giuliano said. "A good contract is quick. It's hi–bang–'bye."

79

"No bang," Katarina said.

"No bang," Giuliano agreed. "I said, 'Morning, Barnie'—he was in bed, sitting up, expecting me maybe. An old man, old men wake up early. And I say, 'All set? There you go,' and I pull the trigger and nothing."

"You had the safety on?"

"That's what Barnie said." Giuliano shook his head. "I checked. It was off. I tried again: no click, no nothing."

"Let's see that gun," I said.

"That's what Barnie said," Giuliano said. "So I did that."

I grunted. I could see it now. It was still mostly me but the others played good parts, too, after all. Giuliano wanted my approval for not taking out Barnie for hanging Button (hey, Giuliano is old—hey, Giuliano is sick) and I didn't grunt. Wacko wanted me to back him when he set up his desire to kill "just one bad guy" and I grunted. Barnie wanted my approval for setting himself up for Wacko in case Giuliano kept chickening out and I grunted. So it was mostly me setting off this vengeful course of action, but there's still the chaos backing me up, there's still chance going any which way, there are still gods playing dice.

Proof? The Walther didn't fire. I liked that. I mean, I don't mind being mostly me when these big moral decisions are being made but it's nice sharing fate.

"You gave Barnie the gun that you wanted to shoot him with but it failed you," I said.

"Sure," Giuliano said. "So he fixed it."

"What was wrong?" I asked.

Giuliano shrugged. He explained it was no fault of the gun. A burr on a cartridge rim got the deadly projectile to stick in the breech. Barnie flipped it out and the next cartridge popped up from the clip and fitted fine.

"Barnie gave you the gun back?" I asked.

Katarina nodded. "But then Giuliano couldn't do it any more.

Don't you think that's nice?"
    I grunted . . .

    Giuliano's heart gave in shortly after. Wacko, Katarina, and
I sprinkled his ashes into the cove. Do you know that even
bad guys' ashes turn pink as they twirl down toward the coral?
Wacko got two months off, half of it with pay, and toward the
end of his leave a puppy wandered into his yard. The puppy
looks like Barnie: porcupinesque, cantankerous, crusty,
repressed, apologetic but somehow, in its own way and with
due reservations, not altogether unloving. Wacko's wild
raccoons consented to let Barnie II into their dogfood.
    So that's okay. None of us forgave the human Barnie, but if
he wants to come back as a dog we'll put up with his new
form. When Wacko's on duty, I take the new Barnie boating.
He doesn't like it much but it's better than being left alone in
Wacko's yard. He's allergic to fleas, but Katarina washes him
with medicated shampoo. He doesn't like that, either.
    What he does like is visiting Parrot and doing the arf and
huhhuh-huh together.

MR. XYZ

Doing away with Bad Daddy and Dirty Joe could have been fun, but it turned out I had nothing to do with it. No, sir. Not me. I'm a harmless old codger and the idea of popping Bad Daddy's big head and breaking Dirty Joe's spine wouldn't melt in my mouth.

Although, you know, I don't know. Take the deer hat, for instance. I didn't actually go out and buy the hat–I only, in a roundabout way, mentioned that the hat was available. The deer hat and the decoys were images that merely sort of shaped themselves while I was trying to be helpful, rocking away on the porch, staring at nothing.

Ever seen old folks staring at nothing? I bet you think the poor blighters are all hung up in a senile void.

Ha HA!

One day you'll be really old, too, maybe and you'll see what us harmless old folks are staring at.

Enough preliminaries. Okay, let's introduce a few characters, define the here and now, sketch out some plot.

First, there's modest me. I'm retiree Jannie, born in Rotterdam, The Netherlands, oh, a great while ago, brought up in Boston, where I made a mini pre-Trump career before retiring in Florida, in the Keys, on the most glorious little island of them all, Egret Key, a subtropical horseshoe-shaped stretch of lush wetlands. You've got some fine old houses here, crafted by ship's carpenters a hundred years ago with finicky gingerbread ornamentation between tall white posts holding up a simple tin roof, and some fine old gardens overshadowed by flowering hibiscus, frangipani, orchid trees, and traveler palms.

You've also got a couple of moldy shacks in the mangroves, surrounded by cans and bottles and suffocated by poisonous Florida holly, acid-dripping buttonwoods, and peeling punk trees. Bad Daddy lived in one shack and Dirty Joe lived in the other. Daddy was a bulging man with a matted beard and mean little eyes. He looked like Father Christmas gone wrong. Joe was a skinny character in ragged jeans that were held up by string suspenders. When you asked Joe something, he would take his teeth out of his goatee/moustache combination, study them while shaking his head vigorously so that his long earring rattled, then put the dentures back. Dirty Joe looked like a pirate on a Bahamian rum label. They both liked to carry twelve-gauge automatic shotguns and Bad Daddy had a machete stuck into his belt.

Bad Daddy called Joe and himself "natural" men. They hunted and fished. They also drank. When bicycling by their shacks I often saw them staggering about between the palmettos, raising bottles at the moon, laughing raucously between gulps. Daddy owned a red Subaru Brat with the gear stuck in reverse. One Saturday morning he came by four times, full speed, back-to-front in the wrong lane, waving, with broken teeth showing in his beard.

First pass: "Hi, Jannie. This is the whiskey run."

Second pass, waving his square black gallon of Jack Daniels.

Third pass: "Forgot me smokes."

Fourth pass, waving his carton of Marlboro Lights.

Years ago, when Daddy and I happened to run into each other on a shore path during a glorious sunset and were both at peace sitting down on the same log of driftwood, he told me that discovering square bottles had been a big event in his life. His elbow touched my side. "Always annoyed me, Jannie, having round bottles roll about in the car. Once I switched to flat bottles, life got a lot better."

This is America, everybody improves on doing his own thing. But then others do, too, and all that egotism might just start getting in itself's way.

Deputy Sheriff Wacko shares Egret Key with me, with the memory of Bad Daddy and Dirty Joe, and with a bunch of rich folks who descended during the last decade: leftover rich folks. Their providers, having provided, died and left little old widowed ladies watering palm trees, middle-aged spinster daughters watching soaps, and beautiful aging boys milking their trust funds. Most of them share their loneliness with little dogs. I admit little yappy dogs are annoying. I like to bike along Egret Boulevard and the dogs scurried about my wheels. I also like to row about the cove and the dogs set up a squeaky chorus on the shores. They also messed up sidewalks. Then they all disappeared.

Now wasn't that amazing?

The sheriff had a lot of phone calls from the bereaved of Egret Key and as Deputy Wacko lives right here he was charged with the investigation. How come the Chihuahuas, Bichon Frises, Miniature Schnauzers, and other undersized pedigrees were no longer driving us crazy?

"I didn't do it, Wacko," I said.

Wacko, a wiry little man, is shiny bald, although young. Wacko is fierce. His parents beat on him, his friends betrayed him every which way, his wife foulmouthed him all around, then left. Wacko fiercely dislikes most human life forms. Wacko loves wildlife. His special pets are a tribe of raccoons that sits around his veranda every night to consume free handouts. He hermits in a tower of junk sculpture, a work of art tied to a large number of long nine-inch poles that landed up on his beach somehow. He says his home wouldn't have been a tower if he had had a saw.

"You look like the archangel that's been showing up in my dreams," Wacko said when he came to interrogate me about the lost dogs. "You play the trumpet, Jannie?"

I whistled a Miles Davis ballad on my rear porch while we watched pelicans plunging in Egret cove. Wacko drummed lead bongo. My parrot filled in some cool scat behind us. I brought out my cowbells. We cracked a few alcohol-free beers, rolling the bottles around in our experienced hands, careful not to show the labels. Never spoil the All American scene.

"Daddy and Joe got the fuzzballs," Wacko said on a second visit. "They told me. There are no witnesses, the evidence is consumed, and the suspects won't repeat their confessions in court, so I can't arrest them."

I was nodding gently. Harmless old codgers nod gently a lot. It means they understand. I didn't really understand, until Wacko explained.

Daddy and Joe had been catching the dogs by leaving garbage about. Little pedigree dogs just love to roll around in garbage. After Baby and Peedee and Kifi and Mousey and whatever their little names were had rolled around enough, Daddy and Joe whacked them into their fish net. They then called Old Croc.

You've heard about Florida alligators?

Seen them on the nature channel? Alligators are mean. Crocodiles are meaner. There are golf links on the next key and there are waterholes on the links. The little ponds are filled with salt water, fed through subterranean streams. Crocodiles sneak in and catch the alligators sunning themselves around the holes. The alligators roar and snap

86

their mighty jaws, but the crocodile's much mightier jaws have gator by the tail and drag him quickly into the hole.

We have a huge crocodile in Egret Marsh. I've seen him. He isn't nice. He was Daddy's and Joe's friend. When they whistled, Old Croc came out, opened up, gurgled expectantly deep in his primeval throat, and in went Baby, Peedee, Kifi, or Mousey. Old Croc chomped once, gulped once.

"And there's nothing I can do about it," Wacko said, shifting about on my porch stool, making his gun belt creak. "So Daddy and Joe say."

"Nothing," I murmured happily. "Nothing" always sounds like magic to me. Just imagine what would happen if there were nothing left. There'd still be space, you say? No, no—we agreed there would only be nothing. There would still be emptiness, you say? No, no—just nothing. And in that nothing there would be everything, and in that everything would be the perfect way to catch Bad Daddy and Dirty Joe.

"You think I should kill 'em?" Wacko asked.

"Now now," I said, getting the potato chips and the cucumber dip. I'm a harmless old codger, remember? I was losing some harmless ground, though, when Wacko told me about Daddy and Joe trespassing into his beach tower—while Wacko was off for a few days taking a crime-prevention course in Miami—and blasting turkey vultures with their shotguns.

There are some beautiful birds around here. The frigate, for instance. The frigate, on its huge forked wings, planes around forever. The frigate bird is an aristocrat, but turkey vultures plane good, too. Daddy and Joe called the acrobatic vultures "buzzards." They said buzzards make good shooting practice. Daddy and Joe liked to lure them by dragging in cadavers caught in mangrove roots on the shore side of their shacks and then hit the big birds with supershot. From Wacko's tower the shooting was even better.

Bang bang go the birdies.

87

"Daddy and Joe didn't leave prints in your home?" I asked. They had wiped them all off.

Daddy and Joe also didn't leave prints on the raccoon kittens they threw into thornbushes after trapping their parents, or on the dwarf whitetail deer, the pride of our Keys, a truly endangered species—maybe only a few hundred specimens left on the planet.

Daddy and Joe were shooting the little deer.

"You think I should kill the bad guys?" Wacko asked again.

"Now now," I said gently.

Wacko knows I like to watch ducks when I row. We have quite a few species here, including the still common mallard, the less common pintail, the bufflehead—and my favorite, the red-breasted merganser. "They had fifty-two ducks lined up on Little Egret Key beach," Wacko said, "rotting." He looked me straight in the eye. "Some mergansers, too."

"Wouldn't eat tasty ducks?" I asked.

"Nah," Wacko said. "There were some bales of pot floating in last week and Daddy and Joe dried and sold them. Bought them plenty of microwave dinners. No need to dress fifty-two dead ducks."

I got so mad that my bony knees rattled.

Wacko tranquilized my knees by holding them briefly. "I'd like to kill Daddy and Joe."

"Mmm," I said.

The very next day I saw the deer hat in a Duval window. We have these stores in Key West, selling things tourists need, like hats with plastic turds on them, or four-letter-word texts, or texts that will make America better. One hat said NO MORE IMPORTS. The label inside the hat said Made in China. There was also a deer hat. Chinese exporters are clever. They had fashioned the head of a small deer out of cloth and stuck it on a hat. That deer head looked real. A deer-hunter hat, I thought, and I told Wacko about it.

Next thing I hear, nobody has seen Daddy for a while, but there are lots of vultures flying above the mangroves and when a lobsterman goes ashore to take a looksee he looksees Daddy's remains. He radios the Marine Patrol and it is noted that Daddy's remains are topped with a deer hat just like the one I saw in the Duval store, Key West.

"Shot through the deer hat," Deputy Sheriff Wacko, who helped check corpse and scene, noted.

Daddy's death was filed away as a hunting accident. The bullet was traced to Dirty Joe's rifle. Joe said he had been out hunting at dawn on our west shore, near Indian Grave Bluff, and he thought he saw a raccoon. Quick as lightning, he shot the varmint.

"A staghorn raccoon?" the sheriff asked.

Joe took out his teeth and looked at them for a while.

"Bad eyesight?" the sheriff asked.

Joe nodded. He put his teeth back. He said he had lost his glasses, drinking at the Free Beer Tomorrow saloon.

So why didn't Joe go to look for the staghorn raccoon after he shot the varmint?

Another long look at the teeth.

Okay, Joe said. He hadn't felt good. This bleeding ulcer of his got to oozing and cramping again and he had to take himself home forthwith, leaving his trophy unchecked on the bluff.

Pretty tricky. Why would Bad Daddy be moseying along on the most bug-infested part of Egret Key wearing a deer hat in the early morning? And why would Dirty Joe happen to be about at that exact time within sighting distance of that exact location, loaded for deer? My construction is that a certain Mr. XYZ told someone that he had been seeing deer at dawn near the bluff. XYZ was sure that this someone would be drinking at Free Beer Tomorrow that very night, and there tell Dirty Joe. Bad Daddy had been banned from the saloon for beating on small drinkers, so he would be drinking at home and not hear about the deer. XYZ would then be up bright and early the next morning and prod Bad Daddy awake with the business end of his service magnum revolver and march hungover Daddy to the bluff—make him put on the deer hat, make him stagger about on the bluff, so that Joe would mistake him for a deer and pick him off.

Proof?

None whatsoever, but I did stick a length of bamboo into the ground at the spot where Daddy got blown away, a six-foot length. Daddy was six foot. On top of the bamboo I stuck a piece of bougainvillea, complete with bright-red flowers. After that I placed myself where Dirty Joe fired his rifle. What did I see? Flowers only. No bamboo.

Now Joe could have taken different positions from between his mangrove cover, but they would all be lower down than where Daddy was made to march about by XYZ. So all Joe would ever see was Daddy's hat, or rather the antlers on the hat, so he would fire a little lower, to get the deer in the brain. And he got into Daddy's brain.

One hunting accident makes for one less Bad Daddy.

Which leaves Dirty Joe.

It also leaves me, rocking on my porch, still staring at nothing. And what do I see?

I see Joe gunning up his 50-hp Yamaha outboard on the sixteen-foot skiff built in Ciudad Juarez, racing out to blast more ducks. He won't eat them again because more pot has been floating about the coast—the smugglers must have been shooting each other up again out at Bimini. Joe is out for killing merganser ducks. Maybe Joe will be aiming for white-crested pigeons, too, that'll be about to do their spring dance before nesting now and not paying attention.

Egret Cove is shallow, maybe a foot deep at most places, but there are channels—some marked, some not. The unmarked channels are more interesting, for they lead to good illegal lobster spots, nicely invisible to rangers. I've seen Joe's skiff zipping along at high speed where the reef is high and razor-sharp.

How does Joe do it? I've rowed out there and seen his secret markings. They're duck decoys, anchored in the reef, marking a narrow slip-through. Now suppose those decoys would get moved about a bit, then Joe would come zipping along, thinking his propeller would clear the reef. It would get caught on the reef. So here we have Joe's skiff suddenly stopped, with nowhere to go but flip over backward. What would that do to Joe? I mean, him flipping over backward with the skiff, and getting the skiff on top of him. Reef below, boat above. Between a reef and a hard skiff. This is happening at speed, too.

The happening broke Dirty Joe's spine.

Wacko came to tell me about it. "It's okay," he said. "Just another fatal accident again. Relax, old buddy. No one knows you shifted the decoys." I hadn't gotten around to shifting the decoys yet.

Wacko hadn't shifted the decoys, either. I hadn't had a chance to tell him. Wacko couldn't know about Joe's private channel and the two plastic ducks anchored there. He deducted it later, at the scene, snorkeling around.

Wacko winked. "The decoys were marking a very narrow passage, got shifted, Joe zips along, dead Joe."

"Very clever," Wacko said. "You're an archangel, all right, Jannie. You execute your judgments." He patted my knees that were shaking again. "The deer hat was good, too."

I tried my harmless old-codger smile.

"But how did you do Daddy?" Wacko asked. "The decoy murder was kind of simple, but with the deer hat you had a lot of intangibles there. You had to make sure that Bad Daddy was in the right place at the right time—and wearing that damn hat."

"Now now," I said.

Wacko left.

I rocked my porch chair.

So things are not what they seemed to be again. I've been noticing that more and more. Here I thought that Wacko killed Daddy and he didn't. Here I thought that I was getting myself ready to go out and shift the decoys and I didn't have to. What did shift the decoys? Some freak current combined with high tides and harsh winds that we were having at that time? Joe knew about the freak currents and he checked his markers once in a while, but he was getting sloppy, what with finding all that free pot and spending more time at Free Beer Tomorrow—you know how it goes.

So what did happen with the deer hat? As both protagonists are dead it's hard to say, but we do have a common drinking factor here. My bet now is that Daddy happened to be staggering about Duval and happened to see the deer hat. He bought it and that night, drinking in his shack by himself, he put it on for a lark. He wandered about outside, fell down, fell asleep. The next morning he woke up just as Joe was out hunting for deer. Daddy got up, the fake deer head became visible above the mangroves. Joe fired.

Nothing to do with Wacko. Nothing to do with me, either? Did I tell Bad Daddy to buy himself a silly hat and get drunk? Did I tell the freak current to shift Joe's decoys? Could there be a connection between a harmless old codger's thoughts and what actually happens out there?

"Wow," Wacko kept saying, patting my knees. "Got to hand it to you, guru."

Would I bother explaining my innocence to Deputy Sheriff Wacko, my hard-won disciple?

Maybe not. I just sat there, rocking gently on my porch, whistling a jazzy ballad, hardly noticing Wacko leaving, wondering whether I would be staring into nothing again sometime soon.

And if I were staring at nothing, would something show up that might connect me to the Colombian lady?

I mean, would this thing work two ways?

Doing away with the bad guys, attracting the good guys? The good lady, in this case? She is beautiful. I notice her driving by all the time, in the white Mercedes. She's a leftover from the drug wars, a lonely widow, a little over half my age.

Would I will her my way?

I would not, of course. I shook off the temptation. I got up, picked a bouquet of bougainvillea and frangipani, combed my whiskers, put on a clean shirt, phoned, invited myself for tea.

Voodoo, even of the detached guru variety, is for bad guys only. A good lady should be given her chances.

SKULL
& KIMONO

We're at Shark Key, a tiny, deserted, less than an acre mangrove and coral islet situated between Florida and Cuba, some twenty miles out of Key West. Key West used to be an island too until all these bridges toward Miami created a peninsula sticking out from the mainland, like a crooked, bony, hundred-mile-long finger, beckoning Castro, "Come hither, my dear."

Castro huffs, but tourists, often of the foreign denomination—lots of Japanese lately—come hithering in droves. Dear tourists shed dollars as if M. Mouse was the printer, easy-get easy-go folks, like my new friend, old man billionaire Sato-san, and his glowing lithe Miss Kira, the best-dressed goddess this side of Fifth Avenue.

Tourists come here to have a good time, but I wondered whether Skip's arrangement of kimono and skull on the weathered veranda of Shark Key's only cabin was doing much to cheer up Sato-san and Miss Kira. Skip's artwork, to my surprise, was good. Who would ever think that bluff blustering renegade Skip could shape such subtlety? I'm an old man, of

95

course, no longer likely to scare easy, but the sinister swaying twirls in which Skip arranged the red and orange batiked kimono on a structure of tied-together twigs, forming a slender female shape about to rise from a humble kneeling position, and the dainty touch with which he stuck the clay skull-mask on top, making it look up at the spectator, as if the alluring ogre were shyly offering her body to whatever perversion her new master might care to suggest . . . this was unnerving.

The smiling mask was early-Mexican, Aztec art from that ever-in-pain region of magic. The Aztecs were a cruel people, always butchering their own kind to appease wicked gods, then tossing aside the bones, which came back to haunt them. This particular skull image, lacquered gleaming white with inset slivers of transparent blue stone for eyes, silver stone for teeth, looked both woeful and mocking. My first impression was wrong. After Skip dropped us off on Shark Key, and as Sato-san, Miss Kira, and I approached the weirdly constructed life-sized doll beckoning from the cabin's veranda, the artwork's appearance changed. It expressed a threat now. "You once tortured and killed me," the mannekin suggested in body-talk, "but now, my dears, you're mine, and you know just what I will do to get even . . ."

Behind us Skip's heavy outboard started up with a roar. I turned to see my protégé take off in Happy Hour's speedboat, cutting a silver swath through the sapphire sea. The confrontation with the ogre had to be Skip's doing. I had seen the skull-mask before, a tourist item Skip brought back from an ill-advised vacation in bad-bug infested inland Yucatan (the dear boy threw up for a week afterward), used as a paperweight for unpaid bills in his office at Happy Hour. Happy Hour is the decaying Key West hotel that Skip inherited from Old Skip last year. Old Skip was my old buddy.

Happy Hour had by that time worked up a habit of losing money. To fix things up, I became a kind of avuncular

96

counselor to Skip. Old Skip made me that in his will. I was even to be paid: ten percent of any future profits, and as collateral part of the joint got deeded to me. "Turn Happy Hour around, Jannie," Old Skip whispered before breathing his last. "You won't fall foul of the dying, will you Jannie? Make a man out of my only heir."

"Sure, old buddy." Through ninth grade Old Skip grew up with voodoo-ites he recruited from Key West's Little Haiti, where the chicken heads fly. He used to tell me about the spells he could cast. Powerful stuff you learn at that early age is never forotten, Old Skip had me know. I didn't like the way Old Skip directed that last look. It burned into my forehead. Sure, I'd do those two little things for my old buddy. Get his hotel to stay on this side of Chapter Eleven. Do some major restructuring on Young Skip. Twin pieces of cake. "Sure, old Skippo."

After our return from sprinkling his dad's ashes into subsided storm waves curling gently near Shark Key, the only heir parked the speedboat into its slip and marched me down the pier to Happy Hour's office. I was shown the Mexican horror-head, made to marvel at such lifelike details as the mask's high cheekbones, hairline, and indentures at the temples. Skip also showed off the kimono, bought with his last credit card—maxing it in the process—at the expensive end of Key West's Duval, the city's main drag, to "show intent."

I asked if I knew the lucky recipient.

Skip smiled his macho smile.

"Not Miss Kira?"

Skip's intent was pure goodness of course. For what situation did our white knight face here? As Happy Hour's owner, Skip's first concern is the well-being of his guests. Sato-san, rising late, going to bed early, shuffling about between naps on the hotel's back porch, beach, and pier, seems happy enough. But what about his plaything? Sato-san, widowed,

97

childless, entering the twilight zone of arteriosclerosis, lives out his life while globetrotting with this lovely and, Skip assured me, lonely lady–does anyone worry about Miss Kira's emotional needs?

Sure, I thought. Skip worries. Skip, Southern Florida's handout to emotionally neglected erotic beauties. Skip's animal–behold that gorilla chest, that lion's mane–libido will fill Miss Kira's void. Watch Skip handle Happy Hour's twenty-six-foot Chriscraft with the 200 HP Suzuki outboard, sway through his version of the cha-cha-hop to compact disked jazz in the bar at the end of Happy Hour's pier. Ignore Skip's drinking and drugging. Disregard the way he makes no use of his Harvard law degree. Don't think of Happy Hour's state of disarray. Pay no mind to Skip's self-inflicted run of defeats, "my loser's luck," as he calls it.

But then again, I thought, young and beautiful Miss Kira might be looking for some inspiring company. Sato-san is really old, as old as I. Miss Kira's feeble companion smokes as much as he coughs. Sato-san, dragging a leg, goes nowhere without his cane. He nods off between telling the same joke again. I've seen him wearing his dentures wrong way round.

"Right you are, Skip," I said. "When are you giving Miss Kira the kimono?"

Skip already did.

"So how come it's still here?"

Because Miss Kira refused Skip's invitation to hanky-panky. Pure Indonesian cotton handwaxed and scraped to receive each individual organically pounded color, artistically cut into a seductive garment did not perform for bad Skippo. Our loser stared at me, holding up the kimono.

I tsked.

"Can you believe that, Jannie?"

I'm sorry, I got carried away. I should have introduced myself before spilling half this tale of, so far, woe. Hi, this nose belongs to Jannie, former mini real estate tycoon from Boston, now living it up at the lower end of the Florida Keys (as far as a decent man gets away from Miami without taking to water) in a big ramshackle house on Heron Cove, alone with Parrot. My wife died; she didn't like me. At my age I should be out of it too, but maybe, like Methuselah, I'm doomed to live forever: wide-awake longevity for my sins. Parrot didn't like me either but I whistle and dance for him now, grow his favorite sunflower seeds on the back porch, take him for walks on the beach of my cove, play him his favorite tapes (mating calls of the Australian pink-billed cockatoo). Parrot finally gave in and hangs upside down from his perch, sounding off endearing chirps, when I come home from being busy. I make out okay: a recovering egotist, finally engaged in the attempt to consider others, like feeble old Sato-san and his young companion, out for a day's boating on calm and balmy seas, but suddenly, by Skip's mad dash back to Key West, faced with terminal horror. When everything works and the weather is right, little islands like Shark Key are like in the brochure: white sandy beaches, swaying coconut palms, mangrove in flower, long-legged white herons, a reef close-by to snorkel around purple groupers and yellowbacked snappers. Florida delivers. But only when your boat floats. Do these unsuspecting tourists know that they are marooned on an inhospitable fleck of a little isle, furnished with nothing but a weather-battered cabin next to a grove of palms populated by rabid rats and surrounded by ubiquitous mangroves attracting slimy low- and wildlife between the stilts they use for roots? Islets like Shark Key are nice picnic places best left before sundown. Little vampire insects come out at sunset, vultures circle forever, looking down to see if anyone is ready to give up blood or ghost. Watch those seagulls on the little beach where Skip put us off so treacherously just now. Seagulls ravish exhausted people. Skip's boat was still in view, circling us at a distance, like the ever-checking sharks that give the isle its name. "Joke?" Sato-san asked, gumming a denture.

I didn't quite think so.

Skip had to be after Sato-san for ransom, and after Miss Kira so that he could manipulate Sato-san. And me? Skip threw me in as Sato-san and Miss Kira might not have risked the pleasure trip without me. I can think quickly at times. I can also catch the lowest motive. There would be a nice twist here, legally safe, profitable to bad Skippo only.

Have you noticed how things often set out well enough? And then turn out as bad as things can be when the stars of destiny shift positions?

Happy Hour Hotel, Old Skip's lifelong claim to fame, had been doing just dandy for years with beautiful waiters twirling and skidding about on the terrace serving lightly broiled catch of the day, the luxurious pier bar, glorious rooms with a view, and complimentary speedboat excursions for guests in suites, paying top dollar. We all get into grooves—why worry if things go good? It's easy to forget that anything on Key West is Wet Tropics and that our real estate is held up by termites holding hands and that beautiful staff steals us blind as we loll about with the guests and pretty soon those very guests check in next door and the bank manager keeps leaving his card at the reception desk.

Skip, triumphantly home from Harvard, also lolled about with the guests. Then Old Skip took off and the bank manager didn't leave his card but stood on the table in the hotel's entrance and wanted all loans repaid right now or there would be that auction.

Which would be good for me. I've bought abused hotels at auctions for cheap before, made them as good as new again at little expense, sold them dear. That's how I can keep Parrot on smoked salmon and myself on shrimp with horseradish sauce and trimmings for both. Promises to Old Skip? *Make a man out of my son,* says Old Skip. So I bankrupt the hoodlum, then hire him back as a wage slave and won't let go until he shows signs of improving. *Turn Happy Hour around,* says Old Skip. So I just snap up the old thing, run it properly for a change, advertise it right, and sell out to the suckers.

Old Jannie does it again.

But why would he?

As I thought that way, constructively in the capitalist manner, following American optimism, letting the markets decide, adding another two bucks to the pile, I felt a sudden cold shiver. I also sniffed a whiff of tobacco and honey, of what Old Skip used to smoke in his corncob pipe.

"Okay," I said. "Just kidding, old buddy."

More shiver, more whiff.

"Leave this to me," I said. "I may know just what to do, old buddy."

Young Skip would run after me. "Things are bad."

"That's good," I would say, watching him sweat.

"It's good that you see things are bad," I would say, watching him stare.

"Because only then can you change your situation," I would say hearing him go: "Nah!"

Maybe it's today's America. This is an era of no patience. Maybe it's because of the videos we slide into the VCR. Hollywood programs the happy end, and it'll hit us in just another ninety minutes. All the audience ever does is sit back. Maybe it's because of modern travel. Relax, snowbird, give it another hour or so and the nice pilot drops you off on the beaches.

"You promised Dad to fix this, Jannie," Young Skip would say, waving bad bills.

Now, in order to appease Old Skip's spook, frightening poor old Parrot by swishing about on my veranda every time I come back from Key West, I'd better do something.

I tell you, I did plenty. I called on all my strength. I remembered my youthful escapade to the White Cloud Monastery near pre-Communist Beijing and rowed around Heron Cove chanting the Platform Sutra in neo-Sanskrit. I sent my mind back to sojourns on the coast of Maine and burned incense while reciting the Ultimate Power song in Algonquin. I reread the life of Silly Ivan Osikin by Pyotr Davilev O (an essay on how-not-to that eventually made me flee Boston forever). I even made myself a perch and hung it next to Parrot's so that we could roost upside down together and overcome our chasm between lifeforms. I also called on the wisdom of Old Skip himself and whiffing and sniffing together we remembered Pearl Harbor. The various factors taken into account, the solution came to me slowly.

Skip on the bad track. Happy Hour Hotel going down. Very well. One does not swim against the tide.

Tides turn. Just catch the moment.

That Happy Hour still attracted guests who stayed had to be due to its bar in the old boathouse at the end of the pier. Old Skip had it paneled with old rosewood orginally used in the state cabins of a clipper wrecked on a Key West reef a century and a half ago. The bar's glasses are long-stemmed crystal found in another ancient vessel. Happy Hour's bar stocks no bottles, only decanters, crystal too, of course, each with its little chain and silver label and the glow of its fluid magic. The teak counter is a solid plank cut from a giant sugar maple, polished to show the beauty of its infinitely mottled grain, like the Ch'an master's metaphor of the mirrors, each reflecting the entire universe. The bar stools are New Guinea teak, suitably topped with crocodile-skin seats. There's a large-scale model of a Malayan proa, the native sailing vessel, as graceful as a Zen poet's final thought. Miss Kira was standing next to the proa, in a simple shimmering dress, tall, stately, with finely chiseled features, antelope eyes, and the mouth of a Far Eastern elf. Miss Kira is half-Malayan herself.

Sato-san was limping about near the bar, lifting his after-dinner brandy while Miss Kira smiled her welcome. I had known the two for a while now. Sato-san and I shared breakfast on his suite's balcony most mornings, served by Happy Hour's last beautiful waiter. I would cut the number-one guest's grapefruit into segments while Sato-san told me why he didn't collect Van Gogh paintings.

"Jannie-san."

"Yes, Sato-san?"

"Van Goghs are dead now."

I'd pass the grapefruit. Sato-san would bow his thanks, smile, dig in, slurp, look up, laugh. "Departing old men must invest in life."

Sato-san could be very clear at times, albeit briefly, and before going into long dozes, sometimes with his eyes open, and staring at the sea that seemed to give him visions of eternity so enjoyable that he couldn't abide interference, not even Miss Kira's, whom he'd wave away if she moved into his moments.

She'd smile at me then. "Stepping between the infinities, Sato-Sensei doesn't like that." Whenever Sato-san seemed to reach his inner being Miss Kira liked to call him Teacher.

He'd also enjoy his lower levels, while watching pelicans, for instance, when they dive-bombed the surf for their meals of baby fish. Sato-san said he couldn't do that kind of copulation anymore, dive in with such abandon. He'd like to, however. He'd stretch his arms and encompass the entire bay, making it change into the great female receptive. Following up, we'd be another two old men comparing sexual skill of long ago, like Miami retirees who, in parking lots or shopping malls, endlessly discuss what will never be again and most likely never was.

"But there's Miss Kira."

He nodded. So much was true.

I asked Miss Kira what I could get her. I also got my own. Doing our slow dance around the Malayan sailing vessel, holding our long-stemmed crystals, we managed to blend our minds somewhat.

Was I really Skip's uncle?

I said I was everybody's uncle.

Hers too?

Yes. Parrot's too. I told her about my wife. I told her it wasn't enough to make all that up to the bird.

"So you're good now?"

I disagreed. I aim for beyond good and evil.

"Where there's nothing at all?"

I have no idea what nothing at all could be but that's where I am going. Pyotr Davilev O has the shaman claim from the Sixth Platform in neo-Sanskrit that nowhere is where Superior Man may find his values. Not later. Right now.

"You're not being silly?" Miss Kira asked.

I told her I often am indeed silly but that I hoped I was not just then. I also told her how the Chinese characters for Sage and Child are identical.

She rephrased her accusation. "You're an innocent."

I said I liked that better.

"I'm a whore," Miss Kira said. "You want to hear more?"

Old men should learn to listen.

I heard about her father, a Japanese manager working out a contract in Kuala Lumpur, Malaya, running a facility where native girls assemble plastic weaponry that becomes credit card-financed Christmas gifts for the kids in New York, L.A., and Chicago. Japanese-employed assembling girls are colorcoded. Subdued colors, as shown on duck-billed caps and shoulder badges, show higher ranks. Miss Kira's mother's code was a nice pale shade of a demure burnt orange. Manager Ishimura gave her his orders directly and often mentioned marriage, but then, suddenly, his stint was up and he had to go now but maybe he'd send for Miss Kira's mother at an as-yet-not-to-be-specified date. He was making no commitment but this was a target he would definitely strive to hit, maybe later.

Miss Kira was born; her mother saved for many years and flew to Japan. Vice president Ishimura already had a wife in Tokyo. He also had another mistress. Both incumbents were jealous. Ishimura-san also happened to be loaded down with some gambling debts, was due to go to the hospital for a sinus operation, had been summoned for operating his Lexus under the influence of rotgut sake. This was not a good time. "Are you okay? I could come up with enough to pay for a speedy flight home. You're sure? Nice little girl, you really think she looks like me? Why did you call her Kira? That's not a Japanese name. Anyway, from all my *kokoro,* good luck and *sayonara.*"

Miss Kira, caressing the model proa's keel, said that *kokoro* means "heart."

"So what did your mother do?" I asked, beginning a ritual dance around Miss Kira in tune to piped music: Bill Evans on piano, Scott LaFaro on bass, Paul Motian on drums, "Waltz for Miss Kira." She applauded, telling me that I have the endangered-species crane's long spindly legs, and that a crane is a holy bird in Japan, that she trusted me because of my holy legs.

We danced together. A pity I had left Parrot at home. He would have watched upside down. Antique Viking and Modern Exotic, joined by fingertips only, doing pre-Freudian Viennese one-two-threes performed by advanced U.S. jazz.

105

Sato-Sensei came to bow, smile, and leave for his balcony to watch the infinities filtered by a full moon.

"Then what happened?" I asked Miss Kira.

Miss Kira's mother became a barmaid in downtown Tokyo, the famous Ginza. She did well for a while. Miss Kira herself became a hostess. She did better for longer, but all that better didn't add up to much, until she ran into Sato-san.

"You know how I staged that meeting?" Miss Kira asked.

I almost skipped back into dance again to Tutu-tones (Miles Davis now). Such a good word Miss Kira used there: *stage*. It's true that man cannot do much more than at least try to ride the big waves that would otherwise drown him, but there are times that Chance smiles and we can set up a bit of a wavelet ourselves.

"How did you stage a change of fate, Miss Kira?"

"Come with me, Jannie-san . . ."

We're on Fujimicho (viewing Mount Fuji but there's eternal smog these days) Cemetery in Tokyo and Miss Kira has visited her mother's concrete-encased urn. She has seen Sato-san descend from a showroom-condition collector's item Lincoln 1979, "the last of the big ones." She saw him prostrate himself on a reed mat his chauffeur carefully unrolled. Sato-san pays his respects to his wife. Sato-san and Miss Kira are on similar schedules, for the scenes are repeated exactly one week later. It occurred to Miss Kira that something to her benefit could be done.

"I became a Kwannon of the Graves," Miss Kira said. "'Kwannon of the Graves' is a Japanese police term. Kwannon is a bodhisattva of compassion, a lovely lady. Japanese prostitutes, emulating the divine appearance, dress up in flowing robes and shuffle demurely near rich men lamenting loss of spouse. The bereaved male is subsequently engaged in commiserating conversation, aroused, and charged exorbitant fees."

106

"Ah," I said.

I held up my crystal, to be refilled by a charmingly efficient Skip, in whites with an impeccably hand-tied black butterfly—Skip likes to do that at times. The dear boy is not really allergic to work. He single-handedly repaired a good part of Happy Hour's rotted-out pier, doing a good job too, swinging hammers and fine-tuning power tools, but he became despondent. There was the bank manager hounding Skip. There was a bad drinking habit. There was cocaine. There was me, not helping out.

Happy Hour slid back further, even Sato-san took note. Miss Kira was despatched to sample other places. Skip had to hurry.

"Shall I take y'all out for a trip to Shark Key tomorrow?" Skip asked, smiling nastily across the bar. "How would y'all like that?"

There was darkness behind that dazzle. Miss Kira noticed too. "Is he jealous?"

I didn't think so.

"Ah?" I asked. "You charged Sato-san an exorbitant fee?"

"Sato-Sensei charged *me* an exorbitant fee," Miss Kira said.

Aha. A good old man adding some finishing touches on what destiny is about to do to him. Show an ordinary man a trap and he is already halfway caught, but some of us manage to turn fate a tad, to the mutual benefit of all interested parties. So maybe Sato had a right to the Sensei title. The man does have credits. Sato-san's company sells useful gadgets worldwide, cheaper and better than anyone else in his field. He truly loved his wife. He also truly liked what Miss Kira might have to offer. He took her everywhere.

"A daughter-disciple," Miss Kira said.

Beats hanging out in noisy bars and drafty cemeteries, I thought. "You give him a good time?"

"His wife's departing suggestion," Miss Kira said. She touched my holy leg. "Now what, Jannie?"

107

Now what, Jannie?" Here we are on Shark Key, reading the message Skip's skull and kimono demon offers from a twiggy claw. I respectfully took the note.

Tell Sato-san he has a choice, Jannie. Buy Happy Hour for a million and he's back in his suite before nightfall. You and Miss Kira will be picked up once I cash Sato-san's check after the closing tomorrow. Hold on to this note as I'll want it back. Okay? Okay.

I looked up but by that time the villain was far away.

Kidnapping for ransom disguised as a legitimate deal. Skip cashes the check and flees. Sato-san holds a worthless Happy Hour Hotel. Skip's proposed crime earns up to life, and Florida likes you to spend that in a chain gang.

"Hello?" Sato-san asked, wandering about vaguely among the scavenging seagulls, admiring a vulture circle, wafting away a mosquito or two.

I found the cooler and the duffel bags I had hidden in the mangroves earlier on, at daybreak, riding out in a rented cabin cruiser. We had a pot and a pan, a camping stove, plates, cups, and utensils, mosquito netting and sleeping bags, diving equipment, freshly roasted Hawaiian Kona coffee, mangoes and guavas, soy sauce, a tube of wasabi mustard, a yard of French bread, butter, key lime pie.

"Hello?" asked Miss Kira.

"Sashimi?" I asked. "Nap first? A drop of Armagnac for the Sensei? How about a bit of a swim?"

Sato-san wanted all of that, in reverse order. I spear-dived a sizable jewfish that Miss Kira cut up for sashimi. Two snappers became the main course. Sato-san snatched five lobsters. Miss Kira prepared seaweed.

After lunch Sato-san wanted to see Skip's note.

"You knew this would happen?" he asked me.

I did. I had seen Skip's dark look in the bar, the glare of the dear boy's demons. We'd have them turn round. No good getting rid of demons. They're helpful fellows if you can choose their direction. I wouldn't fight Skip. I would go along with Skip.

We slept that afternoon, then Sato-san and I, wrapped in mosquito netting, hid in the mangroves. Happy Hour's speedboat turned up at dusk that changed to darkness as Skip beached the boat and jumped lightly down on the sand, ready to pick up Sato-san and his check. We aren't kidding here. You lose some, you win some. This was a winner. I'll say that much for bad Skippo, he did remember to bring a hamper of food and suitable gear for Miss Kira's and my comfort that night. I had expected no less. No harm in the dear boy. Skip only wanted a million from Satosan's billion. There we have Skip, peering at the scene ahead, looking for his quarry. Nobody home except his own creation. The full moon above the mangroves helped.

Miss Kira's training as a courtesan helped too. She really can dance.

And I can sing. And Sato-san likes the kind of weird percussion you hear as background to Japanese Noh plays: odd bangs and clatters. We had found empty cans and a steel drum after swimming, and Sato-san made a shell rattle that sounded eerie.

Sound effects were good, the dance was great. Skip staggered back as the skeleton in the red and orange kimono, topped with her grinning white death-mask, transparent stone teeth, and eyes shining, slowly raised herself, then tripped off the veranda. Miss Kira cleverly assumed the same starting position Skip himself originally created. To him there was no change in the way he left and found Shark Key. Miss Kira became nasty Pinocchia, in a dance of approaching death, with Sato-san on percussion, Jannie producing off-stage screaming.

109

Skip, having had a hard day, may have been somewhat the worse for abuse of assorted drugs. The spectacle may have completed his worst hallucination. Skip turned. Skip ran.

There were two boats behind Skip now. The first was his own. The second was a Sheriff's Patrol with friendly Officer Wekko at the wheel. Wekko and his grumpy mini-mongrel Barnie are my neighbors, both newborn anarchists who believe in letting things take care of themselves with as much noninterference as bending over backwards may achieve. Wekko, however, is a friend and doesn't mind play-acting if requested politely.

"How're we doing, Skip?" Wekko asked, taking the key out of Skip's speedboat's dashboard.

"Can we talk for a minute, Skip?" I asked.

Wekko, Sato-san, and Miss Kira started cooking dinner as Skip and I strolled about on the beach.

"You set me up setting you up?" Skip asked.

"Dear boy," I said, "you check yourself voluntarily into a drug clinic and get yourself cleaned up while Miss Kira takes over Happy Hour's debt."

We walked arm in arm. There was good coffee aroma around, and the fragrance of broiled fish wrapped in the right choice of seaweeds. Lobster tails cooked. French bread crackled. Miss Kira whipped cream to top the key lime pie.

"Not Sato-san?" Skip asked.

"Sato-san will sign over the million to Miss Kira as a farewell present," I said. "Miss Kira will run Happy Hour until we deem you worthy."

"Shit," Skip said.

"Miss Kira will be holding your paper so that she can foreclose at any moment, and your dad left me a small but controlling interest. Maybe you can come back, but the terms will have to be tough."

"What *is* this?" Skip asked. "You want me to turn myself inside/out? You go screw yourself, old man."

Neatly uniformed Deputy Sheriff Wekko joined us, handcuffs and pistol barrel gleaming on his belt.

"There's the note in your very own handwriting," I said. "There's your very own chain gang waiting on the mainland."

"There's the disease," Wekko said "Natural-born alcoholics and junkies cannot drink or drug. Once they stop they can face their situation. You're not the only one, Skip."

"You too?" Skip asked. "Is that why you make me serve you all that free water?"

"I come for the music," Wekko said, "before you know, you may enjoy your work. Get some live jazz in that Happy Hour's bar. You'll make us all happy."

Sato-san was playing his cans and drum again, shaking his rattles.

"Come and get it," Miss Kira called.

It never quite ends well, but that seems to go with the planet. Sato-san's terminal cancer was diagnosed as entering the painful stage. We saw him float into the infinities on small tumblers of hospital-supplied morphine. Miss Kira held his hands. Sato-san left his fortune to a trust fund in Tokyo, with proceeds going to the fight with earthly discomfort. Skip escaped from the clinic but then tried on his own and is using Happy Hour work as a discipline to stay clean. Miss Kira has Wekko and his self-centered diminutive mutt Barnie over for dinner at Happy Hour every other Thursday. She won't stay at the hotel and married me so that she can stay in the country. Skip comes over to learn to chant the Platform Sutra in neo-Sanskrit and pursue his effort to impress Miss Kira. There has been one important change: Wekko's formerly asocial hybrid Barnie has taken it upon herself to visit Parrot. They howl together. Old Skip's spook has found better things to do than bother me with its whiffs and shivers.

SKULL AND KIMONO

As Pyotr Davilev O and the Ch'an master have it, just try and be a little more negative and you'll find that things are getting better and better.

THE JUGHEAD FILE

Text of a police file used as study material in a detective course at the Police Academy of Kyoto:

A report—drawn up by Inspector Third Class Saito Masanobu, Crime Squad, Municipal Police, Kyoto

Kyoto, 20 April 1979

Alerted by a telephone call made by Kogawa Sujuru, I visited a house, 7–3–5 Kawabata, this morning at ten o'clock. At the house, on the second and upper story, in a room at the rear, I found the lifeless body of a woman, Washino Maiko, 64 years old. Dr. Obata's report, stating the cause of death and a description of the woman's remains, is attached. Several garbage bags, made of grey plastic, had been cut open and tacked to the paper sliding doors and windows in order to block the flow of air. I found a small gas cylinder in the room, of the type that will fuel a cookstove. The cylinder's faucet was open and it contents had escaped. Mrs. Washino lay on her bed on the straw floorboards. Her arms were crossed on her chest.

113

The only other inhabitant of the house, Kogawa Sujuru, a forty-year-old man, told me: "It must have happened during the night. I had been drinking last night and slept deeply. I live downstairs and always spread my bed in the lower front room. When I woke I smelled gas and saw that the small cylinder that feeds gas to the kitchen stove had been removed. I ran upstairs to call Mrs. Washino. She adopted me as her son five years ago and she owns this house. I opened the door to her bedroom but staggered back because of the gas escaping into the corridor. I saw her in her bed, covered my mouth and nose with a cloth, rushed in, and opened the windows. I then called the police. Mrs. Washino suffered from depressions and often talked about suicide."

Kogawa is an artist, a painter, self-employed. I interrogated him in his studio, the rear room on the lower floor. He said: "I feel guilty. Mrs. Washino has never married and is quite well off. People from the neighborhood call her 'Mrs.' but that isn't really correct. It was most kind of her to be willing to adopt this humble person, a struggling artist, as her son. Thanks to her, I no longer have to sell my drawings and paintings in the street. Since Mrs. Washino accepted me as her official son, she made me comfortable here and paid all my expenses. I have been unworthy of her many gifts. I should at least have tried to cheer her up. Now I inherit all her possessions and cannot repay her many favors."

As both circumstances and the doctor's findings indicate that Washino Maiko died voluntarily and by her own hand, I conclude suicide.

A report drawn up by Inspector First Class Saito Masanobu, Crime Squad, Municipal Police, Kyoto

Kyoto, 3 May 1983
Alerted by a telephone call made by Miss Ozaki Jumoko, I

visited a house, 7–3–5 Kawabata, at nine-thirty this morning. Miss Ozaki, a charwoman employed by Kogawa Sujuru, the well known artist, took me to the lifeless body of the owner of the house. It hung from a beam in the studio, the room at the rear on the first floor. Dr. Obata's report, stating the cause of death and a description of Kogawa's remains, is attached. I also attach a lengthy letter I found pinned to the kimono the corpse was wearing. After having ascertained that the handwriting was the same as that on various documents found in the house, and in view of the doctor's report and the circumstances I observed, I conclude suicide.

Letter written by Kogawa Sujuru directed to Inspector Saito Masanobu

Kyoto, May 2, 1983

Friend and Devil who pursues me: You will doubtless remember what I told you when you visited here on the occasion of my adopted mother's untimely and unnatural death. You suspected that I was lying. My lies were convincing enough as I had wrapped them around the truth. My adopted mother died, four years ago, because she choked on poisonous gas and you interrogated me at length. I saw that your ears stand out rather and therefore called you "jughead"–not aloud, of course. The physical flaw that makes you look rather comical impressed me deeply.

You wanted to learn the truth. Did you ever hear the Buddhist tale about the onion? I refer to the comparison here because before you asked me all your questions, you said that you subscribe to the Zen Sect of the Buddhist faith. You treated me politely, even with some kindness, perhaps out of habit but also, it seemed to me, to make me drop my defenses. I own a small statue of Bodhidharma, the first Zen master, who came from India a long time ago. You admired that impressive

115

work of art. I said that I had been given the little sculpture depicting the fat, angry-looking patriarch by my father. My father had in turn received it from the Zen master Gota, the recently deceased teacher who was in charge of the Northern Temple.

Gota often talked about the onion. When we peel an onion, one layer after another comes off until finally only emptiness is left—just as the Buddhist training gradually peels off the ego so that we can enter the great void. You wanted to peel my onion, tear off my lies that, as a scaly hull, cover up my truth. For even I, I dare to presume, have the divine core, the silence that we all share in the end. You sat there so strongly and quietly, like a monk in deep meditation. You wore a dark western-style suit of good quality, tailor-made perhaps, a white shirt, and a narrow tie. You had folded your legs, your head stood straight on your shoulders, and your torso rested squarely on my poor wornout floor. I felt that you didn't believe any of my filthy fabrications, but I made them up anyway, so that you could write them into your report. The death of my stepmother was framed within those lies as a suicide that could not be disputed. I said I was sorry so that my innocence might be clear. Anyone who breaks the law is careful when the police face him in his own quarters. You were my enemy, a devil ready to drag me into hell.

A jugheaded devil? A physical aberration increases the humanity of our appearance. I beg your pardon—I'm not saying that you're physically handicapped, like me. Did you mention in your report that I have a hunch-back and squint terribly?

I don't think you did, although the information could be relevant. To what? To murder. Surely you noticed that my stepmother was hunchbacked, too, and squinted behind her thick glasses. Some people thought Mrs. Washino was my mother long before she officially adopted me. In reality, our similarities must be due to an interesting twist of fate.

Can I tell you something about my life? Even you, an intelligent and well trained police officer, may learn something about the way human relations come about.

My mother died shortly after my birth. My father was ashamed that his son was a crippled horror but he couldn't avoid raising his own child. He designed kimonos for a well known store here in town. After my mother's death, he got up early every morning and visited Zen master Gota. I think my father wanted to know what he had misdone in order to deserve a son like me. Surely my handicaps and my mother's untimely death are consequences of mistakes he had made in previous lives. Master Gota devised some riddles that my father was supposed to solve and advised lengthy meditations so that my father could reach his deeper mind.

My father always had little luck. Now he couldn't even rest after his long hours of work, for which he was never properly paid. I wonder now if master Gota's efforts were very helpful. He heaped more questions on my father's basic query: why does a well meaning man have to suffer in his everyday existence? Zen riddles make little sense—they can't be solved logically and tend to drive the disciple crazy.

Stop the express train from Osaka. Have you ever heard of that Zen riddle? Isn't it rather a cruel command? My father must have thought so, for one day he was found dead on the railroad track. I think he was waiting for Buddha, thinking maybe the Holy One would show himself as a train. The corpse was mangled but I recognized his remains as those of my father. I was fourteen years old then.

The stop-the-train riddle interested me profoundly. Half my being originates in my father's genes—I am the continuation of all of his inquiry. I burn incense in front of his photograph now, but it would be better if I could find an answer to his question.

Stop the train from Osaka. How often didn't I stand on the track on the spot where the hill rises and one can see the ancient Toji Pagoda on one side and the modern Grand Hotel on the other, a symbol of western civilization that has moved us so far forward in time. Time—that has to be the answer to the riddle, time that doesn't exist, but my father wouldn't see that. He still believed that he had to hurry somewhere, but master Gota wanted him to stop himself. He didn't suggest that my father should try to flag down a rushing train.

Shouldn't Zen masters be equipped with some psychological insight? Are such lofty souls allowed to push the silly under a train? I think master Gota was sorry, for he sent his head monk to take me to the temple. For two years I was given board and lodging at the monastery, went to school during the days and spent the evenings with the monks in meditation. They made me get up early so that I could sit quietly in the mornings, too, and whenever I dozed off they beat me with a stick. Afterward I had to bow down to show my appreciation. Beating seems to be part of a proper education. There was an article in the paper the other day, praising the president of a company manufacturing luxury cars. He had beaten a student laborer with a wrench because the young fellow hadn't properly fastened a bolt.

The head monk was an aristocrat. Every time you visited me, you reminded me of him. You wore your tailor-made suit like he wore his robe. It's fashionable in the Zen temples to always wear the same robe, so that outside people can see how little money the monks are spending on themelves. When the fabric tears with age, the monks patch the holes. The head monk spent much time and trouble continuously repairing his robe, and it was a work of art, a most subtle combination of bits of cloth in all possible shades of blue and black. I often painted him, although he refused to model for me. Master Gota would say I wasted my time whenever he saw me busy with my brushes. He would confiscate my paintbox, but I got pocket money from the monks so that I could save up and keep replacing my supplies. When high school was over, I escaped from the temple and began to wander about. For many years I slept under bridges and tried to sell my work in the streets.

I was alone and hated everyone around me. Cripples learn how to hide their feelings, however. The other homeless bums abused me and kept stealing my money. I dreamed about revenge. Perhaps my hatred kept me alive in those days. Street-people die easily enough. They lie down somewhere, embrace themselves, sigh a few times, and die in their sleep. But I still needed life and was strengthened by my fury. I dreamed that I broke the posts that hold up the famous old buildings of our city or that I burned down City Hall. I exploded temples and caused huge holes in busy streets. In reality I behaved pretty well and made nice pictures, showing cute toddlers playing in gardens or darling kittens adorned with shiny bells dangling from velvet collars. The kittens were fat and happy, not at all like the starved creatures people dump in temple gardens thinking that Buddha will take care of them. Buddha never sees them, but the kittens' screams bother the monks, who drown them in the temple pond.

Did you grasp any of this when you stared into my squinting eyes, when you inquired how Mrs. Washino had met her end? I believe you did. I do squint rather badly, as you surely noticed. Passers-by often laugh at me. "Don't you get bored with the view of your own nose?" more than one has asked. The way your ears jut out amused me, too. I wanted to ask, "How is it you don't get blown away when the typhoon descends on the city?"

How did my stepmother and I meet? You asked me that and I supplied you with some of the required information. I said that I rented a room in the old lady's house and that she

119

liked me more and more, and then took me to City Hall one day to have me inscribed as her lawful son.

As her son, I was her heir and her death would be of material benefit to me. So I manipulated her into death. Ungrateful, right? I am now allowed to fill in the remainder of the pertinent information?

I was showing my work in the streets and slept under a bridge, the Gojo Bridge it was at that time, by far the worst shelter the city offers—there are drafts even when the wind dies down and the rats are bigger and more aggressive than anywhere else. The bums are worse, too—drunken muggers and toothless old hags creaking with filth.

I had just started portraying the Buddhist holy men—Bodhidharma leering over his scraggly moustache, the ancient master Hakuin falling apart with age, the retarded Ananda, Buddha's first disciple who always repeated his teacher's words and was therefore called Parrot. Tourists often come to Kyoto because they think that our temples emit a heavenly radiance and holy pictures make suitable souvenirs to bring or show the folks back home. One day I made a fair amount of money and couldn't resist the temptation to buy myself new clothes. I suddenly looked so neat that I didn't dare to go back to my bridge. I wandered about aimlessly until I saw a well kept house in an alley of the Eastern Quarter. There was a sign on the wall, *Room for Rent.*

That was the beginning of the big change. Mrs. Washino opened the door and permitted me to come in. I hadn't been in a proper home for so long that I felt ill at ease. I had to restrain myself for I wanted to grin—Mrs. Washino was hunchbacked, too, and also squinted horribly. We couldn't look straight at each other and had to hang over somewhat to counterbalance the weight of our misshapen backs. The rent she offered was reasonable enough and I said I would take the room. She thought it was strange that I wanted to move

120

in at once, but I had everything with me—my rags in a bag and my work in a wooden cylinder. I thought she might refuse and quickly counted out some notes. She nodded in acceptance. There's something indecently alluring about cash openly displayed.

I wasn't decent, either. Mrs. Washino often came to chat and would offer tea but I always insisted on drinking rice wine. Under the bridges I had become accustomed to alcohol. Fiery rice wine warms the bones and can be inspiring at times. I kept painting holy men and needed to be somewhat drunk in order to get their expressions right. But not too drunk. It was only later that I became really addicted.

Mrs. Washino liked to chatter, and her choice of subjects was rather monotonous. She usually discussed death and ways to die. She often watched TV stuff in which noble gentlemen and ladies of long ago get themselves into trouble and are forced to take their own lives. We would talk of various deadly poisons, knife and sword thrusts in belly or neck, swallowing broken glass, suffocation by hanging, jumping off cliffs, walking into the sea, and other methods. I suggested gas, for she kept gas in her home. I understood, of course, that she discussed her own death, even as she forced all sorts of depressed friends and acquaintances she didn't have, to act in her tales. She didn't know anyone at all.

I would paint until noon and spend the afternoons in the streets. One day she asked me how I made my money. I told her the truth and she shuffled out of the room without saying anything. She didn't even bow. Later that day she came back and accused me of shameless begging. She said I would have to go. I could stay until the end of the month, but not a day longer, for a person who squats on the pavement waiting for passers-by to hand out money was not the type of tenant who was welcome in a nice lady's home.

"If I'm not welcome, I won't stay a moment longer," I said

curtly and began to pack my belongings. Mrs. Washino said she wasn't evicting me but she knew a shed where I could possibly stay. I left angrily and slept under the bridge again. The next day she found me in the street, selling near the Imperial Palace gates. She told me she had been looking for me for hours. She cried and apologized and so I moved in again.

She wasn't a bad woman, you will say, although she might possibly be a little proud and generally limited in her outlook. I agree, with some hesitation. Human motivations aren't always easy to grasp. We looked alike and she may have considered me to be her own continuation. Then again, perhaps she wanted to have me in her power or saw a chance to gain honor through me. I'm not an untalented artist. Haven't I proved my worth since then? My *Cranes on a Rainy Evening* won a prize last year and *Kyoto Art* regularly shows reproductions of my work, followed by lengthy articles in which the experts sing my praise. *Kyoto Art* is the best art magazine in the country, some say. Mrs. Washino would have been proud of me if she were still alive.

When I returned here from my night under the bridge, she and I had a long and serious conversation. I need pay no more rent if I promised not to sell my work in the streets any more. From that day on, she paid for my paint and brushes and brought me all my meals. I was to produce a fair number of paintings and find an agent who could introduce me to the galleries and arrange exhibitions. I did my best and within a year or so my work became known.

Can you imagine what it's like to be attached by a leash to an old woman's claw? Certainly I could paint under favorable conditions, but I had lost my free will. I fought back by drinking more than before and regularly invited other artists I'd met through my agent to help me empty the jug. I became quarrelsome and encouraged her when she got into her death talk again. Whenever I sold a painting I kept quiet, but I made sure that all my disappointments were fully discussed. The subject of suicide cropped up more and more often and I insisted on the providential use of gas.

The cylinder with cooking gas belongs in the kitchen but was found in her bedroom when you came to inquire about my stepmother's death. Who carried it up? She didn't ask me to lug that heavy object up the stairs, but one evening I thought the time had come, and was proved right.

Isn't it amazing how roles sometimes revert? At first she could control me at will but gradually I became the driving factor. My stepmother committed suicide. She unscrewed the faucet after she had pinned the plastic garbage bags on the frames of her door and windows. I only carried the cylinder up. To assist in a suicide is illegal, but hard to prove.

As her only heir I became a suspect, but the truth is that I didn't need what she left me. A week after Mrs. Washino's death, my first big exhibition opened and I knew that I would sell. My hunch wasn't unfounded. My name had been mentioned in the right circles for a while.

So why did I help her make up her mind? I think I did that to wipe out my own past. I wanted to be rid of the disgusting beggar I had been for so long, and Mrs. Washino was the only one who had known him well. Perhaps my misdeed was also caused by the dreams of revenge I experienced under the bridges. Had I finally found someone who was even weaker than me? Or did I long for the beautiful young women I couldn't bring into the house because my stepmother's possessive jealousy barred them from my life? Did I intend to free myself once and for all? Or was it her negative talk getting on my nerves too much?

It's hard to know oneself. You saw me as a potential murderer and kept coming back from time to time. Very clever of you. As a policeman, you certainly knew your duty. You couldn't prove my guilt, but you suspected that I wasn't quite done as yet and stayed in touch in order to prevent further upheavals. You wanted me to know that the State had her eye on me, isn't that right, Inspector? Isn't it your task to protect society? Or were you interested in my case, like Zen master Gota once was when he made me sit in his temple where the monks were beating me? Every one of your visits inflicted severe pain on my soul. Your soft polite voice hit me like a whip. Your gaze burned into the very depth of my being. You are a devil employed by the judges of hell. Doesn't Buddhism claim that only development matters and that pain is the best teacher? Isn't that truth so convincing that we enjoy reading in the paper that a student laborer in a motor-car factory has been beaten by his highest boss with a wrench?

I see you now, with your jugheaded face. If you had normal ears, you wouldn't have impressed me. Unblemished truth-bearers can dazzle us too much. Master Gota suffered from the disease of Parkinson and his trembling hand underlined everything he was trying to show me. Why does Bodhidharma's image fascinate me? Because that great teacher made use of a fat body and a grumpy face and because he slowed himself down by always displaying a nasty temper. The stylized Buddha images mean nothing to me. What do they display but inimitable perfection?

You haven't visited me for a while, but I know that you can drop in any minute now. Your visits were always unexpected and I was never able to prepare myself properly.

I assume that you will read this letter in my studio. Look about you, please. Do you see my latest work? The portraits of the ballet dancer Netsuku? Yes, that's right—on all my sketches the poor girl squints. Netsuku is known for her beautiful eyes that contemplate infinity with their luscious radiance, but in my portraits she short-sightedly peers at the tip of her nose. That failure made me buy the rope that will strangle me. I did keep trying for days on end, I've always been good at drawing eyes but I must have lost that ability for good. If you check my chest of drawers, you will find hundreds of scraps of paper on which I tried to depict Netsuku's eyes. What shows, as you will see, is my stepmother's unhappy squint.

The end of the road. Suicide is always inspired by despair. My father jumped against the thundering engine of the Osaka Express, Mrs. Washino opened up a faucet. I'll be kicking a stool in a minute. When one does that, there has been the choice of the only way out. I can only guess at what went on in the minds of my father and stepmother, and in my own mind the process is not too clear, either. Should I have confessed my crime? What would you have done? A confession alone does not stand up in court, but even if, together, we had collected some proof, my guilt could never have been washed away.

Do I realize now that I must punish myself by cutting short a most promising career? In a way I need to thank you, terrible devil who never gives in, for you destroyed my revenge. By visiting me from painful moment to moment you made me peel my own onion of ignorance. I'm not done yet—there are still tear-drawing skins that need to be ripped away, but does any process ever come to an end? Is the end provided by death no more than a new beginning? I will meet my stepmother again, in another form and under fresh circumstances, for even if there was no connection between us before, this present life has certainly tied us together.

I hear the monks chant again when they began their morning's meditation and a new day:

I myself see where I failed before.

Is there no end to the greed, rage, folly that brought about my birth and determined the place of a fresh start?

I confess my ignorant mistakes now, so that I can keep moving forward.

You'll have to cut me loose, put me down, and write your report. I'm sorry I cause you trouble. Meanwhile, thanks to you, I float away and am finally rid of your infernal but benificent meddling.

HERON ISLAND

Y ou want me to confess?" Professor Suzuki asked
through his interpreter, Toshiko. "I wasn't here in
Amsterdam, Holland, when it happened, commissaris-san, I was in Kyoto. And confess to what? To a crime?
But the crime is the murder of my own son, my only child,
and it was the French couple that did that, the skinheads, arrr
. . . Ninette, and arrrr . . . Pierre, yes, *yes,* commissaris-san?"

"Mere instruments?" the chief of detectives, a neat little old
man, asked politely enough. He was at an advantage of course,
entrenched behind his huge antique desk. He was at home,
so to speak, at Amsterdam's Police Headquarters, a far cry
from his visitor's Kyoto, the exotic temple city, the pure heart
of Japan; although, Suzuki had told him just now, industry
was polluting even Kyoto, darkening the sky above perfect
copies of T'ang Dynasty Buddhist buildings, extinct in China
since the Cultural Revolution, but duplicated perfectly in the
land of the Rising Sun. "Saaah," Suzuki said, admiring a giant
blue heron, preening blue and silver wings on a branch of a
century-old elm tree outside the commissaris's open window,
stretching its snake-like neck, croaking musically. "A rare bird."

"Herons aren't rare," the commissaris said. "In fact, they're a pest. All over the city. They get so bad that we put up signs to warn our good people not to walk under their trees. A good splat ruins clothes. It's the canals that attract our thousands of herons, and the recession, of course. You see, we have all the unemployed now, who like to fish, so Amsterdam stocks her canals with minnows and the unemployed yank the fish out and feed them to the herons."

"So desu ka?" the motherly young Toshiko twittered, too surprised to translate. "Is that so? Herons are *very* rare in Japan."

"I thank you, commissaris-san," Suzuki said, "for solving my son's murder. It is terrible indeed when a man's sole biological successor is killed criminally, and his body is cut up, and found in a trunk, floating in . . . arrrr . . . Brewer's Canal, was it?"

"Yes," the commissaris said, sharing a relaxed coffee ceremony with his guests, handling the heavy silverware deftly: pot, jug, bowl—handing out cookies.

"Oishiiii," Suzuki and Toshiko said, "tasty."

"Brewer's Canal," Suzuki said. "It may be fitting that my son departed there. He did like beer."

"You drink alcohol yourself?" the commissaris asked.

"What?" Suzuki stared over the rim of his coffee cup. "Oh . . . no, don't care for drink . . . but Koichi had the bad gene, his mother's. You know—" the professor spoke in an exaggeratedly youthful voice, which Toshiko immediately imitated in English *"—Out of beer, out of luck . . . All beer is good beer."* He spoke in his own voice again. "My son's favorite sayings."

The commissaris glanced at polaroids on his desk. Some were of a dismembered corpse, one showed Koichi alive, standing on an Amsterdam gable house's stone steps, between sculptured granite lions, squinting awkwardly. The commissaris thought the young man's sullen looks could be due to more than being hung-over. Koichi looked disturbed—the way he held his head to the side, as if someone was about to slap him, defensively raised hands, a too eager smile. The underdog, the commissaris thought, the pathetic creature rolled over on its back signaling: "Please don't hurt me."

"What should I confess to?" Suzuki asked. "Please, commissaris-san, tell me what happened, from the beginning if you please . . . oh . . . Koichi, my son . . . "

"I told you," the commissaris said.

The heron in the elm tree half raised his huge wings, as if intending to float down easily to cool its feet in Moose Canal below, then croaked musingly. The elm tree offered shade. The summer day was hot. He could claim his fish later.

"I tell you, yes?" Suzuki said. "Koichi didn't like to travel, he just drank, in bad bars, so I wanted him to expand his mind, to travel. I sent Tadao with him, Tadao, youngest son of my colleague Sakai . . . arrrr . . . Sakai and I are professors, medical men."

"You paid the trip for both your son Koichi and your colleague's son Tadao," the commissaris said.

Suzuki shrugged. "I am well off. I invested, locked in on my profits a long time ago." He stared at the heron, folded his hands, bowed to the creature.

"There are no Japanese herons?" the commissaris asked.

"We only keep Japanese people on the islands now," Suzuki said. "Other lifeforms are dying out in Japan." He looked down at the commissaris's oriental rugs, then up at oil portraits of ancient Dutch constabulary captains, smiling down from red faces.

There was a silence, first soothing, then disturbing. Toshiko broke it. "Not all wildlife is dead. There are sanctuaries, commissaris-san. The professor owns Heron Island on Lake Biwa, close to Kyoto. It is very famous."

"The snow monkey sanctuary in Hokkaido is famous," Suzuki said, "nobody ever heard of my insignificant effort."

"Your son Koichi," the commissaris said, shaking a pathology report from a plastic file and arranging its pages neatly next to the polaroids, "died of an overdose of pure heroin."

"A new vice," Suzuki said. "To add to the drinking. I worried about my son. I thought a change of environment . . . "

"Amsterdam heroin," the commissaris said, "often comes pure.

"Well," Suzuki said, "so you're saying my son's unnatural death was an accident? I don't think so. Dealer Pierre knew that Koichi wouldn't be able to handle that injection. Malicious foresight, *neh?* They robbed him, *neh?* Pierre and Ninette. You jailed that bad couple?"

"Pierre is dying in the jail's hospital now," the commissaris said. "Withdrawal sometimes does that. Users are in bad shape, they haven't eaten for a while, living on the drug only, and then, when the drug is withheld, the shock kills."

"Ninette too?" Suzuki asked.

"Holland is short of jail space," the commissaris said. "We released her to the custody of her family, in Paris. Pierre prostituted Ninette. She's in a clinic, recovering nicely."

"Good girl at heart?" Suzuki asked suspiciously.

The commissaris lifted a thin, almost transparent hand, smiling gently. "What's *good?*"

"What's good is what's good for *us,*" Professor Suzuki said, thumping his chest.

The commissaris smiled. "For the surviving lifeform?"

"Hai," the professor nodded.

"The polluting lifeform?" the commissaris asked.

"Arrr . . . " Suzuki said.

"Arrr . . . " the commissaris said kindly. "I don't believe holding Ninette improves the common good."

The heron outside, alerted by the professor's loud voice, lifted a wing and croaked loudly. Suzuki's face twitched as he moved forward in his chair. "Listen, police-officer-san. Ninette bought the trunk with a traveler's check taken from a dead body to purchase a trunk to get rid of that same body. My only son's dead body. You yourself told me so. That's how you caught Pierre and Ninette. They killed Koichi Saturday night in their loft on Blood Alley, and Pierre, a butcher by trade, bled and cut Koichi's corpse. You told me that the stores here are closed Sundays and Mondays. The trunk, found floating in Brewer's Canal late Monday, was new. Your detectives traced the vendor at the street market, which is open on Monday. He'd taken a hundred-dollar American Express traveler's check in payment from a French female skinhead. You knew, because Tadao told you, that Koichi and he had been drinking with a French skin-head couple in Blackbeard's Bar at Blood Alley that Saturday night when Koichi disappeared. The connection was clear. Your detectives traced the French couple to their loft and their search produced more of Koichi's traveler's checks." Suzuki's voice squeaked indignantly. "Yes, commissaris-san, *yes?*"

The commissaris coughed. "Please. I'm sorry, Suzuki-san, I really want you to make that confession." He blew his nose. "Excuse me. It's better for you. You will feel relieved."

"You want to arrest me?" Suzuki asked. "You're kidding... arrrr . . . you can't hold me on nothing. I was halfway across the globe when Koichi died. How could I kill him?"

The commissaris smiled. "I won't arrest you."

"I'm a medical man," Suzuki said, "I serve the common good. Why do you blame me? For sending my only son to Amsterdam, with a friend to protect him?"

"I just want you to clarify your motivation," the commissaris said. "I am not blaming you. Besides," he gestured gently, "you did nothing illegal."

Suzuki held up his hands. His eyes blazed. "So why this confession?"

"To clear your mind," the commissaris said.

"For the common good?" Suzuki asked.

The commissaris nodded.

"I don't follow you," Suzuki said. He turned to the pleasant-faced Toshiko. He muttered furiously. "Suzuki-san," the interpreter, stepping out of direct-voice mode, said briskly, "says he doesn't follow you."

"Tell Suzuki-san," the commissaris said, "that he does. Tell him I want his confession. Tell him I won't arrest him. Tell him he can go home." Suzuki got up.

"Confession first," the commissaris said. Suzuki sat down.

"Perhaps, if we go through the events again . . . " the commissaris said.

"Okay . . . " Suzuki said. "Where are we now? My unemployed son Koichi and his friend Tadao Sakai, a medical student, vacationing in Amsterdam, visit a bar. Koichi drinks. Tadao abstains. Blackbeard, who tends bar, sells Koichi marihuana. Koichi smokes the joints. Tadao does not. A French couple, in leather clothes, with shaven skulls, enters Blackbeard's Bar. The couple indulges too, sidles up to the rich Japanese tourists. Pierre offers drugs that he keeps in his loft. Koichi leaves with the French couple. Tadao returns to the hotel alone. Koichi doesn't show on Monday morning. Tadao informs our ambassador, a Kyoto native who happens to be an acquaintance of mine. The ambassador alerts the police."

"More coffee?" the commissaris asked.

Suzuki's trembling hand made his cup clatter on its saucer.

The commissaris poured.

"What do you want of me?" Suzuki asked. "Yes, I know I accused Tadao of kidnapping Koichi, when the ambassador phoned me in Kyoto. I overreacted. I've explained the situation: my colleague Sakai has been losing a fortune on the stock market. He's back in debt, his house is mortgaged to the hilt again, the continued study of his four sons is in jeopardy. I'm the rich guy. I first hear my son is missing, then that his dismembered body has been found floating about in a trunk. I don't know about a French couple. I do know about Tadao. Maybe Tadao had Koichi tied up in some basement here and wanted me, in return for my son's release, to pay for his, Tadao's, studies, or maybe I was to finance Tadao's father's debts. I imagined that Tadao might have killed Koichi by accident, by binding him too tightly. It could be, couldn't it? And Tadao studies surgery, he knows how to cut up a human body . . . to get rid of the evidence?"

"Really. . . " the commissaris said, shaking his head. "Really, professor . . ."

"Far-fetched," Suzuki said. "I know. Tadao is a good boy. Besides, my hypothesis was unlikely, as you explained. There are no empty basements in Amsterdam, the city is overcrowded. Besides, Japanese are conspicuous foreigners here. How could one conspicuous foreigner molest another? Wouldn't someone have noticed? Wouldn't you have been informed?"

The commissaris sipped coffee.

"You didn't arrest Tadao," Suzuki said. "You want me to confess to accusing an innocent party? My motive is jealousy? Very well. I confess." Suzuki thumped his knee. "Why does my associate-professor Sakai, my inferior, Sakai the foolish gambler, have four excellent sons who study hard, four heirs to have pride in, and why am I damned with misfit Koichi?"

"Thank you," the commissaris said.

"Can I go now?" Suzuki asked.

"That was only the first part of the confession," the commissaris said.

Suzuki was shouting. "You want me to admit to manipulating Koichi to die by sending him here to Amsterdam, a magic city of sin, where dangerous drugs were bound to reach him? That I was sure that Koichi would go for heroin? That he would surrender to that evil French couple? Show them his roll of traveler's checks? Set himself up to get murdered?"

"We dropped the murder charge," the commissaris said. "There is no evidence of conscious planning. These things mostly just happen, you know. There's no proof that Pierre knowingly injected an overdose into a willing client. We have Tadao's testimony: Koichi was bragging he was used to heroin."

"Pierre should have noticed that Koichi didn't inject," Suzuki said.

"You think Pierre checked Koichi for needle marks?" the commissaris asked. "In a dark loft in the early hours? Everybody is drunk and stoned already, and Pierre has just wandered all over Amsterdam looking to buy heroin and needles, not easy products to purchase, even here?"

The heron was looking at Suzuki. Suzuki covered his eyes. *"Kudasai . . . kudasai . . . "*

"Please . . . please . . . " Toshiko translated. Suzuki dropped his hands. He stared at the heron. "I protected you, remember?"

"You're almost there," the commissaris said.

Suzuki was calmer, sitting back, hands clasped on knees. "It hurts too much to tell you my truth."

The commissaris smiled helpfully. "You know why the truth hurts?" Suzuki asked.

"Because we cover it up by lying to ourselves?" the commissaris asked. "But lies are transparent. The truth moves underneath, it keeps wanting to get out."

"It twists about in pain," Suzuki said.

"So?" the commissaris asked.

The heron had flown away. The commissaris looked out of the window, beckoning his guests to join him. Six stories below, the bird stood next to a man in a red hat, dangling a fishing rod above Moose Canal. Man and bird.

"I love birds," Suzuki said. "Koichi hated me. He wanted to hurt me. He was drunk, he was on my island, shooting my birds."

"What had you done to him?" the commissaris asked.

"I didn't marry his mother," Suzuki said. "She gave him to me after my wife left me. Koichi's mother hates me too but she thought I would pay for a good education. I paid for everything. Koichi wasn't grateful."

"Should he have been?" the commissaris asked.

Suzuki raised a shoulder. "Maybe I pressured him, eh? Pushed too hard, maybe? Wanting him to do well? Wanting to show off a good son?"

"Thank you," the commissaris said.

Suzuki danced, using the commissaris's large oriental rug as stage floor. First he danced Koichi, drunk, crazed, firing an automatic shotgun. Then he danced a wounded bird, flopping about between the pine trees and ornamental bushes, shrieking in agony, trying to stretch its broken wings. The commissaris noticed how heron-like Suzuki was himself, with his wavy silver hair brushed up over his ears so that it tufted backward, with his long arms that perfectly imitated wing movements, with narrow trouser legs and tall-shafted tight boots, stepping about stiffly.

The shot heron died, falling into the professor's chair. The professor sat up painfully, croaking: "arrrr. . . "

"I see," the commissaris said.

"See what?" Suzuki asked.

"I see what you mean," the commissaris said. "I'm very close to my pet turtle, dear little fellow who lives in my garden, closer than I am to humanity, perhaps."

"Now your son shoots turtle," Suzuki said.

"Now I kill my son?" the commissaris asked.

"So now what do I do?" Suzuki asked.

•

Both parties met once again, at Suzuki's invitation, at a restaurant facing the southern gate of Amsterdam's Vondel Park, a conglomeration of large ponds surrounded by clusters of trees and shrubbery that provide optimal habitat for the capital's many species of birds.

"Commissaris-san," Suzuki said, "I thank you."

"Are we done?" the commissaris asked.

Suzuki bowed. "My mind is clear."

"I'm glad," the commissaris said.

"So am I." Suzuki smiled. He touched Toshiko's arm. "My adviser here tells me that it's time to move ahead intelligently. She also tells me that intelligence is the capacity to make the best use of a given set of circumstances. I still have the island with a recovering population of splendid birds. With Koichi gone I have no heir. You told me that your detectives, when they visited Tadao at his hotel, found him developing photographs of herons, taken while he was hiking about in Vondel Park?"

"Tadao told Adjutant Grijpstra," the commissaris said, "who likes to paint waterfowl as a hobby."

"What style?" Suzuki asked. " . . . Arrrr, Hondecoeter's style perhaps, the old master . . . ?"

"The old master," the commissaris said. "Tadao told my adjutant that herons, in Japan, symbolize the ability to fly out to higher spheres."

Suzuki nodded.

"A sensitive boy," the commissaris said. "This Tadao."

"My colleague Sakai would agree," Suzuki said, "to give me one out of his four sons. It would be beneficial to all parties. I would pay for Tadao's education, and maybe lend his father some capital to sort out his present mess."

The commissaris, limping slightly due to a rheumatic condition, leaning on a silver-tipped cane, walked Professor Suzuki and Toshiko back to the city's center through the park.

A giant blue heron, its long neck curved back gracefully, broad wings stretched widely, hovered effortlessly above.

HUP THREE

Handsome, successful Frank Nullish and his brand-new super-automatic Volvo had a choice that fateful day. They could take a left turn after leaving the clinic where Frank's wife Betty-Baby wasn't being cured and go home. Home was Frank's spacious top-floor apartment in a four-story condo in the luxury suburb of Amstelveen. The apartment overlooked a well kept park lined by ramrod poplars and ever mown lawns surrounding a clear pool with shiny white Peking ducks on top. Left turn was nice—the Volvo would sit in its underground garage and Frank, teeth clenched on the old meerschaum, would watch ducks from the balcony, Cat hanging bonelessly across his arms.

Frank smoking, Cat purring. Ducks quacking down below.

A right turn was not so nice, meant getting caught up into a web of narrow one-way streets, crescenting alleys, steep bridges that led into the inner city of Amsterdam, originally of Seventeenth Century gable-housed splendor, subsequently abused by the greed of commerce, recently revamped as a quaint old-worldly center, of interest to tourists and pleasure-seeking locals, a region of hup-ho, hanky-panky and goings on.

There was a choice: left/right. The Volvo turned right. Frank smiled happily for a moment, then worriedly for more moments.

Frank liked to see himself as a detached introvert, a homebody who's got it together, a lone watcher of ducks. His wife Betty-Baby watched lonely TV, but that was a while back now, before she got too sickly fat and was hospitalized in the private clinic. A brief daily visit, after work, to his ailing wife was part of the detached introverted got-it-together loner's life, which wasn't a bad life at all.

How long had Betty-Baby been away now? Frank calculated, reaching for figures and dates, payments of medical bills going out, insurance payments coming in. While he calculated, the Volvo waited behind a truck that burped up foul smoke.

Frank pulled his sun roof shut. The truck's rattling exhaust burping oil-smudged air into the Volvo's vents hardly bothered him, of course. No point in fretting about unavoidable aggravations when things are going good. Frank smiled sagely at the truck's enormous rear doors that denied him passage and view.

The truck moved. The Volvo didn't as yet, but then it did, with Frank nodding via his rearview mirror at the angry driver behind. She filled a small car. The car beeped, the truck burped. Frank laughed out loud.

Things still couldn't be better. Wasn't he making a fortune on what Betty-Baby's dad once called "our modest but profitable lines?" The lines consisted of specialized hooks and needles used in art needlecraft by rich ladies with a need to embroider cushion slips, prepatterned wall hangings, bellpulls to summon servants that had left, keyboard covers for pianos nobody played. There had to be quite a few of them, Frank thought: bent-over grannies and aunts in slipping wigs and shoulder scarves, buying the strangely adapted hooks and needles that his company turned out so diligently. All the products had been hermetically patented. The machinery making them was paid for years ago. Quantities weren't big enough for big business to even consider worrying about. An

140

easy little product, a high margin, no competition, a steady, abundant flow of cash into Frank's company.

His company? Well, Betty-Baby's dad's company, but the old man kept forgetting his own name these days. It was okay when Wuffo the dog lived, for Wuffo brought her doddering master home after walks. But Wuffo herself got old and forgetful, too, then died, so the old man went to the nice nurses in a nice home, fulfilling nice needs. Frank signed the nice checks with pleasure. With power-of-attorney passing to son-in-law Frank and with only child Betty-Baby ailing, who owns what?

But there was another question just now that got away. Catch the question, Frank. How long has Betty-Baby been sick? Maybe three months? Is she missed? She is not missed. Mostly invisible housekeeper Mrs. Bakker keeps good house. May the good life go on forever. So why the Volvo's wrong turn? Why this almost uncontrollable anger all of a sudden? Wherefrom this glowing desire to step on the gas and ram the smelly truck, shift gear, and reverse into the little beepy car?

Hey, a parking space ahead between elm trees at the side of a canal. Get in there. Don't worry about signals. Ignore the little car's wagging lady finger. While you're at it, ignore the lady lips mouthing "Asshole."

Frank, getting out of his vehicle parked inches from the canal's quay, recognized his surroundings. Formerly the company was located here, before the inner city exchanged grimy business for glitzy pleasure. Now the refurbished merchant mansions, warehouses, and workshops held cozy bars, tourist hotels, arty galleries behind spiffed-up gables. Frank checked his watch. Galleries would be closing by now, bars would be very much open. What now? Guzzle a gallon?

Frank hadn't guzzled in years. Guzzling requires buddies, good old boys who shout welcomes and thump you around a bit before opening up the inner circle. Frank remembered himself as "Tarzan," raising a tulip-shaped glass of juniper-flavored gin to toast mustachioed and earringed "Pirate," squat, military-dressed "Stinky," and a bartender known as "Saturated Fats." Twenty years ago, these were important people on Frank's stage. The stage collapsed, the actors wafted away—not quite, though, for Frank recalled running into Pirate again recently, and the new image, bald-faced and with no earrings, cheerfully mentioned one wife, three kids: "The five of us, Tarzan, having breakfast every day."

"The three of us, Pirate," Frank could have said. But Frank, huddled in his British raincoat, with his blown-dry hair wavy in the breeze, didn't say that. It wasn't true, anyway. Betty-Baby and Cat didn't breakfast, but slept in, snoring gently, hand in paw, while Frank gobbled precooked and slurped instant in the living room, one eye checking the paper to see how his stocks were doing. Not that they were ever really doing. Dutch boring beer and boring banks, electronics, oil. As permanently safe as the royal Netherlandic House of Orange. If the shares dip, wait five minutes. Up they pop again.

"Still drink beer, Pirate?"

"No. No beer." The man receded into the crowd, on his way to smilingly earn more tribal breakfasts.

Frank, standing between the Volvo and a doggie-crusted elm tree, faced a cinema poster showing a nude woman approaching a warty alligator. See the movie? But shouldn't he have dinner first? Grab a nuked bite somewhere close? Why not go home and share one of Mrs. Bakker's filets mignons with Cat? Sauteed chanterelles on the side? Cheese and crackers for leisurely afterward? Real whipped cream on fresh fruit? Java coffee? Cuban cigar? View of the park? Another pleasant evening watching more ducks? What was he doing here in this hole of hell?

General Frank curtly ordered himself back into the Volvo. The troops demurred, said "Nah."

Frank wondered whether a woman was wanted, perhaps. There should be quite a few bare-shouldered, bare-legged, bare-bosomed women waiting in the alleys all around, framed by neon tubes, illuminated erotically by pink- or purple-shaded spotlights hidden under window sills: a multicolored selection.

Frank muttered defense to himself. You're not in your right mind today. You want to get sick?

He tried compromise. Take out a blue movie and stick it into the VCR at home. But the saints kept marching on, on narrow sidewalks behind phallic metal posts installed by the city two feet apart to protect peaceful citizens from bad traffic. He touched the posts' smooth tops gently, begging off their urge. He passed bars filling up with bright young people. Being forty years old was bordercase, maybe? Wouldn't his clothes make him stand out?

He stopped in front of a small store, put on rimless gold-stemmed spectacles, and appraised his looks mirrored between the window's display of high-heeled boots, shoulder bags, and other leather items for gay tourists. His light-grey three-piece suit seemed fine. Silk-maroon tie? Nice. Button-down pure-cotton pink shirt? Neat. Hair? Thinning, sure, but still covering well. Frank frowned. Why would he concern himself with being accepted by little people? Wasn't he the country's monopolist of profitable needlecraft hooks and needles?

He walked on, stubbing toes on cobblestones, limping for a bit. He recognized the gable he leaned against. It shielded the patrician's mansion where he had started work twenty years ago, fresh from business school, for Betty-Baby's father. A while later the building was sold and the company moved to the modern business park on the city's outskirts where he bossed it around today, but it was here Frank's career started.

Frank laughed too loudly, then frowned furiously. Why was he out of control if he hadn't started drinking yet? He clearly heard the opening line of a sad jazzy tune. Did the music originate in a sound system active within the building or was old Frankie cracking up? He shook his head to get rid of a depressing but fascinating ballad, played on a row of double basses handled by tall men with hollow eyes.

In order to rid himself of these frock-coated musicians, Frank appealed to the wall he leaned against, feeling it tenderly with his fingertips. He remembered the building as a ruin, but now its surface had been filled in and varnished, its doors repainted, its rotted windows replaced. The tall mansion's imposing entrance showed seven brass pushbells with elegantly lettered nameplates, one for each story. So there were apartments now, instead of Betty-Baby's father's tatty office, the clerking rooms, and storage for finished product. The basement, where machinery once thumped and stamped, had become a bar.

Frank rethought himself into the nineteen-year-old bright young fellow finding his gateway of success here: Stepping through—stepping right into it. Into marriage, too.

He didn't know about Betty-Baby then, about the sole heir. Betty-Baby was learning manners in a Swiss college at the time, but about to return to provide her entrance.

Stepping through.

Did you arrive? Frank asked Frank. How do you like the other side?

I do. I do, Frank told Frank.

Now he was rich, and Betty-Baby was nuts. Frank, waiting for the electricity in his toes to subside and the gloomy bass players to finish their tune, saw the face of Betty-Baby's doctor. "Physically," the face said, "there's nothing wrong with your wife." The face smiled. "My colleagues are in full agreement, of course." So what about Betty-Baby's itching, stomach cramps, dragging leg, weight problem, breathing troubles?

"I would like to recommend a psychiatrist, Mr. Nullish."

Frank pushed himself off the wall, stubbed his toes again, staggered backward into a passerby, turned around, apologized.

"Join AA," the passerby said. "They're boring blowhards, but can be helpful at times."

"Yes," Frank said.

"They sure helped me." The passerby said, pointing at the bar's entrance close by. Frank noticed a strong smell of gin coming from the bar and the passerby's mouth. "I can resist the attraction now," the passerby said, holding up a stubby chin. "I don't have to enter the bad places any more. I can go home." His red-rimmed eyes squinted. "Okay?"

"Yes," Frank said.

Sure Betty-Baby was crazy, just like his brother Pete and his wife Suzie. Another story of success. Pete, through Suzie, stepped into a sole agency for Japanese dike-repairing machinery. Suzie tired of exercising her credit card in shopping centers and started seeing a shrink. Pete was invited to show up, too. Pete came to Frank. There was Pete, in Frank's office, silhouetted against the showcase filled with needlehooks and hooked needles.

Pete's faee shone with the sweat of fear. "Shrink wants to make me crazy, too, Frankie. Not me, Brother, not me. Liberty for me." So Pete bought himself a plastic replica of a Duesenburg 1931 convertible and picked up girls in the inner city to go sailing with in his plastic mini-schooner.

We have all gone crazy, Frank thought.

If he could ever have known that he would be selling needlecraft hooks for a living—being useful to old ladies at eight times cost. It was a good thing he didn't believe in heavenly justice. As long as he didn't believe, he wouldn't have to amuse Saint Peter.

Saint Peter: What did you busy yourself with down there, sir?

Frank: Eh—with making money?

Saint Peter: Is that so, sir? Specifics?

Frank: Yes. Well, I kind of cornered the market for hooked needlecraft needles, the kind with those little chromium-plated catches at the end, you know? Mahogany handles?

Saint Peter: What else did you do, sir?

Frank: Eh—nothing?

Saint Peter, leading a choir of angels wielding flaming swords: Hahahahaha.

They probably wouldn't even bother to shove him into hell, but cruelly ignore him instead, let him wander about like he was wandering about now.

Frank wandered into the bar. The bartender reminded him of Saturated Fats, but this was a younger man, although even more blubbery, more overflowing his pants. The bar was antiqued—seats and counter stained in yellowy browns and shotgunned into worm holes under sagging smoked-over beams carrying a partly white-washed ceiling. Teak wainscoting added for elegance. A copper rail lined the bar for parking unsteady footsies on. Spittoons in all corners.

"Draft?" Saturated Fats II said, sliding a mug toward a tap.

Frank raised a hand. Beer is for canals, comes out like it goes in, without even being polite enough to change color. "Whoa, Fats. Whiskey. American. Ice, no water."

"Sir," Fats said, "the name is Edmond." He wasn't reaching for the beer tap any more. He wasn't reaching for anything.

"Edmond," Frank said, gently edging forward to reach a barstool between Longhairs smooching on each other and Cleavage in a lace blouse being stared into by man with Loose Teeth. "I am sorry, Edmond."

146

Edmond's bellies cascaded. "You wouldn't just be saying that, sir?"

"No," Frank said.

"Not sorry?" Edmond asked.

"Yes, sorry."

Edmond poured from a square black bottle and moved ice about with a silver stirrer. Frank smiled. He hadn't been drinking for a while. Or smoking. Now he would smoke again, too. He looked at the tobacco display behind the bar and pointed at Black Belgians. Edmond opened a pack, tapped out a cigarette, pushed a candle across.

Frank coughed, waved the loosely stuffed cigarette through dense smoke, and coughed again.

"Being bad?" Cleavage asked, ignoring Loose Teeth's protest.

"Sir?" Edmond asked, half closing his eyes in disgusted disbelief. "Sir? Could you arrange the denture?"

"What *is* this?" female Longhair asked, watching Loose Teeth's coated tongue frantically trying to correct the position of his over-turned denture.

"Fellini," male Longhair said.

Within the third bourbon and the fifth Black Belgian, Frank found himself afloat on pure joy. A flashing insight promised that he could step back to the exact moment that marked the beginning of his wrong direction. The step had to be in time only, for his present location was right. The exact moment happened right here, twenty years ago. Up until then, the time was fine.

What good times were coming back! Nothing to care about then. Young Tarzan hangs out in happy jungle, rides the magic streets of Amsterdam on his shiny Harley Davidson, lives in an attic listening to Dizzy Gillespie on LP. He wears corduroy pants, a leather jacket, no tie. He goes for Jane.

"Me Frank, you Ravena."

"Ha!" shouted Frank, banging the bar with both hands. "Ha!"

"Sir?" Edmond asked.

"Edmond," Frank whispered, "Edmond, I thank you. This magic third drink, the house drink, is showing me what's what. Thank you, Edmond. Have one on me." He raised his glass. "Hup one." He raised it higher. "Hup two." He put it to his lips. "Hup three." Immediately there was a third flash of insight. Find Ravena. Things had gone wrong after Ravena, so he would have to get back to Ravena to start again. How simple. Bring her magic presence back into his life. Start again. Total turnaround in two easy steps. "Edmond? Got a phonebook?"

Ravena wasn't listed.

Frank rested his hand on the page. He was doing well back then, before turning right instead of left. True to type, daredevil type, young Frank had faced Betty-Baby's dad in his gloomy office. The old man lectured about attitudes, about young Frank's double-exhausted, rumbly, wide-handled, all-victorious American Harley Davidson motorcycle. Betty-Baby's dad explained that an employee being trained for business management shouldn't be imitating Marlon Brando. Betty-Baby's dad, in his pinstripe suit, made weighty words flow heavily.

But did young Frank Nullish pay attention? He did not. He was looking at Betty-Baby's dad's new secretary's long light-brown legs with tightly curved calves, her supple body in a short skirt and tight blouse, elegant hands poised above the Remington's keys, dark eyes, raven-black hair.

Frank had met Ravena in the corridor that day. They held hands briefly. He secretly read her application letter in the clerks' room. Born in Borneo? Frank saw palm leaves, heard parrots screech and the slow flap of foxbat wings, an exaggerated sunset splashed in blood-reds and soft-orange tinting slowly giving way to silver shades as the full moon sails in. Ravena steps out, naked but for a batik loincloth.

Shell anklets click. The Remington's keys click. Betty-Baby's dad had spoken and Frank is sent off to sell the bike, get a decent suit, behave, remember the future.

But not yet.

Frank stepped out of the past for a minute to enjoy more bourbonically clear insights. "Edmond?"

The square black American bottle poured more clarifying potion.

Frank sucked insightful black smoke, reentered the past.

Betty-Baby's dad went off on a business trip. Frank bought six yellow tulips and had a student clerk deliver them to the presidential chamber. The messenger, for a small consideration, promised not to say that the tulips were bought by Frank. Mystery goes with true love.

Next move. Meeting in corridor.

"Would you like to have dinner with me at the Chinese restaurant of your choice?" future executive Tarzan asked secretarial Jane.

"No." She brushed past him. Her huskily vibrant voice made him see birds-of-paradise spreading brocade wings, a pouched tree kangaroo pogosticking across a glade, giant orangutans tossing banana peels, a tiger partly hidden in bamboo shadows.

Of course. This Dayak (he remembered Borneo headhunters from a geography lesson) princess was too exotic to give in easily. His own shameless hurry disgusted him. How could he even dare to expect so much so fast?

Next day, another six yellow tulips.

Waited for her in the street. Offered to take her home on the Harley's saddle, designed for maximal physical contact

She preferred public transport.

A day passed. More anonymous tulips were accepted but every direct approach got blocked by curt refusals. Maybe she thought he was too young. Frank checked Ravena's application again.

She was twenty-three years old, against his nineteen. But what the hell? The mature princess and the ardent young prince. Possibilities were still endless. The form also gave an address. He rode out on his Harley. She had her own mini apartment with a front door and private steps. She wasn't home.

The clerks were low people, caught in drudgery, scribbling all day before grinding home on rusty bicycles. Frank refused to laugh at their crude jokes. He wouldn't go out with them for coffee breaks, reading avant-garde poetry at his desk instead. Resulting hostility exploded into a nasty joke. A clerk sidled up. "Say, Frank, been on the roof yet?"

"No."

"Come with me—you should see the view."

"Okay."

There were small hinged steps leading to a skylight the clerk obligingly unhooked. "You go first, pal," he said.

The minute Frank reached the roof, the trapdoor behind him slammed shut. Underneath, there was mumbling and laughing. "Nice view, what?" clerky voices asked. The view was not nice. Frank could see other roofs and bare trees reaching up sadly. Ragged washing dried on sagging lines. A rear garden displayed heaped garbage between slimy tree debris. The roof's streetside showed grumbling traffic, released by a green light.

Frank waited minutes. The skylight stayed shut. Rain drizzled coldly. He squatted so that he could hear better and heard Ravena's soft laugh. She, too.

Angry, he was angry—but anger alone wouldn't break his trap. He walked away from the trapdoor to the edge of the roof, where fear of height stopped him. The laughing voices underneath the skylight egged him on. He jumped to the next roof, across a narrow but gaping depth. His smooth leather soles made him slide and he almost toppled backward, but managed, by mowing his arms around windmill-fashion, to stay upright. He forced his trembling legs to inch toward the edge of the next roof. Seven stories down a rear garden covered with junk pushed against a sagging fence. Under the gutter near his feet, a window had been left open. If he—but, no, he couldn't accept the challenge. Say he swung from the overhanging gutter forward and backward once—twice, maybe—trying to work up momentum to propel his reluctant body into the window? What if the gutter broke, dropping him down into rotted-out boxes and rusted bicycle frames a hundred feet below?

So, back to the skylight, kneel and knock, beg the clerky people for mercy?

Never.

Fresh bright-orange streaks of fury burst through Frank's brain and burned away most of his fear. He hung from the gutter, after careful squatting that, because he began to slide again, brought him quicker to the edge than he dared to. So far, so good. His fingers slid through the gutter's gooey contents before grabbing hold. Sooty leaves creamed in messo of bird. So far, so better. Now for the best part, swinging Tarzan-style. The tension made him grin. Pity he had forgotten the apeman's war shriek. But he could make up his own. Yuuu-aayuuuuh? There we go. Hup ONE! Hup TWO!

At hup three, his fingers released the gutter, his body shot through the window, and his heels aimed for and hit the floor. The room contained a bed, a chest of drawers, a washstand. There were no signs of an occupant. A boarding-house room, waiting for the next guest? Frank slid on worn linoleum, slowed down to a casual walk, left hand in trouser pocket, opened a door, followed a corridor, descended narrow stairs. He lived here and was on his way out for a stroll. If he met anyone, he'd say, "Hello—how are you doing?" non-committally but friendly enough, and meanwhile keep going.

Descending floor after floor, he met no one. The street door opened easily. Outside, he turned back to the office.

There they were, all the king's men and woman, waiting gleefully for Frankie's pleas from above to open the skylight, waiting for Frankie's surrender.

Frank quietly joined the giggling crowd, maneuvered himself next to Ravena, and took her slender hand. She looked up at him, her dark eyes gleaming. "You! Where did you come from?"

"I flew."

That was all he would ever say about his feat, even to Dayak princess Ravena, even to Jane of his private jungle.

Ravena often asked him about the miracle when he lay next to her in the wide bed of her apartment, opened to him after the clerks' defeat. He stayed with her until Betty-Baby's dad moved him to associates in Paris for a while to learn tricks of the trade. While Frank was away, Betty-Baby's dad sold the building and moved the company to modern premises.

He also got rid of Ravena. She wrote to Frank in Paris, mentioning another lover, a man with a sailboat who might take her far away unless Frank came back at once to take her even farther. He didn't go back at once, and when he eventually did Betty-Baby's dad made him crown prince.

Rumor reached him that Ravena got dumped off the sailboat somewhere and came back to Amsterdam, but Frank didn't see her again. He saw pink, dimply Betty-Baby instead, who bought him the condo. Years slipped by. There was no reason to hunt about in the alleys of his past.

Until now.

Frank studied the phone book. No Ravena Simons. Sam Simons—would that be Ravena's brother? He dialed.

"Frank Nullish," Frank said. "Remember me, Sam? I used to be with your sister."

"Sure," Sam said. "You're rich now, Frank?"

Frank nodded.

"What?" Sam said.

"Yes."

"I'm poor." Sam gave the number.

Ravena's voice was low and vibrant.

"This is Frank Nullish, Ravena."

The silence was low and vibrant.

"You remember me, Ravena?"

"I remember you, Frank."

"So how are you doing?"

"Well—" she said. "Okay, I guess."

"That's nice," Frank said. "Meet me? Now? Here?" He gave her the bar's address. She said she needed half an hour.

Frank dipped the tenth Black Belgian into the fifth bourbon and inhaled alcoholic nicotine. Ravena came in. She wore a silk orange-red suit and her hair down, hiding most of her face. What he saw of her skin had wrinkled. She'd be forty-three. The hand that clasped his was clawlike, the claw of the bird-of-paradise.

So what? Old Ravena. Me old Tarzan. You old Jane.

A lovely lady. A matured exotic. They'd start over, build a gazebo in a banyan tree, turn the lights low, spray perfume. Keep an ape.

Edmond's chins trembled. "What would the lovely lady like to imbibe?"

Ravena ordered whiskey.

Edmond's pudgy hands manipulated the square black bottle with ease and abandon.

"How nice that you phoned," Ravena said.

She needed more whiskey to say more. She told Frank she had a daughter, who left and wasn't doing well, and that she

153

had no man, except Uncle Joe. She lived close by. She hoped Uncle Joe had not followed her.

"Is there an old man, looking in?"

Frank asked Edmond. Edmond said there was. "His head shakes."

"Parkinson's disease," Ravena said.

"Very old," Edmond said.

"Eighty," Ravena said. "He gets nervous without me."

"In shirtsleeves," Edmond said.

"He should be wearing a jacket." Ravena excused herself and went outside. Frank saw her admonishing a shabby old man, marching him off. Uncle Joe's bald head shone like a reluctant moon, his arms swung widely.

She came back after a while. "Naughty Uncle Joe. I put him to bed. He'd better stay there." She looked at her empty glass. It filled up again. The bird-of-paradise claw touched Frank's arm. "How about you, you got kids?"

"I married Betty-Baby," Frank said. "No kids. It isn't working out. She's sick all the time."

"The company is hers?"

"In her name," Frank said.

Ravena nodded. "So all your property is Betty-Baby's."

He nodded, too. "In a way, in a way, but I'm starting over again." He touched Ravena's shoulder meaningfully. "I phoned you, you know. Can we go somewhere?"

"Uncle Joe will be nervous," Ravena said. "It's better in the morning. He sleeps late. We have a big apartment."

"Uncle Joe's apartment?" Frank asked.

Some gold in her teeth gleamed. "In a way, in a way." She looked up. "There's a hotel nearby. But tomorrow would be better."

Frank overpaid Edmond. Outside, they both stubbed their toes on cobblestones on their way to the Volvo.

Frank drove off carefully, aware of possible police and Uncle Joe in his mirror. "Which way's the hotel?"

"The other way." She looked over her shoulder. "Oh, dear, he got out again. Stop the car."

Uncle Joe's face pressed against Ravena's window, mouth moving like that of a fish about to die in the bottom of a boat. "Ravena, where are you going?" the fish head asked.

"I'll have to go with him," Ravena told Frank. "Phone me tomorrow morning, we'll work something out . . ."

"No?" Edmond asked when Frank sat down again. "Last drink? I'll be closing soon."

The black bottle did its job. "You sure you like that lady?" Edmond asked. "I've seen her here before. Got to know her, so to speak."

"Tried her out?" Frank asked. "One morning, Uncle Joe still asnooze?"

Edmond winked. "Now now, sir, now now."

Frank stood next to the Volvo. A copcar stopped. "You wouldn't want to be driving?" the copcar's loudspeaker whispered.

Frank crossed the quay again, tentatively pushed the building's door leading to the apartments. The door would be closed, of course, but wasn't. He climbed all seven flights of stairs, reached the skylight, lowered its steps, walked up the steps, pushed, reached the roof. The roof was still old, with peeling tar sheets showing decayed tinplate and moldy gutters.

Frank was happy. He was back, he had reached the starting point. He would jump to the next roof, slither about, squat down, be a hero again. He would dig his fingers in the juicy contents of the rotten gutter, lower himself, swing his rejuvenated body into the neatly made bed of the boarding-house room below, Ravena's bed, and they would fly off together on bird-of-paradise wings, away from the battlefield where pathetic clerks' corpses stank pitifully.

Hup one. Hup two—

The gutter broke.

"Yuuu-aayuuuuh!"

"Can we take him now, Adjutant?" one of the paramedics asked the portly police detective. "We haven't got all night."

"Wait," the younger detective with the wide moustache said. "Wait, Grijpstra, tell me again why we shouldn't investigate the corpse and location further. I know you told me before, but you were eating that hamburger." He glared at the paramedics. "You guys wait, okay?"

"Sergeant De Gier," Adjutant Grijpstra said, "you've been upstairs. There are tracks on the roof, the victim's tracks only. The subject jumped off all by himself. Accident? Accidents are okay. Suicide? Suicides are okay."

"Prints say the subject hung from the gutter by his hands," Sergeant De Gier said. "As his swinging broke the window's glass, I may surmise that the subject was attempting to swing himself into the room below. Maybe he was a burglar and a rapist. Maybe he's listed and we can now cross him off our list."

"You checked the subject's wallet," Adjutant Grijpstra said. "Credit cards, cash, valid driving license, papers that go with the Volvo parked at the quayside. Photograph of a large lady. A Boucheron gold watch. A Leyden House suit. The subject's visiting card calls him managing director of a corporation making needlecraft needles. The company's name is known to me. My own mother and my own ex-wife use those needles. They're good needles. You still say he may be suspect?"

"There was a woman in the apartment the subject didn't get into because the gutter he was hanging from broke on him," De Gier said. "He tried to enter the woman's room intending badness maybe. She saw him swing in and pushed him out again."

"Self-defense is kind of okay," Grijpstra said. "But it wasn't self-defense. Why not? Because the woman says so. She was asleep in another room, heard the glass break, heard someone shout *"aa-yuuuuh,"* opened the broken window, looked down, saw the body, and phoned us. We confronted her with the body. She says she never saw the subject before."

"She lied?" De Gier asked.

"Ugly women have no reason to lie," the second paramedic said.

The sergeant thought. "Yes. So why did he force himself into a fatal accident, this handsome, well dressed, still youngish, reputable needlecraft-needle-business-owning subject?"

"Who cares?" Grijpstra asked. "Fatal accidents are okay."

De Gier's sensitive brown eyes shone pleadingly. His moustache curled in gentle protest. His perfect teeth showed in a humble smile. "I care," he said.

"Please," Adjutant Grijpstra said pleadingly. "The subject is some forty years old. He is doing fine. He has been making and selling needlecraft needles for years. He is looking at selling even more needlecraft needles for even more years. But why? He already has a Volvo and a Boucheron watch. He is beginning to wonder about his effort, his direction—his destiny even, maybe. One day he goes home, but he doesn't. He comes here. He drinks to cheer up. He cheers down. Events swing him by the arms. We'll ask the bartender in that bar tomorrow. Not that whatever he'll say will matter much maybe."

"Edmond," the first paramedic said. "Fats Edmond, but don't call him Fats or he'll beat you up. We took subjects from there that were beaten badly."

"What will Fats say that won't matter much maybe?" De Gier asked.

Adjutant Grijpstra shrugged. "That the subject got drunk maybe, met a woman maybe, it didn't work out maybe. That he drank more maybe, he was a sporty type once maybe, he was going to show himself he was still a sporty type maybe?

"That *aayuuuuh* the woman heard could be Tarzan's goodbye cry maybe," the paramedic said. "I wanted to be Tarzan, too. I still do maybe."

"Don't drink," Grijpstra told him. "The vine you're swinging from may break."

"I only drink beer," the paramedic said.

"What brand?" De Gier asked.

The paramedic smiled knowledgeably. "All beer is good beer."

"So?" De Gier asked Grijpstra.

"So," Grijpstra said, "Mr. Frank Nullish, married to the bland blonde he keeps in his wallet, got himself into a situation that reminded him he once was Tarzan, swinging happily from a vine in the Amsterdam jungle. He does that again, Sergeant. Watch this." Grijpstra reached up into an empty and uncaring sky, lifted a huge leg. "Hup *one.*"

The first paramedic nodded at his partner. They each grabbed their end of the stretcher.

Grijpstra reached higher into the empty and uncaring sky and lifted a huge leg higher. "Hup *two.*"

The paramedics lifted the stretcher. There was a moment of reverend silence, then the stretcher slid into the ambulance while adjutant, sergeant, paramedic one and paramedic two sadly shouted: "Hup *three.*"

THE GREEN-HAIRED SUSPECT

Algar was a well behaved boy until he grew into a well behaved man. The process could have taken no other way. His mother, a devout Christian, lost her husband, then lived on his pension, supplementing that meager income by babysitting and scrubbing floors in church. Algar became her little man.

He learned diligently at school, greeted his authorities politely, picked up firewood from the streets, did most of the shopping, and said his prayers before going to bed. He also mowed lawns. His mother included Algar's earnings on her tax forms.

God was Algar's father. Algar showed him his school reports, holding them up against the panes of his attic windows. Algar never failed his exams.

That way he grew up, until he was over six feet tall. He had wide shoulders and excelled at most sports. When his team won, his mother applauded, and when, on occasion, he lost she would kiss him anyway. Algar's good grades in high school admitted him into the Police Academy, where, as an honor student, he earned a handshake from the Inspector General. Because his appearance was both military and handsome, he was asked to model for posters that advertised the police and his image smiled from walls all over the country. His mates were jealous, but they liked him, too, for Algar was modest, soft-spoken, always willing to lend a hand.

Before Algar did something he judged the activity on its merits. If the verdict was "good," he would apply himself. If it was "bad," he would attempt to sidestep the assignment. His first posting was in the capital, which was good because that godless city had to be the worst place ever and whoever had a chance to do good in that hellhole was in an excellent position to earn all conceivable credits.

Algar rented a room above a vegetable store, with its own entrance to the tiny apartment, and fixed it up so that the quarters were worthy of a proper man's presence. He also bought a junk car, resprayed and polished it, and had the engine replaced. Whenever Algar had a few days off, he'd drive to his mother's cottage in the country. During one of those visits, he met a girl named Mona. Mona was a regular church person, too. She dropped her bag in church and Algar picked it up for her. The bag-dropping had been arranged by Algar's mother. Once the dropping and picking up of the bag was completed, the priest, playing his part in the plot, introduced the young people and before Algar knew what was happening to him he was half of a future couple.

But the marriage kept being postponed. Mona taught school and needed to pass a fresh set of exams so that she could improve her position. Mona didn't like the capital, which she saw as the center from which all sin was spawned. Algar promised her he would apply for a transfer to a country town with a good reputation, the right environment for their future kids. The future was mapped out. Good luck came to those who tried for the best. The road ahead would surely lead to heaven.

Algar sometimes considered heaven, wondering what it would be like up there. In his thoughts, and sometimes in three-dimensional, subtly colored dreams, he saw himself parading on a neatly clipped field. Uniformed colleagues blew trumpets and beat drums. Algar took three controlled steps forward, stood to ramrod attention, and, with perfectly arranged rows of recent dead behind him, was introduced to God.

God said that all was well. Those blissful words were the start of a party. Souls who had been around in the higher spheres for a while served delicate and tasty foods and poured sparkling glasses of a nonalcoholic beverage. After that, a blessed eternity opened up. Algar strolled along shadowed paths and saw lions gamboling with lambs on the glades, supervised by Hell's Angels who had repented in time.

Hell's Angels were the worst people Algar knew. But there were other types of sinners he abhorred. Punks, in Algar's view, were no less than earthbound devils, who prayed to Satan, that destroyer of harmony who has been supplied with abundant power on earth. God gives Satan free play in order to test Algar, to make sure that Algar deserves the potential grace held out by heaven.

Most people are content to dangle between good and bad, and what their ultimate fate may be is by no means clear, but Hell's Angels and punks would for sure find themselves in the roaring fires of a forever-lasting hell. The police, Algar believed, does more than merely restore law and order. Its strength, if properly and constantly applied, makes examples of its members. Algar's daily work as a constable serving his fellow beings was a spiritual exercise that would lift him beyond all selfish greed. He daily polished the emblem on his uniform cap, the sword of justice rising above the holy book of law. He cherished these signs of the high and truly

161

mighty and detested the evil symbols that dangled around Hell's Angels' and punks' necks.

Although Algar thought along these straight and heavy lines, he never talked that way, preferring to follow the right path in silence. In the precinct canteen, he kidded around just like everybody else, and during an evening off he could be seen playing cards or pool in a cafe not far from his room above the vegetable store. A glass of beer, some mild rough language once in a while, innocent flirtations with girls who smiled at him in bars or on the street, a modern novel, an off program on TV–Algar did make exceptions, catching himself if he thought he was sliding back from the way up. There were personal tests that he failed now and then, and when that happened he visited his priest, who forgave him in the name of heaven.

There were accidents, too.

Called out to a sudden upheaval in one of the worst parts of the city one night, Algar slipped and fell into a knife held by an opposing party. The Hell's Angel didn't really intend to wound the charging policeman, but he didn't wait to explain his side of the conflict. Algar, seriously wounded, was ambulanced to the intensive-care unit of the closest hospital. Unable to break out of his coma, he wandered contentedly in surroundings so pure that it had to be disconnected from earth. An angel was his constant companion.

The angel was female and wore her green hair in tight little curls. Algar knelt down to adore her, but she raised him to his feet, snuggled into his arms, and whispered important secrets that weren't so secret after all. Algar remembered having once known those truths but he must have forgotten them while he was down below. A divine melody welled up from their bodies and made them dance in perfect rhythm. Together they floated in exotic and beautiful skies that, once she explained them to him, he remembered as well. Then their link was broken. The divine presence that, Algar tried to explain to the doctors who pulled him back, was part of his inner being, faded, and evaded his feverish grasping. He saw the green-haired angel smile sadly while, in vain, he struggled to loosen the doctors' viselike grip. "He's not altogether with us yet," one of the doctors said. "He'll need plenty of rest now—the trauma has been severe."

Algar's insides healed and the stitches were removed from his wound. There was no excuse for not returning to earth, but, half drugged, Algar cried and tried to resist becoming part of lower life once again.

The priest was called. Smoothing the folds in his robe before he sat down, he said, "So what seems to be the trouble?"

Algar's hands fitfully caressed his pillow and sheets. "I've lost her! Please help me find her again."

"Who?"

"The angel. She has green hair."

"Nonsense," the priest said. "You've had an overdose. Now you see what happens to those who abuse dangerous drugs. You belong in the land of the living, my boy. You're needed here. There's a reason for your return. Get better."

Mona visited, too. She couldn't stay long because her exams were coming up. She brought him a gift, made in her scarce free time. Algar had trouble recognizing his fiancee. She sat next to the bed with her hand on the sleeve of his pajama jacket. She placed her gift—a cross stretched from strands of thin green wool within a polished wooden frame—against the window. She kissed Algar and said she really had to go.

Algar stared at the cross which seemed strangely alive. As his strength returned, his daily meditation on the cross led to several violent visions. Unexplained powers possessed the green strands—pulled them out of shape so that the cross changed into a face, and later into a complete and radiating shape. The being was female, the companion angel who had guided him when he was free on the other side of life. One evening the sun sank away behind the hospital's garden wall and a deep red light shone through the wooden frame of the woolly cross. Algar, groaning, reached for the angel, for the halo that still hovered after the last rays of the sun were gone. Then a nurse came in briskly and made sure he took his medication.

Algar sighed and collapsed against his pillows. In his half sleep, he saw the angel step out from the cross. He began to groan. He didn't understand. When they'd been together before, their shared pleasure was different from what she offered now. He watched her veils split slowly and admired her lithe movements as she pranced round his bed. Was she luring him away? Didn't he have responsibilities down here? What about his planned, positive life, the obligations to his mother and his bride-to-be?

Hearing Algar's moans, the nurse came back and switched on the light. Algar asked her to telephone his priest.

The priest smoked a cigarette with short, hardly inhaled puffs. He was in a hurry. Now what seemed to be troubling his errant disciple?

"I keep dreaming of this green-haired woman."

The priest hardly listened. "You're dreaming of your fiancee?"

Algar shook his head weakly. Mona was plump with a slightly squashed face that could hardly support her glasses. She wore her wispy hair up in a bun.

The priest continued. "It's only natural that you long for your betrothed. Be patient—it won't be long before you're married."

"This woman is different."

"Interesting." The priest stubbed out his cigarette and lit another. "What does she want of you?"

"She wants me to join her." Algar's eyes gleamed.

The priest took an interest. "Hold on, my boy. Has she got hold of you? You must shake yourself free."

"I love her," Algar whispered. He pointed at Mona's handiwork. "She comes to me from that cross."

"Amazing," the priest said. "All I see is a rather frayed abstract conglomeration of wobbly lines." He shook his balding head. "It's rather tasteless, if I may be frank. Maybe Mona should switch to a more practical hobby. Can't the woman knit?"

"This woman," Algar whispered, still pointing at the window, "is so beautiful."

"Yes?" the priest said. "Tell you what. I'll take that horror with me and get rid of it somewhere." He held up a trembling, nicotine-stained finger. "Now you make an effort, my boy, and get better soon. You're needed in this world."

When Algar left the hospital, his superiors granted him another two weeks' sick leave. He telephoned his mother, whose sister was staying at her cottage. "But you're always welcome, son," she said.

"No," Algar said. "I'll take my leave here. I've missed some lessons, studying for my sergeant's exam. I'll use the time to try and catch up."

The papers discussed imminent riots. Considerable unrest had been brewing. Red brigades fostered a general revolution, claiming that the present society was corrupt to its roots and had to be brought down with ruthless force. Several fires were started in municipal buildings and a bomb exploded in a government car, causing loss of life. Squatters forced themselves into a brand-new hotel and other activists urged the unemployed and restless to use any excuse to provoke the police. Large, boisterous crowds formed in the heart of the city, obstructing traffic and disturbing peaceful citizens. The police, the papers said, were being reinforced by specially trained squads mobilized from all over the country. Algar reported to his precinct but the inspector in charge sent him home again. "Not on your life," he said, "you're supposed to recover."

"Sir," Algar persisted, "can't I be of some use? I could hide in a strategic location and radio information to mobile colleagues. I could note and report on hostile movements."

"Stay out of it," the inspector gruffly commanded.

Algar studied in his room and went out for walks when the material threatened to block his brain. He walked under the plane trees of the city's main square. Looking up to admire a golden lute that rested on the gable of a spacious hall reserved for classical concerts he saw the pale-blue sky formed a calmly detached background for the spires and curved roofs of the buildings around. Suddenly he felt joyful in his dark-blue windbreaker and tight new jeans, bouncing on the soles of his expensive jogging shoes, a powerful giant at large in a void. Whatever happened had, by orders from his superior officer, to pass him by.

And quite a lot was happening. A convoy of armored trucks climbed up onto the sidewalk and parked on a wide lawn, forming a protective circle. Policemen in battle dress jumped out of the sliding doors, whooshed their long rubber sticks through the air, jostled each other with cane shields, and broke up only when bellowed commands called them to order. A captain appeared, hulking above the helmeted riot troops. His bass voice, amplified by a megaphone, roared at the scurrying warriors, telling them to prepare for the fight. Military police, distinguished from their municipal colleagues by white straps wound around their leggings, marched from their vehicles parked on the other side of the square.

Two square heavy cars trundled along, waving water throwers from turrets covered with steel mesh–short-barreled spouts manned by grim gunners, safe behind their armor, searching for a target. Minibuses, filled with bulky detectives selected for their physical strength, drove quickly around the square before veering off into sidestreets. The nimble little cars ignored traffic lights and signaled to each other with two-toned sirens.

Algar continued his stroll, turning a corner.

He could hear the armored vehicles behind him but the rumble came no closer. I'm going the wrong way, he thought. Good. I've got nothing to do with that commotion. I'm just out for a walk.

The city's principal boulevard, an active thoroughfare at normal times, was quite empty now. The civilians have fled, Algar thought, but I'm no civilian. —I'm no policeman right now, either. The authorities don't recognize my presence. I'm invisible. I'm out of everything.

Some murky figures darted across his line of view. Algar grimaced when he saw the hair ridges on their skulls splashed with odd bright colors, the dirty, worn leather jackets, baggy pants, and heavy boots. Beer-bottle caps dangled from paper clips stuck through their earlobes. The punks had blackened their faces with soot. Their eyes were bloodshot pools staring from dark holes. They shouted slogans and four-letter words.

One group was led by a slender girl, dressed as shabbily as the others. Her hair was dyed green and permanented into tight little curls.

"Tear gas!" one of the punks screamed and wound a dotted Arab scarf around his head. "Watch it!" Algar jogged along. Behind him on the square, police constables fired gas cans from their raised rifles. The popping sounds seemed innocent enough, but the small cylinders bounced onto the sidewalk ahead, exploding into foul clouds. The gas hissed as Algar ran into an alley and kept running, for the wind picked up the cloud and blew it under his running feet. He aimed for a cafe at the next corner. The door was locked. His knuckles rattled on the glass. A waiter peered out suspiciously from inside.

"Gas! Open up!"

The waiter opened the door and Algar slipped in, followed by the girl with green hair, who coughed into the mottled scarf she pressed against her face.

"Out!" the waiter yelled at her. "Your sort isn't welcome!"

The girl wiped her face with the rag. Tears streamed from her eyes. She coughed and tried to spit out the gas.

Algar was only aware of sharp particles stinging the skin of his cheeks. He put a restraining hand on the waiter's round shoulder. "It's okay. She can't harm anyone in here."

The cafe was crowded with people fleeing the trouble in the streets. The waiter stepped aside to make room for clients wanting to look through the windows. Algar pushed through to the bar and passed a beer back to the girl, bending down so he could look in her eyes. Her face was narrow, with high cheekbones and a full, strongly shaped mouth. Her leather coat was smeared with dirt and coming apart at the seams. Her luminous irises were surrounded by pure white. "How're you doing?" Algar asked.

"Fine." Her voice rang like a clear little bell. She gulped down the beer and grinned. "We started some streets back and worked ourselves closer in. We set two streetcars on fire and pushed over some cops. But now all this stuff's coming at us so we better retreat for a while."

"Smoke!" someone at the window cried. "Look at that! Pitch black, coming down the street! The whole city must be on fire!"

"You should have seen the flames," the girl said. "Bright yellow shooting high in the air. We were lucky. A truck unloaded oil. We got hold of some barrels and fired them with newspapers and bits of wood. There are plenty of stones around, too. The municipality is repairing streetwalks and there are stacks of tiles everywhere. If you drop them, they break into good-size pieces—very easy to throw. I got all the windows of a bank." She wiped the foam off her mouth with her hand. "Thanks. I've got to go now. See you later."

Algar sipped the last of his beer, smiling at the image the girl had left behind—her slender body in the oversized dirty coat. Her long hands and black-lacquered nails. A punk angel.

Then he was back on the street. A police motorcycle and sidecar flashed past, the constable in the sidecart taking photographs with a long-barreled camera. One of the mobile water guns aimed a pressurized spout down an alley. A dull-grey tank, twirling the cannon above its square body, raced around trees that offered cover for ragged insurgents. Algar turned and ran, remembering his escapes from the school fights of his youth, heeding his mother's warning not to damage his nice clothes.

He sped around a corner, stopped, swiveled, and rushed back. A military-police squad, in an attack formation, came at him rhythmically hitting their shields with their twisted-leather sticks. Algar saw the girl with green hair racing ahead. She tripped and fell. She didn't get up.

Algar hurried to her and squatted. "Are you hurt?"

Her hands clawed at his trouser leg. He grabbed her shoulders and pulled her up. "My ankle." She tried to hop away.

"Here." He slid his arms under her back and thighs and ran, effortlessly carrying her light, limp body. Dark uniforms and white helmets loomed at the end of the street. Algar swerved and rushed up stone steps leading to the portal of a mansion.

"You're so strong," she murmured.

"What's your name?" Algar asked.

"Lucy."

"You're from here?"

"No, from the country. Me and my group arrived early this morning. We don't know the city well. We should have planned this better."

"Stand behind me," Algar said, putting her down as carefully as he could.

Military policemen rushed the steps and peered into the darkness of the recessed doorway. A hard, pointed stick prodded Algar's belly. "Ouch." Algar's scar tissue was reacting with a sting of white pain. "Hello. You guys doing okay?"

The corporal grunted and dropped his plastic visor which was spattered with paint and mud, backed off with the others down the stairs.

"You're with them," Lucy said.

Algar shook his head. "I study law."

"There is no law." She showed him her fist. "Don't you know that yet? Why pretend? We have to wipe out the stupid illusion–torch our mistakes, clear the rubble, allow nature to start all over again. Not bend it to our self-made rules, go with it for a change!"

Algar moved away from her, risking his head for a glance down at the street. The minibuses rushed to and fro, howling their sirens, pushing blindly through the thick smoke thrown up by an abandoned burning truck. Detectives pulled collapsed punks up by the hair and kicked them into their cars. The motorcycle carrying the photographer rushed by again.

"Look at that," Lucy said. "Subhuman automatons–robots *we* created to keep us down."

"Stay behind me," Algar said, touching her curls gently. "We'll make a dash for it when things quiet down. It won't be long now. The battle keeps shifting ground."

A dozen constables in leather coats charged past the steps, fanned out across the width of the street. There were dull thuds as their sticks hit fast retreating punks.

A tank trundled along. The tank aimed a gigantic plow at a hastily thrown-up barricade defended by screaming youngsters. The street was clear. Algar put his arm around the girl.

"Let's go," he shouted.

Lucy stumbled along, dragging her painful foot. Algar wanted to pick her up again. She pointed at a bicycle, dropped by a fugitive, lying across the sidewalk. "Let's ride. It'll be quicker. I'll sit on the luggage carrier."

She picked up the bike. "Here, get on."

"But it isn't ours. The owner will come back for it."

Her eyes opened wide. "What?" Then she smiled, forgiving him his ignorance. "Everything's the property of the masses. That's us—the masses."

Algar rode the bike, Lucy leaning against his back. "Will you take me to the train?"

Algar rode faster.

"Hey!" she shouted. "Don't you have a name?"

"Algar." He turned his head. "You'll be safer if you stay with me. You can trust me."

She laughed.

"It's true. Your foot is hurt. Maybe you need to see a doctor. You can rest at my place. It isn't far."

He parked the bicycle against the vegetable store's gable and picked her up. "The staircase is steep," he explained. Her face was against his cheek as he held her with one arm and searched for his key with his free hand.

"You're strong," she said again.

"You're beautiful," Algar said, opening the door and stepping inside.

"Really? Even the way I look now?" Dimples appeared on her dirty cheeks. "You think you can trust me? Perhaps I'll steal everything you keep in your home."

"Feel free—it's all yours."

She looked about her in the small space, saw the framed photograph on his desk. "Your girl friend?"

"We're engaged."

Lucy laughed. "Your fiancee. I've got a steady friend, too."

"What would you like?" Algar asked. "Want to take a shower?" He opened a whitewashed door. "Here you are, the geyser works. The water will be nice and hot. Would you like a cup of tea? A beer?"

"Do you have a bathing cap? I don't want to wash the dye from my hair."

"Hmmm," Algar said. "No, no cap."

"Never mind." She prodded her curls with her fingertips. "You can see me the way I used to look. I can always replace the color later. Good thing the water gun missed me—my mates would have laughed at me, but with you I don't mind."

"No," Algar said. "Stay the way you are. I've got a plastic bag." He opened a drawer. "Here. You can fit it around your head."

"You're kidding," Lucy said. "Your type only likes what present society prescribes. Anything out of the ordinary's got to frighten you to death."

"Put it on," Algar said. "Please."

She took off her coat and unzipped her pants. Her face twitched when she tried to pull the pants past her swollen ankle. Algar bent and guided it gently.

"Is it bad?"

Algar had passed a course in first aid. He felt the ankle, studied the bruises. "It could be worse. Maybe it'll be all right by tomorrow. I'll bandage it for support."

"Let me have my shower first, okay?"

Algar put on the kettle, with his back to the open shower door. Lucy sang softly while the hot water cascaded down her shoulders and back. Algar dropped teabags into his cracked earthenware mugs and arranged the milk bottle and

172

the can where he kept his sugar on the table, grinning at the thoughts that admonished him from a far past. To hide and take care of the enemy was a serious crime. But he wasn't really here—he was out, out from his self—and his conscience meant nothing now. To test himself, he imagined a set of scales and placed his mother and Mona on the left, the girl with the green hair on the right. Mona and his mother dangled high in the air. To make quite sure, Algar added the priest to the left. The scales stayed tipped. Would he dare? Why not? Algar threw in God. No change. But then God has no weight.

She embraced him from the rear. "Here I am."

Algar wanted to ask if she wanted tea but stuttered meaningless sounds. He coughed and nervously cleared his throat. He picked up the mug and turned within her arms.

"Put it down." she said. "It's time for a kiss."

They kissed. He had to bend his knees so that his lips could find hers. The boots he had pulled so carefully from her feet must have been high-heeled for without them she was even smaller than he expected. Her hand reached around him and turned off the gas under the kettle.

They ate afterward, the entire contents of a family-size can of pea soup, from bowls that clicked against each other as they sat on the bed with her legs folded through his.

She looked at his alarm clock. "I can still make the last train home."

"Pity," Algar said.

"Would you rather I stayed?"

"Where's your friend?" Algar asked.

"In jail." She frowned. "He's a Hell's Angel. They keep catching him on drugs. He's been in for months, but next week he should be out."

"I'm supposed to be back at work in a week," Algar said.

She playfully poked his chest. "I thought you were a student."

173

Algar waved at his law books, part of the course that would one day make him a sergeant, arranged in a neat row on a rough board above the bed. "Isn't study work, too?"

"And the girl you're engaged to?"

"She lives far away from here," Algar said. "She never comes here. That would be indecent. She's very strict about what we can't do."

They fell asleep when the sun drew stripes across the windowsill toward the floor, and it was almost noon before they woke up. Lucy washed her clothes in the sink while he made coffee. A cheerful radio voice announced that the riots were over. Hundreds of troublemakers would be judged within the next few days. Harsh punishments were expected. Arrests were still being made and all citizens were requested to keep a sharp lookout for suspects. Any information was welcome.

"We lost the battle," she said. "You guys are still too strong. But we'll try again."

"*You* guys?" Algar asked. She opened his closet. "Isn't that your uniform? Aren't you a cop?" He nodded.

She shook her head. "Why are you against the renewal the brigades will bring about? Were you a spy yesterday? Is that why they left you alone?" Her voice was gentle.

He showed her his scar and told her he was on leave.

She kissed the ragged red line. "Are you sure it's healed?"

"I'm fine," Algar said.

He kept his pistol in the closet. She got hold of it while he poured the coffee. He could hear the weapon click and looked round. The barrel pointed at his chest.

"Sit down on the bed," she said coldly. "I loaded your gun. I know how to do that. I'm a professional freedom fighter— I've been trained well."

Algar reached out to touch her shoulder but she stepped clear. "No joke." Her eyes narrowed. The gun trembled a

174

little and her voice was a razor-sharp whisper: "You're almost dead."

"Let's have coffee first," Algar said.

Her finger applied pressure to the trigger. "Put down that mug."

"Dearest," Algar said, "you should pay more attention when your instructor tries to show you things. The clip is empty."

She threw the pistol back into the closet. "Bah."

"Would you really have shot me?" he asked as she took the mug.

"I might." She smiled. "I was thinking of a book. About the Russian Revolution. You were an officer of the Tsar and I was a Red soldier and we met after the battle near the Dnieper." Her forehead wrinkled. He smiled back.

"Then what happened?"

"We were both exhausted and there were only the two of us left. I had a bad scratch and you bandaged me before you looked for food. We found a tent and I helped you put it up. It was summer. We kissed a lot but I had to tease you before you took me. We lived on supplies the Army left behind–officers' rations. Oysters and caviar, vodka and champagne. We had such a good time."

"Yes," Algar said, reaching out to take her hand. "Did it last?"

She sipped her coffee. "We swam in the Dnieper–that's a clean river, not like the smelly water here. Herons with tufts on their heads stood on the rocks. It lasted a week and then your troops came to recapture the island. You forgot me, shouted out to them, and waded out to their boat."

"No," Algar said. "*No*. How could I?"

She kicked his ankle. "You did. I was a serf's daughter, a slave–a criminal who stole something that didn't belong to her."

"What?"

"My liberty."

Algar shook his head. "I would never leave you."

She kicked his ankle again, lightly. "You did and I killed you. There was a rifle in the tent. I shot you in the back."

The coffee spilled from his mug as she kicked him again. "You were dead. 1 saw you go under. Your blood colored the waves."

"What happened to you? Did you come out okay?"

"Ouch."

"I'm sorry." He held onto her hand.

"I got away," she said. "I became an officer, too—a hero."

"You forgot me?"

She shook her head.   .-

"But, listen," Algar said. "That was long ago. Before we were born. It wasn't now."

She looked into his eyes. "It will always be now. You'll leave me again. Throw me to the dogs."

"And you would shoot me again," Algar said. "Right now. If my mates came in looking for you."

"I would," she said. "But I need some bullets."

Algar dressed and went out. At the bank, he withdrew his savings. He drove her around the city that day and later rented a rowboat at a marina on the river. He strained at the oars and later they floated back with the current. She trailed her hand in the water. During dinner in a cafe, she was stared at and discussed in angry whispers.

"I think these good people would like to beat me up," she said. "We better get out before they call your mates. I saw photographers yesterday. I'm a ringleader—that's what they most like to catch. Maybe I'm in your files."

"Not yet," Algar said.

They walked through a park and held hands on a bench. A thrush sang for them. Later, back in his room, she half dozed in his arms and he told her about his visions, how he had met her before they met.

"Oh, I knew you, too," she murmured.

"Tell me."

"You were directing traffic in your uniform, as bright as the sky. You were so tall and handsome, so strict, so correct. I was still a little girl then and we lived on a wide street. There were chestnut trees in bloom. I walked up to you and you smiled and I knelt down."

"What for?"

"I'm too tired to talk any more now," she said. "Tomorrow maybe. Before you take me to the zoo. I don't want to see the animals who are sick in their cages but there's a nice aquarium. The fish don't know they're caught. We can watch them swim."

The next day, he left after breakfast, found a fashionable store, and bought her a pair of jeans and a blouse–he also found her a hat.

On his way back, two constables waved at him from a squadcar. He walked over and sat in the rear. They told him about wounded mates, kicked by punks after they went down. The constables were out hunting punks now. They showed him a file of photographs. "Seen any of these?" they asked.

Algar leafed through the stack. The colored photographs were quite clear. He saw Lucy, helping to roll a drum, spilling oil, to a streetcar. Another photograph showed her throwing a rock at a store.

"Recognize anyone?" the constables asked. "It's our turn now. We've got to get them."

"No," Algar said. "They all look the same to me with their dirty faces."

"Go by the hair," one of the constables said.

"I'll slip through their hands," she said when he gave her the clothes. "You really want me to wear these silly things?"

177

She picked up the hat. "Maybe I should. I'll be no good in jail. There'll be other riots soon. There's so much to do."

Algar saw himself explaining to the priest. The priest didn't listen. He spilled ash on his robe. "Do a good job, Algar. Defend society. Society pays your wages. Protect the good citizens' lives and property."

She kissed him. "Thank you for the clothes."

"You're welcome," Algar said.

They visited a museum of antique toys that day. There was a puppet show. She laughed when the puppets beat each other up with sticks. There was a policeman puppet, too. "Boo!" Lucy shouted. Her foot felt better and they went for a late walk. He bought her drinks in a cafe at the docks.

The morning broke quietly. A vine had crept up a gable and the early breeze made its small flowers flutter. A friendly chickadee buzzed their heads.

"Why don't you stay with me forever?" Algar asked.

"I can't, can I?"

"Time passes through me," Algar said. "It hurts me with its claws. It tears up our last days."

"Maybe there is no time," Lucy said.

"There is. It eats us."

Her hand found his. "Then let's pretend not to notice."

They passed a church later and Algar stopped to look at the cross on its tower. He crossed himself. "Don't do that," Lucy said, pulling him along. "There's nothing there."

"No God?" Algar asked.

"Silly. Don't you know He died? We killed Him because He made us wrong. But we can make ourselves again, start over."

She thinks the other way around from me, Algar thought. He almost said it aloud. He wanted to convince her now, tell her they should marry, and afterward she'd put on a nice dress and stand at the side of the field while the commissioner called him out and made him a sergeant. After the parade, the commissioner would come over to congratulate her, too. They would be together–she would grow old with him and they'd be happy every new day. If they belonged to each other, they would belong to society together.

Algar kept quiet. In three days he had to go back to work.

They found his car and drove back to his room. On the way, a squad car passed them, searching for the green-haired suspect.

"Bastards," Lucy said.

That night they ate in a French restaurant, with candlelight. She enjoyed the wine sauce on her steak. He took her to a concert–a pianist in evening clothes played Bach.

"A fool in a monkey suit," Lucy said afterward. "But the music was good. It all fitted, did you hear? It was like the little squares and lines on the lino of our kitchen floor. I used to look at them when I was little. Big blocks, little blocks, all in nice colors."

The last night came. They tried not to fall asleep. Algar kept getting up, to make coffee, to light her cigarettes. He had bought champagne, which they sipped slowly, looking into each other's eyes, kissing in between.

He was just going to close his eyes for a minute. When he woke, she was gone.

The pistol lay on the little table next to the bed, at the same level as his head, pointing with its hollow metal eye. He swept the gun into his hand. The clip held five cartridges and the chamber the sixth. The safety catch was off. Algar jumped out of bed and opened the closet.

On the stack of handkerchiefs he used to cover his ammo lay a curl of green hair.

He washed and shaved, put on his uniform, and reported at the precinct.

"How do you feel?" the inspector asked.

Algar said he felt fine.

"You still look pale, constable. You're on office duty." The inspector grinned. He was glad to have Algar back. So was God, Algar's mother, and Mona—and the priest, of course. Algar thought he should be happy, too—pleased that he knew where he belonged again.

The inspector brought out a thick file. "All the constables will be out hunting today. Check all these photographs. Check our suspects, too—there are a bunch of them in the cells. Release the subjects we have nothing on."

He found her. She wouldn't look at him. Algar walked back to the office.

"She wouldn't give her name," the inspector said. "She was picked up at the railway station earlier today. Ugly green hair under her hat and a roll of punk clothes under her arm."

"She doesn't show on any of the photographs, sir."

The inspector nodded.

"Let her go, we're short of cells."

"You can go," Algar said. "We're sorry you were detained." She walked past him into the street.

"Pretty girl," the inspector said. His tone disgusted Algar.

Algar stumbled and fell. An ambulance took him to the hospital. "A massive internal bleeding," the doctors said. They worked hard on him.

In a few days, the riots flared up again. The police were outnumbered. They fired plastic bullets into the crowd and rammed their vehicles into massed punks that kept charging.

The priest came and listened to Algar's raving.

"He keeps mumbling about this angel," a nurse said, "an angel with green hair."

Lucy saw the attack but was slow to move away. A plastic bullet hit her chest and knocked her over. An armored car buried her in mud.

180

The doctors ordered an autopsy and had Algar's body stored in the morgue. Lucy's remains were dumped on the stretcher next to his.

His left hand and her right flopped down and touched. They were clasped as rigor mortis set in.

MADREMONTE

Meneer Haan never got to see bookkeeper Storz' corpse, or Storz' wife's dead body, or the carcass of Felix, Storz' dog. By the time the Curaçao-based certified accountant arrived in Bogotá all three bodies had been disposed of. Bogotá, a smog-covered sprawl of skyscrapers and shantytowns covering a high plateau surrounded by mountains is the capital of Colombia, a metropolis housing five million people in South America's most dynamic country.

Mrs. (Sjaan) Storz' body was buried, following instructions in a note that Karel Storz left in the couple's bloodied bedroom. The suicide note, insisting that Storz' own body should be burned, didn't mention the dog, so Felix' remains were taken out with the garbage.

Storz kept books for a Dutch-owned im- and export company called Impoco. Detective-lieutenant Rodriguez' report said that Storz and the dog were shot through the head, wife Sjaan through the heart. All bullets came from a Smith & Wesson revolver, found in Storz' hand. A chemical test proved that Storz fired the weapon. The teniente's report further stated that Storz bought the gun from the doorman of his apartment building in Fontión, Bogotá's super suburb, on the eve of Storz' final day. Although 'groping in the dark' (Rodriguez liked clichés) the police did at least solve that initial part of the puzzle. Teniente Rodriguez of Bogotá Municipal Police, interviewing potential witnesses, noticed that the uniformed doorman of the Storz' high-rise apartment building seemed abnormally nervous. He questioned the man closely, found out about a sale of an illegal firearm, arrested his protesting suspect. So some justice was done, Rodriguez told his young wife Margarita after coming home from another hard day's work. There was not much to be done about the suicide and murder part–sinner Storz would be having his crime sorted out in purgatory. That's to say, if purgatory applies to gringos too. Maybe not, eh? What did Margarita think? Hadn't she been frequenting early mass lately? Women are so much more knowledgeable than men. And in any case, what does a police investigator 'up to his neck in human filth on a daily basis' know about 'holy levels where the spirit soars'?

The teniente's beautiful wife, after assuring her husband there is, indeed, a purgatory for foreign caucasians known as gringos, asked about Storz' suicide note. What did the blood-bespattered note say exactly?

Rodriguez' favorite term of endearment, in spite of a considerable difference in age, was *madrecita*. Oh, nothing much, *little mother,* just that Storz, after shooting wife & dog, was about to shoot himself now. Reason given? No reason given. Apologies? No apologies. But never mind–it was nice of Storz to leave a message. All investigating police-teniente Rodriguez had to do was compare the dead man's handwriting with something Storz wrote down somewhere else, in this case in his office of the business firm Impoco, and if the scribbling was identical (and it was), and there were no other suspicious circumstances (and there were not) Rodriguez is done for the day. Bogota's star criminal investigator submits his report in triplicate at Headquarters. He subsequently goes home, to eat 'Palo a Pique', a rice and beans dish, from a can that madrecita Margarita was kind enough to micro-wave while he, her provider, was washing his hands.

And kind enough to serve a fresh salad, Margarita said, that she, the dutiful home-maker, personally prepared. She would have done better but it was the day the terrarium needed cleaning. Rodriguez shouldn't complain, only the other day he had told 'madrecita *de vida*' that that was exactly what Margarita meant to him. 'Mother of life'. And that her very presence invigorated his daily living. And just to show that she cared about the teniente's daily doings: what was the dead Gringo Storz' motivation for all that bloodshed in the cozy Fontibón apartment that he shared with his wife Sjaan and Felix the dog? The apartment was cozy?

Cozy gringo-style, Rodriguez confirmed. Nothing like their own refined taste, his and Margarita's. The Storz apartment contained no entertainment center molded in green plastic, no gold framed terrarium (home to Margarita's big pet frogs), no embroidered upholstery on elaborately sculptured seats and couches, no alabaster Jesus in a glass bell, no Salvador Dali reproduction of the disciples eating *pan de yuca* and *buñuelos,* an immense plexiglass-covered print that filled up the rear wall of the Rodriguez *salon.* The Storz quarters weren't palatial and furnished in fine taste, like those of the Rodriguez' (as described just now). But the Storz' place wasn't bad. Okay, it was nice. Nice-gringo, maybe.

Costs money? Margarita asks.

Right, the place must have cost a pile of gringo dollars, real currency that bought the automated kitchen, air conditioning, gigantic TV and other components on steel and glass shelving, marble-tiled floors, oil paintings of windmills in a swamp, a large print showing a group of unwashed people wearing torn caps, farm workers eating potatoes around a heavy table (Rodriguez was surprised the dim scene was signed 'Vincent' –he always thought Vincent van Gogh painted sunflowers only), simple-patterned thick woolen rugs, white leather furniture, a slide through a wall in the apartment's corridor for garbage disposal ... Is that where Felix the dog went? Margarita asked.

No, Felix the dog went out in a gray plastic bag.

So, a nice apartment, a nice job, no niños?

No, no gringo dollar-consuming kids.

No alcohol? No signs of *la droga,* the fluff-happiness that goes up the nose and drives people crazy? Margarita asked.

No traces of any of that. Clean-gringo. Straight.

So where was the problem? Why all the corpses?

Her husband raised his manicured hands and looked through his spread fingers at the Salvador Dali disciples chatting away as they ate their root bread and corn-beignet cookies (that's what the food looked like to the lieutenant, he claimed he didn't know about the Israeli way of cooking). "Who cares, madrecita de mi vida?"

Margarita did: the life-giving mother cared about her world where she sends her *teniente,* her minor male substitute, to report on the state of things. Margarita's favorite term of endearment was *mi hijito.* She likes extending herself in her little son. Being beautiful all day in a small apartment is not exciting. A TV set for a mirror? Margarita doesn't *really* care about TV. What her teniente brings back is madrecita's soul food. So what does the teniente think himself about the dead gringos? What could have happened, hijito?

Rodriguez, back to shoveling his rice & beans, helpfully vents suspicions. How about this hypothesis, madrecita? How about we make Sjaan Storz a thoughtless wife. (Rodriguez secretly smiles). Even better, we make her downright bad. Bad how? She is soap opera-addicted. She is a habitual shopper for not-needed articles. She listens to New Age *mierda-de-toro,* bullshit, music. She is this mechanical cook, sliding cheap cans into her microwave. Can you imagine, Margarita? An irritating home demon poor Storz cannot get rid of–an ever-continuing, steadily increasing aggravation? So one day hard-working Storz buys a heavy caliber handgun and shoots a big bullet through his house devil's ugly mug?

"Hijito," Margarita objected, "I may be all you just said but you love my beautiful face, and you're in awe of my creative powers." Madrecita (she takes language from a TV Language & Literature, the last episode discussed the opus *Divine Irony*, by the laureate Argentine poet, Ignacio Lopes Cardozo) "How you enjoy our home, *the temple you allowed me create to celebrate our joining of souls.*"

Margarita folded her hands. She frowned. She waited.

"Hmmm?" Rodriguez enquired innocently.

Waking up, by the sudden temperature drop in the room's *ambiente,* to the painful falseness of a possible similarity between Margarita's and Sjaan's wifely routines, Rodriguez smacked his own head before pleading humbly for madrecita's forgiveness. He accused himself of outright stupidity. Besides, the motivation he described would probably not apply to the gringo mode. Only Colombians shoot their wives for microwaving canned Palo a Pique for dinner. The teniente lifted his left arm and patted the part of his jacket under the armpit, caressing the bulge made by his .45 automatic pistol.

His petty/chauvinistic attempts at sarcasm cannot hurt Margarita. She is smiling.

Rodriguez thanks his madrecita that she showed him his hypothesis is wrong. He flicked the faulty structure away with almighty fingers. He called up a replacement. In the new theory Storz no longer shoots Sjaan for personal reasons. Rodriguez shows Margarita how the new theory works out visually. He points at the wall of his salon where the disciples are having dinner. The wall becomes a large empty screen, that lieutenant Rodriguez can fill at will. Superimposed on the Dali disciples sharing pan de yuca and buñuelos with Jesus,

Margarita is now shown how Storz, in the Impoco office, is 'cooking the books'. The ingrate is embezzling his employer Impoco, a business company specializing in distributing imported industrial solvents. But, we can see by the way Rodriguez directs his movie, something is going seriously wrong. Embezzler Storz seems agitated. Storz has just become aware that Impoco, personified by its director (who Rodriguez refers to as 'el senor Schelten' and who is played, on the wall screen, by an older portly actor) is getting wise to Storz' illegal and self-serving manipulations. Storz seriously suspects he is being seriously suspected. His feverish brain suddenly fills with horrible hallucinations. Storz sees himself in Bogotá Jail.

Margarita had been shaking her head slowly and rhythmically. Now, still watching Rodriguez' projections on the wall in front of her, her body temporarily freezes. Madrecita's dark eyes gleam in deepening sockets. The facial skin tightens. Her nostrils glare, change into little dark tunnels. Her face resembles the skull-masks Mexicans wear on their 'dia de los muertos', the day when the angel of death enters their lives.

Lieutenant Rodriguez, watching his wife's reaction, smelled decay while he told her of the cheese-faced gringo's fear of being tortured by money-extorting guards while rats scurried in the cell's dark corners.

The teniente, although frightened by his wife's change of manner, even shape, while participating in his projections, still persisted in pursuing his analysis. Does Madrecita now see what must happen next? Storz can't stand the vision of what will occur when el señor Schelten will have him arrested. Embezzler Storz slinks out of the office, runs home like a madman, bursts into his apartment, grabs his newly acquired gun, shoots his helpless dependents, kills himself.

Margarita looked loving again. She got up to rearrange a bouquet of leaves and flowers in a vase. She admits to being impressed by her husband's lucid imagery but there are still questions. Why would Storz embezzle his employer Impoco? Isn't he, like all gringos, being paid in daily dollars? Margarita reminded Rodriguez that Storz has no need for extra money. Didn't the teniente ascertain that the dead man had no bad habits or costly kids—no doubt he earned a large salary, collected a yearly bonus, enjoyed regular paid leaves.

Gringos, teniente Rodriguez explained, as he presented yet another theory for madrecita's approval, are without good taste and marry without foresight. Teniente Rodriguez closed his eyes while he, reluctantly, called up the dead gringa Sjaan —shied away from the sight of stilt-like legs, higharched finger-toed feet, small breasts that looked like insignificant dollops of vanilla ice-cream. Once again the teniente shivers as he hurriedly releases the corpse to the waiting undertakers, watches them lug the body away, stop to tie it down better, set the stretcher upright in the elevator. Sjaan's head, with the short blond permanent curls, once again falls limply forward. The blue eyes stare one more time—silly-blue, like an unlikely sea on a cheap tourist postcard.

Margarita strokes her long black hair, looks down at her bare strong feet, somewhat flat as they should be for comfortably standing on, feels her trim wide muscular hips, makes her smile show Rodriguez her square strong teeth.

The lieutenant pays momentary attention, then continues fitting known facts into hypothesis # 3 (noting, in his male methodical mind, that # 1 'daily aggravation' and # 2 'fear caused by greed' are now definitely rejected).

Back to the beginning. Why did Storz commit violence?

As Sjaan's physical appearance must clearly disgust the gringo, Storz will be tempted to rent the pleasures of beautiful Colombiennes of the Bogotá night. Unfortunately Storz gets rented the Disease too—Rodriguez now argues—and it won't go away with the pliant Colombienne who passed it on, and maybe Storz shares the deadly virus with his wife Sjaan. Habitually visiting the gringo doctors who maintain her asparagus-like body Sjaan has a blood test. She furiously confronts her husband with the viral truth of rapidly approaching death. Storz foresees confronting his unfaithfulness during the next few years of joint terminal suffering. He chooses to speed up the process. He kills both parties involved.

"What's the Storz dog's name again?" Margarita wanted to know.

Felix. The dog's name is Felix.

Storz gave Felix the virus too? Margarita wants to know now.

Who, the teniente asked his wife Margarita, would look after an old poodle/terrier with a moth-eaten tail, soon, for lack of support group, to become homeless in Bogota's bleak streets? Rodriguez looked accusingly at Margarita's tigrillo Ludzilla. Watched the cat-size Colombian panther yawn back at him from its stack of brocade tasseled cushions.

Madrecita Margarita suspected her rebellious husband/son to suggest similarities again. She enquired whether Sjaan Storz did go out to work, make any money herself.

Sjaan did not, the teniente says.

Because—Margarita wanted to know—she, his wife, some-times forgot to cool his guava and curuba juice or didn't pour enough aguardiente on his icecubes and he sometimes had trouble handling his macho-temper the pet would have to get shot too?

Rodriguez was thinking he might strangle the varmint.

Yes? Margarita asked icily.

The lieutenant answered sweetly that he wouldn't ever shoot Ludzilla.

Margarita wanted know if the Storz case is now to be closed by authorities.

Rodriguez lifted a decisive hand, pushed an imaginary door shut, while he scraped the last of his canned Palo a Pique off his plate with the other. Policia Teniente Jaime Bolivar Rodriguez' final word is decisive. Rodriguez' word is that the Storz case is closed.

So now what happens?

Rodriguez shrugged. *Nada.*

Nothing? Margarita shrugged too. Don't bookkeepers keep their employers' books? Don't books reflect the state of the employing company's financial health? If she were Impoco's director—this 'el señor Schelten' that Rodriguez mentioned—she would want to know why her keeper of treasure died by his own hand.

Rodriguez agreed. How smart madrecita is in her divine wisdom. How smart he was, to trade her out of the nightclub where Margarita worked as a live-in hostess, and computered the club's books in her leisure moments. He, the smart but dutiful police teniente Rodriguez, guardian of the city of Bogotá's welfare, has already advised Impoco's resident shareholder and director, el señor Schelten, to hire a certified accountant out of Curaçao to plug the hole in his bag of gringo dollars.

Margarita's delicately curved eyebrows arched. He now wants her to think *again* that it was the mere gringo dollar that killed the gringo?

Rodriguez sighed at this brief sign of abysmal ignorance that he never expected to exist in the mind of his mothering goddess. No suicide/murder case is ever simple and money is always involved but money, by itself, is nada, nothing but inedible paper printed with absurd numbers and faces. Money only has value as a granter of wishes. The Storz homicide case is closed (the suicide note, the position of the bodies . . .

191

all clear enough) but it would be interesting to delve deeper. What desire/sickness would Storz have been suffering from? What illegal urges made the silly gringo steal from Impoco and fall foul of el redoubtable señor Schelten?

"But we are now talking theft," Rodriguez said disdainfully.

The lieutenant saw himself as a certified killer hunting killers. Running after mere thievery was below his status.

It takes a certified thief to catch a thief.

Rodriguez laughs. It takes a certified accountant (haha) to catch an accountant (haha).

Margarita smiled. Yes, hijito. But why would the lieutenant, her very own teniente, the substitute she sends out into the world to be her eyes and ears, want el señor Schelten to hire a certified accountant all the way out of Curaçao?

Ignorant Margarita ... doesn't she know that the luxurious Caribbean blue-sky island is filled with gringo financial experts ever ready to swarm all over South America at the drop of a gringo dollar? We're not dealing with Colombian pesos here, Margarita. At seven hundred of those little things to the dollar no gringo accountant, certified or not, will take the trouble to pick them up if they drop.

Storz may have been dropping a lot of gringo dollars, Margarita agreed.

Rodriguez, encouraged, is holding forth again. Impoco is one hundred percent gringo and so is el señor Schelten, the director—so were Storz and Sjaan, Rodriguez says. There should be some gringo concern here. Only Felix the dog was Colombian and he went out with the garbage.

The lieutenant smiled. The Storz murder case was closed. As a public servant, however, he would do more, to protect the interests of a Colombian resident with vested interests in the country. He had suggested as much to el señor Schelten. Bring in a government tax inspector to have the Impoco books checked officially? Of course there might be a chance that a government audit would reveal funny facts, not directly dealing with the mystery of the three dead Storzes.

The teniente's all-seeing eye noticed an Impoco invoice for chemical solvents on el señor Schelten's desk. He now put his finger on the document (the varnish on his nail reflected sunlight). Industrial solvents are used in the manufacture and refinement of many products, like paint, like nail polish-remover, like cocaine. Solvents became severely restricted imports in the eighties. Firms like Impoco that had been importing such materials for a long time indeed would still be able to import the solvents, sell them to bona fide industry. In quantities, of course. Not a drum here, a drum there so that the small coco leaf farmer may be preparing la droga in his barn. This invoice right here, was, for let's see now, ah—it says so right here—240 barrels containing 200 liters each? That would be okay then, but say the inspection found small invoices, for just a few barrels at the time? As Rodriguez said, maybe at this point a thorough official enquiry into Impoco's books might be both justified and revealing. The teniente, if el señor Schelten was agreeable, would be happy to arrange for such procedure.

"Ha!" Margarita said.

Yes, madrecita, the teniente had been given a wad of gringo dollars not to oblige with an official enquiry but to satisfy himself with a copy of an interim report to be signed by a registered accountant. El señor Schelten was good enough to appreciate such leniency on the part of the lieutenant.

Rodriguez indicated the side pocket his jacket. Notice the slight bulge?

"Aaaaah," Margarita said. How convenient. She had been wanting some new clothes for the autumn.

The lieutenant was about to accompany his wife to impress the sales ladies in the designer stores on the Avenida Jimenez with some considerable purchases. It's Thursday, the stores will close late tonight. There's no rush, still plenty of time for coffee and a shot glass of aguardiente.

Rodriguez fingered his thinning gray mustache as he bent down to kiss his beaming wife's ample cheek. He was thinking about el señor Schelten's position again. He, the lieutenant, didn't have to feel guilty. He had done nothing to worsen the director's position. Bribe or no bribe, the director still had to fax Curaçao.

Look at it this way, Rodriguez told Rodriguez. El señor Schelten was only a minor shareholder in Impoco. The majority of the company's owners lived in Curaçao or Amsterdam. In due time they would hear about this violence that might have diminished their property and insist on a clean bill of health for Impoco. In order to protect his own position el señor Schelten would have to call for an official audit by an outside accountant at once.

The Curaçao accountant, Rodriguez thought, smiling, would swoop down like a hungry *chulo,* the Colombian vulture. "What led up to murder and suicide here?" the chulo would ask.

Rodriguez, an experienced detective, could read el señor Schelten's worried mind. So far Storz' alleged dishonesty didn't seem to have left traces in Impoco's accounts, not to el señor Schelten's knowledge anyway, and he had checked Impoco's books again and again. Now the chulo would sit down, flap its dark wings and scrutinize expense account figures, possible bad debts that had been collected in cash (and pocketed by Storz), faulty profit calculations, exaggerated acquisition figures or blown-up depreciation of stocks. Mr. Chulo would investigate lists of special prices for big customers, or for discontinued or damaged goods that were sold out at discounts. Storz' fraud may have bankrupted Impoco. Somewhere there was a hole, that let gringo dollars seep into where? A thought of a lighter note struck Rodriguez. Where would a deceitful bookkeeper be spending his 'ill-begotten gains'?

By now the couple walks down the Avenida Jimenez.

"We should be careful with the money, hijito," Margarita said gently.

The lieutenant laughed. He leant down to whisper into his wife's ear. "Why worry, Madrecita. That's the way money flows. Down the hole. Up the hole."

"Desgraciado!" Margarita pushed her husband away. She doesn't like him talking dirty, but Rodriguez explained that the expression entered his mind as a respectable quote from an art discussion with el señor Schelten.

The lieutenant, during his first call on the Impoco office, noticed a mural on the director's office wall. The valuable artwork, el señor Schelten told the lieutenant, represented *Madremonte,* mother of the mountains, a pre-Christian Colombian goddess who likes to surround herself with giant frogs and mini-panthers. The teniente had never heard of his own pre-Christian goddess? No? Amazing. Madremonte is the protectress of women, she who pursues and punishes errant lovers, who abuse, lie and wander. Madremonte lies on her side, on a bed of moss and leaves. Her face is partly hidden behind criss-crossed branches. Her compact and fertile form centers in private parts that are a symbol of entry and exit, something, el señor Schelten explained, to do with access to another dimension. Through the opening between her luxuriant and pliant legs, all and everything appears and disappears.

Down the hole up the hole.

"See? Madrecita?"

Margarita wasn't listening. She stopped to admire a silk dress seen in the display window on the Avenida Jimenez. The dress was hand-painted, Margarita told Rodriguez as she affectionately clutched his arm, hand-painted with a pattern

of moss, leaves and haphazardly crossed branches. She liked
it.

•

At meneer Schelten's telefaxed request the firm UniaccC
(United Accountants of Curaçao, the three c's get twisted into
an interesting logo) selected meneer Haan to perform
Impoco's audit. Haan's special qualifications, of course, helped
to land him the job. Being a bachelor the man could leave at
a moment's notice. His Spanish was fairly fluent. He could,
correctly, and taking no more than a minute, add a column
of telephone numbers listed on any phone directory's page.

Tickets were booked at once, first for the Fokker F-100 Royal
Dutch Airlines uses to connect Curaçao and Barranquilla,
secondly for the DC-8 Stretch Avianca uses to connect
Barranquilla with Bogotá. On both airplanes Haan sat next
to *la bella Helena* who, in both cases, requested a steward to
get her the seat. Such a special looking man, Helena told the
stewards, pointing her delicately shaped nose at the athletic
golden-maned figure. The attraction of opposites? Nordic
Medicine Man meets Dark Latino Witch? "You do me a favor,
señor Steward? Si?"

Si, como no. Yes, how could we refuse? The stewards, sensitive
types, swept up by what they took for raw female passion,
had no choice but to grant the darkly beautiful lady's fervent
wish.

Viking Haan knew la bella Helena as the Colombian *duena*
of a Curaçao store selling Colombian ponchos, gold and
emerald jewelry, jars filled with giant fried ants (raised on
honey), shoulder bags of shiny leather trimmed with fur, toy
autobuses complete with passengers and luggage, sheaths for
the Colombian macho weapon of choice—the machete. The
store the radiant Helena owned also sold statues of a two-

sided female figure, sweet and smiling under a crown of moss and flowers on one side, cruelly snarling through a mask of twisted branches on the other. On her dark side the Madremonte figure wore a necklace of bleeding skulls, on her light side she caressed a frog seated on a small-sized panther. The figure's vaginal opening interconnected both divine aspects. Customers, noticing a likeness, sometimes asked Helena if she had modeled for the statue but, working her noisy cash register, she never seemed to hear that question.

It's cheaper of course to buy these tourist items in Colombia itself but the country no longer has a reputation for safety. These days tourists prefer to nip out of their cruise ships in Curaçao and shop with Helena.

Haan was flattered by Helena's attention. He found her Colombian mannerisms fascinating. His quiet scholastic mind had always been attracted to the great country being so close to his little island of Curaçao, yet so far. When it was his turn to say something he told Helena about the dead Storzes. The world of South American well-to-do society is small, its members meet on the luxurious shopping islands of the Caribbean Sea. Helena didn't know Karel Storz personally but, alerted by her less fortunate countrywomen, had noticed him cruising about the island.

Haan sipped tonic water and ate peanuts while Helena was telling him—she did not know why, she thought she had come to Curaçao to make her fortune—she had become involved in protecting the inmates of Curaçao's prostitution quarter. Parts of the quarter are traditionally staffed with Colombian brides earning their dowry during the two weeks their entry permits allow them to stay on the island.

Karel Storz, Helena told Haan, frequented Campo Alegre. He liked to abuse the inmates. So did his wife. The quarter is sometimes obliged to cater to perversions. The Colombian brides have little protection. They can only stay a fortnight, the money they make is to set them up for life.

But why, Haan asked, wouldn't the Storzes attempt to satisfy their low lusts in Colombia itself?

Helena smiled, frightening her travel companion. Her teeth seemed very sharp all of a sudden, her eyes dark. The fingertips that held Haan's wrist were so cold they hurt him.

The airplane landed. La Bella Helena was gathering her bags. On Bogota's El Dorado airport she was soon surrounded by her tourist-item suppliers, small servile men in dark suits and hats, welcoming their client. *"Doña Helena, como está usted?"*

•

Haan himself was welcomed by a tall over-straight meneer Schelten, reminding Haan of a carrion-eating stork-like bird, walking about with measured little steps under neatly folded wings. The marabou used to frighten him when he visited Amsterdam zoo as a child.

Driving his new Lincoln model 'Town Car' to Bogotá's Tequendama Hotel meneer Schelten reported on his traumatic confrontation with the dead Storz bodies. Incomprehensible at first. Such a neat little fellow. Impeccable behavior, meticulous work through many years of, how many, eleven? twelve? years of faithful service. Right up to the end. All books perfectly balanced.

Haan, politely interested, said 'Ah'.

Meneer Schelten complained about his dueling with Police Teniente Rodriguez and the appreciable cash payment extorted to avoid further trouble. A beautiful country, but corrupt. A multitude of rules and regulations, never enforced until the right moment. To benefit who? The petty officials— give the little assholes a chance and one may as well pack one's bags, close up and go home to Holland.

So why did the Storzes end up prematurely dead, meneer Schelten?

Who knows? But listen here, certified accountant Haan, you must have heard that Bogotá is a dangerous city now. The citizens, including a peaceful fellow like Storz, reluctantly arm themselves. Proof? Here is proof. Meneer Schelten showed his bare fingers to his guest. Why bare? Because he had been held up and forced to strip off and hand over his rings at gunpoint. My God. Imagine. This was in Teusaquillo, at the crossing of Avenida Quince and Carrera Treintados. An elegant part of the city, daylight. Please God. Isn't that sort of thing likely to drive a perfectly good man out of his perfectly good mind?

It is. Now then, all of us here have our stories to tell but what overcame Storz was particularly nasty. First, just a week ago, he gets relieved of his wallet by a pseudo-cabdriver. Can you imagine the nuisance? New driver's license, resident's papers, credit cards and so forth? What comes next? Relieved again of his wallet by a pseudo-cabdriver. This on top of a burglary, in his own condominium supposedly well-protected. Two fellows just walk in, frighten poor Sjaan, make Felix nervous, take the family silver home. So Storz buys a Smith & Wesson but what does a bookkeeper know about heavy caliber revolvers? Never had a shooting lesson in his life. That evening Storz fiddles about with the damn thing, accidentally shoots Sjaan through the head. Now what?

Can a meek man like Storz (mind you, Sjaan was, well ... no comfort, no ... kind of a bitchy woman if you forgive my language, witnesses could be found to prove that Storz had reasons to be rid of her perhaps) can our unlikely wife-killer suspect face a Bogotá-style murder investigation? Can a dear man like shy old Storz put up with being kicked and beaten, starved, share a cell with bad guys who ...? Surely not. Facing his dead wife he can only decide to shoot himself, too.

199

"Heavy trigger," Haan said.

The Lincoln was faced by a battered bus, roaring along from the opposite direction, overtaking another battered bus. Schelten's vehicle got forced halfway up on the sidewalk where vendors jumped, kicking their suitcases that spilled glittering merchandise. Policemen, perched on traffic towers, blew their piercing whistles. Pedestrians, feeling threatened by the careering Lincoln, yelled curses. An old man poked his cane at the car. A side mirror got torn off by a lamp post.

Driver and passenger were carefully pronouncing guttural Dutch curses after the Lincoln bumped back into the roadway and rejoined traffic.

The Lincoln was easing along, approaching a crossing. "You see what I mean?" Schelten asked. "Life in Bogotá made Storz nervous. You were saying, meneer Haan?"

"Heavy trigger," Haan said. He told meneer Schelten he had handled revolvers in the Dutch army. In order to fire the gun that killed Mrs. Storz several conditions would have to be met. It would have to be loaded. It would have to be pointed at Sjaan's head. Considerable pressure would have to be exercised to pull its heavy trigger.

Meneer Schelten pointed out that Storz wasn't good with machinery. As he talked a junkie stumbled off the sidewalk just ahead of the Lincoln. The car, swerving to avoid the woman, nearly hit a new-looking powerful motorcycle, carrying two well-dressed young men, that was overtaking the Lincoln. The motorcycle braked, then sped up again. Car and motorcycle were riding abreast. The motorcycle's passenger opened his guitar case to show a short barreled machine gun to meneer Schelten. Both young men smiled politely. The motorcycle's driver advised meneer Schelten not to swerve so suddenly in future. *Entendido?*

Entendido *perfectamente,* meneer Schelten said. The motorcycle took off. Meneer Schelten said that this sort of thing happened all the time. It was depressing. It made peaceful men like Storz lose their minds. He assured Haan that he had checked Impoco's books carefully and found no trace of any embezzling that Storz might have wanted to escape from by killing himself. He hoped that Haan would be satisfied with a perfunctory check of the Impoco accounts and take a few days for a guided tour of the surroundings perhaps. The quicker this thing was over now the quicker anybody could be on his way again.

The dialogue continued in the Tequendama bar. Meneer Schelten drank a double imported Dutch gin, Haan sipped a tonic water.

"No alcohol?"

Haan said he preferred tonic water and fruit juices. Meneer Schelten's eyelids dropped a little before his long birdlike face assumed a helpful, friendly expression. He would give Haan a tip, valuable advise. In Bogotá it's customary to freshen drinks like tonic water with *pitaya*. He would order some of *la fruta* from the waitress. *Señorita?* Here we are, looks a little like a large softshelled chestnut does it not? Try a little, cut it like this, spoon out the pips, the fleshy contents. How is that, eh? Delicious? Truly refreshing? Downright heavenly, no?

"Señorita? Mas fruta. More pitaya, if you please."

Meneer Schelten had some too, although pitaya, he explained, does not go well with alcohol. Wonderfully refreshing, an old Indian secret, in the old days the fruit was specially grown for kings. No more for me, thank you, as I said, la fruta doesn't go with Dutch gin, but it just loves tonic water. Haan, the next day, arrived late at the Impoco office. There had been some trouble. Having slept deeply Haan woke up with a slight rectal urge, nothing special. Haan thought he could shave first. Haan liked the early morning ceremony of shaving, using piping hot water, lathering his face leisurely, applying even strokes with his new Gillette razor. He was doing that when the rectal urge re-announced itself. Maybe some gas. Okay, lift one leg gently, allow a little vaporous pressure to escape. We will sit down later. No rush.

What was planned to be ventilation became a true explosion. Pitaya, although a single slice goes nicely with a soda, is mostly used as a powerful laxative. It works exceptionally well on the unwary stranger, exposed to an elevation of nine thousand feet. The Bogotá plateau is an unusual habitat for a tropical island dweller. The victim's intestines, activated by an overdose of *la fruta,* voided in seconds, while Haan jumped about, attempted to avoid faeces ricochetting off walls and ceiling. Cleaning up took time. Resting up took more time.

"There he is," meneer Schelten said when Haan came in after lunch. "Oh dear. You don't look well. Same old story, it's so hard for you flatlanders to be suddenly exposed to the rare air we enjoy. Didn't sleep well, did you? Diarrhea? Oh dear oh dear. When is your return flight? You still have three days? You could use some of them for a rest."

Without la fruta, that led to suspecting meneer Schelten of an attempt to debilitate a potential opponent, Haan, after checking Storz' computerized files, might have signed an interim balance sheet and taken the rest of his stay off. The humiliation caused by the tasty pitaya infuriated him, however. However, Impoco accounts seemed to be in perfect order. Meneer Schelten was smiling. Sign the document, go home to Curaçao, everybody is happy.

So why the diarrhea-dose of *la fruta?* So why did the Storzes die?

Meneer Schelten smiled sadly. As he said, a depression. He hadn't told Haan everything yet. Sjaan Storz and the doorman. Yes, sad indeed. Sjaan had other lovers too. And Storz being Dutch Reformed Protestant, brought up in Holland's bible belt. You know what I am trying to tell you, meneer Haan? I

Still think it was an accident though. Pointing the gun, accidentally pulling the trigger.

"So," meneer Schelten said glibly, "you've scrutinized my books, you've counted the stocks, you've spoken with the customers, you've faxed with the suppliers, you've verified every comma and zero. Now sign the document if you please. There is work to do. There's getting on with our lives."

"Curaçao," Haan said. He had heard the Storzes liked to regularly visit Curaçao.

True, meneer Schelten said. True enough. At their own expense Karel and Sjaan Storz visited the Dutch island of Curaçao a lot. At their own expense.

Haan checked and rechecked, re-calculated, compared physical files with what Impoco's bookkeeping screens told him. Meneer Schelten became a little irritated.

Haan entered meneer Schelten's vast office, stopped for a moment to contemplate the sculptured image of Madremonte. Meneer Schelten was glad he could vent more of his knowledge of Colombian pre-Christian religion and art. Madremonte, meneer Schelten explained, was known for several aspects. She was the mother of life, the mother of death and she was the crazy mother.

"Puerto Berria," Haan said.

How's that, meneer Haan?

Haan said he was puzzled by Storz' travel expenses. There were all these bills for airfare, hotel and restaurant bills, entertainment of agents, even the expense of a company car parked in Barranca Bermeja, the nearest airport to Puerto Berrio. Haan, checking a map, learned that Puerto Berrio, a port on the Magadalena River, two hundred miles north of Bogotá, is situated close to small rural industrial centers.

Yes yes yes. Meneer Schelten knew that. Over thirty years in Colombia, one gets to know where is what.

Now, why would Storz, Haan asked, at Impoco's expense,

frequent a small town like Puerto Berria, where there is only one customer, Colorama?

Potential big client, meneer Schelten explained.

Potential big client? Really, meneer Schelten? Not according to the books. A small client, rather. Two or three orders for solvents per year. A couple of hundred drums. Nothing special.

There was interest on Impoco's behalf to buy Colorama, meneer Schelten explained. That's why Storz kept visiting.

Because Colorama, a small wholesaler of chemical products, could be retailing chemicals as used in the refinement of cocaine, for instance? Haan asked. Sell solvents in small quantities? A drum here a drum there? Maybe even a gallon here or a gallon there? At some incredible mark-up?

Going where? That mark-up? Haan asked. Would that be split with Impoco?

Importer/wholesaler Impoco was going for the retail profit now?

Please. Meneer Schelten wove his long narrow hands. Impoco was a nice company. Meneer Schelten was a nice company director. Just another Dutch trader who believes. In what? In continuity. Anything to do with *la droga* is bad business. Would meneer Schelten be likely to deal with small-time hoods liable to catch bullets?

Haan was thinking. Catch bullets like the Storzes did, and little Felix?

Haan lived with a dog himself, a little dachshund called Max.

•

Looking a bit better, the nun Angelica thought, as she stood next to the patient's bed in a small room of the small Puerta Berria hospital. The gringo was still mumbling his magic mantra 'Co-lo-ra-ma-Co-lo-ra-ma' so his mind might still be wandering, but after having, intravenously, most of his fluids replaced, the patient was improving.

"Mister?" the nun asked, holding the sick man's hand. "Mister?"

Haan spoke Spanish. "Matador-bus."

Killer bus?

The nun Angelica listened to Haan's halting Spanish. She heard, holding his hand, how Haan arrived at Barranca Bermeja airport where he couldn't rent a car. The car rental agent was polite enough. "You need a credit card, señor Haan."

Haan had just given his Visa card to the rental agent but the man couldn't remember. "You need a credit card, señor Haan."

"You have got my Visa, you put it in that drawer."

"You need a credit card señor Haan. *Siento mucho.* Sorry, señor Haan. Company rules. No card no car. Siento mucho. We can't accept cash here."

So Haan took a bus. The bus driver said *Siento* too, he sold roof space only. There were seats free in the bus but they were *reservados*. So Haan rode on the roof, between boxes, crates, suitcases, birds in cages. The driver kept aiming the bus at the side of the road so that tree branches could sweep his vehicle's roof. The merchandise and luggage didn't offer Haan much protection. Haan's face and hands were getting badly cut. When the bus slowed down climbing a steep slope Haan jumped down.

He walked. A jeep picked him up. The jeep's driver and sideman wore Viet Nam-style pith helmets pressed from straw and were armed with rifles. Where did the gringo think he was going, wearing a white shirt with pens in his pocket, carrying an attaché case. Was this a remake of Falling Down? The movie? Michael Douglas walking across Los Angeles? No? The Mister was going down to Puerto Berrio? They could take him most of the way, *no problema*. The jeep stopped for lunch at a roadside restaurant, serving catfish and green bananas, rice, a large salad, with fresh green leaves, freshly washed in water scooped up behind the restaurant's outhouse. The *bandidos*–they said they used to be *bandoleros* but they didn't need munition belts anymore, the modern assault rifle shoots bullets from a clip, so they were just bandidos now–drank Bavarian beer–free Bavaria for free bandidos. Free beer makes a man sleepy so the bandits drove the jeep behind a hedge and everybody slept for some hours, and then it was night and the jeep's lights had been shot out, so the bandits drove back to the roadside restaurant for more Bavaria. They danced with the waitresses to Cuban blues sung by Flora Purim and trumpeted by Mr. Gillespie. Haan danced too, a samba, partnering an Indian woman who appeared from the jungle. The woman's hair was braided, the braids swung as she danced and pulled faces and sang when Flora Purim didn't. Haan slept in a hammock. He woke up with belly problems. The bandits were kind enough to stop when requested, so Haan could sit between the palmita bushes, to be a little pink blob within a million square miles of luscious green. He got too sick to ask and began to roll about in the back of the jeep, becoming more dirty and smelly. Haan vomited and trembled. The bandidos said *Siento Mucho* but they had to turn off the highway now. They left Haan propped up against a tree trunk.

That was all Haan knew. "How did I get here, Madre?"

An old woman in a cart brought Haan in. A mule, white with age, pulled the cart.

Madre Angelica sat next to Haan's bed, she was old and smoked a short pipe. The nun laughed. "I am smoking you." Tobacco? No. Pot? No. Weeds, mister Haan. *Yerbas.*

Haan liked the smell of the weeds. He drifted away on the smoke while more fluids were dripped into his veins from a machine that a nurse checked from time to time. The nun's gnarled hand was stroking his wrist sometimes. Haan saw animals, panthers that changed into frogs, then into a lizard. The lizard seemed friendly but Max the Curaçao dachshund entered the dream and backed away anyway, grumbling to himself.

The next day Haan was on his legs, leaning on the madre's arm. They visited the hardware store Colorama and asked to see the owner.

The young man minding the store's counter said señor Storz was in Bogotá on business but could be back any day now. He also said they weren't selling any *solventes* now, el señor Storz had left *ordenes* to that effect. The young man was sorry. Siento mucho.

"You want to see the *policia* now," madre Angelica told Haan.

The local police *sergante* wasn't too helpful at first but madre Angelica kept sitting in the shade of a palm tree and the shadow of a palm leaf kept brushing across her face. The sight of that moving shadow seemed to make the sergante nervous. The police station's cats, great spotted animals, behaved strangely. The cats were yowling whenever the nun smiled or even just glanced at them, yowling in an affirmative manner, Haan thought. Frogs croaked in the brook behind the police station. "Madrecita," the sergante pleaded.

"Que diga," the old nun said. "So tell señor Haan why you, illegally, allowed Colorama to sell solvents to the farmers."

It wasn't him, the sergante said. Okay? He was just the sergante. There were others, officers commissioned by the president of the republic, to defend the law. But the law was different every day. It was okay for a hardware store to sell industrial solvents in small quantities, to make paint, paint remover ..

"La droga?" madre Angelica asked.

Yah. Si, madre. Maybe. Maybe not. It was okay for such a store to have owners. Si? A store must have an owner. Si? But not a gringo owner, then si, yes, a gringo owner, if he paid

207

special taxes. To the police officers, not the sergante, he was only the sergante, si?

"So tell us, hijito, *then* what happened?" the nun asked patiently.

So el señor Storz, from Bogotá, bought Colorama, the hardware store and next thing the sergante knows is that every bush farmer is coming in to buy the solventes, and el señor Storz is flying in and out from Bogotá, and la señora Storz too.

"The parties, hijito, you forget the *fiestas,"* madre Angelica said.

The sergante said that he had protected the fiesta girls that the Storzes ordered for their pleasures, because madrecita said so.

"And el señor Schelten?" Haan asked. He got up and walked, like Impoco's director, like the marabou in Amsterdam zoo, with little steps, bent forward a little, his hands folded on his back, looking to the left, looking to the right in a dignified but alert manner. The sargente excused himself to the nun, then laughed.

"Schelten was here?" Haan asked.

The big gringo was, the sergante said, just a few times. El señor Schelten didn't own the hardware store. The sargente thought, however, that the big gringo, stork-like Schelten owned the cheese-faced Storz, the little gringo. "Si. Yes, madrecita." And a police captain out of Barranca Bermeja came to change the law again and close down the solvent business of Colorama, privately owned by the Storzes, then raise the solvent sales tax, to be paid monthly, then to tell the little gringo, el señor Storz, not to leave the country for awhile, then to serve papers on el señor and la señora Storz, papers that confiscated their private property and invited them to report at a jail sometime in the near future. All sorts of papers. Who knows exactly what papers are served by profit-sharing police-captains from Barranca Bermeja on gringos that own a droga-connected hardware store? But el señor Storz wasn't selling solventes to droga-farmers anymore, no madre. He began to twitch and stutter and to shout at la Señora Storz and then they both flew back to Bogotá and stayed there? Isn't that how it goes, madre Angelica? He was only a simple sargente in a town that falls off the map when it rains but all this harassment of little gringos was a warning maybe to the big gringo el señor Schelten to pay higher sales taxes to the police-captains in future?

"Gracias, sargente." Madre Angelica said kindly.

"De nada, madrecita. For nothing, little mother. I have done nothing. I am only the sargente. I know nothing, madre Angelica and when *la droga* kills us all in Puerto Berria give me free passage. To where? To heaven, madrecita.

•

Within two weeks UniaccC arranged a meeting in the Oester Bar, Amsterdam. Impoco owners bought registered accountant Haan dinner. Haan sipped tonic water while the owners toasted him with their tulip-shaped glasses filled to the rim with ice cold Dutch gin, in appreciation of a job well done. After the fried soles au Picasso the owners signed a Thank You/Farewell note to meneer Schelten and another that appointed the youngest (and most minor) owner as Schelten's successor. The owners shuddered as the new director presented Haan with a check that went with appreciation of a job well done.

Schelten retired in the Dutch village of Vinkeveen.

Statistics gathered by the Dutch Ministry of Economics prove that retired company directors live an average eight years. Meneer Schelten contributed to keeping the average as low

as it is by dying within two months from the date of retirement.
Schelten broke his skull, after slipping off Vinkeveen Dike.

Haan, on leave in Amsterdam at the time, happened to hear
about the accident. Curious as to whether Madremonte could
reach a Dutch dike he made enquiries in Vinkeveen. Witnesses
to the accident said meneer Schelten was attacked by a spotted
cat, stepped back on a large frog, slid off the dike, broke his
head on a moss-covered rock between some bushes. Nobody
had seen a brown skinned woman.

USING PEOPLE

B oris Baldert, sipping pisco sour at Lima's three star
restaurant Pollo Dorado's number one table, the table
with the best view of the restaurant's rose garden,
arranged color polaroid photographs that showed a young
man tied to the frame of a metal bed. The young man wore
no clothes. Some of the polaroids were close-ups of various
parts of the young man's body. The whitewashed wall behind
the bed was splattered with blood.

Businessman Baldert, waiting for his guest, Rural Police
lieutenant José Moreno Llosa, (although moved by the photos,
but he had seen them before) was thinking how easy it was to
solve situations. All it takes is people. Money takes people.
Especially Peruvian people. Especially dollars–money.

Dollars, tycoon Baldert thought, I can buy with my guilders.

The problem, trader Baldert thought, is how to buy the
absolute minimum number of dollars, without appearing to
be stingy, of course.

There was another problem too, that he wasn't considering
for now, but he'd get to it. In due course. Problem number 2.
One problem at the time.

He turned the polaroids over, stacked them.

211

USING PEOPLE

US dollars weren't the currency of Baldert's choice anymore, hadn't been for a long time, the stuff had yo-yoed itself down to unacceptable levels–but for the citizens of Peru dollars money was still all. All and everything, Baldert thought. Total happiness. Total motivation. Baldert sipped his drink. How he liked pisco sour. It reminded him of the good years, the sixties, when he had made the first of his millions, right here, in Lima, capital of Peru, sometimes right at this very table, with a waitress handing him the telephone, smiling, waiting for a greenback, a ten or a twenty, that he would stuff into the breast pocket of her blouse. He always did, whether the deal came off or not–his fingers always lingered, the waitress never pulled back.

Not that Lima was heaven. Heavens no. Baldert smiled. Lima, curse of the Incas. How did the legend go again? Pisarro, the Spanish conquistador with his small band of mounted roughnecks, managed to bring down the advanced Inca empire in Peru. Pisarro impressed the Inca ruler by claiming to be a god riding a mythical beast, a horse. The ruler had never heard of horses so far. Or of guns, killing lightning rods with triggers that could only be pressed by divinities. So the Spanish roughneck, for a palace-full of gold & jewels, humiliates and kills the ruler. He then upsets the entire empire of some twelve million people who he starts killing off methodically. Now general Pisarro needs a capital from where to organize his gold and jewel gathering expeditions. Where will he order the Inca slaves (soon to be known by the swear word 'Chollos') to build his metropolis?

An Inca architect, a nobleman, on his knees, in chains, points at Lima's present location. He convinces the godly generalissimo that the coastal desert spot, indicated by his trembling index-finger, will be the ideal foundation for tall and proud buildings to house the divine Spanish marshal. Most of Peru's coastal strip is bare, a yellow desert that assumes a green shade at the best of times but the skies are blue, the air is clear. Only Lima sits under eternal clouds, filled with moisture, about to supply rain that will make luscious gardens grow, water plantations, bring happiness, wealth, about to ...

The Inca architect was taking revenge. The eternal cloud is always about to ... the promised rain never falls. The clouds never lift. Lima lies, forever, under a ragged wet blanket that may leak a little some days, thickening the fog, causing drizzle. Window wipers swish-swash swish-swash, maddening the driver as he peers through fog that clings to his car's hood. That is, if he has window wipers, for they get stolen all the time, by 'churres', street kids, spawned by Lima's immense 'barriades', the slums.

"Señor señor," calls the churre, "I saw the black child steal your wipers just now. I know where the maldito nigger churre lives. Give me money now, I'll bring your beautiful window wipers back to you. I am your little *amigo*. Please? Señor?"

Sure. New window wipers are expensive. Hand the churre his coins, Peru's worthless soles, "golden suns." Get your window wipers back, and your hubcaps. Drive the brand new Cadillac cabriolet, the 'space ship' the Chollos called it, to the office and make another fishmeal million.

It was mostly fishmeal then. Baldert smiled. He remembered the trucks racing around Callao harbor, big open trucks, topped up with smelly powdery reddish-brown fishmeal. He saw the pelicans zoom in low, huge beaks wide open. He saw the birds shoveling away, stealing, feeding. Who cared? There was no end to the zillions of sardines pushed close to the two thousand mile shore of mother Peru. A great ocean current did the pushing. The pelicans got a lot of live sardines too, by diving into waves, even if it was more effort than stealing from the fishmeal trucks. There were other birds too, voracious cormorants, sea gulls of all sizes, any kind of sea-duck and goose, diving, feeding, gorging themselves, defecating on islands and beaches. Those birds had been shitting for a thousand years, leaving a thick layer of decomposed *guano* that the Chollos dug up, into ships that Baldert directed by phone and telex. The fishmeal was more profitable so he gave up on the birdshit, concentrated on the meal, shipping it all over the world as fodder for ever increasing herds of cattle feeding ever increasing multitudes of people. Millions of dollars were made by the likes of Baldert, in US dollars that were much bigger then.

Baldert got up to greet his guest. "Buenos dias, mi Teniente."

"Buenos dias, Don Baldert," lieutenant José Moreno Llosa said. "Encantado. Delighted, I'm sure." The lieutenant, although out of uniform, clicked his heels, stood erect for two seconds, bowed from the waist.

They sat down. Good, Baldert thought. The Rural Police lieutenant, stationed in Talara, a thousand kilometers north of Lima, close to the Ecuador border, was delighted to see him. Baldert smiled. He called over the waitress. The waitress was part Inca, part black, with a touch of the conquistador Pisarro, the delightful mixture that Baldert liked to use. He had used it many times, in the old days, the good days, the days that everything was fresh, new, not repetitive. Life now, in Amsterdam, was more or less the same everyday, didn't present a challenge, although now perhaps, wait until .. well, wait till he showed the photographs to the police lieutenant. Teniente Moreno. The guy was supposed to be formidable. So said lawyer Sanchez. Sanchez was supposed to be excellent, so said the ambassador of Holland, a wise old owl, cynical, go-getting, eager to serve his friends.

Baldert and the ambassador went back a long way.

Moreno ordered beer. Cheap local beer, although, in a restaurant that merits a star in the Michelin guide, nothing is cheap.

"You won't join me with the pisco sour, mi Teniente?"

"No gracias, muy amable, prefiero cerveza."

Amazing, Baldert thought. He studied the slender young man with the raven black hair, dark large slanting eyes, (angel-eyes, Baldert thought), the enormous mustache that hid the upper lip, noticed the lower lip pushed a little forward. Aggressive? No. Moreno's eyes were calm enough. They did seem to glitter a little. Could be the light. Baldert noted the young man's military look, even in immaculate black cotton jeans, a recently buffed leather jacket, a freshly laundered and ironed blue/gray American work shirt, collar unbuttoned. The latest fashion, eh? Good, Baldert thought, this man needs money. So he drinks cheap beer. He still needs money.

Host and guest studied the menu together. The lieutenant ordered chicken roti, with side-dishes of rice Castellano, Chili olives, macadamia nuts from Hawaii. Good straight food but there was better. No partridge? Sole al Pisarro? Vicuña chops with lusuma-fruit and a herbal salad with a Catherine Deneuve dressing?

"No gracias, Don Baldert. Muy amable."

That was right, muy amable. There we have Baldert, kindness incorporated: make a million, hand out a hundred thousand, make another million, make that a couple of hundred grand, try to figure out a way to get the two hundred grand back. Get to know the people involved, use them to serve. The Pisarro approach. Baldert smiled. He hadn't lived in Peru for nothing. Replace the general's horse for the trader's Cadillac.

"Salud." Glasses were raised.

"Ahhhh ... " Glasses were put down.

They drank a little more, just sipping now. Baldert couldn't understand how anyone could prefer cheap beer to the one and only worthwhile Peruvian invention, pisco sour, the delicate amber distillate mixed with a little very fresh lime juice, chilled, beaten till it foamed. That delicate tart taste, not quite quenching, gently titillating, delivering its powerful whop a few seconds later, clean, short.

Refreshing too. After three, four pisco sours Baldert knew why he was alive, understood the goddamn universe, and more, he understood non-imaginable universes, ruled, owned, by his very own non-imaginable divine self.

Baldert put on his widest smile. "A military man likes his rough beer, right?"

"One strong beer, yes," lieutenant Moreno said. "I like more too but I get drunk. An unfortunate truth I had to realize already in my student days." He returned Baldert's smile with white even teeth. He spoke clearly, as if on stage. "One cold beer and a fried chicken, a feast. In Talara, like everywhere else in Peru now, the food is poor. The farmers get robbed by the guerrillas and killed by the army for feeding the guerillas. My guardias, the rural policemen I have the pleasure to command, fish in the harbor. Talara's harbor is dirty, however. It's like all the world's refuse finishes up on our beaches. Unspeakable *suciadades*. The fish we catch is diseased. The vegetables are better, even if grown in poor soil, within the protection of my station. Gracias, Don Baldert, for this feast." Moreno dropped his smile abruptly. His face looked sharp now, ready for battle. "So you know my uncle, the lawyer Sanchez? He works with your embassy sometimes, Olanda embassy, from Holland, si?"

To business, was it? Baldert thought. Very well. The food came. They ate. The lieutenant finished his beer, the waitress came, he asked for water. Baldert had another pisco sour, a small glass, and water too. His sole was a little salty, musn't quench thirst with alcohol, couldn't afford to get drunk in front of this little lieutenant.

"The matter has to do with the disappearance of my son," Baldert said, burping. He excused himself and sat back. He frowned, made his big red cheeks droop a little. "Let me

216

explain, mi Teniente. Your uncle, the great lawyer Umberto Sanchez, probably explained my case better. Correct me if I explain wrong, I just thought it never hurts to fully explore a situation. Excuse me, mi Teniente. I'm no more than a simple trader. You are a ranking police officer, in charge of an entire district of this beautiful and ancient country. A large number of tricky cases, beautifully solved, has made you the experienced detective I have been hearing about."

The lieutenant bowed. "You are too kind, Don Baldert."

Baldert gestured. "No no. This is what appears to have happened. My son disappeared a month ago. The Vianca plane that he booked on, Lima-Amsterdam, arrived without my son. Not seeing him appear at Schiphol Airport I was worried. I telephoned and faxed with the Dutch embassy. The ambassador was kind enough to use the services of your uncle Sanchez. Lawyer Sanchez ascertained that, yes, my son left his hotel, arrived at the airport, was detained by Customs officers, could not board the airplane."

"Cocaine?" Lieutenant Moreno asked, touching his mustache. "Six one pound plastic bags. Three strapped to each leg?"

Baldert held his large head to the side. "So we hear, but there was no charge, mi Teniente. Your Uncle tried the courts. No charge had been filed. But my son was handed over, by Customs, to the Military Police, who treated Henri roughly, according to witnesses interviewed by lawyer Sanchez. Henri was handcuffed, pushed, hit in the face."

"Then you received a letter in the mail, I believe? Anonymous. Sí?" Moreno asked. "With photographs? Later there was also a trans-oceanic telephone call? Your son, Don Henri, he spoke to you? Told you what happened?"

"A few days after I received the letter," Baldert said. He called the waitress, ordered Java expresso, another small pisco sour, cigars.

"Cuban, señor?" the waitress asked, sharing her little smile with him, that might lead to a big tip, maybe more, who knows, who can foretell the future when capital meets beauty?

"Como no." Why not? We're in South America, Baldert thought, a good Cuban cigar will bring out the right *ambiente*.

Lieutenant Moreno leaned forward. The fox was awake. (The waitress saw it too, she whispered to another waitress "fox meets pig," she and the other beautiful waitress quietly giggled).

The waitresses watched the fox leaning toward the pig. "Could I see the photographs, Don Baldert?"

The polaroids were back in the inside pocket of Baldert's cashmere blazer. He brought them out again, arranged them like a fan, turned his hand, dropped them where Moreno's plate had been. Moreno studied the photographs. His eyes widened. His mouth fell open.

"Santa madre puta," the lieutenant whispered. *"Santissima puta Maria."*

Baldert thought the combination of the evoked images peculiar, but understandable. In the misery of Peru maybe even the holy mother was seen as a mere prostitute. Or was this the other genuine aspect of the holiest of women, like in Hinduism where the female principle, Kali, is shown as a white angel, but turn the statue and the mother of God becomes a horrifying black demon, with fangs, and skulls around her neck. Her bare feet trample an abject male body. Kali's long pink tongue lolls as she invites her followers to possess her.

Puta Maria. Why not? After all, the Christian goddess prayed to in Peru did allow Henri to be tortured, as the polaroids proved.

Lieutenant Moreno had lost his crisp look for a moment. His angular face looked suddenly haggard. He mumbled. "But why? The MPs burn a prisoner with cigarettes? They whip your son? Did you see the prisoner's swollen testicles?"

Baldert nodded. "That's why I am here, mi Teniente, to ask you to stop this horror. Henri is my only child."

Moreno looked at the polaroids again. "But ... por que?"

"Why?" Baldert asked. He allowed his face to redden, his fist to hit the marble table top. "For money, mi Teniente. For *my* money to be exact. You, better than I, must be aware of what goes on in this God-forsaken country—since the ocean currents, due to climate changes, deviated, and pushed the sardines away, out of reach of your boats, and pushed the fish deeper, out of reach of your nets. So now you have your Chollos grow cocaine, to make up. With the change of product you have lost your manners. You never had too many manners in the first place. In the old days you stole my window wipers, now you're after my hard-earned money. Crime is contagious. In the old days you would interrupt my telephone service. I would complain. Some Telephone person would appear, tell me he was my amigo, offer to fix the problem for free, but there would be another Telephone person, an invisible entity, blocking the way, and this Higher Mr. Phone had to be paid off, of course. Now you kidnap my son, and the lawyer appears, Amigo Lawyer, and then the detective, Amigo Detective."

"Señor ..." the lieutenant had been saying, gently trying to interrupt the foaming Baldert "... Señor ..."

Baldert took a deep breath.

"Yes, mi Teniente?"

"I am with the Guardia Civil, the rural police, not with the Military, Señor. I did not kidnap your son. Don Henri was smuggling cocaine, a bad drug, he was committing a crime, he was arrested by the Military Police."

"No!" Baldert lowered his voice. He dried his sweating skull. "No, mi Teniente. My son was set up. This matter has been

219

discussed at length with the ambassador and your uncle, lawyer Sanchez. I must explain ..."

He briefly touched the lieutenant's hand. "You see, my son and I ... father and son ... his mother left me ... I raised the boy. I keep him short. He works for my company, he has a salary, an expense account, not much. I am training him, like I was trained, on little money, he may feel that he should show me that he does not need the small salary I put him on, that he can make his own wealth, so what happened was that Henri was approached, in the hotel, by a stranger ..."

Lieutenant Moreno smiled sadly. "Yes, I heard, Don Baldert, I heard such things happen. They made your son a *mula,* a dumb animal that carries cocaine out of the country on his body."

Baldert sat back, sipped his refreshing drink. There were cigars on the table, long hand-made cigars. He offered one to the lieutenant.

"No, gracias." Teniente Moreno lit an Inca cigarette, rolled with cheap black tobacco. The packet was crumpled. The match broke, Moreno patiently struck another.

Baldert lit his long cigar with a single flick from his silver lighter, puffed. "It is worse, mi Teniente. There is perversity here, this is as low as ..." Baldert pointed at the floor "... evidently you don't know, but your Peru has become *desgraciada,* what happens now is that your national income is derived from crime only. Peru is a drugdealer now, nothing else. You're poisoning the world, and the rest of the world protests. You beg for help and the rest of the world gives that help: food, blankets, machinery, anything you beggars need, but ..." Baldert held up his hand "... on conditions. The international community insists you stop your export of cocaine, so what do you do? You make a mule out of my son, then you catch him. Prisoner in hand you make big whoopee, you tell the newspapers you've caught a big-time *narco,* with a big load of the evil powder strapped to his legs. It was probably just sugar. Why would you risk real stuff on a masquerade? And while everybody cheers a thousand tons of real cocaine are shipped quietly out."

Lieutenant Moreno coughed out some smoke. "Whoopee? But your son disappeared, Señor, he was not made out to be an example ... "

Baldert grimaced. "Worse still ... I see you are an innocent. My son told me on the phone what happened. He was taken to a room, stripped naked, a plastic garbage bag was slipped over his head, he was beaten, yelled at. This is routine ... "

Moreno was shaking his head. "I have to find fault with your hypothesis, Don Baldert. If your son was set up, Señor, then the Military Police, they knew he was innocent ... Why beat the unfortunate, why cause unnecessary pain?"

Baldert smoked his cigar. "Why? I'll tell you, mi Teniente. Because with your MP colleagues rough treatment is routine. Because you never know ... this gringo may be somebody important, be, for example, my son. A good excuse for blackmail. Imagine the scene. Two, three uniformed cops are doing everything possible, mentally, physically, to hurt the prisoner. To shake him. My son Henri is yelling, telling them anything that comes into his mind, anything that might alleviate the pain. He tells his devils about being sent here by me, the big time fishmeal dealer who used to live in their own Lima years ago. He tells your sadists that I, Don Baldert the big time Trader, sent Henri to see if there is truth in the rumor that Peru is building bigger ships with better nets to catch sardines in new locations. That business can still be done here. They smell money, right?"

"Please ..." teniente Moreno said.

"Yes?"

Moreno sighed. "I understand now. As I said, I have heard of such things happening. Kidnapping, by us, the dreaded *uniformades,* the very authorities that should protect the country. This is sad, Señor. This is anarchy. The government becomes evil." The lieutenant shook his head. "Your son is still in Callao, in jail close to the airport?"

"He would not have survived," Baldert said. "Callao prisoners usually starve to death. Your uncle persuaded the Military Police, with the extra aid of some fifty thousand dollars, to transfer their prey to a place in the North. Punta Negra. A kind of camp."

"Yes," Moreno said.

"Your territory, Teniente." Baldert smiled. "Punta Negra, the peninsula twenty kilometers from Talara."

"How high is the ransom, Señor?"

Baldert looked grim. "One million US dollars, to be deposited into a Swiss bank account."

Moreno looked up. "You do not wish to pay the ransom, Don Baldert? They will free him when you pay, they must free him, or the news is out that they're not reliable and future ransoms will not be paid, by future parties."

"One million dollars?" Baldert asked.

"Your son is not worth a million dollars?" Moreno's eyes glittered. "You have many millions, I hear."

"No," Baldert said. "I won't pay a million. I will pay two hundred thousand, half to your helpful uncle Sanchez the lawyer, already taken care of, that he shared with the MPs, and the other one hundred thou to you, my friend. That's good money I offer, it should get Henri out of Punta Negra and out of the country, just a few miles from the camp. Take Henri to me. I will be waiting at the Equador border, a hundred meters South of the airstrip of Macara."

"You have your own airplane?"

"The company's Learjet," Baldert said. "The plane is too valuable to risk in Peruvian airspace. I had myself flown in by rented Cessna. Nobody except your uncle Sanchez and yourself know I am here."

The two men sat quietly. Baldert puffed his cigar, sipped pisco. The lieutenant smoked a third Inca, sipped water.

"Not enough, mi Teniente?"

Moreno looked up, still deep in thought. He didn't seem to see Baldert.

"I will not pay more," Baldert said. "You know what my money is? It's my stored energy. I'll open my larder for you, help yourself, but I'll be there to restrain your hand."

The silence returned. The waitress brought more coffee.

"I know Punta Negra," Moreno said. "An abandoned fishmeal factory called *Angeles del Mar* is now a camp, a prison. A busy place once, before the sardines disappeared. There are fences, wooden towers with machine guns. I have arrested drunken soldiers in Talara, they were picked up at my station and taken to *Angeles del Mar*. Later the soldiers were free again. They told me there were different departments in *Angeles del Mar*. One part is reserved for *politicos,* another for wealthy *gringos*. Most foreign prisoners get to eat each day, receive cigarettes, sometimes swim in the sea, do exercises, are kept healthy."

"They are beaten too." Baldert looked grim. "To make them cry, on the phone. Henri was crying. 'Pay the money, Pappie. Please Pappie. Get me out of this hell.'"

"Yes," Moreno said. "I have heard such things, the soldiers told my guardias. I wouldn't believe them. Such things dishonor my country."

"Free my son Henri," Baldert said. "Your uncle says you can find a way. I left ten thousand dollars in cash with him. You'll have another ninety thousand for the body of my only child, dead or alive. Your own ticket to freedom. I hear you have plans to leave your dishonored country yourself?"

Moreno stood up. Baldert remained seated.

"Sí," teniente José Moreno Llosa of the Guardia Civil de Peru said quietly, standing at attention, "Yes, Señor. I'll deliver

Don Henri to you in Macara, Ecuador, Señor. It will take me
one week."

•

There were only two ways, Baldert knew, while waiting in
a comfortable room, in an inn owned by a German couple,
in Macara, Equador, in which the teniente could free Henri.
The lieutenant could choose between force and deception.

Baldert, like the waitresses in Pollo Dorado, associated
Moreno with a fox. Humberto Sanchez, the lawyer, when
recommending his nephew to the Dutch ambassador and
Baldert, had praised the lieutenant's intelligence. He had
mentioned other factors. Moreno, as a boy, had wanted to
become an actor. His father, an Air Force marshal, squashed
that desire. There had to be a military career. José Moreno's
eyesight wasn't good so the father had to compromise. José
was to rise to the rank of a Guardia Civil general. All attributes
were available. The Moreno family traced itself back to the
days of Pisarro. There was money, invested in the fishmeal
industry. There was a capital villa in Lima's garden suburb
San Isidro.

Cadet José Moreno Llosa earned high grades at the
Academy. He was popular as an amateur actor, playing villains
and good guys with the same talent and conviction, delighting
audiences of Lima's high society.

Everything was just fine, just fine ...

"Ah," Humberto Sanchez said, covering his eyes, bending
his head for a moment, "the debacle, Don Albert, such bad
luck ... "

Peru, at the time, had turned against America and befriended
Russia. It had bartered fishmeal for half a dozen MIG jets.
Peruvian pilots were trained by Soviet aces, but the aces were
sidetracked by being exposed to Air Force tours of ancient

Inca cities, high in the sierra, to Naval merrymaking on battleships of First World War vintage, to Army polo matches on the Peruvian prairie, the llanos. Everywhere there were beautiful women and Chollo waiters shaking pisco cocktails. Soviet teachers forgot to tell Peruvian pupils how to read MIG dashboards properly.

At the demonstration, presented by Air Force Marshal Miguel Moreno Llosa to the president, to the president's lady, to the ministers, to the dons and duenas of the great families, to the famous artists, to the movie- and popstars, to the generals and admirals, the leading Peruvian pilot made a mistake, his five following pilots copied his mistake and the six MIG jetplanes hit a mountain, and changed into little blurbs of smoke, accompanied by six little bangs, that reached the audience three seconds later, because of the distance.

"No!" Baldert said.

"The air marshal," lawyer Sanchez said, "shot himself. Shortly afterward our family lost their money, because of the fishmeal industry coming to a full stop. Now, don Baldert, we see my nephew stuck in the miserable town of Talara." Sanchez had changed the subject.

.

Knowing all this, Baldert thought, as he enjoyed German cuisine in Ecuador, the equation can be completed. My servile lieutenant will play the game. He wants to leave. His reputation is ruined by his father's blunder and his country's extreme poverty, anarchy, terminal insanity.

Baldert remembered his walk through downtown Lima. There was garbage everywhere, even corpses. That the Pollo Dorado restaurant still functioned was due to a corrupt clientele able to pay in dollars. Most of the stores Baldert saw between the restaurant and the embassy were closed. That he hadn't been molested by street robbers was thanks to bodyguards, provided by lawyer Sanchez. The Dutch embassy was a closed fortress, under siege.

Baldert's reward money would secure uniforms so that Moreno, and two of his guardias from Talara who wanted to desert, could dress up as a colonel and his aides. More dollars would secure a helicopter. Moreno's knowledge of the military bureaucracy would supply him with the right forms and missives to be faxed just ahead of his majestic entry in the concentration camp of Punta Negra.

"The prisoner Henri Baldert from Olanda, if you please, *mi capitan.*"

There might be time for pleasantries, for a drink, for compliments on the way the camp was run. And off they are, with poor Henri still in chains, hobbling along, crying, begging.

•

"Your son, Don Baldert."

"Your money, mi Teniente. Thank you for all you have done, how are you, Henri. Poor boy. You can refresh yourself in that little building over there. That man will take you. Mi Teniente, I had a few refreshments prepared by my pilots. No? I understand. You have to be on your way, too, Lieutenant. We want to leave soon, too. We're too close to Peru for comfort. Let me embrace you for a job well done. Good luck to you, my friend."

The jet was starting up when the former Peruvian lieutenant José Moreno Llosa rode a horse off the airstrip. A sound made him look back. Jets don't backfire do they? The sound was like the crack of a gun shot. A handgun going off? A .45 automatic pistol? Perhaps. Yes, a pistol.

Moreno made his horse wheel around but the jet was moving already.

Two men, one pushing a pistol into his belt, the other with a rifle slung over his shoulder, came out of the shed at the side of the airstrip. Both carried spades.

Moreno rode off. Low above the airstrip a black vulture, turning a slow circle, was joined by others.

•

The note reached Baldert's desk at his headquarters on the Heregracht, the Gentleman's Canal, an elegant address in Amsterdam's center, some six months later. The note was accompanied by a check for $98,000. The note was signed José and expressed regrets. José Moreno Llosa regretted that he had assisted a father in killing his son.

Baldert, that night, talked to his bedroom mirror. He was drinking pisco sour that he had mixed and chilled earlier on. He kept refilling his glass as he wandered about the room, striking poses, hitting his chest, shouting, at the fat sweating man unable to get away.

"So, what else could I do, pal?

"Listen, Pigface.

"Yes, I admit it, he was my son, cute little fellow, I once liked Little Henri, I took him everywhere. Three years old. I would carry him, like this, he'd sit in my hands, dangle his little legs. Sweet little kid.

"Then what! It started at high school, when he was stealing from me, drinking, causing trouble all the time, nothing spectacular, the little shit was stealing pennies, lying, smoking pot.

"Wanted to study history, so, sure, that's what he does, I paid for it, I always paid, and what did student Henri do? You tell me. Right, nothing. Smoke more sweetsy dope. Didn't

227

even drink alcohol, the coward. Sit around, luvvie duvvie. Bring all those pals home, that used my house, my phone, fouled up the place, every time I came back from somewhere Henri's luvvy pals had taken over. I would kick them out, change the locks. Next time they'd be back again, using my resources. Everybody doing cocaine.

"Right. Using me. ME. Ironic. You're so right, pal. Ironic.

"Right. Then Henri is sorry, wants to work, change his life, so I believe it. Give him a job.

"He's clever now, pretends interest, all he wants is to go to Peru on some pretext, something I could believe in, like checking on the fish, but really out to corner the cocaine business, the idiot, show Old Dad what's what, show me he can do it ... and he gets CAUGHT, goddammit, and next thing I have to fork out a million to get him back, humiliate myself, suppose I had paid, eh? Those Peruvian government gangsters would have used him again and again, to suck me dry.

"Using *me* ...

"Nobody uses *me*. But nobody ...

"So the honorable lieutenant sends me back my money. A gentleman and an officer, is he now? Two thousand short.

"Probably what he had to spend to get into Angeles del Mar, the concentration camp. To get Henri to me, so I could use the Equador Chollos to kill Henri. So that Henri could never embarrass me again.

"Probably will be sending the two thou too, later maybe.

"Won't let me use him.

"Prove me wrong ...

"Wrong to who, eh? To his forefathers? Mr. Moreno has Indian blood all right, touch of the tar brush, yes sir, so what does he want to be a gentleman for? To impress the Inca kings? Power freaks? That quarreled and split their empire so that Pisarro could take over? Is he trying to impress Pisarro

228

who invited the kings to a party and killed them for their gold?

"Oh please ... do me a favor, mi Teniente. Who needs your money? Who needs you?

"Who needs me?

Baldert kicked the mirror as he came to the end of his monologue. The mirror broke. Baldert cut his foot. He fell asleep on the floor, unable to tend to the wound. Baldert bled badly that night but the maid found him in the morning and telephoned for an ambulance. The emergency room staff repaired the damage.

•

Baldert is back in business but, amazingly enough, not doing well. After a series of wrong decisions his corporation recently applied for protection from its creditors, the court is not sympathetic. He may have to file for bankruptcy and, as he is the sole owner of his corporation, made personally responsible for his company's debts. Baldert has stopped drinking and jogs in the "Amsterdamse Bos," a national park.

Lawyer Umberto Sanchez was killed by 'churres', Lima street kids who he refused to give his wallet too.

José Moreno Llosa became a Hollywood B movie Bad Guy. He gets bigger parts now, starring as a subtly sadistic Mexican or Colombian, often with a bizarre sense of humor, intent on destroying the North American dream. Although in regular life Moreno is happily married to a former Los Angeles waitress, is devoted to their two little sons, lives on a small farm, drives a pickup truck, won a prize for growing the biggest local tomato, he is always mean on screen. When asked to explain his successful portraying of intelligent evil Moreno says he had good teachers.

THUNDERHOLE
EXIT

The year was 1956, the location Southern England. As a young man I lived in St. Ives, Cornwall, for a while. The picturesque coastal town of St.Ives attracts many artists, writers, aspiring thinkers even. Imagining myself to belong to the latter category I was 'reading philosophy', going through some thirty books on and by Western seekers, as suggested by my London professor. I had chosen Cornwall as it has better British weather: some sun, mild winters. There's such a thing as a Cornish palm tree. I swam in St. Ives harbor at Christmas.

That, in addition to diligently pursuing my studies, I had become a tool in an international vendetta of the area was not immediately clear to me.

I rented a small apartment and my motherly landlady, Gail, St. Ives' leading herbalist, worried about my status as someone 'from away', introduced me to a fellow 'continental'.

Herbert Auerbach was a former Luftwaffe gunner, who parachuted into the English county of Cornwall in 1942. He was eighteen years old at the time, an enthusiast, an early believer in a United Europe where things would be better. The British disagreed and Herbert jumped from the tail of a

Dornier bomber that had been disabled by a Hurricane fighter plane. The idealistic warrior, after landing, got his foot caught in parachute lines, a mishap that made him bump about a field on his head, until stopped by a farmer.

Instead of thanking his savior Herbert shouted "Heil Hitler." "Young chap has gone mad," the Cornish farmer told the elderly Home Guard soldiers who came to pick Herbert up. As he kept shouting "Heil Hitler" the prisoner was taken to a camp for hostile madmen. At the prison camp Herbert was certified as temporarily crazed, partly due to shell shock, by a fat female psychiatrist. "She was right," Herbert told me, "bumping about that field on my head possibly aggravated a schizoid condition." The psychiatrist recommended art as therapy and saw to it that Herbert was provided with plywood, left-over paints and a set of used brushes. The prisoner stopped heiling Hitler and painted flaming fields for awhile. From there he progressed to depicting nude women modeled on the psychiatrist. After the war Herbert chose to stay in Cornwall and was, fifteen years later, becoming known as a talented neo-expressionist. When I met him he was in his 'Coastal Egg' period, filling large canvases with yellows on white against green and blue backgrounds. I thought he was good. Walking about his large studio in the coastal village of Zennor filled me with energy. His work had begun to sell then and would soon hang in important galleries all over England and Europe.

When I arrived in St. Ives Herbert seemed to take a liking to me. He and a Swiss girl called Gretel were the only foreigners in the area at the time. Gretel's sister, nicknamed 'Hansel'– her real name was Annie–had recently disappeared. Hansel liked walking on wet coastal ledges. Had she slipped and been carried off by treacherous currents?

I understood that 'Hansel and Gretel', beautiful blond blue-eyed sisters in their twenties, were art students from Zürich,

232

learning the art of woodblock printing at St. Ives workshops. They had signed up for a year. When I arrived Gretel still had a few months to go. Hansel, according to my landlady Gail, a cheerful widow in her sixties, known widely as a healer, liked to 'sleep around' more. Hansel and Gretel both, Herbert told me, narrowing his eyes a little, as if to warn me of useless attempts on my part, 'preferred more mature men'.

Herbert was 35, bald, and rather heavy. I was 24. I liked gymnastics. While walking about the area I was always looking for barriers and hindrances I could have fun with. I knew that my sudden jumps, feints and somersaults tended to put people off but found it hard to restrain myself.

Herbert and Gretel often met me in a St. Ives pub called The Dinghy. We would sit at a corner table and talk German. I thought we were friends.

Taking a break from thought-structures conjectured by Kant, Husserl and Schopenhauer (my London professor's favorites) I was finding solace in the thoughts of Nietzsche. Trying to digest 'the meaning of no meaning' I had begun to wander about the narrow streets and alleys of old St. Ives, a town that dates back to medieval piracy, at odd hours. One early morning, with seagulls greeting the coming day with eerie cries and the surf crashing against the port's breakwaters, listening to my solitary steps reverberating on dew-covered cobblestones, the concept of Nietzsche's Void excited me. I felt so elated that I jumped across a fence that was part of a sports field, did a handstand on a park bench, and spun around a high bar between two posts at the harborside. My performance (I also sang and whistled) was observed by Constable Bob. I got myself arrested. The charge was 'disturbing the public peace'.

Constable Bob was a tall man, darkly/impeccably uniformed, wearing a pointed cloth-covered 'Bobby' helmet, who, in keeping with the British principle of understatement, carried no arms, not even a stick. His authority, nevertheless, was immense.

I wore a tattered duffel coat, hadn't shaved for awhile, needed a haircut and spoke with an accent. Meeting this apparition of spotless power (that politely wished me Good Morning) I was glad to have an audience. I took out my collected Nietzsche, pounded the book enthusiastically and excitedly told my fellow human seeker that "there is no demonstrable cause to see the universe as either lacking or possessing intrinsic meaning, and that all 'values' we read into our existence are therefore relative, of no absolute use at all, so that, at the very most, our self-made 'values' can only be read as symptoms of our own present condition," I told Constable Bob, "and as evolved by frantic attempts at being self-important." I raised my voice. "But what if there is no self?" I pointed at the gleaming buttons on the policeman's tunic. "Can you imagine the relief?" I put the book back in my pocket and clapped my hands loudly. "No self to carry no self? Liberation at last? "

Constable Bob spoke softly. "Your papers, if you please."

I did own a valid resident permit, but it was lost between my books in the small apartment I rented in Virgin Street. I was escorted to St. Ives Police Station where I spent time in a cell while Constable Bob contacted the Immigration Office in Southampton for confirmation of my statement.

A copy of the permit arrived in the mail the next day.

When Constable Bob brought me hot chocolate I again tried to demonstrate the joy experienced after grasping the concept of 'no meaning, no purpose.'

"My self-created purpose," Constable Bob said, "is to arrest you, and keep you in safe-keeping, for having no purpose."

Conflicting, and overriding home-made values, however (as expressed in British Law), forced Constable Bob to let me go.

"Reluctantly," he said darkly.

To celebrate my freedom I bought a second-hand motorcycle.

A few weeks later beautiful blond blue-eyed Gretel consented to be taken for a ride through the Moors, the boggy lands covered with low bushes that flower yellow, that cover most of the Cornish south coast. Constable Bob waved us down.

"Your papers if you please."

My overseas driving license wasn't really valid (it would have been if I'd been a tourist instead of a resident) but Constable Bob didn't seem to mind this time. He only issued a written warning.

A week later the mail brought an invitation to visit Constable Bob at his station.

I showed up at the appointed time.

"Are you getting your British driving license?"

I showed proof that I had passed local tests and that the required document was about to be issued.

Constable Bob seemed disappointed but cheered up again soon enough. "It has come," he said softly, "to our notice that you have been washing dishes and scraping pots at the Lobster Pot in Land's End. Your resident permit specifically states that Student Status does not permit the bearer to perform work."

"Is that bad?" I asked.

"All values," Constable Bob said, "are arbitrary. There is no such thing as 'bad'. Am I right?"

I pondered the proposition.

"You agree," Constable Bob said, "that I can make up my own meanings, and the meanings of those who find themselves under my jurisdiction?" He frowned. " I mean the meanings of those like yourself, Mr. Kalkman. As my ward I now order you to make a meaningful visit. The Commander, as you probably know, lives in Rose Cottage in the nearby village of Zennor. I believe you know the Commander. Now visit the

Commander and report to me afterward. If you fulfil your meaning the Queen and I might decide to let you off with a written warning again but meanwhile your deportation order is pending."

I knew the Commander as a former naval officer now living on private income. The Commander was gentlemanly handsome with a full mustache and beard, resembling postage stamp images of European royalty. The Commander liked to drink and could often be found at The Dinghy.

Before visiting the Commander I called on Herbert at his Zennor studio and told him about Constable Bob's mysterious order. Herbert knew the Commander, who lived a little further down the coast. What could be up?

"You're a philosopher," Herbert said and picked up a brush while eyeing a freshly framed piece of blank linen. "Find out for yourself."

I ran into Gretel during grocery shopping. I asked Gretel to explain Herbert's rudeness. "Jealousy," Gretel said. "Now that we've been on your motorcycle together he suspects we are sleeping together too. Herbert thinks he owns me. I just seduced him once or twice."

"I would love to sleep with you," I told Gretel.

"You old-fashioned boy." She smiled. "You're so direct."

I told her about Constable Bob's order.

Gretel smiled again. "You check on the Commander first. Then you collect your reward."

"But why investigate this Commander?"

"You're studying to be a professional thinker," Gretel said, "find out for yourself." She gathered her shopping bags and whisked herself away.

I wondered why my fellow-foreign-friends were leaving me to fend for myself in hostile country.

I left the grocery store too, hoping to run into Gretel again in one of St. Ives' narrow alleys. Remembering her smiles I planned to kiss Gretel's moist full lips, hold her trembling luscious body against me, ride her to the Moors on my powerful motorcycle, and make love to her between the flowering bracken. It was just the day for an outing. We could have tea and muffins afterwards, in the inn at Land's End, make love between the flowering ferns again, then eat steak and onions in my room overlooking St. Ives harbor.

No Gretel.

I did meet my landlady, on her way back from the Moors carrying a basket full of herbs. I asked her about the Commander. Gail took me home to lunch and told me about Marilyn. Marilyn was a 'nicely-stacked' (Gail said) young woman from London, formerly employed at The Dinghy as a barmaid. Marilyn owned a large and fierce dog. The Commander enticed Marilyn and Mutt to live with him at Rose Cottage, as 'a housekeeper of some sort' (Gail winked heavily, shaking her head simultaneously so that her white ponytail bounced about). Marilyn quit her job and was seen around town for awhile, running errands for the Commander, or walking her giant poodle/terrier. Marilyn and Mutt would come in on the bus, or in the Commander's small Austin. Then both weren't seen anymore. Questioned by Constable Bob the Commander said there had been some trouble and that the useless woman and her ungainly mongrel had left, returned to London for all he knew.

The next morning Constable Bob stopped me again.

"I might remind you that you are in violation of your resident permit's conditions, which is an arrestable misdemeanor," Constable Bob said softly, "and that I can put my hand on you and hold you in St. Ives jail while I arrange for your deportation. Have you seen the Commander yet at Rose Cottage?"

I thought about leaving the country but I hadn't finished reading my thirty philosophy books yet and wanted more teaching in London so I rode my motorcycle to the Commander's charming cottage, enjoying the country- and seaside.

There was no reason to feel nervous. The Commander and I had been talking before. When, in The Dinghy, he 'had a few' the Commander welcomed an audience and I, for one, liked to listen. The Commander's favorite story went as follows: One foggy morning, late in World War Two, off the French Coast, he himself, then a mere lieutenant, was in charge of a Motor Torpedo Boat. The MTB was looking for German cargo vessels worthy to be destroyed by expensive torpedos, but instead met with two German 'Raumboote'. 'Raumboote' were wooden Kriegsmarine vessels, heavily armed. The lieutenant knew that his MTB was no match for the larger and faster German craft.

"Intelligence," the Commander said loudly, after drinking another beer and ordering yet another, "is making optimal use of a set of a given circumstances. Am I an intelligent man, meboy?"

I banged my glass and cheered.

"Right. So. As I said. It was a misty day. A particular thick bank of pea-soap like fog was about to envelop those two big bad Raumboats and single Silly Little Me, so I ordered full speed ahead, aiming for a position right between those two Nazi bastards, and ordered my crew to 'fire all guns, port and starboard'. A perfect double Rat Tat Tat pumping out the wicked shells, meboy. Both sides. So the Krauts, being shot at, returned fire, right?"

I applauded.

"And Silly Little Me kept going full speed ahead and was out of there while the Bad Boys were sinking each other." The commander laughed. "Haw haw HAW, meboy."

I agreed the Commnder's strategy was brilliant.

Mollified (for he was in fine fighting shape, reliving the Victorious Moment, shaking his fist, yelling and stamping) the Commander had invited me, any time I happened to pass his abode, 'to drop in for a spot of something or other'. The barman heard the Commander invite me. My landlady Gail had told me The Dinghy's barman was Constable Bob's brother. The barman must have told Constable Bob—feet up near the woodstove, the two brothers sucking their pipes peacefully, two redoubtable powers at home on their own turf, moving me about, me, an expendable foreigner, a mere peon in their war game—that the Commander had invited the witless Dutchman to visit him at Rose Cottage anytime. Now then ... just a little prodding ...

There I was, riding a Norton between flowering bracken.

But it was all beyond me then, how could I ever learn to understand British innuendos. And why?

I sighed, checked my map and rode out to Rose Cottage, snugly set on the Cornish sea coast, some five miles out of St. Ives, overlooking a cove.

"My fine fellow," the Commander said as he looked up from splitting firewood in his front yard. "Just in time for a spot of lunch. How nice to see you. I get lonely out here, you know? Isn't it a splendid day? How do you like my simple dwelling? An old miner's cottage, dating back to a time when it paid to dig for tin here. Every beam, post, tile, stone a priceless original, and me their trusted keeper. Come in and have a pew, my boy. A drop of port? Watercress salad? Care for some almonds? Hot lamb, cold chicken or both? Home baked bread or froggy fries? Frogs, haw haw. The French, you know."

The lunch was just fine. As the Commander poured beer to go with the lamb chops I looked up, thinking I heard thunder closeby, but the sky had been clear as I rode out of St. Ives and it was the wrong time of the year for thunder.

The Commander laughed. "Tide coming in again," he explained. "Thunderhole acting up."

The center part of the cove, where the cliffs cut down sharply toward the sea, was white with spray that burst from large rocks. The Commander explained how tides and currents force the water in and out between large granite boulders, having cut, through the ages, a tunnel that surfaces just behind Rose Cottage, on the far side of a sea wall. The roof of the tunnel caved in near the shore, so during High Tide enormous waves come thundering up. "A splendid sight," my host said as he walked me to 'Thunderhole' after lunch. He showed me the stone wall that bordered his garden. The wall was some five feet high. The thundering water got pushed up on the other side of the wall, every four minutes or so. "Did you see what I have there?" the Commander asked.

We were back at the table in the cottage's main room, sipping 'Froggy' cognac, smoking Cuban cigars. The Commander got quite excited. "My own private connection to the fourth dimension is what I have there." He shouted, banging his fist on the teak tabletop: "Yes, meboy. There's a good old exit there. For good riddance of bad rubbish. HawHAW, HAWhaw."

Of course, he explained after refilling our snifters, the fourth dimension has many connections to the third, our own realm. The oceans in themselves—and the oceans cover three quarters of the globe—are one gigantic connection. "Like I proved with the Raumboats?"

The Commander became thoughtful. "The entire German Navy got cleaned away that way." He banged his fist again. "The Japanese Navy too for that matter. Can't have enough destruction, you know."

Did I care to hear my host's private philosophy? Yes? Here goes.

Anything at all, the Commander told me, that irritates or annoys, especially if it shows up as female, that despicable though seductive side of the creation, can be gotten rid of by

240

tossing it into the fourth dimension. Boats, as everyone knows, are female. Sometimes females are useful, but the Raumboots were the wrong females so off they went. One could also burn unwanted items. He pointed at his stone fireplace. Another connection. Burnable rubbish? Into the fire with it. Burnable rubbish will never bother again. But some items are best dropped into the Thunderhole. He had heard I was a philosopher too. Could he ask for my comments?

I said his theory was fascinating but that I would have to go home to further study its deeper contents. The Commander was jumping about by then, waving wildly, cursing German and 'slit-eyed' shipping, British and Swiss women who tried to 'bed him down' and large mongrel bitches that bit his toes at night. The Commander was singing too, about a bottle of rum and Yo Ho Ho.

"You know how bitches go?" he asked as I was thanking my host for an excellent lunch. He took me to the garden and demonstrated how dogs go. Bad female dogs will jump at your throat, and while they are suspended their fore paws hang down. What you do is dive under your canine adversary, grab her by the paws and simply flick her over yourself, across the wall into Thunderhole. "Down the hatch!" the Commander shouted. He dropped his voice, stepped closer, caressed my hair, whispered innocently. "I like you, meboy, but you could be a traitor. Now, dear lad, confess. Do you or don't you happen to be a *faggot?*"

Riding home I remembered Gail saying that the Commander was quite an athlete. He swam in his cove most days and had been a member of the St. Ives fencing club but got suspended because of overly aggressive behavior. In my present awed, trembling state, I might not have been a good opponent.

Constable Bob was waiting for me in High Street. He waved me down again. I switched off my engine, took off my helmet,

241

moved up my goggles. I scraped my throat. "The Commander ..." My voice was squeaky.

"Not here," Constable Bob said softly. "Slip down to the station."

I reported. Afterward Constable Bob poured hot chocolate. "But there would be no proof," I said. "That Thunderhole ... wouldn't that powerful current roaring in and out through a granite tunnel grind a body beyond recognition?"

"Don't know what you're talking about," Constable Bob said.

"You might thank me," I said. "That was a dangerous mission. Here I am, innocent bait and your Commander is stark raving mad. Tosses people 'down the hatch'. He could have come at me. More foreign fish food."

"What would you have me thank you for?" Constable Bob asked softly.

"Okay," I said. "Maybe the risk was minimal. I'm neither female nor faggot, and you know that I'm good at swinging around bars, jumping fences and so forth. So you may have figured that I would have tossed *him* down that hole? So there is really nothing to be grateful for? I should thank you for being allowed to form part of your sport? Well, thank you for nothing." I made ready to leave.

"Mr. Kalkman?" Constable Bob asked softly. "May I remind you that I have charges pending? That your job may not be done yet?"

"Now what?"

Now what was Gretel.

Gretel telephoned from where she stayed in nearby Zennor. She invited me to dinner.

I rode out to the cottage Gretel had shared with her sister Hansel, a working farm's outbuilding, next to a haystack.

The dinner was minimal but Gretel kept pouring wine. When I made my move she excused herself. Due to female peculiarity she could not fulfil her promise that night. I thought

242

I might better go. Gretel thought drunk riding of heavy motorcycles on narrow rural roads would not be a good idea, especially with Constable Bob around. As I lay sleepily on Gretel's couch she said she heard I had lunch with the Commander. She mentioned her sister Hansel who had lived with the Commander, Hansel who disappeared. I may have told Gretel about Thunderhole, the Commander's problem with the female principle, about 'down the hatch'. I slept on the couch. The next morning Gretel felt better. After a Swiss breakfast she took me to the haystack nextdoor and suggested 'to fool around'. Muesli and cheese melts seemed to heat up her blood. The combination also made her unstable. As soon as I approached her Gretel pushed me away, ran off, suddenly turned, screamed with rage and charged me.

I remembered the Commander's demonstration. As soon as Gretel was close enough I grabbed her wrists, put a foot in her stomach, fell backwards and swung her over my head. She fell in hay, shook herself, jumped up, tried again.

"Very nice," Gretel said after she got thrown a few more times. "Be a darling. Rush me for a change. Would you do that?"

We reversed roles. Gretel had some trouble tossing me over her head at first. We were both tired. I changed tactics. She finally opened up. Afterwards we dozed off.

"That was payment in advance," Gretel said, shaking me awake. "Back to work, you lazy fellow."

That afternoon we built up a four foot high wall of straw bales and pretended Thunderhole was behind it.

We practised again. I attacked Gretel. She made the right movements: grabbing wrists, foot in stomach, falling back. My body flew lightly: 'down the hatch'.

"I can do it now," Gretel said. "Thank you."

•

The Commander disappeared.

Constable Bob made routine enquiries. Gretel had been seen visiting Rose Cottage but she denied that there had been anymore than casual contact. She recalled that the Commander told her he planned to travel. To Chile perhaps? No. Liberia? Nigeria? One of those places? Gretel couldn't remember for sure.

Constable Bob asked me, 'just for the record', if I had, by chance, seen the Commander lately.

"Commander Fishfood?"

He didn't laugh.

Gretel completed her course in woodblock printing. We would go out on my motorcycle together, and enjoy picnics on the seaside. She mostly refused further advances. I saw Gretel off when her train left Penzance station. Herbert didn't show.

One evening I spotted Herbert at The Dinghy. He tried to ignore me. I shouldered myself next to him at the bar. I told him that there was no reason to be rude. If anyone had a right to be nasty it would surely be me. Herbert should have warned me away from Constable Bob's dangerous scheme. Wasn't Herbert my friend? And why feel jealous? Hadn't Gretel used me too?

"We're talking values here?" Herbert asked. "What about guru Nietzsche you are always quoting? How did that mantra go again?" Herbert quoted: *"Life neither lacks nor possesses intrinsic value. All 'values' we read into our existence are totally relative, of no absolute use at all, so that, at the very most, our self-made values can only be read as symptoms of our own condition ...?"* Herbert grinned. *"... evolved only by frantic attempts at being self-important?"*

I left the pub.

Gail, back from her rock altar in the Moors where, she said, she met a herd of wild longhaired goats who reminded her of

Druids, sorcerer-priests of the pre-Christian era, said there might still be value to "values."

"How so?" I asked.

"Don't knock relative value," Gail said, looking wiser and holier than ever. "If it's home-made it may be tasty. Look here, my dear, I agree with your pain. Isn't Herbert petty? Here he is, a stranger in a magic land that cured his insanity when he fell from the sky from where he was trying to hurt us. And here you are, another stranger who came here in search of wisdom. And instead of guiding you Herbert never warned you of Constable Bob's dangerous plan to rid ourselves of an evil presence. And when poor Gretel compensated you for your trouble this small-minded Herbert allowed himself to get jealous?"

"Petty," I said, trying to weigh the word.

"*I* don't say so," my landlady said. Maybe you don't say so either, but he will say so himself."

"Herbert?"

"Right."

"Subconsciously, Gail?"

"Right, my dear." She laughed. "He'll want to be purified by pain."

It was almost time to leave. I finished up my reading, made Gail a present of flowers, paid my debts and caught a train back to London. Not a week later there was a note from Gail, saying "see?" The note accompanied a newspaper clipping.

MAN NEARLY DROWNS IN A GLASS OF BEER.

Herbert Auerbach, local artist, nearly drowned in a pint mug of bitter, last Saturday evening, at The Dinghy's counter. Our reporter learned that the neo-expressionist painter hadn't taken off his backpack, heavy with a load of groceries purchased to last him a week. The pub being crowded Mr. Auerbach was squeezed against the bar, leaning forward to take a sip from a full pint of bitter. An acquaintance, whose identity is not being recalled, greeted the artist boisterously. HELLO HERBERT! The extraverted reveller then slapped the unfortunate painter heavily on the back and moved on. More clients entered the popular pub at that point and Herbert Auerbach, his face firmly wedged into his mug that had been filled to the rim with his favorite brand of bitter, was unable to retrieve his mouth and nostrils. Awhile later the barman, noticing that Mr. Auerbach hadn't moved for awhile, reached across the bar and separated face and mug. The unconscious artist was raced to hospital and emergency staff managed to restore life to the patient's oxygen-starved body. According to Dr. Smudgers Mr. Auerbach is doing well and a full recovery is expected.

I mailed Herbert a get-well postcard. He sent me a photograph of Thunderhole, his latest painting, the large canvas now on display in The Tate Gallery, in London. When the white foaming spray is studied carefully a pink tinge may be noticed, getting darker in the spout's center.

PRAWNS WITH EVIL FACES

Real estate salesman Joe was nervous when inspector Skates of the Brisbane Municipal Police questioned him about a dead cyclist on Greenpine Subdivision Lot 16. Normally Burton didn't think of the law, and its enforcers, other as a phenomenon that happens to be a around, like he, Joe Burton, happened to be around, and never the twain do meet. That Sunday, however, the twain kept clashing. Thrice.

First, there was the motorcycle cop, a grim cleanshaven powerful young man, crisply uniformed, riding a sleek Japanese late model Kawasawa, who stopped Joe's little Mazda. Joe was driving his wife Mary and his four year old Rebecca to the park where Rebecca wanted to feed 'duckies'. The policeman stopped Joe because the rear window in Joe's Mazda was cracked. An offense. Blocks the view. Dangerous. Would have to be repaired soonest. The officer issued a written warning and wouldn't smile at little Rebecca as he thumbpressed his four-cylinder super bike into action again. After that, there was the sergeant in Kangaroo Square ordering Joe to 'move along now if you please'. Joe, on the way back from the park, had parked the Mazda, bought icecream cones for his family, and was walking back to his car from the Italian icecream cart when he noticed a disturbance near the cute-colored shelter where Brisbane citizens wait for the city bus to pick them up and take them places. A tall uniformed foot-patrol constable was clicking handcuffs on a bum while his supervising sergeant was looking on. Joe stopped to look on too. There was something frightening/exciting about watching one man taking another man's liberty away. The other man was a bad looking tramp, of course, and unshaven hung-over individuals in rags shouldn't be littering a nice bus-shelter with their unseemly presence, not on the edge of a nice park on a nice Sunday morning, but even so.

"Nothing to look at here," the sergeant told citizen Joe while the tall constable pushed citizen Tramp, none too gently, into the rear of a patrol car, summoned out of nowhere by the sergeant talking into his two-way radio, a neat gadget clamped to his breast pocket, next to war medals.

Joe, clutching the dripping ice cream cones, walked back to the Mazda.

"What did the man do, Dad?" Rebecca asked and Joe didn't know. The man didn't seem to be doing much except being a man. The wrong sort of man maybe.

The Sunday moved along—in the evening Joe drove to Greenpine Subdivision. Joe worked for an agency that developed land all around the city of Brisbane and Greenpine was Joe's baby. Joe had to make sure he, and his team, made sales there. The Agency urged her salesmen to make at least two sales a week. There were almost a hundred Greenpine lots to sell when the subdivision opened. Sales were brisk during the first few weeks but now, almost a year later, the pace had dropped right down. There was still quite a bit of land left.

"What's wrong, Joe?" the sales manager, known as 'Uncle

Tatty', asked at the end of yesterday's meeting. Joe hated Saturday morning sales meetings. Saturday should be a day off but the Agency didn't recognize a salesman's human rights. "What's wrong, Joe?" Uncle Tatty asked, using his irritating British-born accent. "Why isn't your team selling? Why aren't *you* selling? Getting slack, Joe?" Uncle Tatty, ever since Bob Big, the Agency's owner, had made him a partner, had forgotten he had been a salesman too, with ups & downs, and how enervating his downs had been. Uncle Tatty's tactless prodding still hurt that Sunday evening and Rebecca was being cranky because of TV cartoon violence Mary wouldn't allow the innocent child to see, and Mary was accusing Joe of having an affair with a client, so escapist Joe drove out to Greenpine to get away from it all. Maybe make a sale too.

The Agency did good advertising that attracted prospective clients who would roam Greenpine's quiet roads at odd times. Joe could wave shopping cars down, to point out available lots, wave his map, and big color pictures of a church, a school, a park with slides and swings, planned items that would show up once all lots would be sold. Here, Sir, this is where your trout fishing stream is, here, Ma'm, is the park.

Charismatic Joe waves his magic wand and clients see their bright & beautiful future in priced-to-sell Greenpine. "Step right up, folks." Joe carries a satchel, with contracts, and pens, and receipts for down payments. "Sign here if you please."

Joe sold Lot 16 that way, to Miriam and Steve Maslow, still married at that time. The as yet not unhappy couple, alerted by one of the Agency's full page ads, came driving into Greenpine to check for themselves and there happened to be salesman Joe, contract ready, pen poised, mouth wagging. "Let me show you around. You like this lot here? To carry your future home? Excellent choice, folks."

Miriam signed. She was the one with some money, also with the education, Miriam was about to graduate as a clinical

249

counselor. Husband Steve was just tagging along, a nothing, a loser, Joe understood. Husband Steve drove a delivery van for a living. The man was a mistake. Joe found long-legged Miriam quite attractive. "Thank you Ma'm. Congratulations on your purchase."

Now, as Joe parked the Mazda, a full moon lifted itself, just like that other Sunday night Joe first met Miriam. Joe walked between huge pine trees, leftovers from the forest the Agency had chainsawed down, that graced every individual lot. It wasn't eight yet. There was a soccer match on TV that night, played in Melbourne, that would be keeping any clients away. Joe didn't mind. The subdivision was peaceful, until Joe screamed, after stumbling across the dead man. Mike Herring, partly hidden in tall grass, lay next to his bicycle, next to a juniper bush. An orange rag waved from a branch.

"Oh dear oh dear oh dear," Joe sobbed. Joe used four letter words to comment on little mishaps, when things really went wrong he used Sunday school talk. "Oh dear oh dear oh dear." He kept saying that as he got into the Mazda, drove to the nearest convenience store, pushed coins into a phone, dialed Brisbane's emergency number.

He might have driven home instead, but Joe thought that was too risky. There was a retirement home on a hill, overlooking Greenpine, old folks would have noticed his white Mazda ambling about the subdivision; nosy old folks, witnesses to the fact that he had run away from the scene of a crime.

"Brisbane Police," a pleasant female voice said softly.

"Dead man in Greenpine," Joe reported. "South of Bridgehill," Joe said. New subdivision. Milepost Seven. I'll be going back there. A white Mazda. I'll have my blinkers going."

A patrol car arrived: uniformed constable at the wheel, a middle aged man in a linen suit on the back seat. The passenger introduced himself as inspector Skates, Homicide, happened to be on call tonight, you found a body, Sir? Skates looked around, directed technicians and a doctor, who arrived in other cars, to the corpse, then asked Joe to meet him in his office in Brisbane's downtown Bowery Building. "Have a chat?"

The dead cyclist was located on Lot 16, Joe told inspector Skates in Police Headquarters, third floor, a grey nondescript room, that Sunday evening at eleven. "Yes, I knew him." Joe knew Mike Herring because he, salesman Joe, sold Lot 15 to Mike, about a year ago. He remembered Mike because the deal had complications. In order to finally close the sale Joe visited his client in Mike's shed, out of town, near Pig's Harbor, where Mike kept his old prawn fishing boat.

"Anything odd about Mike Herring?"

"Yes, you could say so. Bit of a drunk, Inspector."

"Weak heart?"

Oh yes, Joe told the inspector. Mike had showed him the scars of a triple by-pass heart operation.

"You said you sold Mike Lot 15," inspector Skates said. "But you came across Mike's body on Lot 16, right?"

Inspector Skates, while walking about the subdivision had figured out what was what by checking with the Greenpine map Joe had pulled out of his Mazda. The map was on Skates' desk now. "We found Mike's body on Lot 16 but Mike owned Lot 15, the lot with the house on it. So Mike had a nice new house built on his lot?"

"Yes, Inspector."

"But the house is empty." Skates said. He knew. He had walked around it.

"It isn't quite finished yet, Inspector."

Joe stared at Inspector Skates, thinking the man looked different from the other policemen he had encountered that day. What hair Skates had left could do with some cutting.

The crumpled linen suit showed food stains. Inspector Skates' beady eyes were heavily lidded. Joe thought the man looked wild, doggish.

"So what was Mike Herring doing dead on land he didn't own?" wild-doggish looking inspector Skates asked, using a faintly menacing growly type of voice.

Joe, after some thought, suggested Mike could be admiring his new house, ogling his luxurious property.

"Right." Skates briefly closed his eyes, as if to analyze the scene Joe called up for him. "You'd make a good detective, Mr. Burton. It figures. You're a good salesman, aren't you? We both learn to figure people out." Skates' smile was encouraging. "So you reckon Mike put some distance between himself and his castle, so as to widen his view?" The inspector's beady eyes glittered. "And why the bicycle, Joe? Didn't you say Mike lived in Pig's Harbor? That's some way from Greenpine. Five, six miles?"

Joe said Mike always rode a bicycle. Mike had been riding a bicycle when Joe first met him.

"No car?"

Not that Joe knew of.

Skates frowned. "An unshaven older man in worn jeans and a pale blue work shirt with frayed cuffs, a soiled bush hat, battered boots, on an old bicycle, a man who doesn't own a car, building a house on an expensive piece of land? Three bedroom, two bath, full basement, front- and back porch, carport?" Inspector Skates paused. "Would that be prawnfishing money, you think, Mr Burton?"

"What else?" Joe said. Questioned further, Joe admitted that he had been a bit surprised when Mike, during that first meeting, produced wads of soiled small notes to establish his credit. The money had been in the bike's canvas saddlebag. And Mike performed another trick. He demanded a discount. Middleclass Greenpine buyers almost invariably bought on the time-payment system which weakened their bargaining power. And now some tramp offers cash and wants a hefty rebate? But a sale is a sale. Sales keep the Agency's sales manager happy. Joe described, for Inspector Skates' benefit, the Agency's Saturday morning torture meetings, with Uncle Tatty wielding the whip. In this particular case Uncle Tatty wasn't even happy. Taking ten percent off indeed! How about five? It had cost Joe several visits to Pig Harbor till Lot 15 sold.

"At five percent discount?" inspector Skates asked.

"No, at ten." Joe said. "Mike wouldn't give in."

Skates winked knowingly. "You split the ten percent with Mike?"

Joe scowled.

"That's a 'no', Mr. Burton?" Skates asked.

Joe was quiet.

"Summing up," Skates said, "a small time prawn fisherman scrapes up a thousand pounds to buy Greenpine 15 and then puts up a ten thousand pound home. How so, Mr. Burton?"

Joe shrugged. He just sold blocks of land. Mike won a lottery? Mike robbed a bank? Who knows what Mike did? Who cares, inspector?"

"Now Mike is admiring his property, Skates said, closing his eyes again, visualizing the scene. "He can't stand it? He dies?"

"Heart attack?" Joe asked. "Didn't I hear your pathologist say that to you just now?"

The inspector nodded. "Yes. A heart attack due to what? Mike must have been used to being a house owner by now. He saw it grow slowly. A gradual joyful process doesn't cause trauma, Joe. A sudden shock does. Did Mike see something fearful? What do you think, Joe?"

Joe said he wasn't thinking.

"What else do we have?" inspector Skates asked. "An orange

rag on a bush. Does your Agency use small pieces of orange cloth to mark land boundaries? A flag? There is a purpose?"

No purpose. Joe had checked the piece of cloth, too. The Agency sometimes used orange luminus tape to mark land, but this rag seemed to be made of cotton.

Joe swallowed what threatened to be an elephantine yawn. It had been a long day. He would have to work in the morning. The orange rag was garbage, blown about by a breeze. Could he go now?

"In a minute," Skates said.

Joe answered a few more questions. He told the inspector he had cut down on his drinking so that he couldn't go to the bar for a few cold ones with his mates, but he couldn't always stay home either. He and Mary and Rebecca lived in a small apartment, part of a converted house in the suburb of Bowen Hill, near the railway tracks. There were shunting trains, even on Sunday. What with Rebecca's tantrums and Mary's screaming and the trains clanging their bumpers he sometimes preferred walking about quiet Greenpine.

"You're on commission only, Mr. Burton?"

And expenses, Joe said. He got a few pounds for petrol and free parking in the garage that the Agency owned in Queen Street. Joe needed his average of two weekly commissions to keep his ladies fed. There were few windfalls. There had been a seven-sale week but recently he had been missing out. The Agency didn't tolerate sales-missing salesmen.

"They get fired?" Skates asked.

"After a few warnings by Uncle Tatty they do."

Joe sighed, while looking at a bare wall behind the questioning inspector. The bare wall felt like his mind. He said as much. Skates smiled, got up, excused himself, shook Joe's hand, thanked him, walked him to the elevator. "Sleep well, Mr. Burton. Thank you for your assistance. Ah yes, one last question. This other lot interests me, the lot Mike Herring died on. You sold Lot 16 too? Who is the happy owner?"

Skates blocked the elevator door while Joe unrolled Greenpine's map. Joe put a finger on Lot 16. He grunted.

"Yes, Mr. Burton?" the inspector asked.

Joe shook his head. He didn't think he had sold 16. Maybe someone else had sold it. He could check at the office.

"You do that," inspector Skates said. "Thanks again." Skates stepped back. The elevator door closed. "Oh dear oh dear oh dear," Joe whispered. The elevator felt like his coffin, zooming down into the nether spheres.

•

"There you are, Mr. Burton," inspector Skates said, next Tuesday, when he hopped onto a stool next to Joe at a cafe's counter. The meeting took place in Rats' House of Prawns, a hole in the wall two blocks down from the Agency in Queen Street. Joe was allergic to shellfish but he enjoyed Mr. Ratsiaficas' anchovy lunch rolls, washed down with strong tea. "You know, Mr. Burton," the inspector said, winking as if he were sharing a joke with a friend, "Never mind what the learned pathologist says—blow that autopsy report. I am the sleuth here and I think Mike Herring got himself killed Sunday night."

Joe spilled some tea on his pants. "Ah?" he asked politely.

Inspector Skates ordered tea too. "The secretary at your Agency said I might find you here. You don't mind, do you? This continued questioning is not interfering with your digestion?"

Joe smiled weakly.

Inspector Skates stirred four cubes of sugar into his tea. "You and I are alike," Skates said happily. "We both corner clients and we both close sales. But I am less greedy. I'll let you get away. I'm just curious. I like to know what goes on. Fill me in and I'll be out of your hair."

Joe was spilling tea again. "Mike Herring died of a heart attack, I never touched him."

"Listen," Skates said. 'Maybe you and I should study some psychology, like the buyer of Greenpine 16, your lovely Miriam. It might give us some insights."

Joe put his mug down. He burped. He excused himself.

Inspector Skates winked. "So you like Miriam Maslow, do you? And you didn't want me to know? So you didn't tell me you sold Lot 16 to our suspect?"

"Miriam Maslow," Joe managed to look puzzled.

Inspector Skates scratched his chin. "She who, for her own account, as she is divorcing her husband Steve, recently bought Mike Herring's house, Greenpine, Lot 15. You know how I know? Because I checked Brisbane's Land Registry. What else did I learn? That Miriam already owns Lot 16. What did I remember? That you couldn't remember that. What did I conclude? That you were lying, dear Sir. What did I do this morning? I visited the wonderful woman. What did I hear? That Miriam Maslow bought Greenpine 16 from 'some salesman'." Wild-dog Skates barked excitedly. Dingo Skates stopped barking. His paw prodded a sheep's chest. "That's you. How do you like that, Joe? You tell me you can't remember her, she calls you 'Some Salesman'. Next question. Why does Miriam Maslow buy Mike Herring's house?" Inspector Skates was laughing/barking again. "It doesn't make sense. Why didn't she build a house on her own land, Joe? Where do you fit in? You sure you don't recall her?"

"I deal with lots of clients," Joe said.

"I carry a badge and a gun, Joe," Skates said. "I use them to find out things. Only an hour ago I called on the builder of what you tell me was Mike Herring's house. He never heard of Mike Herring, the good man claims that his client is Miriam Maslow."

Joe shook his head. He wanted to say he didn't know what Inspector Skates was talking about He scraped his throat a few times. "Ehhh ... "

Inpector Skates ordered prawn ragout on rice with pickles and olives on the side, the most expensive item on Mr. Ratsiaficas' special gourmet menu. "I like to eat well," the inspector said. "I can afford to because I'm a lone lean hunter. You should see the way I live, Joe, rent-free in a loft above a race horse stable. I sleep in a hammock. I read free library books. I ride a bicycle, like Mike Herring." Skates smiled. Joe didn't like the inspector's teeth, the canines looked too big, the man was indeed a wild dog. Joe felt sheepish. Dingos like to dance around sheep before they kill and eat them. Joe had read that somewhere, in a magazine article on what aboriginals believe. Native Australians claim to know that every human can summon his special spirit animal as a guide. The article said that people advised by dingo spirits are particularly tricky.

"I keep my expenses down," the inspector was saying, "that way I don't have to join the ever-needy ever-consuming herd. Doing things my way work can be a hobby. You know what my hobby is? My hobby is figuring out why sheep get themselves all twisted up."

"That's nice," Joe said, pushing his body away from the counter. "I've got to go now." He tried to match his tormentor's smile. "Maybe I can find some grass today." He attempted a wink. "Lead my family to pasture?"

Inspector Skates moved his tea cup out of the way so that Mr. Ratsiaficas could put down a large plate of prawn ragout, decorated with fresh parsley. Skates pointed his table knife at Joe. "You sit down, mate. I have news for you. You know your mistress Miriam is pregnant?" His fingers squeezed Joe's biceps as he pushed the salesman back on his stool. "Yes, mate. But not to worry. Miriam tells me the baby could have one of several fathers. Since she sent Steve home to his mother she has 'been trying things out'. She says she wants to be a single parent. She says she doesn't care much for the company of men. How does that sound, Mr. 'Some Salesman'?"

Skates speared a large bright orange prawn. He showed it to Joe. The prawn still had his head on, and its small black eyes seemed to be peering intently. The inspector bit the prawn's head off, grabbed it gingerly between index finger and thumb, put it down on the counter.

Joe left the cafe.

•

That afternoon Uncle Tatty asked Joe to step into his office. The Agency's sales manager was a born Englishman, a true "Pom," who liked to wear a tweed jacket on cool days, sported a bristly mustache, fancied a 'landed gentry' cap that he pulled into his eyes, enjoyed pouring 'half pints of bitter' into his red face, about every hour or so, work permitting.

"Joe!" Uncle Tatty said happily, waving a pencil. "Have a pew, old man. Let's have a bit of a powwow."

Joe sat down.

Uncle Tatty held up photo-copied documents. "Something amazing here, Joe. You know that I check real estate sales, that's part of my duties. Your sales manager has to see what's going on in the market. Keep you informed. Hey what? Old Chap?"

"Too right," Joe said grumpily. Joe was a true Australian, he detested Pom talk.

"Now then," Uncle Tatty said. "Ever since your prawn fisherman kicked the bucket I've been wondering about that bloody sale of yours. Mike Herring, got a perishing big discount on Greenpine 15, paid the Agency in small notes." Uncle Tatty stabbed his pencil at Joe. "Next thing Mike dies on Greenpine 16, facing a new house on his own Lot 15, and you, of all people, find the bloody body." The pencil clicked against Uncle Ratty's false teeth. "I've been wondering, Joe, about your illegal client Mike. How come he died, for instance?"

"Heart Attack," Joe said. "Read yesterday's *Brisbane Australian.*" Joe frowned furiously. "And what's illegal about paying in cash?"

Uncle Ratty's eye, close above the pencil that he aimed like a mini rifle barrel, peered at Joe. "Joe, please. Your sales manager knows everything. My mansion is on the river, close to Pig's Harbor. Once I knew who he was I kept an eye out for Mike and many a time have I seen his unregistered tub fish in closed waters. Your client was asocial, Joe. He circumvented normal distribution channels and sold his poached prawns directly to little places, like Rats', right here in Queen Street." The pencil clicked between Uncle's teeth again. "I avoid places like Rats. Know why? Mike's prawns could be bad. Like Mike's money."

"You took it," Joe said.

Uncle Tatty put his pencil down. He dropped his voice. "Why give a discount to a bum like Mike Herring, Joe?"

"Because Mike paid in cash," Joe said. 'I know you think I shared the discount but cash transactions are so hard to prove." Joe grinned. "Besides, blokes like you love cash too, don't you? When you or owner Big happen to make a sale yourselves you always try for cash, am I right?"

"What?" Uncle Tatty asked softly.

Joe sneered. He was glad he understood how company owners channel tax-free cash into their own pockets. "The sale registers with the city so the client gets his land but the Agency forgets to record it in its own administration. Before the End of the Year balance sheet is signed all records of a cash sale disappear smartly. The deal never happened after you and Mr. Big help themselves. You spend the loot together. On holiday in Tahiti, with Gauguin-painted floozies."

Uncle Tatty grinned. "So we are art critics now? You're so clever, Joe. Now be clever again and tell me how Mike Herring had a house constructed on Lot 15, with money he can't have made on those few bushels of prawns he has been selling to the likes of Rats'?"

Joe held up his hands. "Nothing to do with me."

"No?" Uncle Tatty squinted at Joe. "I hope so." He moved papers about on his desk, re-arranged his pencils and ballpoints, stacked some envelopes. "Listen. As I said, I was checking real estate sales at Brisbane City Registry again. About a week before Herring died his Lot 15, house and all, was transferred to an abutting landowner, another dear client of yours, a Miriam Maslow. Lots 15 and 16 resemble each other like peas in a pod, same size, same pine trees, same juniper bushes. Want me to tell you what happened?" Uncle Tatty's face approached Joe's as he dropped his voice to a whisper. "You helped Miriam grab back her own house, the building on Mike Herring's lot that got put there by mistake, the property Mike wouldn't sell to her unless she paid big money. Don't tell me you weren't involved, Joe meboy!"

Joe bared his teeth. "This is crazy."

Uncle Tatty nodded. "It's even crazier, Joe. I had the city clerk find me the transfer papers. I know your handwriting, Joe. Look at this photocopy I brought back. Your t's slope backward, and there are big loops on your g's. You filled in this paper on behalf of the buyer. Your client Miriam Maslow hired you as an expert." Uncle Tatty pounded his desk. "The Agency pays your expenses while you make dishonest money. Can't have that here, Joe."

"You checked Mike Herring's signature?" Joe asked.

"Ha!" Uncle Tatty shouted, waving his paper about. "Our in-house crook confesses! So this *is* your handwriting, okay?

And you're right, filling in transfer papers isn't illegal, it's the seller's signature that counts, and the signature was Mike Herring's. Is that what you're saying?" Uncle Tatty's fist kept pounding his desk. The British accent was even more noticeable now. "Speak up, confounded scoundrel!"

"Mike sold, Miriam bought," Joe said. "Attorneys are expensive. I helped two of the Agency's clients to save a few hundred pounds. So what else is new, Uncle?"

Uncle Tatty's fist kept abusing his desk top. "This transfer paper pre-dates Mike's death so he could have signed it, but he didn't, Joe. The man was a drunken simpleton. He could probably hardly write. His kind of signature is easy to fake."

"I faked Mike Herring's signature?" Joe asked. "And then I killed him?"

Uncle Tatty sighed. "You didn't?"

"Mike died of a heart attack," Joe said. "There was an autopsy, Uncle."

Joe was getting up.

"You leaving?" Uncle Tatty asked. "Why are you leaving, Joe? We aren't finished here ..."

Uncle Tatty asked his office door, that was closing. It closed with force. The glass in the door broke.

•

Next Thursday Inspector Skates had ordered prawn ragout again, and a Greek salad, with red onion slices and black olives and some white cheese. Joe sat next to him. Joe wasn't eating.

"Miriam Maslow is about to graduate as a clinical psychologist," inspector Skates said, "but she doesn't always aim to cure her fellow beings, that's where I was wrong, Joe. She sometimes wants to kill them." The inspector shook his

261

head. "You know why I had her down as a suspect? Right from the start?"

Joe shook his head.

Inspector Skates arranged the giant prawns on his plate. They had been served in a circle, looking in, now they were looking out, were fixing their little black eyes on their victim.

"Because you lied about her, Joe." The inspector nodded helpfully, as if he were pleased he could explain things to a friend. "But why am I going on like this? Mike Herring died of a heart attack, so far we're in the clear, but now for the rest of that autopsy, Joe." Skates was shaking his head. "Joe, was that old codger ever in bad shape. Cirrhosis of the liver. Peptic ulcers. Pickled brain. Victim must have been nuts, a wreck like him wanting to live in a suburb like Greenpine. You think Mike was nuts?"

"Don't know," Joe said.

Inspector Skates pleaded. "Please. Share some knowledge. You have a wife and a TV at home. All I have is my work. This has nothing to do with why Mike got murdered. You must have figured out what motivated the crazy codger."

"His grandparents owned Greenpine farm and forest," Joe said. "As a kid Mike had good times there."

"You knew the man," the inspector said, after spearing another bright orange prawn and spitting out the head. He chewed thoughtfully. "You had reason to visit Mike Herring again and again. Ever since Miriam discovered that she had pointed out the wrong lot to her expensive builder, that the house she was paying for would be Mike's property, that she was wasting the inheritance her father saved up for her. Legally Miriam was nowhere, right? *If I improve another man's land whatever I put in is his to keep.* Skates nodded seriously after intoning the words. "Such is the law of the land, Joe."

Joe didn't seem to be listening.

"Good," the inspector said, intoning again. "Never say

262

anything that can be used against you. But here is what was going on. Listen, Joe, as soon as you said you didn't know who owned Lot 16 I knew you were lying, and therefore involved with Mike's corpse somehow." He patted Joe's shoulder. "You had just told me you were the chief salesman for Greenpine Subdivision and that you had been supervising selling the land for nearly a year. And then, ten minutes later, you say anything to do with Lot 16 is a blank in your tired mind? Come on." The inspector shook his head. "Please, Joe. So I checked. The city's registry had Miriam Maslow's name on that lot. What do you say, Joe?"

"Hmmm," Joe said.

"Yes," the inspector said, "hmmm is ever so right. This is Brisbane, Australia, mate, the town where the men drink beer and play soccer and the women watch TV or the kiddies in the park, and you're Mr. Handsome and Miriam is Mrs. Attractive and she has already filed for divorce. An affair. The two of you. Bang bang bang. Okay?"

"Hmmm," Joe said.

"Right." Skates's fork felt another prawn's back. "Miriam's little apartment is driving her crazy. Through you she had bought Greenpine 16, using some of her dad's inheritance, and the rest was to go on her house, but then, distracted by frantic goings on perhaps, she gets muddled about Lot 16's location and tells the builder to put her house on Mike Herring's lot. Ha." Inspector Skates winked. "Ha ha ha, Joe."

"Funny?" Joe asked.

"Pathetic," inspector Skates said. "I'm not laughing at you or Miriam or her dad or Mike, I'm laughing at happenstance. I'm laughing at the way things just damn well happen. Nobody planned this mess, you know. Miriam's panic. Your confused passion. Mike's greed. Miriam wants her house back, Mike wants to enjoy her 'gift'. So you, Miriam's white knight, try everything to make Mike switch ownership of 15 to 16. What is the swap to Mike? The land looks the same. The old codger keeps refusing. Miriam gets you to fake paperwork, notarization and all, that was clever, using your Agency's notary stamp, shows us what all our protective red tape is worth, hey? ... and file the transfer with the City of Brisbane."

Joe coughed. He excused himself.

The inspector went back to his prawns, spearing them, biting their heads off, arranging future victims so that they could look at Joe. Skates looked at Joe too. "Tell me, Joe, what went on exactly? You can tell me. We're both white Protestants. I know most of it already. I spoke to the other fishermen in Pig's Harbor. They told me about Mike's recurrent attacks of *Delirium tremens.* Poor fellow saw all the prawns he ever caught crawl all over his poor painful body, 'fixin' him with their evil little eyes'. But Mike had clear spells too, and he wanted to change his life, get back to his happy childhood on Greenpine farm. You got that dream fulfilled for Mike. That was some sale: the cash, the discount, Uncle Tatty and Mr. Big giving you a hard time. What does the sales-manual say? 'Good luck comes to those who keep trying?' Next sale is Lot 16 to Mrs. MiniSkirt—commission plus pooky. The salesman's dream."

Joe was watching the prawns on inspector Skates' plate, there were still quite a few left, peeking out of the pale colored stew. Joe looked pale himself.

"You got into Miriam," the inspector said. "You spent time in her apartment. Nice. I've been there, Joe. But I didn't like that cage full of rats. Part of an experiment for Miriam's master thesis. Rats watching you while you're trying to do it. Maybe Miriam bothered you too. Did she want you to kill Mike so that he couldn't stop the transfer you had arranged for his land? Or was she going to kill Mike herself? How, Joe? All Mike had was a heart attack. You guys didn't touch him. What did you do to Mike?"

264

Joe was trying to drink his tea. His hands trembled.

"I'm sorry," inspector Skates said. "I know I'm bugging, you, mate. I'm not blaming you, please believe me. I would go for Miriam too, if she let me. And you didn't frighten Mike Herring into his death, I can see that. Why would you? You like your wife Mary and your daughter Rebecca. Miriam's pregnant but her husband must be the father. You couldn't have been. The timing is wrong. I was just trying to shake you when I brought that up. There's nothing serious between the two of you. I've spoken with your neighbors in your apartment house on Bowen Hill. You helped Miriam out with that fake transaction out of the goodness of your friendly heart. And then she killed the old codger so that he couldn't run to the city and dispute that bill of sale. But how did she do it?" Inspector Skates looked grim. He stubbed another prawn, bit off its head, put the head on the counter. The prawn's head looked at Joe.

"Women are tough," inspector Skates said. "Miriam had to defend her house, her baby. What else could she do? I'm not blaming you either. What else could *you* do? Miriam may have been threatening to phone your wife Mary. She probably paid you money, too. Car trouble, Mary's asthma treatment ... sales had been off and Uncle Tatty is on your back, its okay, Joe, but tell me how, please, how do you think Miriam killed Mike?"

Skates looked at Joe.

Joe was sweating. "I don't know, Inspector."

"You mean you really don't know?"

Joe nodded.

Joe was looking at the prawns' heads looking at Joe.

"You know," inspector Skates said, "I swear I'm not going after Miriam. Good luck to the woman. She is talented and energetic. She'll be a good psychologist, like she was a good dancer, chorus line, a professional in the Sydney musicals.

Did she tell you that? That's a hard life, Joe, swinging those long legs night after night." The inspector hummed while tapping the counter. He looked up. "But I have to know what Miriam did to terminally freak out Mike. Think back, Joe. That evening on Greenpine, under a full moon, with Mike ogling the house he never paid for. Sipping hooch from his flask. Muttering and drooling. Did delirium hit him? Did Miriam provoke deadly jitters?"

A bright orange van happened to pass the cafe. Joe noticed Mr. Ratsificias was wearing a bright orange shirt. The bright orange prawns were staring at him from the counter and Skates' plate.

"Think back, Joe," Skates was saying.

Joe saw the bright orange rag fluttering from the juniper branch on Greenpine 16.

Joe threw up.

"Hey!" inspector Skates shouted as he jumped away from the counter. Mr. Ratsiaficas rushed up, sponge and paper towels ready, yelling warnings in Greek.

•

"Yes," Miriam said, at home, on the phone. "My pregnant prawn dance. I danced Mike to death. Do you mind? It couldn't have gone any other way. Freud said that, Joe. The future, Freud said, is too complicated to predict, there are too many factors, but looking back there is only one way."

"Oh dear oh dear oh dear," Joe kept saying.

"Shut up Joe," Miriam said. "you told me Mike had that delirium that made him see crawling prawns with little evil eyes." She laughed softly. "So I made myself a prawn suit."

"Oh dear oh dear oh dear," Joe said.

"I was lucky," Miriam said. "You said Mike liked to come

out on Sundays. I was waiting for him. The moon, the intoxication, me singing the prawn song ..."

"You left a piece of orange cloth stuck on a bush," Joe said. "Inspector Skates has it."

"He has?" Miriam aked pleasantly. "You told him what it was?"

"He figured it out himself."

"After you puked in his plate?"

"Oh dear oh dear oh dear .."

Miriam hung up.

Joe dialed again.

"Now what?" Miriam asked. "Are you taping this?"

"I'm on a pay phone in Kangaroo Park," Joe said. "Skates won't follow up. He doesn't like making arrests. He lives alone on a loft, above a horse stable that belongs to his brother. He doesn't care about his career. He likes to read free books from the library. You impressed him. You two should get together." Joe paused. "You aren't sorry about killing Mike, Miriam?"

Miriam sighed. "Yes. Some. It would have been better if the asshole had just died, but he was kneeling for me, and rolling around, begging, screaming, he thought I was both a prawn and the Virgin Mary, and I had to keep dancing to aggravate his condition. I had to have him die on me, I need my house, Joe. So does the baby."

Joe groaned. "Oh dear oh dear oh dear .."

"I like inspector Skates," Miriam said. "You happen to have that horse-stable's phone number, Joe?"

QUICKSAND

Capetown, May 1955

to Count Gerrit van Abcoude
    Castle of Abcoude,
    Abcoude, The Netherlands

Dear Uncle:

Your emissary visited me yesterday and will no doubt send
you his report on how your ne'er-do-well Nephew is doing in
fascist South Africa. By the way—your interest in my welfare
flatters me of course—where did you find the spy? He said he
works for your bank here in Capetown but he looked like a
Dutch Reformed Church minister, all pissy-eyed and pussy-
mouthed. Don't believe the asshole, Uncle. Believe *me,* your
only relative in the Universe after Mother (your noble Sister)
died. You and I are most intimately connected and when you
die—I'm happy to hear from Nurse that you're recovering

from the stroke–I'll be your next incarnation, whether you disinherit me or not. You have been threatening ... and I've been genuinely upset–no longer, however. I will still be the next count, that's all that matters, right? But what's a count these days?

Is a title worth holding on to?

Here is something, you know that counts are nothing special in Capetown?

There's a Dane here, my good friend Ole Segestrøm, who just inherited his countish prefix from his father being dead in some genuine medieval castle in Jutland. Ole has a fullgrown Scandinavian accent. Ever since the good news hit his hashished brain old Ole has been jumping all over town shouting "I'm a cunt, I'm a cunt". The next thing was crowns on his underwear, embroidered in gold, to impress Jane, but Jane is mostly with me now.

I tell you, I'm better than Cunt Segestrøm. Nobody knows I will be a count one day too. I take after you: quiet, modest, self-effacing, hard-working, hell-bent on always pleasing Heaven. I even look like you (wide shouldered, curly haired, tall, handsome etc.). Your photo (as a young man) is on the shelf in the villa's number one bathroom here. Jane thought I was a little too narcissistic bowing to my own image before brushing my teeth three times a day. I told her the picture portrays you and now she wants to make love to both of us at the same time. I told her she is a little too Aphroditical.

Don't believe whatever your mealy-mouthed bank manager-spy is writing to you. Whatever he says ... the opposite is true. Do you know that I've been doing extremely well, since you fired me last year! Wasn't that silly of you! First you send me to Capetown to learn how to be rich and famous like you, by identifying with and slaving for one of your many overseas companies, and then, just as I am beginning to learn that all business is founded on the principle that a merchant sells for (at the very least) twice costprice less a small discount (never mind the product), you have me thrown into the street. Knowing full well that I had been spending the low wages that you paid me. Were you trying to teach me humility? Well, Sir, by exposing me to a cold and heartless world you awoke my nihilistic instincts. First your nephew thought himself rich; then (thinking further) he thought himself into being a murderer. Yessir, thanks to your interference, and the subsequent change in me I managed to kill lieutenant Boelie van Rooyen, South African Police, Capetown Constabulary.

Which is probably a good thing.

Do you mind? Look at it this way. Boelie was a practising racist Nazi. A bad guy, Uncle Gerrit. And you and I are good guys. You were a true officer and a gentleman, colonel with the Hussars van Boreel, weren't you? With feathers on your bearskin hat and a horse and a saber? Pity you were too old to fight the evil Germans, and I too young, but now I killed Boelie so at least somebody did something again.

Okay?

Not okay? Well, let me explain what happened here. Let me rationalize it away. Make it sound right. I know you believe in morals but that's a strut, Uncle. I don't want to kick your strut away though, you're an old sick man and the only person, except Mother and Nurse, who ever cared for me. Some sentimentality should be excusable.

No, don't pretend you aren't interested. Nurse and I have been writing to each other and she claims you are interested in my career (or lack of same) and have been spying on me. The visit of the bank manager is an example. Ha! That bank bird left with a hat full of question marks. How come I live in this palatial villa in the genteel suburb of Rondebosch? And the brand new Harley Davidson, eh? And beautiful Jane, running about in her nothings, attentive to my slightest needs. (Jane is great, when your manager was here she put on high

271

heeled shoes and was strutting around him, serving tea and muffins. He tried not to stare at her breasts. Ha!) How can I keep such a beautiful woman with no ready cash?

I didn't tell–but all this is thanks to you, and to positive thinking. Your own preaching, Uncle. Dale Carnegie and *How to Make Friends and Influence People.*

You see, watching you in your castle made me think. Here we have a nobleman who managed not only to hold on to his fortune but to multiply it by a hundred, and is he happy? Dear Lord, he is not happy. Okay, sometimes he is somewhat content, when growing split peas on his own chickenshit in the castle garden or looking up Nurse's starched skirt–but all in all he is miserable. Lonely, shyly defensive, nasty, devious, frightened probably (of what? of death? Death should be a release to a man in your position).

So did I want to be like you?

No.

What did I want to be like?

I wanted to be like nothing. You always said "you have to be something" but something didn't work for you so why should it work for me? I began to entertain the idea that "being nothing" is the answer. If I am nothing I have nothing to lose. No dear Mother who dies of the flu, no dear dog that dies of old age after having epileptic fits all the time, winking at me and drooling and pissing. Such a good dog too. Only friend I ever had.

But nothing = nothing. How can I live with nothing, without a body for instance? Or with a body but without food and shelter? Believe me, Uncle, I gave this problem a lot of thought, to the point where it nearly drove me crazy. When you die I may get your empire: a castle, a dented Rolls Royce, ducks in the moat, lots of business companies and other investments, the imitation Delft blue jar on your nighttable that you keep filled with peppermints. So I will have all these

272

somethings, that I may lose, that have to be taken care of, serviced. I will have an army of employees, 'babybirds' as you call them. Babybirds with their beaks open, open beaks that form holes that can never be filled, not by the most generous of employers.

How can I carry all that without having to suffer like you do, on a diet of Maria crackers and skim milk, worrying yourself into ulcers and burst blood vessels in your brain that give you a stroke, change you into an old cripple, a prisoner within your own Castle of Abcoude—how do I do it, Uncle? By not caring. It's an attitude. A lack of attitude. It's trying to have no attitude at all, which is an attitude again, the ultimate negative attitude. How to get there? By applying the power of negative thinking.

Indifference? Never. Capetown has its 'poor blankies', indifferent white folks who live in the gutter. They're uncomfortable people, uncomfortable within themselves. Blacks can't help being poor here, they're beaten into misery by police lieutenant Boelie van Rooyen. For whites it's harder to be poor, but when you dismissed me, for refusing a transfer to Johannesburg of all places, that miserable gold heap, why would I want to live there? But when you dismissed me I had to face the possibility of being poor, of living in the gutter. Capetown is a nice city but we're having a bit of a depression here, none of the business firms are hiring staff. I can't do menial work, that's reserved for blacks. No sweeping of streets or mowing lawns for Nephew, Uncle.

That was a moment. Thanks to your move I had no money for rent. I had to return my car to your company. I couldn't eat, smoke, drink alcohol.

So what to do? I tell you what I did, I backpacked/hitchhiked to Blauberg Beach, a beautiful but treacherous strip of Cape coast that consists of quicksand and slippery boulders, avoided by sensible folks, and thought negatively for three days. About what I did not want to do. Not work for you. No apologies to you. No transfer to Johannesburg. No work of any kind, really. And no poverty. You see, Uncle, I do have curiosity, this life as a human on Earth interests me and I do want to use the opportunity of a human birth to do some philosophical research, but I'm no hermit.

So within my negative thinking there were some reasonable requests, for food and drink, clothing and shelter, sex and transport. In order not to clutter my mind with lots of different images I just set a figure, so much money per month. And a lump sum up front to buy a motorcycle. I also thought of Jane (for sex) and one of the great villas here (for shelter). Maybe I overdid that a bit, eh? Jane is too much sex and this villa is just too enormous.

Don't you think this is funny? I imitated you, like you always wanted me to–you raised me after all–but instead of reading American get-rich business books I applied Buddhist methods. Ever heard of Zen, Uncle? Or Taoism? Hinduism? Basically they're all the same thing, it seems. The older, and wiser (slyer?) religions talk about Nothing as the only reality, and Anything as the great illusion. You can meditate out of painful Anything into painless Nothing and that means figuring out what's what. Negative meditations, supposedly, lead to extreme happiness, a true euphoria of owning Nothing and therefore having Nothing to lose.

On Blueberg Beach I also read Dostoyevski. It's a pity you're old and ill now so there's no point in suggesting you should read Dostoyevski's *Young Devils*.

There's some talk in all this Eastern Thought of doing away with desire, if possible. There are some basic desires though, as I already mentioned, for food, shelter, etc. The basic desires you were using to intimidate me by taking away my income. So I needed money. Sitting there on Blueberg Beach, watching seals and dolphins play in the surf, and barbecueing sausages, remembering your infatuation with 'thought power' I thought up some money.

Thought Power strikes like lightning.

Noblemen are supposed to help each other out, and colleague Cunt Segestrøm became instrumental in getting me money. He is in the insurance business and sold me two policies, before he became titled and before I lost my job. One policy covered accidents and the other insures my property. Hitchhiking back to Capetown the truck I was riding on turned over and I hurt my foot. Some metal ripped off quite a bit of skin, the wound got infected: gangrene set in, a mess, Uncle. Almost lost my foot. That's bad? Here is a little side note. Because of my foot problem a black man lost his life. He had been knifed in a drunken fight and got to hospital before me but because of my skin color I was taken care of first and the black guy bled to death.

The insurance came up with money up front and a monthly payment for as long as the wound hasn't healed completely (which can still be a while, my fellow nobleman Segestrom is a most meticulous fellow). The insurance came up with more money because all my possessions were stolen from my room while I was doing the negative thing on Blueberg Beach. All those three-piece suits you picked out for me, the cashmere blazers, the gray flannel slacks, the white shoes with tassels, the gold cufflinks that belonged to your grandpa, the silk shirts and ties, the antique Bible bound in leather, all gone, Uncle. More money from the insurance.

Back to desire. You're not bored are you? You do want to know how I killed the police lieutenant, the bad guy. I put that in to keep your interest, and its true, I assure you. I did kill the asshole. Why?

I'm not too sure. Lieutenant Boelie was in my way twice, personally I mean. The first time was when my possessions got stolen. The thief was a colored man, and got caught. The lieutenant called me to his office and I saw what he had done to the thief. They use torture here to extract a confession. The colored man was handcuffed to Boelie's steel desk and got beaten some more while I was there. I protested. Boelie told me "you're not in focking Holland nie." The double negative comes from Afrikaans, that got influenced by French, in the old days when Dutch Boers and French Hugenots populated this beautiful country and impregnated it with their repressed puritanism. "We must nie sin nie." Double negative, Uncle. That's one positive for Boelie.

The second time I met Boelie he hit me. I got arrested in a municipal bus for saying something against the Nationalist Government. A plain-clothes policeman dragged me off the bus. Boelie's station deals with subversive activity by 'uitlanders' so I got hit in the face a few times. He threatened me with deportation.

Personal revenge, yes, but there something else. During the German occupation you and I saw a lot of atrocities, perpetrated by the SS, Gestapo, Gruene Polizei and so forth. Remember the little boy who got beaten to death right in front of us once? Because he had pulled funny faces when German troops marched by? And there was nothing we could do. You were 65, I was 14. I wanted to do something, I wanted to kill Nazis.

Frustrated desires live on. They're potent, you know. I always wanted to have sex with Nurse and she still pops up in my dreams and Jane is a younger version of Nurse. Looks just like her. Like police-lieutenant Boelie van Rooyen looks like all the bad Nazi guys who dragged old ladies by the hair, starved us (yes, us, imagine you and I eating boiled sugar beets and tulip bulbs and little trash fishes, but we did, didn't we?) and killed your retarded bastard son in his asylum.

Revenge.

Some desires are too deep to be eradicated by negative thinking. Only way to get rid of them is by fulfillment. Being an only child, and then an only nephew, always alone in that huge castle of yours, alone with your grumpy silences and the rustle of Nurse's stiff white skirts I must have longed for brothership, even if it meant visiting my halfcousin in a mental institution.

I set that up here, this brothership, this modern Dostoyevski-type Young Devils II. Cunt Segestrøm owns a Harley Davidson, and a couple of other friends in my age group ride heavy motorbikes so I got one too, 750 CC, Uncle, a Liberator HD, same type of machine the US Army used in the war. Hear her mighty rumble, and gurgle when she idles. A very female machine, complete with a kind of choke/clitoris gadget that has to be titillated before she'll start up.

What do motorcycle gangs do? Go for a spin on Sundays? Drink beer, smoke hashish, roll in the hay with Jane-type women? Yes yes, but as the leader I had to use a detached type of care. Jealous Boelie was after me and he rides a Harley Davidson too, and he is Police. He can arrest us. He tried to various times but we were sober, flashed valid registrations and licenses, Jane was properly dressed (she is only naked on the premises here) and Robbie, my second in command, is the son of an assistant attorney general. It all helps.

Boelie wanted me to race him. That was an idea.

More negative thinking first. During our "spins on Sundays" we sometimes pass garden parties, of the more elegant variety, in houses like the one I live in now, surrounded by park-like gardens. Villas. Oh yes, your bank manager didn't find out how I can afford this villa in the elegant suburb of Rondebosch —the truth is I don't have to afford it. I was hired as a caretaker, I get paid to live here. The villa belonged to an old lady who stays in an ashram in India. She sold the place to pay her guru's fees. The new owners want to pull it down and build a condominium but they haven't come up with the money yet and meanwhile I take care that the villa doesn't get vandalized. There's quite a lot of stuff here that's valuable, Victorian mouldings, paneling, fittings. You should see me here, Uncle. I sleep in an old four-poster in the main dining room, the motorcycle is parked next to the bed. I sleep in my jeans and a T-shirt. I get up in the morning and jump straight on the bike, ride it out into the garden, hit the fountain's switch on the way out, circle the big fountain on the front lawn, using it as a shower, roar off to breakfast at the Greek place around the corner. Sometimes Jane stays over and she jumps on behind me.

Sundays and holidays our gang roams about the suburbs. Young Devils II like to disturb garden parties. There are quite a few of us now, twelve, fourteen maybe, all 'intellectual' types. Garden parties float on alcohol here and the thing to do is to arrive late, when the company is properly pickled. We don't roar our engines, we look neat in our clean jeans and shoe-polished leather jackets. Our girls look nice too, especially the Lesbian couple on the twin-cylinder BMW. So we are always let in, welcomed even by grinning hosts, fat alcoholics. We usually know a few people, say hello, walk about, make conversation, eat a little roast pig, sip a dry white Cape wine, flirt with the women. Our girls flirt with the men. We make bad trouble that way. Jealousy is a fact of life, wealthy wives getting on in years snarl at their husbands, husbands yell at young mistresses trying to seduce us bikers. We just walk about quietly, make things worse, push over a table here and there, sometimes we do a stomping kind of dance with the garden party ladies. Handle them a little bit roughly. Maybe a dress gets ripped, but by that time we are leaving, not in a group, not with roaring engines, almost silently, well-behaved, after thanking the host for his hospitality and kissing his mistress on the lips.

Honestly, Uncle, I dont know how we do it but everytime I look back (from my Harley Davidson's saddle) on one of these socialite parties the thing is a shambles. Those nice people are fighting each other. Sometimes there are sirens in the distance, of police cars racing in.

The power of negative thinking.

I tried not to kill lieutenant Boelie but the desire was too strong. He also kept asking for strong measures. Opposite where I now live is another big house that employs a lot of black servants, who live in their own quarters in the back of the property. The butler was accused of laziness by his master. As the black butler wasn't changing his ways the master called Boelie's office. That's usual here. Officers moonlight as punishers of servants. Lieutenant Boelie van Rooyen arrived in his jeep and beat the old dignified butler with a bullwhip. Nearly killed the man. I heard the butler scream, whimper, beg for forgiveness but that whip just kept swishing.

And there was my fellow-biker Guenther. Guenther, amazingly enough, is German. I actually have a German motorbike gang colleague. Guenther was in the war, as a Hitlerjugend soldier, firing obsolete 'Panzerfauste' at superbly armored American tanks. I don't quite know why Guenther's tainted past doesn't matter to me. Because Guenther was a child then?

Anyway, Guenther applied for a position in our gang. We all go through an 'experience' before we are accepted. I had the truck accident and nearly lost my foot. Jane, a nice shy type of well-brought up young lady, had to be a naked waitress at my mansion (she never stopped being a naked waitress, she seems to like it). Guenther, a rich boy, he came here to direct his father's toy factory, lost his new Mercedes. We had a barbecue on Blueberg Beach and I marked a false path, that led straight into a bad patch of quicksand. We arranged that Guenther would arrive after us so when he pulled up on the highway he saw us far out on the beach, with our motorcycles and cars parked around some giant boulders. The path to our location was marked with rocks. Wanting to show off his huge car Guenther raced toward us. He got stuck halfway on the path, managed to get out of the car and reach us by dragging himself from rock to rock but the Mercedes was sucked into the beach, very slowly. We pretended not to notice anything. We laughed, toasted each other, ate more Frankfurters on hot buns, pulled beer from the coolers, and Gunther crawled along slowly, fighting for every inch of life while the huge German Victory Chariot disappeared behind him.

The insurance wouldn't pay as Blueberg Beach is not a public road but Guenther's father got him a super Jaguar and Guenther got himself a beautiful black girlfriend so all was well again, for awhile. Until lieutenant Boelie pulled the girl in, had her beaten and raped at his station, and deported Guenther. Young Devils II lost a valuable member. Guenther was the only brother who could read Nietzsche aloud in musical German. Guenther told me that Sartre was wrong when the French philosopher said, sadly, 'nous sommes *condamnes* a la liberte'. Guenther, watching his Mercedes sink into oblivion at the time, realized that it is a joy to be free of purpose. He told me, with tears in his large blue eyes, that only Nothing matters, and that Nothing includes Mercedeses lost forever in quicksand. Guenther's experience of liberation got him another car. Back in Germany he now has a Javanese girlfriend. It is, Guenther writes in a letter, 'Job on the Dung Heap all over again'.

"And your father's wealth?" I wrote back. "What if you lose that? No more replacement of lost luxury cars, no more exotic women."

He referred me to the event of you, Uncle, dismissing me, depriving me of my income and how my attitude of detachment worked out just fine.

Good old Guenther, and he didn't like watching his girlfriend being abused by Boelie van Rooyen's constables.

How I killed Boelie, Uncle?

By thought. Remember how you, religiously, read Dale Carnegie's essays on positive thinking? In the Southern tower of the Castle of Abcoude?

I religiously read the Heart Sutra, in the turret on top of this villa. You drank a cup of mocca coffee, I drank a cup of orange pekoe tea. This is what I read:

when the bodhisattva Avalokitasavara
was coursing in the deep rajnaparamita
(perfection of understanding)
he perceived that all five skandas are empty
thereby transcending all suffering

Yes, I learned from you. Ceremonies are important. They focus our thought. I don't think I read the sutra correctly though. All I heard, when I read, was "empty." I kept visualizing lieutenant Boelie on his motorcycle, approaching emptiness. I didn't even imagine that on purpose, I just saw the abyss open. Then the abyss opened. Young Devils II were out on the Ocean Drive, on the Cape Peninsula, and the sun was low into our eyes, and we were approaching a curve. The lieutenant overtook us on his motorcycle, speeding like crazy for he was the Law of the Land. There happened to be repairs up ahead, big pits in the road, screened by red/and/ white police fences but a bunch of drunks had taken the fences down to the beach to form a racetrack for dune buggies. As the lieutenant overtook me I happened to be reciting the Heart Sutra line

281

he perceived that all five skandas are empty

All five pits, where the road crews had been digging to replace the Ocean Drive's foundation, were empty.

Boelie, all broken up, died slowly.

He looked as if he finally understood something that he had understood all along, but forgotten.

Now Death reminded him, and he seemed pleased.

So, I'm doing all right, Uncle.

Never mind what your spies say, I am the suitable continuation of the life that now ebbs away in your incarnation.

What else is new?

I'm coming to the end of my stay here, Uncle. I'm not sure what comes next but this is all too nice now: Jane, the motorcycle, the villa, the beach. After finally killing my Nazi I need to break free of further destructive desires.

Send me some positive thoughts, I'll send you some negative thoughts and together we may overcome all thoughts altogether.

Don't you think that as long as we think something we still aren't nowhere?

Love to Nurse.

Take care, Uncle.

Your loving nephew,

Gerrit II

CRIME AND PUNISHMENT
IN TIMELESS JAPAN

As a young man I spent some time, quite a bit of time it seems to me now—intense awarenesss kind of stretches in memory—in a Zen monastery, in Kyoto, Japan. The Buddhist monastery was part of a temple compound and each temple had a priest in charge. The priests had ranks and the higher the rank the more colorful their robes. Once a month they would all come to the ornate head temple (which wasn't the monastery, the monastery was a training school where the young fellows got twisted into enlightenment by meditation and other hardships) and dance.

I used to watch those priestly dances. Some of the young monks, who were my mates in the monastery, took care of their music. There was a drummer, a percussionist, a guy on gongs, and everybody sang. The singing was what you hear in surrealist Japanese movies these days: high-pitched notes that would end abruptly, as if someone suddenly cut the singer's throat—hoarse groans, popping sounds, and occasional jazzy bursts of scat, rap, even vocalese where every drum beat has a lyric to go with it. While the monks did their musical mime, flapping the wide sleeves of their simple black robes, portly priests shuffled about in brocades and tailored silks. One priest, a *bonze* called Roku, was brighter and fatter than anybody else. He lifted his flat feet amazingly quickly, pivoted his bulk with astounding ease, even performed solo pieces while his colleagues were softshoe-ing, backing him up. This star-performer was of high rank. He was the only priest who owned a car (this was in the fifties, very few cars about in those days). Roku-sama impressed me. He also impressed the monks and they grinned enviously, patting their butts (a gesture of low-class Japanese derision) as they watched Roku's antics. From the gossip I gathered that "funeral priest" Roku did pretty good out of taking care of dead rich folks, assuring their souls' safe passage to Buddhist high heavens. I was troubled by leg cramps and hemorrhoids (that go with meditation in an attempted lotus position), so I didn't research the career of the dancing priest at the time, but a question was formed.

Questions form answers, this particular answer showed up in a dream. The dream answered other questions too, for although Zen doesn't bother much with good and evil but hints at a void that's beyond crime, revenge, punishment even, and prefers the excuse of ignorance to accusations, I kept wondering whether religious adepts should be greedy.

Maybe I have a visual mind. There was plenty of corruption in the temple compound, lots of practised human weakness to choose from. Priests dressed up in suits and, hiding their bald pates under caps or hats, climbed walls and scurried off to the pleasure quarter to squander offerings from the ever-suffering laity, the papa- and mama-sans who showed up on Sundays to share their savings. Hot dogs were consumed in vegetarian kitchens. Black tobacco cigarettes were dipped in rice wine before being sucked empty of crazy-making smoke. Early-model mini radios were hidden in sleeves and minute phones stuck in ears to while away meditation hours on thumping rock. None of that bothered me, but the priest Roku, whirling in the temple courtyard, orange and red silk scarves flying, sleeves gesturing grotesquely, sunrays causing a halo above his sweating fat head, made me wonder whether there was any righteousness left in the Tao, the wise way of nothingness I was supposedly pursuing.

I mean, a man can ask ...

Time passed. I left the monastery and stayed with a French businessman who lived in an affluent suburb of Kobe. The mansion's kitchen, run by a Chinese cook, fed me endless noodles (with everything on the side), in return for sorting out my host's art collection. Working hours were short and I enjoyed free weekends. I even had my own bathroom and I would sit there, between walls of gleaming white tile, enjoying the spring breeze, pausing from reflecting on the weekend paper's comic section's wisdom to gaze at woods on an elevation at the horizon. I could never quite make out what I was gazing at. Was there a shrine there, hidden between pine trees, a small Buddhist temple with a sloping roof? Did something move about the shrine, a gray shape? A dancing shape?

I also spent time watching, through the bathroom's small and discreetly opened windows, paper and wood houses being assembled below. The Frenchman's villa rose from a hilltop and looked down on this development that grew quickly, being artfully fitted together from prefabricated parts. The picturesque old-Japan-style-village-with-modern-comforts, I was told, would house middle-echelon government workers. Soon the chosen ones arrived and I saw the men, comfortably dressed in cotton kimonos, enoying their weekends, squatting on straw-matted floors of artfully empty and therefore spacious rooms, being served green tea and seaweed cookies on red-lacquered trays by their graceful kneeling wives, while the kids hung out in moss gardens, between decorative shrubs. I also saw an older man grabbing his chest and keeling over, his wife or housekeeper run to the phone, an ambulance arrive too late and a Buddhist priest in time. The priest's chanting voice and the fragrance of incense wafted over to the Frenchman's mansion.

That night Monsieur de Monnaie, my benefactor, entertained, and his Chinese cook made all the dishes T'ang emperors were said to habitually overindulge on. We also drank all the liquor before breaking into beer. My host spoke about his glorious past and present pursuits in many languages and kept losing his new teeth that clattered on the floor and were retrieved by Korean servants. Overcome by the spectacle and my own participation I managed to stagger to my quarters where I plunged into troubled sleep.

The dream showed me traveling in Japan's inhospitable West. I was a monk. The Zen master of the Kyoto monastery had recalled me from the temptations of Kobe and sent me to harsh country for further training. I had walked, on tattered sandals, through freezing swamps all day and was glad to reach a shrine shadowed by pine trees on a bit of high ground. An old toothless hermit in a patched gray robe didn't exactly welcome me.

"Reverend sir" I said, "I am a humble monk of the Rinzal Zen Sect (as if he couldn't see, I was wearing the same bone ring on my robe as he did himself) looking for Buddhahood in general and a night's lodging in particular. How are you doing and please oblige."

The uncouth fellow gruffly referred me to a village below.

The villagers had better manners than their hermit. Some fifty people were gathered in their municipal building but they sent out a selectman who took me to his house, fed me and bedded me down.

"Excuse me, reverend sir," the selectman said, "but there's

a bit of a ceremony going on at the main house that requires my presence." He hurried off.

It seemed that I had only slept a few minutes when my host was back again. "Excuse me, reverend sir."

"Yes?" I rubbed my eyes.

"Please." He was in tears: "My father, the headman here, died today. As, even if your eyes are blue and you mangle our language, you are a holy man, and you were tired and hungry, I couldn't worry you with our trouble so I let you sleep a few hours. But it's getting close to midnight now and all the villagers are preparing to leave."

"Some extra problem?" I asked.

"You have to leave with us, reverend sir." The selectman explained his predicament. Apparently there was some taboo about dead people in the village: they had to be left alone for the night. There was a barn a few miles down the road where we could all rest in comfort. Then in the morning we would return.

I didn't feel like tramping off again and remembered I was a monk. "Please show your honorable father's body, selectman-sama."

The old man was dressed in his best clothes and rested on a trestle table. Candles burned and incense smoldered. Rice cakes and various sweets were heaped in bowls.

"I'll stay here," I said, "and chant appropriate sermons of death and rebirth."

"We'll pay you in the morning, reverend sir."

I raised my hands in horror, remembering Kobe and other traps of illusion. "No pay."

The villagers rushed off and I folded my legs next to the corpse, assumed the proper posture (spine erect, belly pushed forward), arranged my robe, hit my bell, sang my song. Midnight came and I must have dozed off but a chill woke me up again and I became aware of a gray squat shape entering the building. I struck my bell but there was no sound, I tried to sing but my uvula was frozen. The gray shape bent over the headman's head and sucked it up in one gulp. The rest of the corpse wan inhaled too and the shape started on the offerings. All I could do in protest was tremble. The ghoul stood in the open door for a moment, groaned, bowed, took his leave.

At daybreak the villagers returned and weren't at all surprised to see their headman gone. "It's always like this," the selectman said. "It saves the burial of course but we don't like it much all the same. Thank you for staying, reverend sir, can you tell us what you saw?

I told him, and the villagers. A beautiful young woman knelt devoutly and begged me to relieve the village of its curse.

"Nothing for free, of course," the selectman said.

I remembered Kobe and my harsh Zen master who, knowing my weak spirit, had sworn he would send me on spiritual errand until ... until when? The master never said. The young woman smiled sweetly. I squinted furiously. "No pay, if you please."

"Such a holy man," the young woman sighed.

Which reminded me: they had their own holy man. I asked about the hermit on the hill.

"Who?" the villagers asked.

"My fellow Rinzai sect member," I said. "Old codger with a bone ring on his robe." I touched my own. "Like this."

Blank stares.

"Has a shrine on that hill." I pointed.

No shrine, no hermit, no ring, they all assured me. I left and walked back to the hill. The shrine was there all right and so was the hermit.

"You," I said. He was the shape who ate the headman and the cookies and he was fat shiny Roku, the dancing priest in the Kyoto compound. He was, he told me, all of the high-rank dancing priests who "do funerals," promising an easy transfer to heaven, collecting padded bills, racing about in Cadillacs, Rolls Royces, Infinitis and Lexus if must be, visiting geishas on the sly.

The easy life. The fat of the land.

"But look where it got me," the hermit wailed. His shape faded as he spoke, so did the shrine.

"Help me help me." His weak voice pursued me as I tramped onward on my journey up snowy slopes, down icy paths. I remembered the beautiful young lady's plea, the predicament of the villagers, the admonishments of my teacher.

"Oh very well," I said, "I'm suffering so much I may as well take on your pains too. Roku-sama, go on, go to heaven."

One has to be careful with giving in like that, even to please damsels of dreams. Even attempts at holiness are self-serving. Besides, nightmares don't forgive. Soon I was a ghoul, about to devour a corpse in a village. I woke up.

That day I begged off from sorting treasures and went for a walk behind the Frenchman's mansion. Beyond the village I found the woods I had seen from my bathroom. There were pine trees there but nothing else. I had, at the very least, expected to find a cracked gravestone, covered with lichens, stating, in hardly legible characters chiseled ages ago, that a monk was buried here. A greedy monk.

So I walked back. That evening, looking out from the bathroom, I did see a strange almost transparent blur again, between the pine trees on the horizon. A shrine, I thought. And from the shrine a gray blob appeared, dancing and bowing. It waved, lifted a leg, jumped away, was gone forever.